Fantasy Girl

Wartime Druid Saga, Volume 3

Shawn McGee

Published by Assetstor, 2023.

FANTASY GIRL

First edition. October 3, 2023.

Copyright © 2023 Shawn McGee.

ISBN: 979-8215406366

Written by Shawn McGee.

Chapter 1—Rebecca

The lesson I learned upon waking from a deep slumber was never to ask the universe for a diversion, even when faced with matters like telling your best friend about a lie and your grandmother being hospitalized. Urgent knocks reverberated through the room, startling me awake. A voice called out, "Scion Rebecca Adams, may I enter? I am Peridot from Celestia, and the world needs you."

My groggy head forgot that I had accepted the position of Celestia's representative on Earth as the Scion of the True Church. Reflecting the golden glow from Peridot's proximity, my body woke me abruptly, snapping me to my new reality.

After turning on a bedside lamp, I remembered I was in Corey's bed, still in my pajamas. As Corey slept on his outdoor druid bed despite the winter weather, the room was available. This room had become mine because of my frequent training nearby, even though it held bittersweet memories of dating him.

With the bedside light on, I sat up and let my legs dangle over the side of the bed, becoming awake enough to think. What could someone from Celestia be doing here at four-thirty in the morning?

The recent attempt on my grandmother's life caused me to toss and turn until late. As I struggled to wake up, I mustered a response with as much energy as I could gather. "Yes, please come in."

The door swung open, revealing a radiant being bathed in golden celestial light, and compelled me to rub the sleep from my eyes. "We must hurry. The Outer Realm's war has spilled into your domain."

Glowing gold was new and hindered me gathering my scattered thoughts while searching for clothes. Sensing my predicament, the celestial being spoke again. "I shall meet you on the patio with the others."

With determination and haste, I dressed in a jean skirt, top, sweater, and a pair of flats. Stepping into the hallway, I ambled toward the dining room with the glass sliding door that led to the patio. The presence of lights and movement from the patio informed me I wasn't the only one awake. The scent of coffee filled the frigid air, and Wesley handed me a large cup of hot coffee. Corey and Rachel emerged from the weapons cache, grasping their weapons with a sense of awakening muscles that dulled their usual prominence.

"You're glowing," said Wesley. I must have looked sad because he said, "it's not bad."

A familiar voice, belonging to a Daoine, spoke.

"Fionnestra?" I asked. She was one of the two I knew.

She smiled, a hint of amusement dancing in her eyes.

Three other citizens from the Outer Realms stood on the patio, resembling elves with their slender figures, pointy ears, and auras that distinguished their races. The Empyrean emanated a resplendent golden light, and must be Peridot. There was an Ellyll and an Elpys with the other two. Besides the glow, they all looked like elves. Slight, about five feet tall, and pointy-eared.

I knew not to refer to them as elves, but I couldn't tell them apart because my body glow enhanced Peridot's glow and that's all I saw for the auras.

Peridot stood next to me and he had a scar on his face and a fresh wound on his arm.

"Do you need a heal?" I asked, giving him a *Healing Touch* when he nodded.

"You're the only one here that can heal me," he answered. "I'll teach you to control the glow when I show you angel and Celestia communications when we depart."

Wesley got my attention. "Albios, Celestia, Elysium, and the Fey Spring Court have formed a combat alliance, which is why they're all here. They're a strike force taken from the front line during a counteroffensive."

I was desperate for a swift update. "Earth is under attack?" The events unfolded around me, yet they seemed to lag, considering the gravity of the situation.

Corey and Rachel were part of the Fey Spring Court, and I was part of Celestia. The alliance explained why the four beings had come. The term 'Outer Realm's war' had been only a term until a few minutes ago. Also, I hadn't seen an Empyrean, Ellyll, or Elpy until a few minutes ago.

Nicole tidied the remnants of their druid bed she shared with Corey while Corey braided Rachel's hair.

"Yes, we can explain on the way," Peridot said, his golden glow gentler on my awakening senses.

Fionnestra handed Corey a piece of paper. "Here is the address of the inflection point," she said. "It's the Second Chance School past Brookwood."

Corey assumed his position as the Tactical Leader of the Southeast Territory and planned our departure. "Rebecca, would you mind driving as well?" he asked.

I took a sip of coffee and grabbed my keys as we made our way out. Corey issued more instructions, assigning tasks to the others. "Fionnestra, ride on the back of Rachel's motorcycle." Then, with a firm glare at Nicole, he added, "Pregnant women will not exit the car when we arrive."

Nicole, his pregnant fiancé, was still adjusting to her new condition and not accustomed to being ordered around. They did not plan her pregnancy, but when you connect your house to the Fey Spring Court with its thousands of fertility faeries, pregnancies are likely.

Corey continued issuing orders. "Peridot and Scorpia, accompany Rebecca. Everyone else, pile into my car. They surprised us, but we can handle this." He gave a rallying cry. "Let's kick some ass!"

The weight of the impending battle had yet to settle upon me, leaving me ill-equipped to help Nicole handle being sidelined. She couldn't stay alone because the Delta Vampires still had her as their primary target, and she was an empath, not a fighter. Sitting in a car watching your friends fight would be nerve-wracking for a take-charge person.

Also, it was too early for a battle cry. I'd wait until I was in the battle.

The silver hued Ellyll, Scorpia, pointed towards Wesley. "Realms Master, ride with us," she beckoned, surprising Wesley with her request. Reluctantly, he followed, his shocked expression overriding any protest. "I'm not a fighter," he warned.

We settled into the soft leather of my car, and as the car radio started, the music picked up where I left off. The gentle strains of Für Elise filled the space. I lowered the volume to a backdrop level, allowing room for conversation. With Corey's vibrant orange GT Mustang leading the way, its convertible top down despite the bone-chilling temperatures that hovered at six degrees below freezing, we embarked on our journey.

Peridot's voice appeared in my head. "Sorry for your abrupt indoctrination to your new role, but the Outer Realm's war is not going well." He shifted and turned towards me, even though he started conversing in my mind. "Like we are communicating now, there are multiple communication channels available to beings from the Outer Realms. In your human form, you can only hear this one, the Celestia channel. When you take your angel form, you have the angel channel and the channel reserved for angels who have not fallen. Focus on the channel to turn them on and off. You can focus on a being who has access to the channel to give a private message. Also, you may focus on your angelic features to turn off the glow from Celestia." He turned off his glow.

My indoctrination was quick, but I had a couple of basics learned.

He whispered to me, "the channel for all angels hasn't been used since the fall."

I figured off how to turn off my glow and the car looked normal with the soft blue light of my dash. With that problem solved I moved to the next issue. "Help me understand," I said. "It's the dead of night, and citizens from various realms have awakened us, thrusting us into an Outer Realms battle that spilled over near an Earth school?"

Scorpia gave a reassuring response from the back seat. "You've grasped the crux of it."

"I have prepared notes," Peridot said, casting a touch of celestial magic that materialized as a golden scroll floating before him. "Peridot, join forces with cousins from both the Outer and Inner Realms, accompanied by a group of exceptional humans possessing the spark. Your specific task is to team up with Rebecca Adams, the Scion of the True Church. She is the Earth representative of Celestia. Provide her with a concise explanation of the universe's rift, the battle raging in the Outer Realms, and the criticality of our mission. You'll find her amiable, even if her friends are a tad uncouth. She blends into our culture."

The scroll vanished, and Peridot added, now settled in the vehicle, "Of course, embarking on a journey to battle, cocooned within the confines of a beautiful vehicle while indulging in lovely music, demonstrates that you fit into the culture of Celestia." His gaze shifted towards Wesley. "Could you summarize the Outer Realms conditions, Realms Master?" he asked.

Wesley, taken aback by the sudden demand, hesitated before relenting under Scorpia's gaze. "Very well," he agreed. "Quick multiverse background. Our universe is a bubble in the greater universe. It spun off soon after the initial universe creation. Another bubble bounced into ours, and those denizens are trying to steal our energy before the quantum entanglement repulses the two universes apart. This is why things have been chaotic, and will end abruptly."

"Concise and accurate," said Peridot.

He gathered his strength. "I need to perform my one job. Let me see if anyone is going to die." He slipped into a trance and his face contorted in pain. He witnessed each of his friend's death and with his information we could alter the circumstances to prevent them.

As the others in the car exchanged concerned glances, Wesley reached for his phone. "I need to call Rachel," he said. He and Rachel were a new couple and navigating the challenges of their relationship. We all tried to support them because they made a cute couple, even though Rachel possessed the fighting ability and muscles, while Wesley pursued a degree in artificial intelligence.

After he concluded the conversation to send her to the battle faster, Wesley slipped back into a trance-like state in the back seat, to foresee deaths and envision alternative outcomes in battle.

Rachel zoomed past us on her motorcycle, defying gravity as one wheel lifted off the ground. Fionnestra perched on the rear seat, gripping Rachel's shoulders with an enormous grin on her face.

"Sometimes I envy the Daoine and the pure joy they experience," said Scorpia.

Peridot swayed his hands along with Für Elise.

Corey's car spun its rear wheels, swerving to the left as he sped up to catch up with Rachel. Though I kept them in sight, driving at seventy miles per hour on an unfamiliar road in the pitch-black night filled me with trepidation. I opted for caution, preferring to arrive later than never at all because of a catastrophic encounter with a tree.

Wesley's voice was heavy. "The two young girls will now survive, but all our fates are unsure. Rebecca, once we arrive, please take to the skies with a diversion. It's the only way Rachel survives."

The realization that our lives hung in the balance intensified the weight on my shoulders. Yesterday, Wesley viewed our deaths occurring on New Year's Eve. That meant something had changed in the past day, something fate could not have predicted.

"You know," I glanced at Peridot, "I've had one training session and one battle since I gained my angelic powers."

Peridot's smile was reassuring as he offered guidance. "If you need to hover, flap your wings swiftly. For speed, lean forward. Block with your shield and strike with your sword," he advised. "Corey, the druid, possesses the skills and power required to seal the Outer Realms portal while on the Realm of Earth. Our mission is to protect him, close the portal, and eliminate any lingering threats."

Scorpia added a crucial detail. "The two young girls the Realms Master saw are playing with a lost book of Outer Realm magic which initiated the portal."

I veered to the right and found myself enveloped in a monochromatic world of black and white, a stark contrast signaling that the battle had already begun. "The Dark Fey have moved the battlefield to the Realm of Shadows," Scorpia informed us. "Will you humans be able to function?"

"Yes, I thought all battles happened when the world shifted to the Realm of Shadow." I maneuvered my Audi into a controlled slide, bringing it to a halt in the parking lot. Next to the columned entranceway to the high school, a dark brown smoke circle of corruption loomed before us; its ominous presence, accompanied by a horde of Dark Fey spilling into our world.

I knew how to get attention, but I hoped Peridot and Scorpia would help me fight. As I jumped out of the car, I cast *Angelic Form*, and I ascended to the heavens as an angel. With shield raised before me and my celestial sword gleaming, my twenty-foot wingspan unfurled, propelling me towards the swirling miasma of the Dark Fey and their sinister bat-like minions.

My voice echoed through the battlefield enhanced with Angelic power. "I am the Scion of the True Church!" In that moment, a radiant beam of Celestia's golden light enveloped me, casting its glow upon the desolate battleground.

The clash of swords and the cries of combatants faded into a temporary silence as the forces of darkness turned their attention towards me—the untrained angel bathed in light that damaged the evil creatures.

In the chaos, Scorpia's urgent command pierced the air, "Realms Master, mark the origins of these creatures!"

Flying beside me, Peridot manifested in his full celestial form, emanating a resplendent golden aura. "Excellent diversion! This plan will hasten the circle of the druid," he affirmed, his voice filled with determination.

Inwardly, I urged Corey, feeling the weight of time pressing upon us. The anticipation swelled within me as Scorpia soared above us, radiating a silver luminescence. In the ground skirmish, I glimpsed the vibrant hues of the Fey Spring Court's emerald green and the swirling dance of blue and green from Albios' magic, showing that Rachel must be fighting alongside them.

My attempt at flight was a mixture of success and inexperience. As I hoped, dozens of flying Dark Fey attacked us and our bright glowing appearance. I hovered, fluttering my wings with desperate determination, but struggled to find the finesse to turn. My efforts brought down one enemy from the dozens that surrounded me, but not without a price. Wounds covered me, a testament to my own inadequacies.

My training was insufficient for this type of battle, but I persevered.

My celestial blade, alongside Peridot's and Scorpia's gold and silver swords, swung at a myriad of enemies. Peridot's *Sanctuary* weakened the surrounding creatures, while Scorpia sent blinding flashes of silver into the enemy ranks. It was too chaotic around me to see the battle on the ground.

Summoning my magical abilities, I called forth a *Healing Deva*, her ethereal form materializing at my side. "***Me servum regni caelestis adjunge***," I chanted.

Bathed in her golden radiance, my wounds mended under her gentle touch. Peridot lent his aid, casting a brilliant golden light upon my wounded frame, restoring me to full health. "They are closing the portal!" he exclaimed.

With renewed determination coursing through my veins, I seized the moment, bashing one foe to the ground with my shield and cleaving through another with my celestial blade. A deafening boom reverberated through the air, dispelling the twenty-foot-high shroud of darkness and the circle within. The concussive force sent me tumbling backward, somersaulting through the air until I lost my balance, crashing upon the asphalt of the parking lot.

Yet, even as I struggled to regain my footing, my celestial blade found purchase in the heart of another adversary. The tide of battle shifted in our favor as Corey joined the fray, decimating the endless hordes of enemies. The once-chaotic battlefield now lay strewn with the lifeless remains of over fifty grotesque creatures: deformed bats, serpentine shadows, and winged crabs, their forms shrouded in the taint of corruption. With their demise, the malevolent smoke dissipated into the wind, leaving naught but fading echoes of darkness.

Peridot enveloped me in the golden light of Celestia's grace, erasing the last of my wounds. The explosion of the portal had sent my healing deva back to Celestia. "Your Deva finished healing me before the force banished it. Come," Peridot held his hand to help me stand, "aid me in tending to the others."

This I could do well.

One by one, we enveloped our companions in the embrace of celestial healing, their weariness vanishing like mist in the morning sun. Yet it was Rachel, burdened with the deepest wounds, who required the most healing. With a tender touch, I focused my energy on her, pouring every ounce of celestial grace into mending her broken body.

Wesley held onto his girlfriend and tears streamed down his face as she opened her eyes.

"What are you crying for?" she teased him. "I'm the one who got beaten up." Her laughter brought a smile to his face. And she hugged him back.

Intrigued by the events that had unfolded, Scorpia turned her inquisitive gaze towards Wesley, her voice laced with curiosity. "Realms Master, what did you witness?"

Wesley, his brow furrowed with bewilderment, shook his head in dismay. "It defies explanation. Dark Fey, their essence—distorted and out of place, intermingled with beings from Gehenna. Neither group were from here... their signatures were wrong." He stammered, expressing his confusion.

The Ellyll, a silver shining emissary from Albios, affirmed Wesley's perception. "You have glimpsed the truth, Realms Master. You've verified the portal breached the veil between universes. This was our fear, but the druid has closed the portal, and we have succeeded. The war will stay off of Earth."

Scorpia patted my shoulder and grinned. "I'd congratulate you, but I'll already need to listen to the troops from Celestia brag about you for the rest of our battle."

However, urgency coursed through Fionnestra's words. "We must not delay, for the front lines beckon us once more."

With a swiftness that mirrored the blink of an eye, the four beings vanished, leaving behind a lingering sense of their otherworldly essence. I relinquished my celestial form and approached the two frightened young girls with a gentle demeanor.

"Am I the only one who saw the anchors of the realms vanish?" Wesley asked.

I shrugged, uncertain of what he referred to. However, my primary concern lay with the two teenage girls. "Corey, the girls might find your size intimidating. Let me take care of them." Kneeling beside the girls, my heart brimming with empathy, I sought to offer solace. "What are your names?"

The girl with light brown hair, tears glistening in her eyes, mustered the strength to speak. "I am Melinda." Her voice was a fragile echo of the pain she had endured.

Her companion, with darker brown hair, wiped away tears with trembling hands before uttering, "It's Mary, but I go by Mare." Their ripped jeans and tattered coats were remnants of the lives they once knew.

"Melinda and Mare," I addressed them, concern etched in every word, "why are you out here? Where are your parents?"

The floodgates of their emotions burst open, their cries mingling with the tears that streamed down their weary faces. Fragmented sentences revealed snippets of loss, foster care, and running away.

My heart ached for their plight, for the losses they had suffered.

I asked Wesley, "will you accompany Rachel back? I will take Melinda and Mare to breakfast, and then we must see Nathan."

Corey placed his arm around me. "Your distraction, which took over half the opposing force, was incredible. Your entry with golden light filling the battlefield saved Rachel, the girls, and me. It takes true strength to have taken that chance, especially without training."

Doubt crept into my mind, as my failures in battle seemed to contradict the notion of strength. "Even though I have proven that I need it, we have to cancel today's weapons training," I acknowledged with regret. The situation unfolding before us, with enemies breaching the borders of Earth from a distant universe, constituted an emergency.

With one last embrace, Corey reassured me, "We will catch up. But remember to call me—for anything."

Resolute, I gathered the two girls, their fragile forms cowering from the magical tome they refused to look upon, which I also collected. Together, we headed to a nearby Waffle House in my car.

The one task I had scheduled for this morning, apologizing to Nicole for a secret Corey and I kept from her, would have to be rescheduled—once again.

Chapter 2—Madison

The Command Center for the Southeastern Territory lay hidden beneath the bustling streets of downtown Atlanta, nestled beneath the Peachtree Center Marta station. Within its secure confines, a palpable sense of angst permeated the air, occupying the minds of the leadership team as they attended to their respective tasks. Madison's gaze drifted to her boyfriend, Nathan, who sat with his arms wrapped around his head, lost in deep contemplation.

With the setup complete for the videoconference, Madison surveyed the room where Nathan had positioned the laptop. The conference room itself exuded an understated elegance, adorned with ten plush red chairs encircling a polished wooden table. A state-of-the-art video conference monitor graced one wall, while a sizable window provided a view of the Command Center. The room boasted impeccable soundproofing, ensuring the utmost privacy and security. Above all, a switch on the wall showed the room's purpose for magical interrogations to discern lies and half-truths.

Curiously, the others avoided the conference room. The team evaded discussions about its use. Even Preacher Jon, the Territory leader, used an alternative table positioned on the landing, overseeing the room. That exquisite cherry wood table stood against a backdrop of black glass concealing intricate computers and connections to the Shared Supernatural System.

It was within this conference room that private and secure actions transpired, decisions that possessed the power to shape destinies. It also served as the central hub for magical connections to the truth detection system, enabling other territories to observe through cauldrons or crystals, depending on their viewing preferences. Each territory had a requirement imposed by the Realized council for such a room.

The morning's activities had been a whirlwind, with Corey and Rebecca soon to join them. Although the fast pace of her new life in the big city and her new identity suited her, Madison occasionally longed for the slower rhythm of Appalachia. So, she made it a point to contribute wherever she could, hoping to win over the affections of those around her and secure her place in this world—an invaluable lesson she had learned during her time in foster care.

Madison limped out into the main room and asked, "Making progress on the hack?" Her voice carried genuine curiosity as she hoped to gain insights into any additional information they had gained. Over the past week, they had learned about the Delta Territory's involvement, but Aaron, who was assisting Nathan remotely, suspected at least one more clandestine group.

"Aaron is conducting tests, and I must remain logged out. So, I'm preparing the Territory Stability Report."

"The Territory Stability Report?" Her interest climbed. She felt an urge to sit, but the lingering throb from her wrapped thigh wound discouraged her. Resisting the temptation to resort to pain medication, she endured the persistent ache—a constant reminder of the dangerous situation they found themselves in. Though she knew the assailants targeted her and Nathan, their identities remained a mystery, individuals audacious enough to open fire with automatic weapons into a crowd.

Nathan, with his left thigh similarly bandaged, propped his leg up on a nearby chair. "This report represents the invaluable contribution of the AI function within the Shared Supernatural System. In the past, prejudices and exaggerations clouded our understanding of the North American Territories. However, with everyone updating their statuses, the AI now compiles a comprehensive report for us, considering the different versions and prejudices," he said, retrieving a few sheets of paper and presenting one to Madison.

"The Canadian Atlantic in upheaval?" She looked over Nathan's shoulder and took in the red highlight on the report.

"Yes, we've received conflicting reports from various sources showing intense battles erupting in Nova Scotia." Nathan exhaled with the news. "That's why Samantha and Morgan had to leave. There are rumors that the conflict spilled over into New Hampshire."

"Samantha and Morgan would go medieval on anyone entering their territory," Madison noted, acknowledging the immense influence wielded by the two prominent witches. Even her Aunt Becky deferred to their authority.

Madison took a sip of water as Nathan continued, "That is our primary concern."

The screen displayed Nathan's data entry. "What about our surrounding territories? You left these areas blank." Her curiosity grew.

"Key West remains stable under Maergran's leadership, although they are contending with a sea monster near Puerto Rico. The Delta Territory remains closed off, and our ceasefire with them is because we don't want war and they fear Corey."

"The Delta vampires are still trying to kidnap Nicole?" she asked.

He winced. "I'm surprised they're the only ones. She's carrying the first new Abernathy druid since our mother, and a global prophecy mentions her specifically."

Nathan knew the global prophecy, but it was a top-secret prediction.

Nathan continued. "Our own territory stands strong despite constant attacks. Leander ensures the Ohio Valley Territory remains secure. Samantha governs New England with unwavering stability, her close friendship with Morgan ensuring the territory's continued solidity. New York faces challenges, but under Clarissa's guidance, it remains resilient."

"You forgot to mention Chesapeake Bay," Madison said, easing herself onto a nearby chair. She had grown accustomed to Nathan's tendency to avoid questions that troubled him.

Nathan sighed, his expression betraying worry and uncertainty. "Yes, Chesapeake Bay is facing its own set of issues."

"Tell me about it," Madison encouraged, offering a reassuring pat on his shoulder. She knew that until Rebecca left the Southeast and took a position in her home of Chesapeake Bay, that territory was in trouble.

"It's too late," Nathan said, pointing towards the camera as Rebecca entered the Command Center, her arms laden with items. Behind her followed two teenage girls.

REBECCA, HER VOICE filled with weariness disguised by a facade of cheerfulness, broke the silence with a hesitant greeting. "Good morning." Madison hurried to her side, taking the bags from Waffle House and the fruit stand.

"You brought breakfast, but you have a story," Madison observed, her gaze locked with Rebecca's weary eyes. "I checked with Chesapeake Bay; the hospital will release your grandmother by dinner." She hoped she'd hear about the battle from this morning that had surprised everyone.

Gratitude flickered in Rebecca's tired eyes as she nodded her appreciation. "If I know grandmother, she's giving them the definitions of supper and dinner and expecting to be out by three." Balancing a weighty tome in her arms, she went to place it on a desk.

"Step back!" Madison recognized the palpable power radiating from the ancient book, a surge that resonated with the forces of the

Outer Realms. Memories of growing up with witches sparked her fear.

"The book the girls used?" asked Rebecca, holding up the evil tome.

"Zonies alive! That book is giving off booger energy from the outer planes. It'll gaum everything! Only Rebecca, with her Celestia tie, can hold it," Madison urged, her Appalachian Mountain accent on full display. She had slipped into her old way of talking in her fear.

Nathan's brows furrowed as he heard those words and viewed a stunned Rebecca. Fingers dancing across the keyboard of his computer, he started a sequence of actions that activated the supernatural and ordinary machinery housed within the chamber.

The room's black glass door, the barrier to the room bridging the realms of the supernatural and the mundane, opened as he guided Rebecca toward a hidden wall. Cooling fans from mundane network equipment, with their lights working alongside supernatural equipment, each with its unique glow based on the type of magic used.

Placing his hand upon a white glowing pad, a concealed safe emerged to safeguard the perilous tome. "Place the tome inside."

Rebecca's fingers released their grip on the ancient book, allowing it to fall into the secure confines of the safe. As she closed the door, a flicker of relief flashed across her fatigued face.

Nathan locked the safe, securing the tome within. Stepping back, they retreated from the protective enclosure, the black glass door closing behind them with an audible click. Nathan's calm demeanor remained intact as he directed his gaze toward Madison, a question poised on his lips.

"You're the only one in the Southeast with knowledge of Realized Witches. What should we do?" he asked.

As if on cue, Corey entered the chamber through the imposing door, his eyes lighting up at the sight of food. "Ah, breakfast," he exclaimed, his voice betraying a hint of joviality, not knowing the seriousness of the situation.

"I'm sorry I spoke in a cumfluttered manner. That book scared me." Madison attempted to regain her composure. She thought through all her old knowledge. "Rebecca, summon your strongest form from Celestia. Use your most powerful healing to cure all those who have come into contact with it. Once we notify Aunt Becky, Leander, Samantha, and Morgan and they can examine it, we can decide the artifact's fate."

A flicker of concern passed through Rebecca's eyes, but she nodded, accepting the weight of the responsibility placed upon her. "Melinda, you will be first."

Rebecca's Celestial form took shape and her wings tucked in behind her back. She chanted in Latin. "***Me servum regni caelestis adjunge.***"

A smaller angel materialized beside her, its radiant essence channeling healing energies toward Melinda. The two girls attempted to flee, but Rebecca gripped Melinda's shoulder, while Corey reacted and hoisted the second girl onto his shoulder, her futile punches landing on his sturdy frame. That boy had been in the war for so long that he was no longer shocked by anything.

A golden glow enveloped the girl, growing brighter with each passing moment. As her head became enshrouded in the celestial light, a shadow emerged from her and took flight, desperate to escape the Celestial magic.

Madison summoned her magical Fey bow, imbued her arrows with Fey magic, and released two that hit the shadowy creature. It plummeted, writhing in its ephemeral agony.

Madison had learned bow hunting from her father as a toddler. Her skills had impressed the other kids when she took part in a contest in Korea, hitting moving targets. Those were the happy times.

Now, instead of becoming a Realized witch, when Corey used enough Earth magic to save her from being sacrificed to a demon, she became a Realized hunter with her powers steeped in the bow. She didn't need magic to be deadly with a bow. However, her skills and magic together made her something else.

Rebecca laid Melinda down, her movements marked by a grace that defied her own exhaustion. She rushed to the side of the other girl, taking her from Corey's arms, her golden glow casting a protective shield over her. Meanwhile, Madison released two more arrows into the dark creature. It would take a lot more to kill it.

Corey traced a circle on the chamber floor, poised to perform a banishment ritual. However, Madison's voice rang out with urgency, halting his actions mid-motion. "Don't banish them! These creatures are not from our universe!" she cried out, her instincts guiding her words.

Corey's bewildered expression transformed into understanding as Madison released two more arrows, piercing the shadowy creature with unerring accuracy. Rebecca's radiant presence intensified, encompassing the second girl in a healing embrace. Corey, assuming the form of a towering ten-foot-tall creature constructed from intertwined sticks and leaves, the very manifestation of the Green Man, struck the creature, his wooden hands crushing its essence. With eight arrows and a few decisive blows, the creature succumbed, lifeless, in this world.

Melinda sat up, her tear-streaked face a testament to the emotional turmoil she had endured. "Thank you. The creature stopped me from warning you. I feel like such a failure."

Yet, their respite was short-lived, as another creature emerged from the second girl. Corey, prepared this time, held it at bay, holding it for Madison's arrows. With a swift and decisive strike, he crushed the creature's essence after it received its share of arrows, ending its malevolent existence. Two shadow creatures from another universe lay lifeless in their world, two young girls sobbing on the chamber floor, and a trio of warriors: Rebecca in her *Angelic Form*, Corey in his *Green Man Form*, and Madison with her summoned bow. The two girls looked on in awe at the decisive victory of the three.

Nathan emerged from the back, his limp, noticeable, his calm demeanor intact despite the wild morning and the pain he endured from a bullet wound. He carried a black box that consumed the surrounding light. "Corey, could you please place the two bodies in this box and seal it for me?" he requested, his voice carrying the same authority as Preacher Jon.

Corey kept his magical form and accepted the task with quiet determination. The hands of the Green Man smoked as he held the creature. Once he secured the bodies within the box, it found its resting place within the protective confines of the safe.

Rebecca sank to the floor, her head buried in her arms.

MADISON WATCHED AS Corey transformed back into his normal form, a muscular warrior trained in fighting and the druidic arts. He lifted Rebecca's limp body, cradling her in his arms. "You saved us once again." He carried her to the table and sat her in a chair.

"You can become a Green Man?" Her feeble voice still carried surprise.

"The Spring Fey Realm appointed me as Earth's Green Man. Those in great need can seek me out and I answer their questions." Corey, moved Rebecca's blonde hair out of her face with care.

"He took that form when we defended the Moon-eyed people," said Madison, helping hold the chair.

The room buzzed with a mixture of anticipation and exhaustion as Corey then assisted the two young girls to their feet. With a tender touch, he guided them over to the table, their hesitant steps echo-

ing in the room. Nathan carried the bags of food, its aromas waft-
ing through the air and filling the space with something other than
dread.

Seated at the table, Nathan's eyes gleamed with delight as he settled himself beside Madison. A vibrant red napkin and matching
plastic ware adorned his place, a cheerful acknowledgment of his
affinity for a "red food day." "Oh good, strawberries," he exclaimed,
his enthusiasm infectious.

Madison couldn't help but admire the unyielding spirit that emanated from Nathan. It was this unflappable demeanor that had solidified her trust in him as a partner. Wincing as he bent his leg, he
took his seat. Mindful of her own discomfort, she said, "we'll need to
change the wraps on our legs today."

Nathan understood Madison was self-conscious about her slips
into a country accent, and he respected her wishes, not to mention
them. He was glad Nicole didn't hear her slip in front of Corey,
knowing Nicole had a jealous streak.

Corey reached for a cluster of large red grapes from the fruit
bowl, plucking them with care before handing them to Rebecca, accompanied by a bottle of water.

Madison could sense the girls' unease. Memories of her own time
in foster care flooded her mind, a painful reminder of the instabil-
ity and loss that had marked her early years. She wanted them to
feel safe. "Girls, I recognize the clothes and the look of foster care.
I spent ten years in the system until I aged out, and every one of
us in this room has experienced the loss of our parents at a young
age. You can talk without us judging you." Though recounting those
years brought forth unwelcome memories, Madison was determined
to help others navigate the treacherous path of the system.

"I have relatives in the Smoky Mountains," said Mare.

"What-what are you all?" asked Melinda.

"I need the simple definitions myself," said Corey. "So, I'll answer. About one percent of the people in the world have what's called the spark. The spark is short for some type of ability with magic. About one percent of those with the spark have a useful skill and use it. We call those people Realized. The four of us," He pointed to Madison, Rebecca, Nathan, and himself, "are Realized."

"Additionally," added Nathan. "Some families, through breeding and lineage over the past few millennia, created specialty Realized that have powers derived from a powerful entity. Corey is a druid whose power comes from Earth. Rebecca is the Scion whose power comes from Celestia, and Madison is a hunter whose power comes from Elysium."

"What's a hunter?" asked Mare, looking at Madison.

Madison gave them a warm smile, showing them a side of her rarely seen in the Foster Care system. It's a magical job. The Earth and the Fey Realm give Corey druid powers and jobs. Rebecca has an angel form and healing because Celestia gave her a job called Scion. Elysium gave me a job called hunter and I have skills with the bow, tracking, and movement. They've told me to protect the Southeast Leadership until I receive more instructions.

"Rebecca and I got the task to save you two this morning, and we brought as many friends as we could find," added Corey.

The girls were confused still. Not at jobs, but at how large of scope their universe became. It was a small world this morning and now they know that the Outer Realms are real, magic is real, and there is a fight between good and evil. These girls needed protection. This wasn't about proving she belonged; it was about helping them.

"Young ladies," Corey always had issues deciding how to address women and opted for respect. "We may seem nonchalant, but we are the tiny part of the world that allows humanity to continue to exist. If we dwelled on every battle, every book that turned out to house evil entities, or otherworldly beings coming to kill or help us, we'd be babbling idiots. Please be comfortable, but I have to know, where did you get that tome?" Corey kept his voice calm, though his face showed wounds from previous battles before arriving here. Still, he wouldn't dare ask Rebecca to heal him in her exhausted state.

Mare reached into her pocket, retrieving her phone. "I sneaked a picture of him," she admitted with rebellion. "We were in a meeting, about to be scolded for wanting to drop out of school, and then he appeared with the book, promising to make everything better."

Melinda's voice quivered as she spoke, the weight of their mistakes weighing upon her. "We're such screw-ups," she sobbed, her vulnerability laid bare.

Corey's reassuring tone broke through the despair, his words meant to offer solace. "Relax," he said. "We're all screw-ups. Well, maybe except Nathan." With a glance at their friend, he added, "Could we run facial recognition through the Shared Supernatural System, along with a separate facial recognition on the normal internet using an offline computer? We need to uncover the truth."

The word "truth" carried another meaning, and Madison knew Corey well enough to know that he feared something, and nothing scared that boy.

Nathan nodded in agreement; his curiosity piqued. "Yes, but will you tell us why you've been acting strange and keeping information to yourself?" He retrieved two laptops and assisted Madison in setting up the Shared Supernatural System.

Corey fetched three plates from Rebecca's collection, a testament to his robust and muscular frame. She noticed Rebecca had gotten one plate for him that was nothing but eggs, which the druid dug into first. Madison couldn't help but find amusement in the dynamic between Corey and Rebecca. They acted like they were still a couple, their unspoken connection clear in the way she knew his breakfast preferences and he knew her favorite fruits. It was a bittersweet reminder that circumstances prohibited them from pursuing a romantic relationship, though their steadfast friendship served as a worthy substitute.

"Girls, take a moment to relax," Madison urged, her voice brimming with empathy. "This may feel like your rock bottom moment, but from here, you can rebuild, with the help of those who have experienced similar hardships." She yearned for the girls to find solace and comfort in the chaos that had thrust them into a world of magic and uncertainty.

As Nathan and Madison delved into their searches, Corey engaged in an animated conversation between mouthfuls of eggs, relishing the nourishment his muscular body craved. "I've been connecting with the Earth, but its information is no longer in line with the Shared Supernatural System," he disclosed. "The Earth tells me of a threat coming from the north of our territory."

A surge of realization dawned on Nathan's face. "Chesapeake Bay," he uttered, his voice filled with a mix of alarm and understanding.

Madison exchanged a worried glance with Rebecca, a silent acknowledgment passing between them. Everyone knew Chesapeake Bay was in trouble, and events were coming to a head.

Corey finished chewing and leaned back in his chair. "I've been prying and paying closer attention during the North American leadership meetings," he confessed. "Last night, everything fell into place. There's a traitor, possibly more than one, among the other territory's leadership." He paused and looked at Rebecca with sorrow. "I'm certain one of them hails from Chesapeake Bay."

"That's why you contacted Rebecca's grandmother in the hospital," Nathan deduced, his voice filled with urgency. "I was so relieved the territories accepted we were at war. I missed this."

"My suspicions came too late." Corey showed Nathan the girl's phone. "He was on my list of suspects I mentioned to Grace."

Corey walked over to a nearby desk, retrieving a lineage book and a signal scrambler. He gulped down a full carafe of orange juice, then spoke with renewed enthusiasm. "I need to burn off those calories, but that tasted excellent," he said with a grin. To the girls, he said, "Grace Addkinson, the head of the Chesapeake Bay Territory of the Realized and Matriarch of the Addkinson estate, is Rebecca's grandmother."

"So, you're the one who's going to fix it?" Mare said to Rebecca, stating what everyone knew. Rebecca's face showed she had not accepted it.

While Corey continued to eat, Madison's search yielded results. "The Shared Supernatural System is fifty percent confident that this person is not among the Realized, but it requires more input," she informed the group.

Nathan, his face etched with shock for the first time in weeks, made a swift decision. "Let's power down both laptops."

Madison powered down her laptop while he gathered everyone's phones, moving them with the laptops to a secure area of the Command Center. With a nod, he showed to Corey that it was time to activate the signal scrambler. "Okay, Corey. We need to understand how you knew to test that. The person you've identified is Masterson Cassidy from Virginia, with a ninety-eight percent confidence. The Shared Supernatural System cannot be so wrong, no matter how bad the hack is."

"Masterson Cassidy is Realized, a high-ranking officer in Chesapeake Bay's defense leadership," Rebecca added, her voice filled with conviction. With a comforting hand on Corey's shoulder, she continued, "I'm sorry, Corey. If he returns to Virginia, they have jurisdiction, not us."

Corey's voice filled with a mixture of concern and determination. "This morning was a diversion. Without the help of our allies in the Outer Realms, their plan would have succeeded."

"What Plan?" asked Madison.

"Sorry. I told you I have to answer questions as the Green Man, so I've been researching all this crazy Outer Realm's war and it ties back to the attacks on us. The barrier between Earth and the Outer Realms is weakest in the Southeast, specifically at Old Donnie's cabin. That's why there are more events here, the attacks are happening here and why we have strong Realized gathering here." Ignoring the fact that his strength caused his druid circles to be sensed around the world, he pointed at Rebecca and Madison.

"Okay, that explains some things," said Rebecca.

"Yeh well, they're trying to take four people out. Your grandmother, Nathan, you, and me." He had answered Rebecca directly. "If they released enough creatures, the Southeast team would have split up to track them all down and we'd be easy pickings."

"Which explains the recent attempt on Grace's life." He looked at Rebecca. "I'm glad your grandmother is going to be fine."

"That you detected traitors while the Shared Supernatural System remained silent suggests something far more ominous," Madison said, her gaze fixed on the Abernathy Lineage book. When Corey started spending more time in it, Madison did as well to help find anything the druid might look for.

Corey had opened it to a page that detailed Old Donnie's liaison, a connection that may have resulted in undocumented heirs. His finger traced a line, revealing an indent. "March," he read aloud.

Rebecca, curious, sought clarification. "March? Is that a name?"

Corey shook his head, a trace of a smile on his lips. "No, this is Old Donnie's frustrated writing style. He pushed so hard that his pen broke."

Ignoring the throbbing pain in her leg from a bullet wound, Madison sprung to her feet, her determination driving her forward. Could she have missed such a crucial detail? Running her finger over the indentation, she confirmed Corey's observation. "He's right. But what does it mean?" she pondered aloud, her voice laced with a mixture of curiosity and concern.

This was worrisome because Old Donnie was Corey's mentor, but was also the Donald Abernathy. Until Corey became Realized, Old Donnie was the only druid for the past one hundred and fifty years.

Corey shook his head. "There is a tie to this word to the weakness in the barrier and the AI system, but I have no proof and don't know the cause. I'll continue with this morning's plan with a workout and then shop with Wesley, Rachel, and Nicole, keeping a watchful eye." Turning to Madison, he continued, "You three need to remain close. I've already alerted Miles and Trish through squirrel communication. Something is going down today, and we need to be alert because something compromised our normal warning system."

Madison took a moment to gather her thoughts, her mind focused on the pressing tasks at hand. "Nathan, you need to complete your territory stability report. I'll settle the girls, find them a new foster home, and enroll them in a school where we know the counselor. I'll also prepare the room for Rebecca's phone call. Rebecca, rest and prepare for your lunch date."

Corey cast a bit of magic, and a squirrel appeared from nowhere, running up to him. Corey described Miles and said, *"Miles, we have two teenagers for your 'Orphan Christmas.' We'll work out logistics."* The squirrel ran off, relaying Corey's message in its unique voice. They had all become accustomed to the druid's magical squirrel network.

To the girls, Corey said, "Some other friends run an outdoors and camping store, and they organize an event called Orphan's Christmas for people away from their families. I hope to stop by. Spending time with a bunch of friendly people is much better than being alone at Christmas."

The girls said little. Too much had happened in too short of a period.

Turning to the girls, Madison reassured them, "This is not a hand-off. I'm going to keep up with you, and I know a family where we can keep you together. I've been where you are now."

Hope appeared in the girls' eyes. They couldn't be over fifteen years old.

Nathan held up his hand. "Corey, you've had a rough couple of days. Are you ready for what's coming?"

Madison understood why they comforted Corey. Circumstances placed Corey in a difficult position. Realized individuals from other territories had to declare their travel first, or it was a criminal offense. The rules stemmed from a time when Realized sought to gather powers unto themselves, and safety required strict regulations. But the territories declared the east coast of North America was now a war zone, and this offense was no longer just criminal; it was traitorous. Corey had used the word "traitor."

Then it hit her. The traitors had traveled to the Southeast Territory, breaking the travel rule to bring an attack to Earth. This went beyond simple spying; the traitors aligned with evil creatures. Corey, as the Battle Leader, was now required to be judge, jury, and executioner of those who sought to destroy Earth. This morning's attack was evidence of that.

"Is there anyone else trained and signed off in the system who could do it?" asked Corey, his tone revealing his knowledge that there was no alternative.

Nathan shook his head.

"Then I'm ready," Corey said.

"But we have training." Rebecca's head almost bounced off the table from exhaustion.

"Remember? Not today," Corey said. He held his former lover's hand. "Your grandmother's plan for you takes precedence."

Madison escorted Rebecca and the girls to the apartments, ensuring they all could rest. Rebecca needed the next few hours to sleep and prepare for her online video date and conversation with her grandmother. The girls needed time to rest and find peace before we presented new options to them.

Meanwhile, Madison focused on helping Nathan prepare the Command Center for upcoming communications. Afterward, she planned to return home and pack. Christmas was just three days away, and she was eager to introduce Nathan to her family and see her parents alive for the first time since she was eight.

She sat down to gather herself. Letting those thoughts creep up on her could show she had baggage.

Her grandparents were old-school evil. They found an opportunity to take over the witches and locked many of them away. Her parents got one last spell cast which hid Madison and Aunt Becky, which earned them mind torture in a time prison. Madison was eight and ended up in foster care, but Aunt Becky collected anyone with witch powers no matter how weak, and defeated her grandparents. Now she was using magic to heal her parent's minds. This was the first time Madison could see them without causing more problems.

Back in control of her emotions, she got back to work. The visit had to go well. One aspect of belonging was not bringing extra baggage from home. If the visit went smoothly and she continued contributing, then she could stay in this place where she was happy.

Chapter 3—Rebecca

My heart fluttered as my phone vibrated, alerting me to the impending appointment. A symphony of Mahler's Fourth filled the conference room, its soaring melodies intertwining with my racing thoughts. I took a deep breath, summoning every ounce of courage to face what lay ahead. The four hours of sleep after the morning's events help me physically. However, the emotional strain awaiting me far outweighed any physical discomfort.

Our conference room looked familiar, but it was where we resolved all the difficult conflicts. There was just enough space between the furniture and the wall, allowing for a twenty-foot run. I found solace in pacing, tracing the intricate maroon and beige pattern painted on the wall, a subtle distraction from the nervous energy coursing through my veins.

As I settled into a chair on the opposite side of the table, my eyes glued to the laptop before me. The clip of Mahler's Fourth continued its melodious journey, now on its third repetition. I silenced it, yearning for a moment of tranquility.

I glanced at the open door, welcoming the sounds from the main room to seep in. This room held profound significance in my journey—a place where my grandmother had entrusted me with the Scion's box, revealing the secrets of my inheritance. It was also where I had shared with Corey the complexities of his relationship with Nicole and the impending doom threatening our world, where we had agreed to deceive Nicole. Fate had now chosen this room as the setting for my online rendezvous—a room I dubbed the "trauma room."

My relationship with Corey had several issues, so it may not have been fair to blame what occurred in this room for all of them. The first challenge was that marrying Corey would lead to the extinction of both the Scion and Druid bloodlines. Druids couldn't have offspring with Scions, and vice versa. The major issue, however, was that if Corey and Nicole didn't get married, the world would come to an end, often with Nicole being the cause. In response to this dire situation, we panicked and lied to Nicole, as well as shield our minds from her empathic abilities. This is why I made a promise to help Nicole remain with Corey, even as he gradually fell out of love with me and into love with her. Trauma room indeed.

I opened the locked box and turned off the deception detection system. If this date went awry, I didn't want him to know I wasn't truthful. Sometimes lies were a young woman's shield against aggressive men, an alternative to transforming into an angelic being and skewering them.

Dressed in my best attire—a maroon twist halter dress—I couldn't help but feel out of place in this Command Center. The exposed contours of my shoulders hinted at alluring sensuality, while the halter design concealed any trace of cleavage. To appear more presentable, I had considered borrowing a pair of Nicole's shoes, but her feet were a size larger than mine. So, I settled for red flats and made a mental note to buy a suitable pair of shoes to complement this dress when spring arrived.

But now, it was time to focus on the matter at hand—I intended to give my best during this virtual encounter, despite my reservations about the trust fund Virginia boys. My grandmother had warned me about their prominent families, unaccustomed to being overlooked, where appearances mattered. In their world, thirty-minute video dates were a small price to pay. Chesapeake Bay was so distant from the war; they'd find it hard to believe that I had fought twice that morning.

I pushed the door shut with a resounding thud. Inside the room, two pieces of paper lay on the conference table, each containing vital information. The first sheet contained basic facts about Lance Tilson, a figure who stood apart from the rest, intriguing me with his uniqueness.

With a glance at the second list, I found a compilation of values I had to prioritize. Strength, as emphasized by my grandmother, took the top spot—a trait of paramount importance. The ability to protect, to engage in battle and emerge victorious, followed. Treating me as an equal, rather than an object, held significant weight in my mind. Though the attribute of being battle-tested seemed outdated considering the absence of threats to the Chesapeake Bay Territory in centuries, it still clung to its place on the list. Flexibility, both in mind and spirit, became a desirable quality, while the final criterion called for a partner capable of confronting the looming threats.

An involuntary roll of my eye betrayed my exasperation. It was a habit I had long sought to suppress, yet it felt justified—Corey's name might as well have been the sole entry on the list. But deep down, I knew this enumeration held little merit. How could I quantify chemistry, attraction, and the way he would treat me? Instead, I resorted to a shopping list of sorts, copied from the one individual who had met my requirements.

My first foray into the realm of online dating had led me to a self-absorbed individual named Sebastian. The man oozed talk of money management, connections, and his extensive experience with lovers. Rejecting him had been effortless, and I classified him as a mere tool within the dating app. His redeeming quality, if one could even call it that, was his choice of attire—a tailored suit.

The second suitor, Filmore, boasted a braggadocios demeanor, flaunting his flabby physique without a shirt to hinder his display. He possessed no redeeming characteristics, his chest paling compared to Corey's rugged appeal.

In stark contrast, my third date proved to be a delightful affair—an encounter with a gentleman aptly named Baron, who exuded an unmistakable air of confidence in his sexuality. Once I had assured him of my discretion, he became a vivacious companion, sharing laughter and a genuine connection. Baron possessed impeccable taste, suggesting I seek a hibiscus-colored chiffon dress—a suggestion I might entertain when we could arrange such a meeting.

And now it was Lance who awaited my call. I banished any lingering concerns about my appearance, reminding myself that Corey had a point—I was a fantasy girl to these men, an embodiment of their desires shaped by my upbringing, wealth, and physical beauty. The events surrounding the Curia had thrust me into the limelight, burdening me with unwanted power and fame within the circle of the Realized. If it was difficult to be pretty, it was downright distressing to be a fantasy girl.

However, duty and responsibility held sway over my desires, compelling me to confront the challenges that lay ahead. In due time, I would assume a leadership position within the Chesapeake Bay Territory advocating for the True Church.

I knew I had ample time to navigate the treacherous waters of expectation. After the holidays, I would allow myself a brief respite, a couple of weeks to recharge, before considering my next steps. The territory and my grandmother deserved my help, but we should move methodically and avoid rushing into mistakes.

The conference room, enveloped in dim lighting, felt inadequate as a backdrop for the forthcoming encounter. Nathan and Madison had arranged additional sources of illumination, casting a flattering glow upon my face. A video camera, equipped with a seventy-five-millimeter lens, stood ready to capture my likeness—an accurate portrayal, albeit with its limitations.

As I adjusted the delicate pendant necklace featuring a charm depicting the one tree, I pondered the hang-ups associated with ex-boyfriends. I refused to let their influence dictate my choice of attire. After all, the necklace was a thing of beauty, and past associations should not taint its presence.

Corey and I had made significant progress in moving past our desire to rekindle our relationship. The way we were moving forward strengthened our friendship, offering the potential for the best of all worlds. However, we both needed more time.

The unspoken question, one that would remain unspoken, lingered—most Realized lived for a couple of centuries, while Druids and Scions could live for a millennium. In two hundred years, Corey and I would still be young.

I reminded myself that I was twenty-five, with the immediate and sole responsibility to produce an heir to the bloodline of the Scion. Eventually, I would step into a leadership role in the Chesapeake Bay. A solid line of succession, with the bloodline secure, meant an end to the chaos. Perhaps starting with a junior position to gain experience.

A persistent chime broke the tranquil silence, and with a curious mix of surprise and intrigue, I noticed the incoming call originated from the philosophy department at Georgetown University. How peculiar. However, calling this number required a secret code.

With a warm smile, I tapped the answer button and greeted the unknown caller. "Hello, this is Rebecca speaking."

The soft glow of the computer screen illuminated his room, casting a gentle light on the worn-out books and scattered papers adorning the desk. The man on the other end defied the mold of a typical philosophy student or professor. His weathered, wise eyes hinted at a life well-lived, leaving room for the possibility of a profound conversation.

With a warm beam, he introduced himself. "Hello, Rebecca, I am Lance Tilson. It's a pleasure to make your acquaintance." His demeanor exuded formality, yet his casual attire and the faint sounds of a bustling office in the background created an intriguing contrast.

"You've already intrigued me, Lance. Your voice carries excitement, and yet I haven't come across your name before." His call's origin and his polite greeting gave this date a promising start.

Lance chuckled, the sound resonating through the phone. "I'm not surprised you haven't heard of me. I happen to be the black sheep of the Tilson family."

A laugh escaped me in response. "You don't strike me as a disappointment."

He recounted his remarkable journey. "I graduated from high school at fourteen and completed my pre-med degree at eighteen. Tired of being discredited because of my youth, I accepted a commission in the army. I served as an intelligence officer in Afghanistan for several years, and now I'm pursuing my PhD in Theology."

"That's quite an extraordinary life for someone who's twenty-five-ish," I said, aware of the disappointment families often feel when a person diverts high potential towards personal happiness.

"Yes, quite right. I am twenty-five, and while I may share some qualities with the person you described in your requirements, I know I don't quite measure up to him." Lance gave a wry smile.

Intrigued by his allusion, I raised an eyebrow. "If someone asked you to create a list of requirements, would you base it on your past partners and select the qualities you admired in them?"

Lance paused, contemplating the question. "Touché. Although, in the Southeast Territory where you operate, you've been on the front lines of the war, as your requirements show. Here, in the safety of our ignorance, nobody comprehends the true meaning of strength."

"If you understand that, then you must comprehend it too," I challenged, sensing there was more to this man than met the eye. Perhaps not enough for a romantic connection, but at least he could hold an engaging conversation.

"Two tours in Afghanistan gave me some insight, and I had a brief encounter with the threats faced by the Realized. But I know enough to realize that I don't know enough," Lance confessed with a humble and longing tone. "In fact, I was on duty when your ex fought the Deer Woman. The power he used ignited sensors in Afghanistan and made others fear him even more."

I avoided talking about Corey. "You mentioned being Realized. What is your power?" I asked. Time was of the essence, and I couldn't afford to be coy during these brief encounters.

"Ah, my power is equally disappointing to my family. Whenever I lay my eyes upon anything of historical or religious significance, I gain all the significant facts related to it," Lance said. "I even blurt them out involuntarily, much to the amusement or annoyance of those around me."

"Don't underestimate the value of information. Two months ago, Wesley's insights saved my life. He foresaw the danger we were in and alerted us, allowing us to change our circumstances and survive. I'm sure you must have a similar story," I probed, hoping to extract more information from him.

"The army classified the circumstances of that mission, but it played a role in enabling me to begin my program at Georgetown three years earlier than planned," Lance hinted, his words laced with intrigue.

Now, that was interesting. "That makes the third intriguing thing you've mentioned during our conversation. However, I can put two and two together. A person doesn't go from pre-med to military intelligence and ends up studying Theology unless the classified item had religious significance," I deduced, waiting for any subtle reaction to confirm my suspicion.

After a prolonged pause, Lance spoke. "I'm sorry, but I can neither confirm nor deny that."

A chuckle escaped my lips. "My family has its share of company and military experience." I chose my words carefully, knowing that Lance would understand my use of the word 'company' as a reference to the CIA. "But enough about me. What questions did you have for me?" I flashed him a sweet and intimidating smile, hoping to divert his attention away from anything but my warmth. Weak individuals often forgot their inquiries when faced with that smile.

Lance, however, seemed undeterred and posed his question, a glimmer of challenge in his eyes. "Well, Ms. Adams, how have your team dynamics changed since the Scion's rebirth?" His smile was sly, as if he had posed a tricky question.

Impressed by his resolve to maintain his query, I rewarded him with a comprehensive answer. "Our team makeup is unique, rendering power levels and comparisons meaningless among us. However, we now have the first full druid in over a millennium, the first bard in over a millennium, and a host of battle-tested members. The Scion's rebirth after a century holds little significance for us compared to those who haven't faced the same threats we have."

"That's intriguing. But only the Chesapeake Bay Territory reveres the Scion as the embodiment of Realized powers. What are the chances of you moving to that territory in the coming years?" Lance asked.

"Zero. My presence would bring the war to people who are ill-prepared. Those I've spoken to in the territory believe politics to be the battlefield. Besides, I need to travel with my team for mutual protection. We're tracking four class one threats and three class two threats. If we're lucky, we won't have any ongoing investigations by January," I disclosed.

Mentally counting the threats we monitored—two imminent vampire invasions, classified as class one, two unknown entities also classified as class one, two Gullah spells predicted as class two, and rumors of a rogue gargoyle sighted by Nathan and Madison—I couldn't forget the confirmed Curia Cardinal attack scheduled for New Year's Eve.

"You'll have quite a busy December ahead," Lance observed. "Would it surprise you to learn that the Chesapeake Bay Territory has issued a stand-down order?"

My eyes widened in surprise. "We have a ninety-five percent confidence that at least two of the supernatural events predicted in the Chesapeake Bay Territory will require military intervention. We're planning to provide emergency support before things get out of hand," I shared.

Corey's warning of something big from the northern part of our territory ran through my mind.

Lance seemed intrigued by this revelation. "Your grandmother would be furious if she had to seek help from other territories," he commented, a hint of fear creeping into his expression at the mention of my grandmother.

"She would be. I can't imagine what the tactical leader is thinking." Powerful families had the authority to make demands, but if those demands caused failure or embarrassment, the repercussions would be severe.

"Our military's proximity to the Pentagon has led to excessive politicization, and there are no strong Realized individuals among the Chesapeake military leadership anymore—just those connected by family ties," Lance said with disappointment.

"When our team assessed the preparedness of the neighboring territories, I had to inform my team that the Chesapeake Bay Territory wasn't concealing its readiness from us, unlike some other areas. They're unprepared to fight without relying on conventional weapons," I said.

A notification pinged on my computer, drawing Lance's attention. His face lit up with a grin. "Ms. Adams, I've enjoyed our conversation, and I'm grateful for this half-hour of your time, even if it was nothing more than a pleasant exchange."

"Thank you, Mr. Tilson. It's been a pleasure getting to know you." With a click of a button, I ended the call and took a deep breath, relieved that this encounter was over. The conversation had been more of an entertaining interlude than a potential romantic encounter.

I could count on at least a couple of months of respite from such encounters, considering a few factors. Foremost, I couldn't visit another territory without security measures in place for them and me, which meant having Corey, who handled the Southeast Territory's defense, by my side. Corey had provided me with a list of requirements, and I was certain no one else would agree with them.

Besides, Corey terrified the Realized across North America, and his reputation preceded him. He was in the top ten most powerful Realized in North America at twenty-five years old. The old guard, all having been in charge for centuries, failed to lock him down thanks to Preacher Jon. My relationship with Corey was how I became infamous even before being given the powers of the Scion by Celestia.

Soon, I would call my grandmother and listen as she informed me that the territory couldn't meet the defense requirements. I would be relieved to report that while one person was a weak match and the other a friendly acquaintance, neither of them was marriage material. And so, this chapter would come to a close, at least until security concerns no longer took precedence over other considerations.

The soft chime of the laptop phone jolted me from my reverie, its unexpected sound piercing the stillness of the room. Curiosity tingled within me as I reached out to answer the call, my fingers trembling. "Hello, this is Rebecca," I spoke into the device, my voice laced with anticipation.

A hushed voice emanated from the other end, and I strained to listen, feeling my heart quicken its rhythm. "Shush, I hear her. Where do I speak?" It was my grandmother. "Oh, my, you went all out for these dates. That is a beautiful dress."

A surge of warmth flooded my chest at her compliment, and I couldn't help but smile. "Thank you, Grandmother. You asked me to take these dates seriously, and I've done just that." Sitting up straight in my chair, I noticed the unexpected nature of this call. Something extraordinary was about to unfold. Grandmother, still ensconced in the hospital, had changed into her normal clothes. Any doctor who kept her too long was going to face her wrath.

Grandmother's laughter danced through the line, a melody of amusement and familiarity. "Excellent, because I had a delightful conversation with Young Nathan and Young Corey. Corey, in all his muscle-clad glory, sweat glistening on his skin from an interrupted workout. Oh, my! Yowza."

The memory of Corey's rugged charm brought forth a genuine laugh. Once upon a time, his appearance would have elicited the exact response from me, but things had changed. "He's been training me with weapons, and that's how he looks when he's about to leave me covered in bruises," I confessed. I couldn't help but wonder why Grandmother hadn't mentioned the call with him last night.

Grandmother chuckled, her amusement contagious. "Well, fear not, for we have found a solution to our dilemma. It seems Corey has learned a new spell from the ancient Moon-eyed people, a forgotten tribe in Appalachia. He can create portals between two trees here on Earth and travel between them. In fact, he has already tested one from his house to a campsite in the Cowee mountains near Asheville."

"That's amazing," I said.

"Yes, since my Realized power can explain any other Realized power, I shut down the objections here." Grandmother could have done it with force of will, but using her power would have added strength to her argument.

My mind conjured images of Rachel and Corey experimenting with their newfound powers during combat training. I had watched Corey conjure a patch of grass, hoping to trip Rachel, but her incredible speed with a new magical spell had foiled his plans. Their laughter echoed in my ears as I remembered how their mischievous antics had brought the training session to an end. "*Tree Transfer* sound incredible," I said.

"Well, here's the plan. You, Adventurous Nicole, and Young Corey will make your way up here. Corey will use his tree spell to return home, leaving you and Nicole behind. Nicole, with her newfound ability to send powerful emotions, can alert her betrothed, ensuring swift responses in times of defense," Grandmother explained.

"It will be wonderful to visit the Virginia house." I replied diplomatically but the prospect of spending time with others who understood the melancholy of the holiday season had shattered. Corey, Clive, and Rachel shared a beer-fueled Christmas morning each year, longing for an end to the holiday madness. That had sounded like genuine joy.

"Excellent," Grandmother said. "If you let me know whom to invite for the luncheon to celebrate your arrival, we can make all the arrangements." Her smile radiated through the phone as she leaned forward, anticipation shimmering in her eyes.

The next date would be in person. I pondered the company I desired. Lance held an air of pleasantness, but the prospect of spending the day engrossed in discussions about dresses and makeup with Nicole and Baron seemed far more enticing. "Well, Baron—"

"Rebecca," Grandmother interrupted, her voice firm yet loving. "I shall arrange a shopping expedition for you, Adventurous Nicole, and Fun-loving Baron. However, it would serve as a second date, a ruse to appease those ever-watchful family eyes. They would see through a man like Baron."

With the allure of a shopping trip with Baron, I conceded, "The excursion with Baron sounds delightful. As for the luncheon, I believe Lance Tilson would be the companion to engage in pleasant conversation."

Grandmother's eyes crinkled with amusement as she nodded approvingly. "Interesting choice. He is the only young man in Chesapeake Bay who the Realized would approve for marriage. I shall invite Lance and his family. And I have a bit of good news for you."

As my heart sank from the word marriage, hope flickered in my chest as I leaned forward, eager to hear the good news. "I could use some good news," I confessed.

A mischievous twinkle sparkled in Grandmother's eyes. "The renowned painter of the Realized, Christopher Murphy, has agreed to include you in his list for a family portrait. He will contact you before the year's end." Her radiant smile conveyed the honor and significance of this opportunity.

"Christopher Murphy, the artist from Connecticut?" I asked, my mind racing with snippets of conversations and whispers of his unparalleled talent.

Grandmother's voice softened with a note of caution. "Yes, dear, Christopher Murphy. He is a sensitive artist from old money, renowned for his specialized portrait skills. His power aligns with his artistic prowess. But be careful; he can be a bit... difficult."

I couldn't help but chuckle at the warning. Considered for a portrait by such a respected artist was an honor beyond my wildest dreams. "I will be cautious, Grandmother." The thought of capturing a moment in time, frozen on canvas, was both exhilarating and humbling.

A delicate silence settled between us, and I seized the opportunity to bring up a matter close to my heart. "Grandmother, may I discuss something with you?" I asked.

"Of course. You know you can always confide in me."

The weight of her words, the unwavering love and understanding behind them, eased my apprehension. "I learned that the Chesapeake Bay Territory has ceased its military activities. We believe the territory will face two or three supernatural incursions before the year's end."

A flicker of concern passed over Grandmother's face, a subtle furrow forming between her brows. "Thank you, dear. I have already spoken with the Colonel, who has served as the Tactical Leader for quite some time. I shall monitor the situation, and if there is any sign of inadequacy in handling the challenges of this new reality, I will appoint a new Battle Leader for Chesapeake Bay."

Gratitude swelled within me as I listened to her reassuring words. The sense of security her presence provided was immeasurable. "Thank you, Grandmother."

"I also want to thank you for paying attention to the territory. I understand your desire to move at a measured pace, but the world may force your hands."

That was a scary thought. "Grandmother, I am doing what I can, making moves where I can. Sometimes it feels like we're constantly fighting the supernatural, leaving little time for anything else."

"Sending you kisses, dear." We both puckered our lips toward the screens, bidding each other farewell as the call ended.

Closing the laptop, I unplugged the camera, the small click echoing in the now-quiet room. As the soft glow of the screen faded, I released a deep breath, allowing myself to relax and reflect on the momentous news that had unfolded.

I opened the unlocked box on the wall and flipped the magical switch to turn the room's magic back on. In every territory, there was a monitored location where lies could not be told. Magic in the room would turn the lights red in the presence of a lie or even a half-truth.

I thought through any half-truths I might have said, but I had been truthful on both calls. Still, better safe than sorry.

I locked the box, ensuring that no one could tamper with it. The room was now a sanctuary of truth and transparency.

Chapter 4—Rebecca

It was a momentous morning, filled with duties that weighed on my mind. However, as the day progressed, I yearned for normalcy. I longed to cast off the burdens of the day and embrace the promise of a relaxing afternoon.

With my planner, its pages marked with a list of my responsibilities, I scanned the tasks that awaited my attention. A sense of anticipation mingled with the weight of responsibility as I adjusted and rearranged the action items, ensuring everything was in order. An email from Kim, representing Chesapeake Bay's IT team, demanded my attention.

I delved into its contents, absorbing the vital information it contained. I needed secure connectivity during my upcoming trip. With focused purpose, I navigated through the tasks, bringing me closer to relaxation. The fact I could perform the tasks on my own without calling for technical support gave me refreshed confidence.

Satisfied I had discharged all my duties, I left the conference room and allowed my gaze to wander across the expanse of the main room. To the left, the upper section revealed a grand conference table in front of the black glass room with mundane and supernatural equipment, the safe where the tome was located, and a peculiar sensor—a device designed to detect Realized, individuals with supernatural abilities, within our territory.

We had a congregation of Realized here in downtown Atlanta and Near Roswell. Buford at the camping store was a hotbed. The friendly vampires in Charleston, The Tribe up in the mountains, and Madison's family in Chattanooga all shone brightly. There were smatterings of weaker signs, but no one else was in the Southeast Territory.

This reminded me of Corey's druidic power—a force connected to the Earth itself. Our team relied on strategically placed sensors to detect the supernatural, in contrast to Corey's more spiritual connection with nature. These signals converged on the monitoring contraption behind the black glass. The same room that housed the tome and those dead beings from this morning.

"I'm going to relax and pack for my trip," I informed Nathan.

Nathan raised a finger in a gesture of significance, signaling an impending development. He placed Corey on speakerphone, casting the Command Center into an incandescent sea of crimson hues. The room hummed with electric urgency.

"I'll pull up the list," Nathan said through his computer's microphone. "Only Grace has sent her signature to travel to the Southeast Territory from Chesapeake Bay. You sound worried."

A sense of foreboding gripped me as Corey's voice, transformed into a hardened iteration of himself, emanated from the speaker. It was his self-defense mechanism when burdened with tasks that troubled his soul. His words reverberated through the room, carrying tension. "This van may not be from Virginia, but I have a bad feeling about this."

"I'll notify Grace, and do not communicate with the Chesapeake Bay team without me until further notice," Nathan ordered.

My curiosity surged, fueled by the events unfolding before me. "What is happening?" I asked.

Nicole's voice joined the conversation through the speakerphone. "It seems to be an unauthorized incursion by the Chesapeake Bay team," she warned, her words laced with trepidation. Preacher Jon's warning echoed in my mind—a haunting reminder of the dangers in the world of the Realized. "Send your signature to every territory you travel to," he had cautioned. "Any Realized discovered in a territory without authorization is a criminal offense. And they don't even need to return your body."

As the weight of realization settled upon my shoulders, the unfolding events grew even more disconcerting. The Territories of North America declared us a war zone, locked in battle with the Dark Fey and those using gargoyles as weapons. Corey had stumbled upon individuals who violated the laws of the Realized by traveling here. He had discovered traitors—where his Earth senses told him they would come.

Though I knew they had discussed this in the morning, exhaustion had made it all feel like a dream. It had proven the Shared Supernatural System compromised beyond our worst fears.

Nicole's urgent voice echoed through the room once more. "Something is wrong," she warned, fear and determination intermingling in her tone. "Rachel has moved to flank them, and Corey... Corey has loosened his belt—a sign that he is preparing to use his knives." She paused. "Oh no, Corey said he recognized someone from a picture and manhandled that person into their van."

The gravity of the situation struck me like a thunderbolt, paralyzing me. He recognized the man who used the girls to open this morning's portal.

"Are the interlopers armed?" Nathan asked.

Corey's voice, resonating with a profound sense of purpose, pierced the air, commanding my attention. "Wesley, you drive their van," he stated over the speaker, his tone leaving no room for doubt. "Nicole, follow us in the car. I'll ride in the van with Rachel. Keep my phone and relay the message to Nathan—we are bringing these Realized from Chesapeake Bay in for questioning."

One part of every Realized recognizing Corey benefitting us now was how few people would fight him. If Rachel, his friend and weapons trainer, flanked them, Realized would know they were unlikely to survive the encounter. Rachel had a few powers, but her fighting skills were supernatural, and she and Corey had fought side by side for a decade.

Nicole's voice, a mix of trepidation and trust, responded over the speakerphone, her words carrying the weight of our collective resolve. "We are all coming in with the... prisoners."

"Loud and clear, Nicole." Nathan clicked off the speaker and handed me a different phone. "The head of the Chesapeake Bay Territory seeks a private conversation with you."

At that moment, I understood the magnitude of the situation.

I gripped the sleek smartphone, finding solace in its weight as I hurried into the room that held my destination—the trauma room. Determined to secure absolute privacy and minimize distractions, I leaned against the sturdy wooden door until it latched with a resolute thunk. Alone in the dimness, I raised the phone to my ear.

"This is Rebecca," I spoke, my voice infused with a blend of anticipation and fear, for on the other end of the line awaited my grandmother, the revered leader of Chesapeake Bay.

"Rebecca," her tone was gentle, yet burdened with gravity, "I had intended to broach this topic delicately, but your earlier question hinted at troubles within our territory. Corey, the Southeast Battle Leader, has stumbled upon an unauthorized incursion. There are two crucial matters you need to know."

My heart quickened its pace as I leaned closer to the phone, yearning to absorb every morsel of information my grandmother was about to reveal.

"We have adopted a more flexible understanding of what it means to be Realized within our territory. Many bloodlines that were once blessed with talent have lost their connection to the spark. To address this, Kim, one of our trusted IT members, will dispatch a secured printout to an Atlanta printer exclusively for our territory members. You will receive a code via text message, granting you access to retrieve and print this document."

"Yes, grandmother." The word trusted floated in my head and haunted me.

"Second, before Corey questions, it is imperative that you confirm the identification of each individual involved. Inform them you are my official representative, present to witness and observe the proceedings. Take meticulous notes, but refrain from interfering with the questioning."

"Of course, grandmother." Confusion lingered within me. The intricacies of the situation eluded my understanding.

My grandmother's voice softened, empathy permeating through the line. "I understand that this may be perplexing, but let me shed some light. If these individuals fall within our Realized list and were caught circulating a picture of Corey, along with his name, within the confines of churches, then the laws are unequivocal. This treasonous act within a war-zone demands strict retribution. If they carry forged orders bearing my signature which call for the murder of another territory's leadership, this is unprecedented. By invoking the Council's Realized laws, I have already assured Nathan that jurisdiction lies with the Southeast Territory."

Her voice grew steely, mirroring Corey's. "By God, if someone from our own ranks started that attack this morning, I will have to take drastic measures to root out any potential traitors within our defense leadership and prevent a war with one of our closest allies."

The weight of her words crashed upon me, the events of the day escalating far beyond the realm of a simple date. Now, I found myself embroiled in judging those accused of treason. "Yes, grandmother."

"Be strong." Her words carried a blend of caution and reassurance. Heavy silence sat between us. "We have detected Dark Fey in Virginia, and they may have compromised our security. This act would serve as the first confirmation of our circumstantial evidence."

As the call ended, my world had shifted within a matter of minutes. Composing myself, I exited the room and handed the phone to Nathan, entrusting its safekeeping to him. Without delay, I retrieved my device and entered the code provided by my grandmother, starting the printing process.

The secure printer hummed to life. Page after page emerged, each containing an entry from the Chesapeake Bay Territory's Realized list. This report spanned twenty pages, arranged in alphabetical order. Every entry bore the individual's name, their position of influence, a photograph, and a concise notation denoting their Realized status, accompanied by a brief description.

My responsibility was to check the prisoners from the list. I'd be present with Corey and the prisoners.

Nathan, his face etched with a gravity befitting our situation, gestured toward the laptop I had been using for my notes. "Please, set up there," he requested. With Madison's help, he draped a thick white sheet over the table's far end. Drops of moisture clung to Madison's hair, remnants of a hurried shower—a testament to the urgency that had brought us together.

Taking my place at the table's edge, I positioned myself before another laptop. Madison settled beside me; her unease barely concealed beneath a forced smile.

The surreal nature of our circumstances enveloped me, realization unfurling in layers. "I am still grappling with the enormity of it all." My vulnerability was difficult to hide. "I am just beginning to comprehend any of this, yet now I find myself thrust into the role of my grandmother's representative."

Madison pulled up the form on her screen and showed me how to save it in the system for each person. Then, her gaze scanning our surroundings, she leaned closer. "Aunt Becky once shared a piece of wisdom with me. She said that once you find yourself entangled in a war, whether by choice or circumstance, your life can transform in an instant. One moment, you may flirt with attractive witches in Glasgow, and the next, you're devising plans for a rebellion to rescue your loved ones. It's best to embrace the tumult and navigate through the chaos while you still have the chance."

A flicker of understanding ignited within me as I absorbed Madison's words, their wisdom resonating deeply. "That is advice I need." I focused with newfound determination. "To navigate this, I must think like Corey, to perceive the world through the eyes of someone who has spent years embroiled in the throes of war. A church bus in a church lot would not have captured my attention, but for Corey, it was all he needed to start an investigation."

Madison's smile broadened, infused with empathy and camaraderie. "When we emerged victorious from the defense of the Moon-eyed people, the magnitude of the bloodshed left me in a state of shock. Even Miles, who had witnessed dozens of battles, stood in awe of the carnage. Corey confessed to feeling nothing—a testament to his battle-hardened soul. The struggle enmeshed that boy for years, while the rest of us scramble to catch up, still fumbling in the darkness."

The weight of Madison's words settled upon me. Our lives had undergone a transformative shift, and now we stood on the precipice of a war unlike any other. With newfound resolve, I steeled myself for the trials that lay ahead.

Wesley led a group of eight individuals, their faces obscured by black bags secured over their heads. Their hands were bound, rendering them defenseless as they shuffled forward into the Command Center. Rachel and Corey followed behind them, adding an air of authority to the grim procession. Curiosity gnawed at my insides as I joined the gathering.

Nicole followed last and handed a bag and two folders to Corey. He accepted them with a sense of urgency. In one hand, he clutched a small bag, while the other held two folders brimming with information.

Nathan read aloud the orders. The gravity of their mission hung heavy in the air as their orders from Chesapeake Bay became clear. They were to surrender Corey Norwood's and Rebecca Adams' lifeless bodies to any church possessing a gargoyle capable of devouring our souls. The group's earlier proximity to a gargoyle lent an ominous weight to the situation.

Nathan reached for a handheld sensor resting on his desk. He scanned each individual, ensuring their connection to the realm of Dark Fey and their encounter with a gargoyle within the past eight hours. "Verified. Each person has indeed been within ten feet of a Dark Fey and encountered a gargoyle within eight hours." Nathan entered the gathered information into the computer, a gateway to the shared Supernatural System.

His fingers danced across the keys as he delivered the chilling revelation, lifting one folder. "This is an unauthorized approval. Grace Addkinson has verified these orders as forgeries."

My heart sank at the realization that Corey, burdened with undeniable proof of treason, carried the weight of a terrible decision. His face turned to steel, an unyielding resolve shining in his eyes. He knew what had to be done. Armed with damning evidence of betrayal, he sharpened his military stance.

This wasn't just about one person or a picture from a young girl's phone. Our team had caught them breaking multiple laws and carrying forged orders, calling for murder. The instigator of the morning's attack among them added to their crimes.

Planning to murder me, the heir to the Addkinson estate, was a significant offense. But attempting to kill the Battle Leader of the Southeast Territory, the third in charge, during a declared war, was a different level of criminality. Their alignment with the enemy and the involvement of a gargoyle pointed to a coup or siding with the enemy.

Corey's voice rang out with commanding authority, piercing the hushed silence. "You shall not speak or communicate. Your sole purpose now is to listen." His gaze shifted to Nathan. "Nathan, please explain to them why they are here."

Nathan's tone softened as he assumed the role of the good cop. "Rebecca, would you be so kind as to enlighten them about the purpose of your presence?"

Surprised by the impromptu request, I collected my thoughts. "I am the Scion of the True Church and the rightful heir to the Addkinson Estate. In this capacity, I represent The Chesapeake Bay Territory under the direction of Grace Addkinson."

A man voiced his objections, only to be silenced by Corey's fist connecting with his chin. The room held its breath as Corey's unwavering gaze swept across the assembled individuals.

"Anyone else forget the meaning of 'listen until we ask you a question'?" Corey's restrained ferocity laced his voice. "We will deal with him last." Stepping back, he glared at the remaining individuals gathered before him. This was why he had taken on his 'hard Corey' persona.

The rest of the group trembled, while two among them succumbed to tears. Corey had mentioned that Old Donnie had trained him for this very moment, a task dreaded yet necessary. But unlike the sterile confines of the Command Center, the crucible of The Tribe forged Corey.

I drew in a deep breath, aware that what I had just witnessed went beyond a mere bad cop routine. Echoes of Preacher Jon's ominous words reverberated in my mind about what would happen should I travel to another territory uninvited. "They don't even have to return the body." The weight of the situation pressed upon me as Nathan resumed control of the proceedings.

Nathan's approach contrasted with Corey's, donning the mantle of the good cop. "Here is what will transpire. You are under the jurisdiction of the Southeast, and we shall adhere to the council's approved plan for questioning. I shall lead you into the truth room, where the lights will turn red in the event of falsehoods. First, Rebecca will establish your identities, after which Corey will begin the interrogation."

Miles entered, carrying a case filled with mason jars, which he handed to Corey. Engrossed in a hushed discussion, Corey and Miles conferred before Corey ushered the case into the room. The implications of what lay ahead were palpable.

Nicole waved to catch Corey's attention. "Corey, Wesley and I will handle the three pm meeting. Call me if we need to cancel."

Corey nodded in acknowledgment. His demeanor caused Nicole to act reasonable and polite instead of playful and challenging. Rachel took charge of escorting a man into the room, and I followed behind, aware of Corey's piercing glare fixed upon the traitor, his grip tightening around a small sack.

Corey's voice rumbled with a low growl. "Rachel, please assist Nathan outside. The three of us can handle the work here."

Without hesitation, Rachel exited the room. The absence of her contagious grin left an undeniable solemnity in its wake.

Madison stood by my side, her trembling form reflecting the apprehension that consumed us both. "If I may, Corey?" Her voice quivered as she sought a place in the proceedings.

Corey nodded, granting her the floor.

"I am Madison Roane, the documenter and observer for the Southeast Territory. Rebecca Adams serves a similar role for the Chesapeake Bay Territory. Corey commands authority within this room and leads the investigation, having received his interrogation training under the tutelage of Donald Abernathy, whose credentials are registered in the Shared Supernatural System."

Her words resonated, underscoring the gravity of the situation. An unease settled within me, a stark realization that this was not my domain. The document Madison had shared, with its references to violence and checkboxes signifying potential death sentences, turned my stomach.

Madison added, "If you look over your shoulder, you'll see representatives from the Ohio Valley Territory and New England Territory observing these proceedings. Everything in this room will adhere to the procedures we were all trained in."

A white sheet draped over a chair drew my attention. As I pondered its purpose, a man locked eyes with me, his voice brimming with resentment. "You cannot allow the uncivilized to treat us in such a manner."

Corey silenced the man with a powerful blow to his solar plexus, and his question hung in the air. "What is your name and position?"

The man's contemptuous expression offered no respite, further straining his already fraught relationship with Corey. In response, Corey produced three purses and a handful of wallets, a visual declaration of the man's refusal to comply with identification procedures. I marked him as uncooperative on the form, noting down the act of violence under 'cooperation violence.' The checkbox for violence was a stark reminder that explanations were not required.

The traitor's stoic facade crumbled as a knife plunged into his arm, eliciting a pained cry. Corey delivered warnings with ruthless clarity, leaving no room for ambiguity. His eyes widened as Corey withdrew a second blade, the air thick with tension. I refrained from correcting Corey's actions as ordered, documenting the act of violence under 'cooperation violence.' The traitor's screams filled the room, shattering the illusion of unity.

With a swift motion, Corey inserted a rag into the traitor's mouth. "I trained with a group of Realized survivalists known as The Tribe in the Appalachian Mountains. Multiple factions attempted to infiltrate them. Just because you have never heard of my interrogations from your ivory tower does not mean I am not to be feared."

Understanding dawned within me as I witnessed Corey's hardened exterior, a product of harrowing experiences. Corey sifted through each wallet, extracting picture IDs as evidence of their owners' identities. The traitor's muffled screams subsided momentarily.

Corey removed the rag, and the traitor's eyes fixed on him as he placed his chaos bowie knife on the nearby table.

"You match the identity of Masterson Cassidy from the Cassidy family. Is this your name?" I prayed silently, hoping the man would make a wise decision.

His response came with a dismissive eye roll, his arm still impaled by the knife, blood saturating his sleeve. Powerless to assist, I could only bear witness to his agony. "His family is significant. He possesses a sonic Realized power, and the sensors should have alerted his presence."

The man's glare intensified; his defiance was unyielding. I, who once questioned the rule mandating the declaration of one's power while traversing territories, now recognized its necessity. An attempt on my grandmother's life, the opening of a portal designed to kill within our territory, and the looming threat against both Corey and me had shattered any illusions of unity. The Realized Territories implemented this rule to prevent such treachery.

Corey raised his hand, signaling the commencement of the interrogation. "Your party concealed their true intentions, violated territorial boundaries without permission, distributed the Southeast's Battle Leader's image to the enemy, and encountered a gargoyle. These are documented facts, and our aim now is to uncover the guilty party. You gave a forbidden tome of outer realm magic to two young girls, opening the Earth to a war from the Outer Realms. This is your sole opportunity to defend yourself."

Once again, the traitor's eyes rolled in disdain, his pain-stricken arm failing to quell his defiance.

"How did he gather himself to withstand the agony?" I wondered silently, before remembering the Dark Fey's association with pain and torture.

"Did you come into contact with a gargoyle this morning?" Corey's voice pierced the silence, his question hanging in the air.

No response.

"Did you provide a banned tome of outer realm magic to those two girls?" Corey's spoke in a slow low volume tone containing his anger.

A thin smile crept across the traitor's lips, but he remained silent.

"Are you aware that I detected your presence inside the church, but not aboard the bus? The council has deemed such an act criminal across all North American territories," Corey continued, his unwavering gaze seeking a reaction.

A device to conceal Realized powers? It seemed impossible! But I had looked at the sensors myself this morning and knew it was true.

Still no response.

"Did you have any inkling that the location you inquired about harbored the entire Southeast Territory, endangering the lives of countless individuals?" Corey's words carried an unmistakable weight.

Silence persisted.

"Failure to answer my next question seals your fate." Corey reached for one of the mason jars containing a viscous fluid. "This is called a Bliss Jar. While its purpose is to grant eternal happiness to those who have suffered, I have repurposed it. By sealing the heart of a living or recently departed being, I can inflict eternal pain. We reserve this for the most stubborn cases."

Corey's words hung in the air, the threat lingering over the room. The traitor's eyes widened, realization dawning upon him.

The man hesitated, his eyes darting around the room, desperate for an escape. Time stood still as his defiant gaze met Corey's unwavering stare, a battle of wills playing out before us.

Finally, he spat at Corey.

Corey's expression remained stoic, the weight of his decision clear in his eyes. "This seals your fate—guilty."

He removed his shirt and shoes, standing tall while the traitor backed into the corner of the room. Corey had positioned the interrogation seat strategically, trapping him. He plunged his knife into the traitor's chest, then cut a circle around the man's heart. The room filled with his agonized screams contained within its soundproof walls. Crimson arterial blood splattered on the window and onto Corey.

Screams of pain wailed in the room when he snapped the wide bone in front of the heart. The noise stopped when Corey reached his hand in and ripped out the traitor's heart.

He held the heart dripping in blood and started speaking his language of magic. The body twitched on the floor. A resounding thunk gave a finality to the questions.

When the druid placed the heart in the Bliss Jar, it did not displace this viscous fluid at all. While Corey continued speaking the Ancient Gaelic words of magic, he sealed the jar and concluded his spell. The heart still pulsed inside.

Corey retrieved a body bag and placed the lifeless body inside, bringing an end to the ordeal.

Chapter 5—Rebecca

"Madison gasped, 'I need five!'" Her footsteps reverberated in the empty hallway as she darted out of the room. My heart pounded, and I muttered under my breath, trying to keep up with her frantic pace.

The restroom door swung open, revealing Madison hunched over the toilet bowl, heaving. The sound reverberated within the confined space, sending shivers down my spine. I splashed a handful of water onto my pale, sweat-drenched face. Just a few feet away, Madison gasped, her retching transforming into dry heaves as she clung to the porcelain bowl.

Leaning against the sink, I caught my breath and glimpsed my reflection in the mirror. My face betrayed the shock and horror that had engulfed me. This small restroom had become a grim testament to the unimaginable sight we had witnessed.

Madison wobbled towards the sink, her trembling body seeking support, and I reached out to steady her. She took small sips of water, attempting to calm her racing heart. Her voice trembled as she spoke, her words laden with fear and uncertainty. "I thought I was prepared for this. I've heard tales of such things in other Territories, and Aunt Becky warned me about the perils of staying with Nathan, a territory leader. But this... this was..."

"It was visceral." At that moment, I garnered the true purpose behind Nathan's white sheets. The innocuous checkmarks on the forms and the video monitoring held a deeper significance. The others expected this horrifying experience.

Madison nodded, tears mingling with the water on her face. She splashed more water onto her pale features, attempting to wash away the remnants of the nightmare that had unfolded before our eyes. "Do you think Corey was telling the truth about the jar?" she asked.

"If he lied, the room would have turned red." I had made sure the switch was on.

"I need a pain pill for this bullet wound." With a deep breath, Madison straightened her posture. Determination flickered in her eyes as she resolved to face the unknown with newfound strength. "Alright, I suppose it's time for me to put on my big girl panties and face the world once more. This is how I prove I belong here with Nathan."

I couldn't find the words to respond to Madison. Together, we walked back into the room, the weight of recent events clear in Madison's limping stride. Corey had positioned a body bag in front of the individuals waiting to be interrogated, serving as a grim reminder of the consequences that awaited those who defied their captors.

There was a spot on the form to test the lie detection was active. "Testing the room. The punishment did not bother me."

The room lit up in red, exposing the lie. We documented the room's truth detection. The jars remained on the table, the one with a pulsing heart within sight of the interrogation chair.

Standing in the doorway, Corey wiped the blood from his hands with a towel, his expression a mix of apology and resolve. "I apologize for not warning you. We selected the individual most likely to divulge information. Those who refuse to answer the questions will face the same treatment." He fixed his eyes upon the two of us. "Only those controlled by the Dark Fey will refuse any attempt at cooperation."

I nodded, my gaze shifting to Nathan. He removed the bloodied sheet, replacing it with a fresh one, his movements deliberate and controlled. Corey wiped the streaks of crimson from the glass window, a visual testament to the stark reality that permeated the Trauma Room.

Nathan reentered the room carrying fresh sheets. "Leander called me and confirmed that, within the bounds of the law, we allow Bliss Jars for traitors. Please make a note of their use on the forms. He is the council's representative today. Morgan viewed the questioning to measure Corey as a Battle Leader. She sends her support for your actions."

Madison took her seat, her face now a mask of stoicism, and I followed suit, our eyes fixed on the next person escorted into the room by Rachel. This newcomer lacked the defiant look that marred the faces of his predecessor. Corey, armed with a fresh towel, wiped away the blood that marred his features.

With each passing moment, tension thickened the surrounding air. The traitors provided minimal answers, interlaced with lies. Corey, his patience worn thin, escorted the new betrayer out of the room, sealing their fate with a guilty verdict. "Death," he uttered with a resolute tone, the weight of the word palpable in the air.

Though writing that word still pained me, it had become a somber duty, a necessity. Yet, it was easier than bearing witness to an execution or even writing "use of Bliss Jar" on the form.

The pattern repeated itself with the next two individuals, sentenced to death because of their cooperation. By the time the fifth person faced their demise, neither Madison nor I displayed any semblance of shock. Corey removed the heart of the woman, who refused to even utter a lie, her actions blending into the macabre routine. My notes showed two members of the Cassidy family were in this group. They were a powerful family in Chesapeake Bay. This would shake the territory and require someone to deal with the fallout for years to come.

Rachel escorted the seventh person, Sheila Patterson, into the room, where she would face questioning. Sheila's resolve crumbled. Her desperation was clear in her trembling voice as she spilled every secret.

They had planned to locate Corey and I, tracking our every move, and uncover alliances. Someone higher up the ranks had struck a deal with the Dark Fey, unleashing a gargoyle as a sinister surprise, an attempt to eradicate the troublesome Southeast Territory and assimilate it under the control of the Chesapeake Bay Territory, with the church as their ally. They called me the false scion and said my grandmother and I would die gruesomely. The sight of the gargoyle had shaken Sheila to her core, leaving her trapped in a web of fear and uncertainty, unaware of how to extricate herself.

The team of traitors floundered in their efforts. They scoured the land, searching for Dark Fey allies within seven churches, yet their search remained futile.

The threat on my life seemed to be a side note to all else. I had enemies, and they had nearly killed me a few times, but now, as my position in the leadership of Chesapeake Bay as designated heir became known, my enemies had grown.

Corey, his countenance a mix of weariness and determination, led Sheila to a side room for further questioning. When he returned, his words carried a hint of compassion. "If Chesapeake has a functioning prison, I'm willing to impose the minimum sentence of twenty years. We lack a Realized prison in the Southeast, so if Chesapeake refuses, death will be her fate," he relayed, his gaze shifting between us.

"Is that for her cooperation?" I asked, my fingers typing the request, directing it to my grandmother.

"Yes," he confirmed, his voice heavy.

As Corey walked out to rouse the unconscious man from earlier, the room bore witness to its grim tableau. Two hearts encased in jars, four souls condemned to death, and Sheila, destined to be held captive within the confines of the Addkinson estate jail until after the passing of the holidays. The weight of their fates hung heavy in the air, an unshakeable reminder of the darkness that had encroached upon our lives.

The last traitor to be interviewed was still unconscious, and we all walked out to view him being awakened. I couldn't help but check the reports for his name. "Corey, he's not on the roster of Chesapeake," I cautioned, my voice laced with concern as I set down the worn sheet and braced myself for what lay ahead.

RACHEL PRODUCED AN ammonia pellet and waved it beneath the man's nose. Corey stepped back, his hand reaching for his tonfa and knife. The room crackled with anticipation as we prepared to face the unknown.

The man stirred from his slumber, his eyes scanning the chamber. Four of his compatriots, bound by chains, and two body bags, were his allies. His skin ruptured, unleashing a torrent of sickening brown corruption, and a Dark Fey emerged from the discarded flesh before their eyes. This creature, with robust legs resembling those of an ostrich and an elongated cobra for a neck and head, emanated an aura of malevolence. Thick, dark brown smoke billowed from its body, coiling around its form as it let out a spine-chilling howl that reverberated through the air.

I envisioned myself as The Scion of the True Church and took my embodiment of strength and authority in my *Angelic Form*, standing resolute in the command's heart center. A celestial radiance, brighter and more incandescent than the luminescence that filled the room, emanated from them. As the creature unfurled its formidable wings, it propelled Corey and Rachel backward, their bodies no match for its sheer power.

"At least it's not a crab shape," said Rachel. "I get sick of those." Like Corey, she'd been fighting Dark Fey so long that these fights bored her where I had to focus to not crawl away.

With unwavering determination, I planted myself, assuming a square stance with my expansive wingspan extended to its fullest. The creature slammed into my shield with an Earth-shattering impact, driving me back three arduous steps. I retaliated with a riposte, thrusting my sword towards its menacing form.

Rachel employed her surujin to ensnare the serpent-like neck of the beast, her relentless pull amplifying the creature's agony. Simultaneously, Corey, wielding his obsidian knife with precision, severed one of the creature's legs.

The celestial light emanating from my blade pierced the corrupted essence of the Dark Fey, causing its corruption marked smoke to dissipate upon contact. As Rachel tore the cobra head from the creature's writhing form, a flood of celestial radiance from my embedded blade poured through the created aperture, illuminating the room with celestial brilliance. The severed leg Corey had removed allowed another surge of luminosity to pour forth, intertwining with the celestial energy already flooding the chamber.

Four Fey arrows, vibrant green in hue, found their mark, piercing the weakening creature from Madison. The beast wavered, its strength ebbing away, until it succumbed to its wounds, collapsing to the ground in a tangle of defeated malevolence. Without hesitation, Rachel, driven by a surge of adrenaline, stomped upon the dying cobra, ensuring the fight met a swift and decisive end.

I surveyed the aftermath of our triumph, my panting from adrenaline more than exertion.

Corey's voice broke the silence that hung heavy in the air. "Some good teamwork puts a shine on a rough few hours."

The sight of the four defeated prisoners, their faces etched with despair, cried out at the appearance of me in my *Angelic Form*. Their cries stirred a pang of empathy within me. I approached them cautiously, my steps purposeful yet laden with compassion. "Even if I were a false Scion, was it worth the lives of countless innocent souls in the Southeast?"

During their anguished cries, the prisoners attempted to justify their actions, their voices tainted with regret. "It was just the druid and Scion," they pleaded, their tears mingling with their words.

Corey, his gaze unwavering, stepped forward, his eyes locked with me. In a hushed whisper, his words resonated with newfound clarity. "They admitted to plotting our demise, conspiring with a gargoyle, and aligning themselves with the Dark Fey. Their leader used the two young girls to open a portal where Rachel almost died, rescuing them before your arrival allowed her to withdraw. Each of them was well aware of the consequences."

The mention of the two young girls sparked a light in me, and I could not judge everything as black and white. I met Corey's gaze, my voice resonating with a mix of contemplation and compassion. "We can still show them mercy."

"Have you considered why your grandmother used you to document the proceedings instead of performing the task herself? She is tough enough and has done it before."

That was not something my mind could consider, and I tossed it aside in lieu of the immediate issue. I stared into Corey's eyes, and the unspoken language between us performed the rest of the communication.

Corey's head shook, a sigh escaping his lips. "I leave the final decision to you. If Chesapeake will accept the prisoners, I will commute their sentence from death to life imprisonment."

I pondered his words, weighing the delicate balance between justice and compassion. In my mind, I formed a plan—a solution that would cause the transfer of five prisoners.

THE SCENT OF DEATH permeated the Command Center as filters filtered the air. I longed for a breath of fresh air, a respite from the stifling atmosphere that enveloped me. It was in this heavy stillness that Nathan's urgent voice cut through. "Please, don't leave," he asked. "Corey, Rebecca, Madison, I need you. Rachel, could you secure the prisoners in the cell room, except for the one with a lighter sentence? Place her in the locking office."

A wave of relief washed over me as they only lost two lives. My parched throat yearned for moisture, and I reached for a glass of cold water, pouring it with trembling hands. The cool liquid slid down my throat, providing a fleeting respite. Yet, deep down, I wondered if I could ever match Nathan's composure in times of crisis.

I was grateful that I wasn't the Battle Leader burdened with Corey's responsibility. "Understood," Rachel said as she marched toward the prisoners. "I was planning to dismantle that van, but I'll handle the situation. Is there any reason for me to stay here?"

Nathan shook his head. "No, you already have all the relevant information." He pointed upwards, as if the ceiling held the answers to our predicament.

With a playful swat on Corey's backside, Rachel lightened the mood. "If you had joined Grandpa Jon after Chattanooga, you'd be aware of all this." A smile graced her lips as she glanced at Corey.

Her expression changed when she turned to the prisoners. "I'm the one who trains Corey in weapons, and don't think of testing me. I can handle the Jars of Bliss just as he can." Propelled by Rachel's resolute demeanor, the prisoners hurried down the hallway.

"That's the toughest side of Rachel I've ever seen," I said. Rachel had always been the epitome of cheerfulness and warmth.

"If you don't mind," Nathan said, "let's retreat to the upper conference table." He dragged himself toward the table. Madison accompanied him, her matching limp a reassuring presence in the room.

The cleaner air helped me collect myself as I sat. A large screen descended from above, and we settled ourselves with our backs against the glass. All eyes turned toward the screen as Nathan projected a detailed map of North America, vibrant hues delineating its various territories. "I apologize for the timing. Our schedule is tight, and I wish we could spare a day for recovery."

Madison, holding a cup of cold water, sipped from it, her pallor returning to her cheeks. Corey and Nathan, their emotions contained, swallowed the turmoil within.

"Look at those beautiful colors," Corey exclaimed, his finger pointing at the vibrant display. "But why is Mexico grayed out?"

Madison answered with authority. "South and Central America don't adhere to the same territorial divisions as the Realized. Only Western Europe, Southeast Asia, Japan, and Australia have similar setups to North America."

"Why are we fragmented? Not just in North America, but worldwide?" Corey asked.

"You might as well ask why we have different countries and cultures, but the short answer is that history has shown not all Realized are models of integrity," Nathan said. "Instead of being governed by those without magic, North America and Europe decided to self-govern and withdraw from the world, except to protect humanity."

Corey frowned. "Is there a possibility of invasion from them?"

"Unlikely. They don't have enough Realized," Madison said. "One reason we enforce strict rules in Europe, North America, the Middle East, and India is to maintain the Realized population. The number of Realized individuals is more susceptible to decline due to mass deaths or a lower birth rate. Powerful women among the Realized don't want to relinquish their own lives. Since there are so few

Realized, a single North American Territory might take control of central and South America if they desired."

"It requires two Realized individuals for a child to be Realized, and even then, it's not a guarantee," Nathan added.

I swallowed hard, suppressing the unsettling thoughts that threatened to overwhelm me. The specter of an arranged marriage loomed, a consequence if I failed to find a partner among the Realized. However, at this moment, I yearned for someone who could comprehend the horrors we faced and offer solace in the darkest moments. It had become an essential requirement in my life.

"Team, I must emphasize that this briefing remains internal," Nathan said. "We've alluded to Corey's war experiences and his role as a wartime druid. But let me assure you, those lines are not hyperbole. Key West is under attack from the sea, and we've uncovered a connection between the Delta Territory and the Curia. Open fighting has erupted in the Canadian Atlantic district."

Corey's voice quivered with concern. "Should we help those areas? We already stretched our resources, and we won't be able to cover the known incursions."

"Not yet." Nathan calmed any panic taking root. "Leander, stationed in the Ohio Valley, is gathering crucial data and acting as a central hub. They're stable and less likely to face immediate attacks, as our adversaries seem focused on the Eastern seaboard." Nathan used vivid shades of red to highlight Florida, the Southeast Territory, New York, New England, and the Atlantic side of Canada on the map. He then emphasized the Chesapeake Bay Territory with a vibrant orange hue.

"But I thought the Curia was our enemy," Corey said.

Nathan leaned back in his chair, contemplating the complexities of the situation. "Corey, did you feel drawn to the church empaths? Your Realized power attracts you to women who possess the spark, correct?"

Corey pondered the question, his lips pursed in contemplation. "They should have attracted me, but no, they were plain and uninteresting."

A revelation sparked in Nathan's eyes. "And Corey, you discovered two thousand vampires in the Delta Territory, whereas the maximum number of vampires with the spark is five hundred." He presented the facts, one by one, laying the groundwork for Corey's understanding.

Vampires no longer needed the spark to be created. Until now, it hadn't occurred to me that the church-affiliated individuals gained their powers similar to the Delta vampires. More than one group held the knowledge to give powers to those without the spark. A sickening sensation settled in my stomach, refusing to dissipate.

Nathan continued in a lower voice. "We've encountered Realized individuals who can traverse borders undetected. The Chesapeake Bay Territory becomes the third affected territory, with unknown powers launching coordinated attacks against us. All this, combined with the elusive gargoyle prowling in Atlanta, evading our tracking efforts, suggests that the church is not the sole instigator."

"I should have connected the dots," Corey muttered, his voice filled with regret. "I'm the one who discovered the possibility of traitors, and that's not even considering what will happen on New Year's Eve."

"Don't blame yourself," said Nathan. "I should have noticed the irregularities in the Shared Supernatural System. It's off-kilter to avoid detection."

"Unless a druid confirms its results using Earth Power," added Madison. "But after the New Year, the incursions should slow down."

"Yes," Nathan confirmed, leaning back in his chair. "The Shared Supernatural System has an online course discussing this. If you want a comprehensive explanation of how our universe is like a bubble within a greater universe and how another bubble has collided with ours, separating in two weeks, let me know. But the short answer is that many of these attacks are happening in the Outer Realms to protect our universe, and the fights are spilling onto Earth."

"Since the Shared Supernatural System is now questionable," I said trying to form a coherent question.

Nathan wasn't about to let panic affect us all into poor decisions. "Let's not go overboard. Only the artificial intelligence modules are problematic. Let's not throw the baby out with the bathwater. Also, the Outer Realms' war isn't what is causing these unknown attacks. There is something else."

"Could this thing causing issues also have caused the Outer Realms war?" I asked.

Corey's face contorted. "There is only one thing that could do that and let's hope not," Corey changed the subject. "Did you discover anything about the hack?"

Nathan's eyes locked onto Corey, a silent acknowledgment passing between them. Corey had an uncanny ability to gather information.

My mind struggled to think of what Corey alluded to. What would scare him so thoroughly he wouldn't say the words? A word floated in my mind—Nephilim. I discarded that. Like Corey, I would not entertain that possibility.

"I'll find that out now," Nathan said, reaching for his phone and dialing a number. The voice that came through the speaker was unmistakable.

"Hey buddy, what's up?" Aaron's voice resonated through the room.

Recognition dawned on me. "Are you Aaron from CJ's IT department?" Nathan was working on the hack with him.

Aaron's response crackled over the speaker. "Yes, that's me. Who's this?"

"Aaron, you're on speaker. It's Rebecca. I never had the chance to thank you. Without you and your team's help, I would never have made it here."

Aaron's voice held a note of familiarity. "Oh yeah, I left the puzzles to the others since I knew who you were referring to."

His admission surprised me. I did not know Aaron was involved in these matters. Perhaps he was part of The Tribe, despite his appearance as a lanky computer guy rather than a seasoned survivalist. Regardless, it was comforting to hear a familiar voice from my past, even if it belonged to an IT specialist who often rolled his eyes at my inquiries.

"Aaron, Corey wants to bring something important to your attention," said Nathan.

Corey spoke with a confidence in technology I had never witnessed before. "While searching for information about the hack and the AI, focus on identifying an extraordinary individual hiding behind it. Someone who possesses exceptional abilities beyond those of a typical human."

"Yes, Druid Norwood," Aaron replied matter-of-factly.

Nathan intervened, establishing Corey's authority for Aaron's safety. "Corey, because of certain circumstances we can't disclose, Aaron is required to follow your orders."

"Damn, sorry about that," Corey said, his gaze fixed on Nathan. "Considering everything Nathan has you working on, please search for any substantial intelligence on an actual entity rather than just Artificial Intelligence."

Aaron's voice carried a sense of relief. "I've hit a dead end in my investigation, so this might just provide the breakthrough I've been searching for."

Curiosity burned within Nathan as he asked, "Why is this significant, Corey?"

Corey's mind didn't work linearly because of his druidic magic. Instead, he followed intricate arcs, connecting unrelated dots. A broken pen, an unfinished name, and an elusive hack that eluded our understanding—these breadcrumbs were enough for Corey to forge a link. Fatigue etched lines on his face, surpassing even Madison's and my weariness. I made a mental note to check on his well-being later.

"I can't put it into words just yet," said Corey.

"It's the best lead we've got. I've had a feeling someone was fighting against me, and now I can follow my paranoid thoughts. By the way, I'm available to head to Canada on the thirtieth," Aaron said.

"Team, we will welcome James Beaton from Grand Prairie, Alberta, on the thirty-first," Nathan said. "Thankfully, Aaron has agreed to journey to the Canadian Shield Territory on our behalf as part of an information exchange."

My mind swirled with the sheer complexity of the situation. How did Nathan keep it all together? I struggled to comprehend the weight he carried on his shoulders.

"So, we find ourselves in a war, facing imminent coordinated attacks," I summarized, my voice trembling with the gravity of the situation. "And there's a possibility that an extraordinary individual is orchestrating it all. We have no allies able to lend support, and it may be up to us to assist them." I pointed to the map above. "That looks like the outcome of last night's meeting, but half the territories refuse to believe this war is happening."

A frustrated Madison interrupted. "We keep discussing vampire attacks, spells, and how busy we are. But as a member of the leadership team, I still don't understand what's happening, except in broad terms."

Corey stepped in to answer. "It's because Nathan and I have been making plans on the known attacks, employing silence spells within my circles. With the AI in the Shared Supernatural System's reliability in question, we build every decision upon layers of contingency and secrecy."

"I'll fill you in on what we know," said Nathan. "The Delta Territory is still attempting to kidnap Nicole, and they have two large-scale attacks planned for that purpose. We're confident that one of those attacks will occur on Christmas day. In addition, a group of Gullah in South Carolina is casting a major spell. It will happen after Christmas, and our allies in Charleston are working to track down the spellcasters."

"There are also two tier-one threats we've never encountered before that we'll be dealing with. There's a chance they might appear on Christmas or later, but we have very little information about them," said Corey. "And I have a gargoyle arriving from the Realm of Darkness on Christmas Eve, but banishing it should be easy."

"Last, there are two Dark Fey we can't track because they've taken possession of human bodies through sacrifice, as well as two free gargoyles," added Nathan.

Madison slumped, overwhelmed. "Does that include New Year's Eve?"

"This is all ignoring the Outer Realms war, and the compromised AI in the Shared Supernatural system," I added, hoping to be wrong.

Nathan and Corey both nodded.

"We know of at least three incursions planned for Chesapeake Bay, so it won't be all on us..." I slumped further. "Except for me."

"No, Rebecca," Corey said. "You always have me. Don't accuse me of having a hero complex when things are this busy." He winked, acknowledging my previous admonishment of his propensity for diving headfirst into fights.

"I have a question since we're in an open question time," I said. "Why am I required to get married for the stability of Chesapeake Bay, while Nathan isn't?"

"I wondered the same thing," said Corey. "Except I was required," he added.

Nathan explained patiently. "There are two reasons. First, you are taking on the roles of both myself and Corey. You'll be a part of the leadership team and you are the bloodline of the Scion. Corey is the bloodline to pure druids. Corey marrying Nicole and her pregnant with a new druid absorbs much of the burden, as we have a new generation of druids coming."

"That's why Rachel and I could use birth control in our relationships, since druids are on the way. We can move at a more normal pace in their relationships now," said Madison. "Corey, if you don't hear it enough, thank you."

Nathan continued, "Absolutely, thank you. The other part is that Corey supports Preacher Jon, and me. He has no aspirations for political leadership. I hope it's not surprising the other territories are wary of Corey."

His thorough explanation left no room for argument. It deepened my resignation.

"I caught something in there that might buy you some time," Corey said. "If you prove yourself capable and defend the territory, people won't challenge you while protecting your grandmother. It might give you the opportunity to stabilize the territory and find a husband at your own pace."

But that still seemed far off, just like everything else. Corey wasn't joking when he said I admonished him for being a hero. He always rushed into fights, saving anyone in need, and he always emerged victorious. They had trained him in hand-to-hand combat as part of The Tribe, while my fighting knowledge came from my days in a Clemson sorority. No one feared me.

Chapter 6—Rebecca

My journey back to the familiar comfort of my apartment building was thankfully short. The tires of my car whispered against the pavement. After I parked, I experienced a deep sense of relief as I stepped out onto the bustling city street. The street entrance beckoned me, and I found solace in the fact that I never resorted to the cold detachment of the service elevator. It wasn't just about propriety; it was about seeking the warm embrace of human connection, however fleeting. Today, more than ever, I craved that semblance of normalcy.

As I approached the front of the building, a gust of wintry wind tugged at my hair, causing my unbuttoned coat to billow open. The chill barely registered on my skin, as I had grown accustomed to the biting cold during my recent stays at Corey's cabin. The resilience within me had grown, adapting to the frigid embrace of nature.

"Good afternoon, Ms. Adams," greeted Barry, the doorman, resplendent in his sharp red uniform that contrasted against the shaded backdrop. Despite the temperature hovering around a mere forty degrees, he stood there, an unwavering figure in the wind tunnel created by the towering buildings. His unyielding dedication to his duty, even in the face of discomfort, commanded respect. "Do you have plans for Christmas?"

Returning his warm smile, I handed him a package, a token of appreciation for his unwavering kindness. I had cast aside the burdens of the earlier part of the day, replaced by an ardent desire for pleasant experiences. It was a balm to my soul, knowing that I had played a part in saving four lives.

"Yes, Barry." Savoring the gentle cadence of conversation with someone I considered a friend soothed my soul. "My grandmother invited me to her estate in Virginia. Nicole and I will leave in two days." Conversations with Barry always delighted me, especially when they strayed beyond the realm of work, for he, too, shared my adoration for Mahler's symphonies.

Finding a rare vinyl recording of Mahler's majestic Fifth Symphony, conducted by the renowned Michael Gielen, had been a fortuitous discovery.

"Barry, since I will be absent for some time, I wanted to offer you this present."

Mrs. Krebbeth, a kind and observant resident, paused nearby, her wise gaze resting upon us. "Dear, that dress you're wearing suits you beautifully. I'm glad you opted for more sensible shoes for your walk, though," she commented, her voice laced with genuine concern for my well-being.

I had forgotten about my choice of footwear, the significance of shoes fleeting in the face of Barry's joy. It was essential to ensure his happiness, for it was a source of my own.

With eager anticipation, Barry unwrapped the present, and his eyes widened with unadulterated delight. "Gielen's mastery with Mahler is unparalleled, and the Fifth Symphony is my favorite!" he exclaimed, his words resonating with an appreciation of the artistry contained within the vinyl grooves.

"Oh my," gasped Mrs. Krebbeth, a faint smile playing on her lips. "What a thoughtful gift indeed."

Caught between the demands of his work and his sheer elation, Barry carried the album to the safety of the front desk. With a heartfelt wish for a Merry Christmas, he bid me adieu, leaving me basking in the warm afterglow of his happiness. A genuine smile graced my lips, a rarity in recent times.

As I prepared to enter the elevator, Mrs. Krebbeth, the venerable woman who had retired two decades prior and recently lost her beloved husband, joined me. Clad in sweatpants and a headband, she had just returned from a spirited pickle ball game organized for retirees. Her heavy navy-blue wool coat enveloped her like a shield against the winter.

"The rumor mill whispers that your friend Nicole is expecting," she said with a wink.

Stepping into the luxurious confines of the elevator, I pressed the button for the fifteenth floor. Nathan had purchased both the fifteenth and sixteenth floors, reserving them for the Territory, a haven for our team and visitors. The dozen designed apartments offered a sanctuary, and I had chosen one on the corner, graced with a balcony that boasted sunlight streaming in from two directions.

Mrs. Krebbeth, the veritable epicenter of the building's gossip, provided an opportune moment to address the rampant speculation surrounding Nicole's pregnancy. Gossip, though inevitable, needed to be tempered, for our team thrived in the realm of discretion. Leaning closer, I confided in the older woman, my voice hushed and conspiratorial.

"I was there when Nicole received the news." My gaze meeting hers, a silent understanding passing between us. "Corey proposed to her, and during a celebratory weekend, they overlooked protection." My words formed a delicate web of half-truths, carefully woven to conceal the true depth of their story.

Mrs. Krebbeth's hand flew to cover her mouth in a mixture of shock and delight. "Oh my."

"The initial shock has settled, and both Nicole and Corey are happy," I reassured her. "Today, they are shopping to prepare Corey's house for Nicole and the eventual child's arrival."

A mixture of sympathy and admiration gleamed in Mrs. Krebbeth's eyes as she absorbed the magnitude of the young couple's journey. "So many changes for such young ones."

Seizing the opportunity, I leaned over, offering her a glimpse into Corey's world. I unveiled a photograph capturing Corey's car alongside Rachel and their beloved motorcycles. "Nicole has given up her attempts to change his car. She will drive a spacious four-seater," I shared, the corners of my lips lifting in a knowing smile.

A spark of curiosity ignited within Mrs. Krebbeth's eyes as she absorbed the details. "Well, good for them," she chuckled, her voice brimming with genuine mirth. "I hope to meet this charming, yet enigmatic man who seems to have a knack for unraveling life's mysteries." The older woman's laughter reverberated in the confined space of the elevator, an infectious sound that echoed through my heart.

"I'll tell Corey that he must have the pleasure of meeting you before Nicole moves out," I vowed, our conversation drawing to a close as the elevator doors slid open, revealing the sanctuary of my fifteenth-floor abode.

With a last exchange of warm wishes, Mrs. Krebbeth bid me farewell, leaving me to revel in another person's happiness. Her gossip would spread, surely, but it brought me a peculiar sense of joy.

THE FIRST ORDER OF business upon reaching my floor was to check on Mare and Melinda. I tapped on the door of the room where Madison had taken them.

"Hello?" A timid voice replied from behind the door.

"This is Rebecca. I wanted to ensure both of you are being taken care of," I said.

"Nice timing," said a voice behind me. Trish, Miles' wife, and her sister-in-law Ada emerged from the elevator.

Mare opened the door, and the three of us entered, eager to greet the two girls.

"We came for a shopping trip," said Ada, a senior in high school who wasn't much older than the two girls. Her powers had yet to manifest, but she would soon become a hunter like her brother Miles.

"It seems I didn't need to check on things," I chuckled.

"Madison organized it on our way back to the Command Center," Trish said. "She didn't want to discuss what happened, so we'll keep Mare and Melinda with us through the holidays and help them with back-to-school shopping."

"I'm glad you came," Melinda said gratefully. "I didn't know how to recognize Trish."

Relieved that the girls wouldn't be alone after their harrowing experiences, I went about my day.

Wearily, I crossed the threshold into my apartment, my heart heavy with a blend of relief, anticipation, and trepidation. Packed luggage awaited me for the upcoming journey—where a whirlwind of festive celebrations awaited. From a Christmas Eve dinner to a breakfast gathering for the children, followed by a Christmas lunch with a date, and then a regular dinner, brunch, and even a shopping trip.

Casting a glance around the apartment, the front rooms remained stark and impersonal, devoid of any personal touches. The bedroom offered little solace, unpacked with essential items and boxes. I wondered when I would move into a home, rather than just a place to stay.

With a sigh, I made my way to the closet in the spare bedroom. There, I unzipped the dress I had worn earlier, preserving its elegance. With practiced ease, I hung the dress on a hanger, ensuring its safekeeping.

I changed into a simple skirt and blouse, symbolizing a shift in mindset. My thoughts entangled themselves with the weight of recent events, the battle against my would-be captors replaying in my mind. As I headed towards the front door, determination guided my steps. The morning's attack emphasized the danger I faced when alone.

With a sense of finality, I lowered the steel bar and secured it in place. Its metallic thunk reverberated through the apartment, offering a modicum of solace. The bar was a constant reminder of the intrusion, an unwavering demand I had imposed despite the building maintenance staff's objections.

But as I stood there, my mind racing, the true magnitude of my earlier actions become apparent. In that critical moment, I had pleaded for the lives of four individuals—three men and a woman—condemning them to face the consequences of their deeds rather than a swift death. These people had intended to end my life, not abduct me.

During the battle in Chattanooga, I had peered through my rifle scope at my abductors, Suit and Red Shirt, prepared to pull the trigger. Yet, fate intervened when Corey neutralized the threats. This left me grappling with an inner conflict, questioning the boundaries of my morality. Why had Corey deferred to me today?

Weighty decisions like these were the realm of Battle Leaders such as Corey. Thankfully, I remained worlds away from such responsibility. Still, the questions persisted, refusing to yield their elusive answers, as I continued packing for my impending journey.

With a sense of purpose, I sent a text to Nicole. "Looks like we're headed to Virginia the day after tomorrow. Shall we share breakfast together after we pick up Corey? How about six?"

"Good idea. Can you believe that man said the baby could sleep outside with him as long as the baby promised not to harm the animals?"

A smile tugged at my lips, grateful for the lightness that Nicole's presence brought. I shared the latest gossip from Mrs. Krebbeth.

She joked back, "Tell her I'm searching for alibis for murder. Also, Corey insists we continue with our workout tomorrow, despite my need to pack!"

As I reflected upon Nicole and Corey's interactions, I couldn't help but marvel at how my mood shifted, mirroring Corey's mercurial nature.

Suddenly, hunger gnawed at my stomach, a reminder that skipping dinner was not an option. Stepping into the bare kitchen, equipped with sleek metal appliances and light wood cabinetry, I retrieved four eggs from the refrigerator, their cool surface offering temporary respite from my mounting worries. In the single pot I unpacked, I hard-boiled the eggs.

While the eggs cooled, I plucked a crisp apple from the countertop. With practiced hands, I cored and sliced the fruit, the rhythmic motions providing a momentary escape from the weight of my thoughts. Peeling the eggs over the trash can, I arranged them alongside the apple slices on a small plate. Realizing I was hungry, I got pulled a pre-made salad out. Placing it all on the dining room table, I adhered to the unwritten rules governing proper conduct for young women, resisting the temptation to devour my meal haphazardly.

In that quiet moment, I couldn't help but yearn for companionship. Madison sought solace in Nathan's arms, finding comfort in their shared sorrows from today's events. Corey's presence, though protective, wouldn't offer the respite I craved. Instead, I longed for the warmth of someone who radiated a gentleness absent from this tumultuous world. Nicole had been fortunate enough to avoid intense interrogation, and Corey had found solace in her embrace. Rachel and Wesley also had each other.

Left with nothing but the promise of an early bedtime to find solace, I wondered what steps I should take next.

Chapter 7—Rebecca

The night had been restless, burdened by unresolved thoughts and worries that plagued my mind. As the first hints of dawn painted the sky with delicate hues of pink and orange, I stood outside Corey's house. The familiar routine of entering his home by punching in the code on the door lock stirred bittersweet memories within me. Corey was a man who valued companionship, granting everyone access to his sanctuary, fearing the loss of those dear to him.

A warm smile greeted me as Corey tended to a crackling fire on the patio. The aroma of eggs filled the air as he prepared breakfast for us. "I'm glad you made it," he said.

Corey surprised me with scrambled eggs—fluffy and slightly underdone, just the way I liked them when scrambled. I waved off the offer of sausage. "Good morning. Thank you for the eggs." To prevent his lecture on my diet before working out, I grabbed an orange and ate it as well.

Nicole bid us farewell as she left with Rachel, heading to the gym where Miles would guide them through their workout routine. Ever since Trish's pregnancy, Miles had taken on the role of her trainer. Nicole appreciated the idea of training with a friend who understood the unique challenges of exercising during pregnancy. One benefit of my deal with Nicole was that our friendship had grown, and she trusted me with Corey. Days like today were an example of our trust.

Once alone with Corey I asked, "are you alright after what happened yesterday?"

Corey shrugged, a hint of resignation in his eyes. "About what?"

"The intense questioning," I reminded him, my voice filled with understanding. Corey struggled with the weight of taking lives, despite considering himself someone who used violence.

With a shake of his head, he sighed. "Old Donnie was right. It has changed me, and I wish I had faced the reality of killing intimately before yesterday. But duty called, and I had no choice. There was no one else."

He was right. "Corey, you did what you had to do."

A hint of uncertainty flickered in his eyes as he picked up the dumbbells. "If someone were to throw a knife at me, missing but still harboring the intent to end my life, wouldn't you expect me to chase them down and eliminate the threat? These six individuals tried to kill us, but also maintained murderous intent. So, what's the difference?"

His argument struck a chord within me, entangling me in its complexity as I struggled to respond. "How did you come up with such an argument?"

"Fitz taught it to me when I trained with The Tribe," Corey placed water bottles next to the towels. "Look, if it weren't for the involvement of the Dark Fey and the gargoyles, I might have paused and considered your perspective. But you saw a deceased man hosting a Dark Fey within his body, and the team pursued us, aiming to end our lives. That's not normal behavior. The entire team could have known about the tome as well, though we can prove it for one of them."

His words hit me, and I searched for an escape from this unwelcome truth. However, the realization dawned on me—I had made the wrong choice. "I sought Red Shirt and Suit in the first battle too and would have pulled the trigger. But the two young innocent girls need an example of compassion. That's what drove me."

Corey's voice broke through my thoughts as he set up the workout equipment near the pull-up bars in the back corner of his grassy backyard. I changed into the workout clothes he had selected, slipping gray sweatpants under my skirt and covering my t-shirt with an unflattering, yet practical, gray sweatshirt. I made a mental note to add workout clothes to my Christmas list, emphasizing their suitability for strenuous exercise according to Corey's standards. Mentioning his name in Virginia would get people on the correct page.

We started our workout regimen, starting with core exercises and targeting different muscle groups. As I pushed my body to its limits, the soreness in my core became apparent.

With each repetition, my muscles strained, and body ached. We progressed through the workout, alternating exercises in what Corey referred to as supersets, a relentless rhythm that kept my heart rate elevated, offering no respite.

Watching Corey tackle the pull-up bar, his body trembling with exertion, I couldn't help but be in awe of his strength and determination. This final set of shoulder exercises pushed him to the brink, etching pain onto his face.

Encouragement spilled from my lips. "Get up! If you can't get up again, how will you get it up for Nicole?" It was the crude yet motivating comment he had been showering upon me throughout our session.

Corey's scream echoed through the air as he completed the pull-up and lowered himself back down. Exhaustion mingled with a sense of accomplishment, painting a radiant smile across his face. "Last set. Let's finish strong."

Pull-ups were a challenge for me. The exercise I started with required hanging on the bar for a minute before attempting to complete two pull-ups. I gripped the bar and my arms quivered like limp noodles as I struggled to hold on. Aching shoulders and tired arms played a symphony of discomfort within me. Yet, I pressed on, for my core, chest, and legs had already endured a grueling hour of physical exertion.

"Okay, two good ones," Corey encouraged, his hands resting on my hips, providing just enough support to help me through. "You've got this. Get up there!"

With my remaining strength, I completed the two pull-ups with Corey's help. My arms gave way as he lowered me to the ground.

"That was a great finish. That's how you work out," he exclaimed, his smile reminiscent of the way he used to look at me after our most intimate moments. Somehow, this affirmation seemed fitting now, given the challenges we faced together. "And we've passed the go-home test."

Curiosity piqued, I asked, "What's the go-home test?" Seated on the grass, I reached for my water bottle, my throat parched and in dire need of replenishment.

"We soaked through a shirt and sweats." Corey peeled off both shirts.

I removed my sweatshirt but kept my t-shirt on. Other women at the gym may have paraded around in sports bras, but it wasn't appropriate for me. The temperature warming up to forty degrees was another good reason. I didn't have the druidic protections from the weather.

"Engaging in workouts like these is how I cope as well," Corey confessed, panting as he took a sip of water. "Without the physical energy to distract me, it forced my mind to confront its own actions. It's easier to face them head-on and move forward."

His words resonated within me, their wisdom seeping into my consciousness. I had made a mistake in overriding Corey's instincts, and I accepted that truth. Though I still lacked the answers to what lay ahead, my previous choice had been wrong. I was grateful I wasn't in a position of authority like Corey; there was still much for me to learn. Yet, I wondered if there was a middle path.

As exhaustion washed over me, the weight of negative emotions faded, replaced by a sense of clarity. I drank from my water bottle, realizing that this experience transcended the expectations of a "proper" woman. There was no time to conform to societal norms. I needed to prepare myself both physically and mentally. It was time to embrace action, to channel my inner Corey. These intense workouts cleared my mind and sharpened my ability to think. They were a crucial part of my journey.

Corey's body sprang into action as he leaped up, muscles bulging as he grabbed two knives from the nearest target. Gripping the lethal blades, he flung one towards the corner of his house, the weapon embedding itself with a resounding thunk into the wooden surface. "You're lucky I had a pair of knives within reach, or you'd be dead," he threatened, his voice dripping with menace.

Interrupting the tense atmosphere, a distinct and unfamiliar voice shattered the silence. "My apologies, but I'm here to see Rebecca Adams." The stranger's words had an accent revealing his northern upbringing.

Corey's eyes darted toward me, seeking guidance as he readied himself to unleash another knife. "I'm down here, out of sight," I called out, my voice carrying across the space between us.

"Oh dear, it seems I've made my first blunder in a lifetime," the man said with a tone oozing with haughtiness. There was no mistaking his audacious confidence.

The stranger's arrogance ignited a wave of anger within Corey, but I gestured for him to hold back, urging him to stand down with a subtle motion of my hand. "Christopher?" I asked.

"Christopher Murphy, indeed. Might I have the privilege of keeping this exquisite knife? It would make a cherished addition to my personal collection. Picture it, mounted on a board with Corey's signature—it would earn a place of honor in my studio," Christopher proposed, his gaze shifting between Corey and me. Corey's confusion was apparent and etched upon his face as he shrugged his shoulders.

"Say yes," I said.

"Sure," Corey said with a confused shrug. "I understand the allure. I wield the Chaos Bowie, a blade that found its way into my gut. Come on in, we've just finished." Corey extended his hand, and with his support, I pulled myself up from the ground.

A tall figure emerged, following the path around the house, skirting Woodrow's majestic black-stained maple tree. The man, with tousled brown hair and a patchy beard, wore a disheveled navy-blue Brooks Brothers suit. His eyes wandered, taking in the surroundings with awe. "All of this is marvelous."

Corey offered his hand, but Christopher failed to notice the gesture, captivated by a particular spot in the yard. "There's Nicole!" he exclaimed, pointing at the measured markings for the extensions.

"We haven't made our final decision yet. Those markings are for discussion." Corey had more than a hint of exasperation in his voice. "But how do you know Nicole?"

I had never seen Corey so flummoxed.

Undeterred, Christopher turned and extended his hand toward Corey. "Greetings, Tactical Leader Norwood. One of my abilities allows me to see glimpses of the past and future, and I envision the extension as a crucial element in a painting I intend to create. It ingrained its presence in the future," he said, maneuvering around Corey's imposing figure. The artist possessed a similar stature to Corey, albeit without the bulging muscles, yet his demeanor exuded unwavering confidence.

"Hold on," Christopher paused, attempting to bring the druid and the artist closer together. However, Corey stood his ground, immovable. I stepped in to relieve the tension and pressed against Corey's back. A palpable wave of heat and frustration emanated from him.

Christopher's eyes lit up, and he retrieved his phone, his finger hovering over the screen. "Kisses, Grace."

Did he possess my grandmother's direct number?

"Yes, everything went swimmingly. And guess what? I now possess a knife that nearly took my life. It's been a morning filled with thrill and passion, and the battle leader remains ready to extinguish me. It's delightful, the way he fumes," Christopher said.

I stifled a laugh with my hand while Corey glared at me, annoyance filling his eyes.

"Yes, indeed. After seeing Tactical Leader Norwood next to Scion Adams, there is a crucial picture that must precede our plans. I need to inquire whether you have space for a grand mural," Christopher continued, listening. "That's precisely why I contacted you. Your question leaves me wondering how I navigate life at all."

"Same here," grumbled Corey, exasperated.

Corey didn't care for the honor being given him by the pre-eminent Realized artist choosing him for a portrait. Despite the aches and pains pulsating throughout my body, this morning had taken a wonderful turn.

"Yes, six by eight feet, capturing the enchanting tale of innocent lovers who evolve into battle-tested comrades and the closest of friends," Christopher conversed with my grandmother and seemed to have come to an agreement. "Indeed. I will make the arrangements to be ready for the plethora of paintings in this area. I expect a lengthy stay."

Surely, Christopher would consult Corey before finalizing any plans. "Corey, I'll explain everything to you." I recognized the need to placate his growing unease.

"Yes, I'll accompany them tomorrow. Kisses, Grace." The man pocketed his phone, signaling the end of his conversation.

"This is truly marvelous." He spread his arms wide in a gesture of exhilaration. "I should gather my notes from inside. It's been ages since I've stayed somewhere as quaint as this—I ought to take pictures for my family."

With that, he opened the door, disappearing into Corey's house before turning back toward me. "Rebecca, you might want to use a mask this morning. The sweat from your hard work has taken a toll on your hair. It would be a pity if the hyenas at your grandmother's estate were to utter unkind words. Celestial magic, unlike Earth Power, does not grant you perfect physical appearances. I can imagine how your ex's hair would dominate any woman's runway." He nodded toward Corey.

"I'm heading out for a run up at the cabin," Corey said, his words forced through clenched teeth, just escaping his controlled jaw.

"Good idea. I'll get him settled, and once you're ready, we'll sort everything out. He'll be joining us on our journey to Virginia tomorrow."

Yet, my attempts at a comforting smile failed to soften his demeanor. Without hesitation, Corey departed, striding into Woodrow's maple tree, the tree that brought him to the Tree Foyer of the Fey Spring Court.

Running my fingers through the left side of my hair, a crackling sensation accompanied the lingering dampness. Today, I would use a mask, ensuring that my hair received the care it deserved. I'd schedule a proper hair appointment, for appearance mattered, even in the turmoil of our lives.

Chapter 8—Rebecca

Not wanting to leave Christopher behind, I spent another night in Corey's indoor bed. The artist accompanied me to retrieve my belongings from my apartment, but it wouldn't have been appropriate for him to stay with me. Instead, he settled into the spare room in Corey's house while Corey and Nicole retired to the druid bed on the patio. Rachel and Wesley, as always, remained in their usual room.

As the night wore on, I set my phone alarm to ring at four-fifty in the morning, determined to be the first one up. With a sense of urgency, I showered and dressed, my mind consumed by an important matter. Sensing my restlessness, Corey joined me in the kitchen, preparing breakfast on the grill. It was time to come clean and admit that not telling Nicole about her involvement in the end of the world was a mistake.

With no battles for Earth or intrusions from other territories, we didn't expect an attack until the following day. If we didn't tell Nicole during the drive up, we might never find the opportunity.

"Look, Corey," I said in a hushed voice. "We have to tell Nicole. It was wrong to keep the truth from her about her role in ending the world."

He averted his gaze, his troubled expression betraying his contemplation. "You're right," he conceded, his voice laced with determination. "I can present the truth that absolves you of blame. I'm engaged to her and should have known better."

"We both should have." I hesitated, uncertain about accepting Corey's version of events.

With sincerity etched in his eyes, he met my gaze, balancing the weight of the situation. "Tell her you wanted her relationship with me to have the best chance, and that you made a regrettable choice. From there, I will handle the rest."

Lost in thought, I pondered his words, grappling with the impending revelation. Before I could respond, Nicole's presence interrupted our whispered conversation. She entered the room, clutching Christopher's suitcase, already showered and dressed.

Christopher stumbled out and Nicole asked for help with some bags. We had a whirlwind in the house now and it gave us a reprieve.

Tension still existed between Corey and Christopher. To ease this tension, I finished cooking breakfast while Corey helped Nicole pack the SUV. As I settled into the front passenger seat, I longed for an uneventful journey devoid of melodrama, except for the humorous kind.

Corey carried Nicole to the car, their affectionate gestures betraying their rekindled adoration. He placed her in the driver's seat, and they exchanged a lingering kiss, her hands entwined around his neck. He was really trying and I think in some months he would love her for real.

Christopher, from the backseat, grumbled about our early departure. "You Southeastern folks sure rise early. Rachel and Wesley are still fast asleep."

"It's already seven in the morning. If it were up to me, we would have been on the road by five. Some things require our immediate attention." Corey didn't stop loading the back to talk. "The others will gather at Wesley's house for a Christmas Eve dinner, followed by a Christmas stay."

Corey and Christopher, as different as night and day, found themselves at odds. The contrasting dynamics between the two held an intriguing allure. Trying to ignite a playful banter, I said, "So, will we witness some clashes between Nicole and Corey during our drive? The shopping trip with the expansion of the house? Making Corey move his beer brewing to the cabin?"

But their overnight reconciliation had dissolved any trace of conflict, leaving love and harmony in their wake. "No, you horrible instigator," teased Nicole. "We settled everything for the house overnight."

"Nicole was right. We don't want children near the hot copper and building a greenhouse with a brewery by the cabin makes sense. Especially considering my ability to use trees to move between locations in seconds." Corey's focus now shifted to ensuring Nicole's comfort.

"And Corey is right that the patio is lovely and young druids should know how to navigate around rocks," added Nicole.

Meanwhile, Christopher settled into the third row of the SUV, putting on an eye mask and ear muffs, determined to escape the waking world.

I turned to Corey in the second row. "I overheard Christopher taking a strange phone call in the middle of the night. Anything odd going on with him?"

Corey looked back to make sure he couldn't be heard. "Can't say I know. But speaking of odd, Clive was in a panic about the holiday rush and needs help when school restarts. I told him I'd look around for options."

Nicole leaned back from the driver's seat. "When you stop by the store tonight, Corey, check on that teenager Isabella too. She's been hanging around the animal shelter more than she should. Trish thinks with her fearlessness, she might end up getting hurt. Maybe you can convince her to be more careful."

Corey nodded. "Christopher's calls, Clive's store, Isabella at the shelter—got it. I'll check in on all of it later." He flashed a cryptic look my way. "I've been meaning to check on weird animal talk around the store."

Nicole started the SUV's engine and we embarked on our journey, I seized the opportunity to ask about a matter of utmost importance. "What's the plan for our housing situation?" I asked. Maybe they hadn't resolved everything. Christopher's slumber prevented him from inciting Corey's playful spirit, leaving me to take up the challenge.

"We have big plans," Corey said with excitement. "We intend to expand the back of the house, adding a ground-floor bathroom and converting the spare bedroom into a second master bedroom for Rachel. Of course, if Wesley—"

Nicole interjected, emphasizing the word "when," instead of "if."

Unfazed, Corey continued, amending his statement. "Yes, when Wesley overcomes his reservations, and without alarming him with any notions of marriage, we'll designate the other upstairs bedroom as his office. And once we've completed the greenhouse and distillery at the cabin, along with a second cabin instead of just a room, we can transform the existing eight hundred square feet in the basement into four bedrooms and a larger living space."

Nicole shared her own vision. "Imagine four children's rooms and a playroom," she said.

The banter between Corey and Nicole amused me, and I teased them about their relationship. "You two are sickening." I feigned exasperation. "It's like you know the result you want, but you have to argue about every detail to get there, and in the end, you're happier for it."

In perfect unison, they responded, laughter filling the air. "We know." Their shared amusement a testament to their union.

We all knew they would have their disagreements, but they had found a method that worked for them. With everyone happy, I believed waiting for the second half of the trip to break the news of the lie to Nicole would be the best timing.

With Nicole maneuvering the vehicle onto the main road, I contemplated the significance of their seamless partnership, considering how I could be of help. Determined to repay Rachel's previous help, I offered my support. "If Wesley gets cold feet, remind them both of Rachel's mother's advice about waiting until Wesley graduates before considering marriage."

"Excellent idea," Corey affirmed. "Those two still need our support."

The drive was serene, having set off early. Corey's phone alert interrupted our tranquil journey. He read the message and informed us of the results of Rachel's investigation. "Rachel discovered a peculiar device on the van last night. She believes it could be the source of the illegal magic. The magical item experts have been called in, and they will examine it after Christmas."

Concerned about the implications, I couldn't help but voice my reservations. "Are we considering replicating the device ourselves?" I asked, aware of the dangers of fighting fire with fire. I had no intention of becoming an accomplice to such a serious crime.

Corey reassured me, his fingers dancing across his phone's screen before he responded. "No, not at all. My intention is to counteract its effects," he clarified. "On a positive note, Madison visited Mare and Melinda at Miles and Trish's store and introduced them to the others. She saw smiles on the girls' faces while they worked with Clive and Coach White."

A wave of relief washed over me. The girls had been through so much, and we couldn't abandon them and move on. "Madison is doing an excellent job taking care of them," I said. However, I couldn't help but ponder the effect it would have on their smiles if they were to discover Clive's vampiric nature and Coach White's lycanthropic identity.

"Let's shift our focus to Christmas," Nicole said.

Corey let out a heavy sigh, his expression filled with disappointment. "This year derailed my Christmas plans," he lamented, revealing a tradition of gathering to bemoan the inclusion of "happy holidays" on the calendar and indulging in morning beer-drinking festivities. But this year, fate dashed Corey's hopes.

Despite knowing it was an impossible desire, I couldn't help but feel sympathy. "I would have loved to join you in your beer-drinking and complaining ritual," I confessed.

"No!" Nicole exclaimed. "We need to prepare ourselves to shower little Donald or little Margaret with holiday cheer. We all have to practice." Her voice trailed off, curiosity gleaming in her eyes. "Wait, Corey, what was that thought about speaking with Old Donnie?" Her empathetic nature always picked up on Corey's unguarded thoughts.

Oh, no. Corey's mentor had died in the summer. In the big battle with the Curia, he crossed the barrier to the source of Earth power, where deceased druids go. If he hadn't mentioned seeing the man he respected the most, this could be traumatic.

Corey leaned against the car door, stretching his legs over the back seat. Weariness painted his face, his attempt to conceal it proving futile. "Let's skip that for now. Instead, let's talk about our friends on vacation." A hint of discomfort flickered across Corey's features, revealing the weight he carried.

This is something that could cause problems. "Corey, if something is troubling you, it's essential to confront it before Nicole gives birth. You can't keep burying your emotions."

"Exactly," Nicole said. "Thank you, Rebecca. Now, tell us what's bothering you, my soon-to-be husband."

Corey rolled his eyes. "When I vanished into the realm of Earth power during the battle, I spoke with Old Donnie."

My astonishment and concern mingled in my voice as I struggled to maintain composure. "And you've kept this a secret?" I stammered. "After wielding a sword of light, soaring with angelic wings, and bathed in celestial radiance looking incompetent, you had something profound to share, and you didn't ease any of the pressure from me?"

Throughout the hours, our allies bombarded me with questions while Corey, Nicole, and Rachel frolicked off to the Fey Spring Court. Everyone seemed compelled to offer unsolicited advice on swordsmanship, as if I didn't already have two expert trainers at my disposal.

Then Corey changed the mood of the car. His voice shifted, mirroring that of his old mentor. "Adults are just oversized children, stumbling through life. Once you realize that I, too, was a mix of mistakes and flaws, but I did my best, you'll take another step toward adulthood. But Corey, know that I loved you, and your heart surpassed all my expectations of a wartime druid. You saved me, allowing me to conclude my life as if I had been a good man. With your help, I fixed many of my problems. However, there is one remaining unresolved issue. I failed as a parent—to children you knew and those you didn't. Please rectify that mistake in my life so my soul can find peace."

Struggling to compose myself, the sheer magnitude of it all overwhelmed me. "You've been carrying this secret?" I stammered, a mixture of disbelief and concern clear in my words.

I caught myself. Everyone knew Old Donnie's greatest flaw was he was a poor father to multiple families over the years. Corey learned everything about being a man from him. No wonder this traumatized him, with Nicole pregnant.

I shifted to helping Corey. "Corey, you get the chance to talk to the man you hold in the highest regard, and you keep the wisdom to yourself," I teased, attempting to lighten the mood.

Corey's body relaxed as I joked. "Laugh all you want, but I'll show up with presents at seven o'clock tomorrow morning and distribute them among the fancy crowd."

Corey failed to grasp the depth of my grandmother's affection. "Grandmother loves you. She'd be thrilled for you to do that," 'Yowza' was not a word she used often.

"That settles it. With your ability to use trees to move instantly, there is no excuse to not show up. Come by at seven, and let's have breakfast and open presents together." Nicole left no room for discussion.

"You'll enjoy the informal breakfast, Corey. Perhaps we can make it a Christmas morning tradition in Virginia," I added, hoping to put him at ease. My mind had a thought. The name 'March' that concerned Corey was in the Abernathy Lineage book. *Did Old Donnie have a certain child that concerned him? Only a fallen angel and a druid could produce the greatest evil, a human Nephilim.*

Nicole maintained her focus as we crossed the border into North Carolina, our only pit stops for gas, ensuring we had enough fuel to reach our destination. The atmosphere in the SUV grew lighter, and our conversation turned to more casual topics, lifting our spirits along the way.

"Well, if you two insist on being dull, I'll browse this dating app and see if there's anyone interesting out there." I postponed exploring the regular app until after Christmas, knowing that the flood of messages would render it useless. Curiosity got the better of me, and I glanced at the profile Nicole had set up for me. "Oh my, Nicole, is this my profile picture?"

Nicole grinned. "And the sexy one. Show it to Corey and see what he thinks."

I scrutinized the image, taken aback by the sight of myself, looking like a contorted doll, with unruly hair and my breasts defying gravity. Corey appeared every bit the charismatic stud, while Rachel seemed poised to witness my imminent crash landing. Handing the phone back to Corey, I sought his opinion.

"Holy crap! Do they post pictures like this for everyone to see?" Corey exclaimed, returning the phone to me.

"She's fully clothed, Corey, just about to land on her rear," Nicole defended herself. "I took it during a training session."

"Only Rebecca can make a butt landing look sexy." Corey chuckled.

"Well, if Corey finds it appealing, then it works as the sexy picture. After all, he's a guy's guy." Never having used a dating app I didn't know I needed a normal picture and a sexy picture.

We continued our journey until we reached a rest area and pulled over, away from the highway. Corey, his hands clasping the <u>Abernathy Book of Gargoyles</u>, cast a discerning gaze upon the rest area.

"Look, that rest area seems promising. Pull over to the right, near those trees."

Curiosity piqued within me, and I couldn't resist asking, "Are you about to banish a gargoyle?"

Nicole's exasperated voice filled the air, carrying a sense of familiarity. "Oh no, I've done a Rachel and forgot to tell you! Corey needs to banish a gargoyle before we cross into the Chesapeake Bay Territory."

As I took a deep breath, I sought to steady my racing heart. This would be my third encounter with these formidable creatures. Corey's duty of banishing gargoyles occupied a significant portion of his time, and unless pursued by the church, we were relatively safe. The fear lingered, for the unleashed fury of a gargoyle had the power to rend people asunder.

I recalled the details from the previous encounters. Corey possessed a book that kept records of when gargoyles could come back to Earth from the Realm of Darkness. He created a circle with an anchor where they would appear. Once they arrived, he bound them to the circle. As long as they didn't break free, he would banish them back to the Realm of Darkness for hundreds of years. Armed with this knowledge, I felt more prepared to face another gargoyle sighting.

Nicole maneuvered the SUV to a halt, parking near the edge of the rest area. With the tranquil spell of Christmas Eve enveloping us, the rest area appeared empty, its silence embracing the chilly air. We opted for a stretch of withered winter grass that led to a cluster of slender trees, away from the restrooms.

This was the life I had embraced—a life intertwined with the supernatural. Stepping out of the vehicle, the thud of the car door startled me. Relax, I reminded myself, striving to regain composure.

Corey seemed unfazed, leaving his weapons belt behind and leaving the trunk open. With graceful nonchalance, he plucked a few honeysuckle twigs from his folded wicker basket and sauntered a few steps into the woods. The druid traced a precise circle on the ground, etching a peculiar symbol upon it three times. Placing three honeysuckle twigs between the symbols, he stood there and spoke his magic in a voice reminiscent of a drunken Irishman.

I positioned myself a few feet behind Corey, adopting a squared stance and standing at ease—a pose that exuded both readiness and discipline. Minutes passed, then a fiery hue lit up from Corey's torc. The world turned monochromatic, devoid of its vibrant hues. The cacophony of highway noises faded into nothingness as a colossal monstrosity, standing ten feet tall, materialized within Corey's circle. From the Realm of Darkness, the gargoyle emerged, its howls reverberating through the air, its frenzied movements a symphony of chaos.

Corey, undeterred by the creature's wild thrashing, persisted with his chant, his eyes betraying an air of boredom. I concealed my trembling hands behind my back, wearing a mask of stoicism, despite the fear coursing through my veins. My hands quivered in silent protest.

Again and again, the beast hurled itself against the barrier, driven by an unyielding determination. Stone body, rending claws, sharp teeth and spiked horns all failed to penetrate the magical wall. Corey's circle held true to its promise, demonstrating its impregnable nature. Minutes that felt like an eternity passed, each one wrenching my gut and twisting my soul, until finally, a resounding pop signaled the gargoyle's vanishing act. It dissolved into thin air, leaving behind the remnants of the circle and the scent of honeysuckle.

"Bingo, bango, bongo," Corey said with satisfaction. He noticed the concern etched across my face. "Is something wrong?"

Shaking, I struggled to regain composure. Corey enveloped me in a comforting embrace and guided me back to the car. Gathering my wits, I mustered the strength to speak, grateful for Corey's support. "Thank you, Corey. I'll manage from here."

"I'm sorry," he said with remorse. "Banishing gargoyles brings me peace. It used to be so simple—me, representing the forces of good, and the gargoyles, the embodiment of evil. But it's no longer that easy." He shuffled toward the trunk of the SUV, burdened by his thoughts.

Nicole handed me a bottle of water, her voice filled with reassurance. "That was a big one. It's all over now. Let's continue our journey."

"You know, that's the same size one I saved Old Donnie from. I thought it was a bear, and that set me on this path when I was nineteen." Corey's eyes held a faraway look. "It's been six years, but it feels like a lifetime."

"You're right, Corey. I must grow accustomed to these banishments," I said. After a sip of water and a glance toward the now desolate woods, I found solace in knowing that I possessed the strength to endure. "But first, Nicole, there's something I need to tell you."

"Rebecca, why don't you take the wheel?" Corey stowed away his belongings in the trunk before settling into the backseat. Retrieving his trusty book, he documented the banishment.

"I knew you two were being secretive in the backyard. What's the big secret?" Nicole asked, her eyes filled with anticipation as I walked around the vehicle and took my place in the driver's seat.

"Corey and I have discovered something, a secret we've kept from you. Initially, it was to ensure your happiness, but we realize it was a mistake, and need to confess." A weight lifted from my shoulders. It was up to Corey not to falter.

With a roar, the engine sprung to life as I started the SUV merging onto the highway. The act of driving served as a soothing balm, instilling a sense of control, however illusory it might be, calming my troubled mind.

In the rearview mirror, Corey sat upright, removing his earring. "I'm taking off my earring so that you can trust every word I say. It was foolish of me to keep this secret. But I've deciphered its significance." His earring shielded his thoughts from mind readers, a necessary protection against enemies, although it caused tension with Nicole, who struggled to trust her empathy around him.

Nicole's gaze fixated on the earring. "Very well, Corey. I'm all ears."

"Do you remember when I returned from the dead? When Rebecca called me into the conference room?" Corey asked.

"Yes." Nicole sat on her hands.

"Rebecca grew concerned when Wesley pointed out that our rekindled relationship altered the date of our deaths. She used her connections in Chesapeake Bay to query the Shared Supernatural System and got a result. She shared with me the summary."

This was the part I had been worried about.

Corey continued, "If I date and marry Rebecca, the world will end within twelve to twenty years. If I remain unattached, civilization will crumble in six years because of nuclear war. However, if I am with you, fate spares the world."

"Alright, nothing hidden there," I said. The numbers spoke for themselves.

"Whoa, what does who you date have to do with the end of the world?" asked Nicole, perplexed.

"I'll explain. The summary included percentages showing each of our roles in bringing about the end. At first glance, you seemed more responsible than me, with Rebecca trailing behind. However," Corey paused, his brows furrowing in contemplation.

"What do you mean?" I interrupted, seeking clarity. The statistics had seemed clear-cut.

He continued, without answering me, "It is I who causes the world's destruction one hundred percent of the time. Both of you will convince me to end the world or at least set me on that path, and that's why the blame falls on you. Then, sometimes, I act of my accord, but it's always me—the catalyst for civilization's demise. However, there's one exception." Corey leaned forward with newfound clarity.

"You're saying you become the harbinger of destruction," I inferred. "You go 'scorched civilization,'" I said using his term—a take-off from the US Military term of Scorched Earth.

"Yes. The stronger I become as a druid, the less I care about civilization. I care about my friends. If the three of you want me to save civilization along with the world, I will. Otherwise, I'm here to save the world. If a city or country stands in my way, I could dispatch them to the Realm of Darkness without a care."

"Corey, I understand it's because of your friendship with Rachel. You two are co-dependent, and if you and I are together, Rachel will be part of our household, ensuring you always have connections to humanity," Nicole acknowledged.

Corey nodded in agreement. "Exactly. The reason Nicole and I being together is crucial is because it ensures Rachel and I never part ways."

"You're right, Corey," Nicole concurred, her arm reaching out to him. "Rachel possesses an unwavering purity of heart. Nothing could sway her towards evil."

"And I vowed to never leave her. If Rachel remains steadfast, so shall I, unless circumstances tear us apart," Corey concluded, easing into a semblance of peace.

"But how does nuclear war fit into this equation?" I asked, grappling with the wider implications.

"Only the two of you are aware of the truth. The stronger I become as a druid, the less connected I am to society. Without the three of you, I will go rogue within a year. It will take both of you time to explore alternative solutions, but eventually, you may have to resort to convincing others to eliminate me using a nuclear weapon. However, things can take a turn for the worse," Corey said. "Nicole's empathy allows her to predict the right words to sway people. That is why she seems so influential. She will employ empathy to convince others to resort to nuclear weapons."

"Three things," Nicole said. "First, thank you for sharing this with me. Second, we are now even for the seed pod misunderstanding. I forgive both of you, just as you forgave me."

"That's fair," I concurred, shifting into the left lane, able to focus on the road with renewed clarity.

"Last," Nicole continued, her voice filled with admiration, "that is a well-thought-out argument. With the information at hand, I find it difficult to dispute. However, I refuse to accept that you are evil without the three of us." She turned, extending her arm towards Corey.

"We've had intense conversations, endured a challenging day, and even banished a gargoyle. For the rest of our journey, indulge me with my Taylor Swift playlist," Nicole said.

It was only fair that she had a say in the choice of music for once.

Corey chuckled, acknowledging Nicole's request. As candy pop tunes filled the car, our minds wandered, contemplating the complexities that lay ahead on our path.

Chapter 9—Rebecca

Nicole dialed the number of a restaurant offering car pickup and placed an order for four salads. A couple of exits later, I maneuvered the car off the highway, eager to retrieve our meal. Determined to arrive by seven, we planned to eat on the go.

"Food, what a splendid idea," exclaimed Christopher. He moved up to the second row, settling himself next to Corey. I felt my anticipation grow, hoping for a humorous interplay between Corey and Christopher.

As our SUV glided into the designated to-go pickup area, the tantalizing flavors that awaited us seemed almost within reach. "Caesar salad with grilled chicken and an extra side of dressing." I extended the creation to Christopher. The next salad was for Corey. "A garden salad with double portions of steak, and no dressing."

Corey wasted no time in delving into the food. Christopher was making an attempt to make peace with Corey. "Surely, one salad cannot suffice for your strenuous workout routine."

A smile danced in Corey's eyes. "This is my first dinner, as I'll be assisting at Miles's store later."

"Christopher, have you gathered enough information for your portraits?" I couldn't ignore a newcomer, especially one accustomed to being treated well.

"I'm waiting for your next set of powers. They'll be coming soon." Christopher ate at a measured pace, less hungry than the rest of us.

Sensing the need for further explanation, Corey stepped in. "Rebecca, the path to gaining powers mirrors mine in the realm of Earth. The Earth grants me a power from each of my four domains within the first year, and seeking guidance from a mentor allows me to gain another. With the help of benefactors and contracts, we gain access to study materials. Every fifty years, the Earth graces us with new powers." Corey's words painted a vivid picture of the journey ahead, filled with countless possibilities.

Contemplating the celestial realm's powers, the process unfolded similarly with my four realms of power: Angelic Form, Sanctuary, Curing, and Belief. "I have yet to find a mentor."

"You have many options," Corey said. "You can choose mentors like Miles, Rachel, senior witches, or those who possess knowledge of unexplored classes. I could guide you in fighting skills, supernatural combat, or even healing. Remember, time is on your side," he said.

"This is a big decision." My thoughts swirling with the weight of the choice before me.

"Don't forget, anyone can learn witchcraft or how to use circles." Christopher paused. "It's interesting. I don't see a future where Rebecca learns to use circles, but there are plenty of possibilities where Nicole learns to use them." He sighed. "This is why the timing of portraits is so critical. I could paint an incorrect portrait."

As our conversation continued, Christopher nibbled at his meal. Sensing a lingering question in the air, he turned his attention to Nicole. "Nicole, I see you and Corey in a captivating couple's portrait. However, I must admit, Corey's portrait seems to miss an essential element."

A playful smile played upon Nicole's lips. "My sister, Rachel. You can't separate them."

I smiled. It had been a challenging first month of dating when I learned about Corey and Rachel's co-dependence and their need to snuggle together. However, they were so platonic, the thought of dating each other caused them consternation.

Intrigued, Christopher voiced his observation. "Ah, unless Rachel possesses shoulders akin to Corey's, I believe there is more to this." The artist, now engrossed in the narrative, left his salad unfinished.

"You're right," said Nicole, a spark in her eyes. "Besides being a bard, Rachel possesses a specialization—a mastery in Shotokan—and she can even train Corey."

Eager to lay eyes upon the woman who captivated their conversation, Christopher asked, "Could I have the pleasure of seeing a picture of her?" Nicole handed him her phone, anticipation and curiosity radiating through the air.

A gasp of astonishment escaped Christopher's lips as his gaze fell upon the displayed image. "Wow! You were right, Nicole. Rachel possesses an indescribable beauty," he marveled, his words accompanied by a momentary pause. "Forgive me. I see the entirety of a person when I'm about to paint them."

Gratitude shone in Corey's eyes as he spoke, directed towards the artist. "You have a discerning eye, sir. Rachel's inner beauty is as pure as one can imagine." A grand smile graced Corey's face, a testament to the artist's ability to soothe even him. Once someone said something nice about Rachel, Corey would forgive a lot of other issues.

Eager to contribute to the discussion, Nicole retrieved Rebecca's phone. "Since we're looking at pictures, let me show you Rebecca's dating profile picture. We heard Corey's opinion, and now it's time to hear yours." She extended her phone to Christopher.

Observing the image, Christopher's eyes twinkled with delight. "Indeed, this is a delightful picture, but the one with the swing captures Rebecca's essence. It is a portrayal of a hard worker; it showcases your beauty, transcending any context. The sunlight illuminating your torso hints at a regal upbringing in rustic surroundings."

Enthusiasm brimmed in Corey's voice as he piped in. "Can I see?" Christopher obliged, handing Rebecca's phone to Corey. "This picture is good because of the way your hair cascades over your breasts." Corey's words provoked a lighthearted giggle, reminding us of the lingering effects of our long journey.

"Surely a picture for everyone," joked Christopher.

"Rebecca, Corey always carries his messenger bag with his spell books and the <u>Abernathy Book of Gargoyles</u>. I rarely see you carry your prayer book with your spells."

This was one area where Celestia fit me well. "My prayer book is much smaller and fits in my purse. When I leave Georgia, I have to take the Ruger LCP out, and the spell book is hardly noticeable."

I pulled out the white book that glowed with a golden light. "Can anyone see it?"

"Just as invisible as my spell books are to others," said Corey.

AS OUR SUV ROLLED THROUGH the ornate gate, we entered the Virginia estate, a world of grandeur awaiting our arrival. The gravel road crunched beneath our tires, guiding us toward the main house half a mile away. The imposing structure came into view, a breathtaking sight. Pulling into the circular driveway, a valet and a small assembly of butlers greeted us, their presence a testament to the grandeur that awaited us beyond the double red doors.

Outside of the car, we stretched our backs and legs with expectations of the splendor within the walls of the Virginia house. Corey, with graceful movements, fastened his weapons belt and adjusted his waist pack, showcasing his preparedness. Chuckling, I couldn't resist breaking the silence enveloping us.

"Someone will be out to handle our bags and take care of the car," I informed Corey, amusement lacing my voice.

"I need to mark the tree and head home. I have a litany of tasks when I'm at the store.

"Be more tactful, Corey. You don't want to sound crude." Nicole playfully punched his arm.

Corey's eyes sparkled, his face transforming into an impish mask as he closed the SUV trunk with a resounding thud.

"Let me spray my man magic on it so I can penetrate it easier," he joked, slamming the trunk and laughing at his own remark.

Caught between surprise and amusement, Christopher couldn't contain his grin, an unfamiliar joy accompanying Corey's unfiltered banter.

"Corey!" I exclaimed. "We're about to enter high society. Show some refinement, please." Although I despised resorting to such terms, it proved one of the few ways to coax a more suitable demeanor from him, especially when Nicole's laughter fueled his exuberance.

With gentle insistence, I guided him up the stately steps, my mind racing to prepare a string of apologies. To my relief, Corey's timing proved impeccable as I turned toward the entrance.

"Sorry. I need to cast my new Plant Domain spell called *Tree Transfer*," Corey said, standing up straight. "This way, I can provide support to our friends so they may have time with family."

My grandmother, a paragon of grace and wisdom, graced us with her presence. "Dear, there's no need to worry about Corey. He possesses an innate eloquence that is always a pleasure to be around." Her voice carrying the weight of experience.

"Grace, you're absolutely right. Corey's presence brings joy to any occasion." Christopher presented a mounted knife embellished with Corey's signature. "Just look, I've already arranged a display for this unique piece proving I was almost killed by the infamous druid!"

My initial concern regarding Corey dissolved in the warmth of my grandmother's arrival, my emotions ebbing and flowing between frustration and relief. "It's a delight to be here during this wonderful holiday."

After the greetings, my grandmother addressed Corey with an apologetic smile. "I'm afraid it's customary for all of you to declare any weapons in your possession before entering."

It was time for them to witness Corey's true character, unfiltered and unabashed. With infectious energy, he bounded toward the grand staircase, wrapping his arm around Nicole. "Ms. Addkinson, worry not. Allow me to present my first weapon." He embraced his fiancé. "This is my fiancée, Nicole."

"Oh, Young Corey, you charmer." Grandmother planted kisses on Nicole's cheeks. "You've been entertaining these ladies throughout the entire journey. You're a fortunate young woman, Nicole."

"Ms. Addkinson, being from the deep south," Corey said with Southern charm, "I know only one way to greet family and friends." He enveloped grandmother in an embrace, his audacity setting the gossip wheels in motion. The scandal of a young man embracing the matron of the Addkinson household would soon reverberate throughout the estate and beyond.

My eyes widened in disbelief as grandmother responded. "Oh my, I can always recognize a genuine hug when I receive one. I must check if I am expecting."

Corey, unfazed by the shocked expressions surrounding him, grinned and laughed at grandmother's jest.

"Take a seat, everyone," he said, pulling off his waist pack first. "Silver sickle, not a weapon. Honeysuckle twigs and trumpets. If you see me holding one, things are about to go down." He unwrapped something resembling a seed pod. "Magnolia seed pod." He placed it back into his waist pack. "Otherwise, I have GPS, multi-tool, search and rescue satellite equipment, fire starter, flashlight, water filter, and two days' worth of freeze-dried food."

Corey moved on to his weapons belt. "These are my tonfa. Well-used. Stun gun, pepper gel, tactical pen, glass breaker." He looked at the man by the metal detector and winked. "Good for turning part of gargoyles to stone, playing on their defense mechanism."

He placed the bags on the conveyor belt with a thunk. Then Corey started pulling out knives. "I used to carry two knives, but they ended up in an enemy with an automatic weapon, and he was in no position to return them. Now I carry more." He revealed eight of his normal knives from inside the holes in his pockets and his calf.

My grandmother giggled at each new knife after the fourth. This was Corey, the wartime druid.

Each knife clacked in the plastic bin the man held out. "Only two of these have killed. The rest are unused. Dead beasts keep stealing my knives." Corey winked at the guard.

He pulled out a new knife much longer than his normal ones. "A man talked so pretty to me, I explained he had to love me from afar as Nicole captured my heart. He stuck this in my stomach and left it there as a present. He had good taste, and I appreciate his gift. It's called a Chaos Bowie."

"Corey, he hated you and attacked you. People who love you don't stick you and leave things in your belly." Nicole rolled her eyes.

Corey showed people the scar from the knife wound, sporting his impish grin. Before anyone could stop him, he turned to Nicole and said, "Why? That's what I did with you." He grinned when Nicole's mouth dropped open.

Christopher, unable to contain his mirth, erupted into laughter. Nicole, her patience stretched thin, leaned in close to Corey and whispered something in his ear, her voice carrying a hint of warning. I hoped it was a threat, a small token of revenge for his audacity.

"That concludes my arsenal," Corey said with a playful flourish. The guard, his eyes betraying a mix of wariness and trepidation, asked about firearms.

"No firearms, sir?" the guard asked.

"Warriors like us prefer the intimacy of close combat, leaving the guns to others." He winked at the guard, further unsettling the already uneasy sentry. He read the man's nametag. "Samson. They should let you grow your hair like mine, with a name like that!"

The guard, Samson, smiled weakly.

Nicole and I were experts with firearms, but now my powers meant I needed to learn melee combat.

Corey consumed the minutes that followed, returning each item to its rightful place, ensuring he stowed his array of weapons. As our group made its way into the opulent grand hall, the twenty-foot Christmas tree adorning the left side of the room drew my eyes.

Grandmother directed Corey's attention to the immense double glass doors leading to the picturesque courtyard. Stepping into the center of the open space, he marked a circle around a majestic tree, his lips lingering on Nicole's before bidding her farewell, his warmth enveloping me in a comforting embrace. Christopher extended his hand, a gesture of camaraderie, while even grandmother yearned for another embrace.

And just like that, Corey disappeared. As Nicole and I exchanged glances, a mixture of laughter and relief danced in our eyes.

"REBECCA, ONE MINUTE please," called out Grandmother, her voice carrying a note of urgency.

"Yes, Grandmother." I hurried to her side. My heart raced, sensing that something important awaited me.

Grandmother motioned to a man standing nearby, burdened with bags. "Take Nicole to her rooms," she instructed, her gaze fixed on me. "Rebecca, come with me." We walked together through the grand hall, its opulent walls resonating with a sense of history and power.

Her grandmother had transformed the room. "This used to be the library, didn't it?" I asked.

"Yes, dear," Grandmother confirmed, her tone carrying a weight I had never heard before. "But now, this is your office." Her words hung in the air, hinting at a deeper meaning.

Sensing there was more to be revealed, I approached the topic with care. "What should I bring into my office?"

A soft chuckle escaped Grandmother's lips. "You are perceptive. Far beyond what I was at your age. Rebecca, events are unfolding at an alarming pace, and you must mature quickly."

I nodded, worried that events pushed me faster than I desired. "In what ways should I focus?" I asked. "I've been learning combat skills since the battle in Alpharetta, where they exposed me as untrained."

Grandmother's tired eyes bore into mine, her face etched with worry. "Yes, continue honing your combat skills, but here we will refer to it as formal instruction called 'Military Tactics of the Realized Training.' Our territory faces greater threats than I had expected. For now, please do not ask for specifics."

I could sense the gravity of the situation, understanding that yesterday's shocking events had taken a toll on Grandmother. But I couldn't ignore my own doubts. "I'm still trying to make sense of everything that happened yesterday. I don't even know if I made the right decision."

Grandmother's expression softened, a mixture of empathy and resolve. "You will soon become the matriarch of the Addkinson estate and the leader of the Chesapeake Bay Territory. Incidents like yesterday will become more common, and you'll need to become more resilient, like Young Corey. The cost of imprisoning those who ally with the Dark Fey is high, and rehabilitation is not an option. These individuals have had their souls manipulated for years before it compelled them to act."

Grandmother sighed. "But above all else, your priority is to find a suitable husband. The stability of our territory and my life depends on it. There has already been one attempt on my life. A solid line of succession will ease everyone's worries. Find a strong man to marry. Unfortunately, we have two years, perhaps just one before an engagement."

Though time seemed limited, I knew I couldn't rush into such an important decision while constantly embarking on adventures. "I've been assessing the men within the Chesapeake Bay Territory. But given the time frame, I fear I may need to extend my search beyond our borders."

Grandmother nodded. "Good. Our territory has seen too many soft years, and our young men reflect that. I'm glad you're already considering alternatives. Once I make an announcement, you'll understand what needs to be placed within this office."

"Thank you, Grandmother," I said.

Her tone softened, and a hint of regret laced her words. "If I had known the painter would reach out to you so soon, I would have prepared you more adequately."

A glimmer of amusement sparked within me. "We managed just fine, although Corey issued a warning to him, threatening his life if he took another step into our yard."

Grandmother shook her head with a smile. "Christopher discovered his powers a decade ago, as a teenager, and he became a renowned artist before even turning eighteen. He maneuvers in the highest levels of leadership, though he is difficult even for those centuries old."

"I will, Grandmother. If there's one thing I excel at, it's dealing with difficult men."

Grandmother chuckled, the sound washing away some of the weight in the room. "Indeed, you do. Now, join your friend. It's Christmas Eve, after all. We're allowed to have fun."

Chapter 10—Rebecca

After settling into our respective rooms, I made my way to Nicole's neighboring quarters. Fortunately, they interconnected these rooms with an adjoining door, providing a comforting and convenient arrangement.

Nicole greeted me with a mischievous smile, her eyes glimmering with excitement. "I have a hidden IP address, and we can gather some information," she said, her tone filled with anticipation. Her years of secret investigations into her parents' killers had honed her spying skills. She succeeded in her mission, with Corey dispatching Bishop Pedrotti. Though her methods were questionable because of her training in deception and empathic abilities, her intentions were noble. If truth be told, her steps crossing the line into questionable activities attracted Corey.

She was a regular member of Saint Andrews and now brought their greatest enemy, Corey, with her. They were even taking the marriage classes to be married in the church. "It still cracks me up how the church marriage counselor said, 'we are Catholic. The first child comes anytime. It's the rest that take nine months.'"

"She is so sweet. Don't tell Corey, but I'm signing the two of us for parenting classes at the church, along with our marriage classes."

"After today, he has no room to argue," I agreed. It was a reminder that we didn't fight the church. We fought a few people who had taken over the Curia of the church.

From her bag, Nicole retrieved a laptop and set it up on a roll-top desk from the Revolutionary War era. She also produced a peculiar device, connecting it to her laptop.

"Bring me up to speed," I said, recognizing the importance of strategizing and gathering intelligence.

Nicole plugged the device into the wall socket and then into her laptop, placing it atop the desk. The screen flickered to life. "When you killed the Monsignor, the church removed his security protocols, allowing me to log back into their network. To maintain continuity, I volunteered to oversee St. Andrew's monthly calendar for volunteer functions, granting me remote access to their network."

Nicole's fingers danced across the keyboard, weaving a complex web of codes and passwords. She dialed her cell phone. "Hello, Nandu. I have connected to CBT-VA-thirteen following Kim's instructions," Nicole informed her contact.

Curiosity piqued, I strained to catch snippets of the conversation on the other end. "Perfect. Thank you," Nicole eventually responded.

Perplexed, I asked, "What was that? How did you find an IT contact here?"

Nicole's eyes sparkled with pride. "Your IT department is huge. Back home, Nathan would set me up, but I couldn't gain exactly what I needed. Here, they allow me to set up and provide me with what I'm permitted to have." She continued typing, orchestrating a symphony of windows and applications.

Taking a seat beside her, I watched in awe.

"Corey insisted I interact with the church's network when I'm not connected to ours," Nicole said while her fingers dancing across the keys. "So, I created an encrypted tunnel to a standalone machine. This hides my identity, location, and bypasses logs while I search for information."

Although computers were not foreign to me, Nicole navigated this uncharted territory with remarkable proficiency. "How did you learn all this?" I asked.

A chuckle escaped Nicole's lips. "It's funny. College was a cover for my quest to uncover the truth behind my parents' murder. Grandpa Jon suggested a major in Finance, and I complied so that he would grant me more leeway. I needed computer skills for the degree, and those same skills were crucial for my espionage. Hence, I ended up with a minor in computer science."

Her voice carried a touch of regret as she added, "It was the worst choice ever! I worked tirelessly, hanging out with computer geeks to learn it all."

"It's impressive. I earned a degree in Classics. My linguistics thrived, and I became familiar with most European languages. I even passed the French fluency exam. My papers on seventeenth- and eighteenth-century Europe seem meaningless now."

"Madison's family has a device that can view alternate timelines if you want to relive those classes." Nicole's fingers continued their nimble dance on the keyboard, the symphony of keystrokes resonating throughout the room. "I'm in, and I can access my volunteer window, where I update the calendar," she said. "Now, I'll connect to the archdiocese system."

Intrigued, I leaned in closer, peering over Nicole's shoulder, my gaze on the screens she navigated. An unexpected revelation emerged, fueling a surge of curiosity within both of us. "This is new," Nicole exclaimed. "Have you heard of someone named Marrianna, spelled with two 'r's?"

I shifted to a more comfortable position on the bed, my mind racing through the repository of knowledge I had gained. "No."

"There's a new connection with that name," Nicole said.

Just as we delved deeper into this revelation, Corey's call interrupted us. Nicole pressed the speakerphone button.

"Hey Baby. Hold on. Isabella? Is something wrong?" Nicole's attention diverted to the phone.

"Mr. Corey has you in his phone as Nicole, the most wonderful fiancé who could exist, and he better not think of any other woman." Isabella giggled.

"I may have set my name as that," Nicole said while laughing. "Corey, is that a dog?" Nicole turned the screen toward me, revealing the enormous canine next to Corey.

"Isabella found this dog who is being put down for being too violent, but it's only misunderstood. I wanted to let you know we're adopting this dog, but she needs a name," he said.

"It seems her name is Valkyrie," I pointed out, recognizing the formidable appearance of the dog. Its eyes showed a past of fighting.

In response to my remark, the Great Dane let out a resounding bark, as if confirming her name.

"Valkyrie it is," Corey's voice resounded through the room, brimming with affection and joy. "I hope the two of you are enjoying the evening."

"You too, sweetie," was how she ended the call.

"We'll get back to Corey," Nicole asserted, her voice brimming with determination, "since I have access to the church's network. I can log in using Bishop Pedrotti's undeleted ID."

Seated beside her, I settled into my role as observer, my gaze locked onto the screens that unveiled a realm of secrets. Nicole broke the silence with a sharp gasp.

The screen transformed into a void of darkness, punctuated by blood-red words appearing as if typed by an unseen hand. "Who dares intrude upon this domain? Pedrotti has passed away," the screen declared autonomously. "Is it Aaron who has displayed remarkable prowess?"

Panic surged within me as the computer communicated with us. I cried out, "Shut it down!"

Nicole complied, her trembling fingers pressing the power button, severing the connection with the mysterious intruder. A shiver coursed through her, mirroring the unease gripping us both.

"We must warn Aaron. I'll call Nathan." I reached for my phone.

"No," Nicole said. "We linked our phones to the Command Center and can't risk it."

Nicole's gaze shifted towards the archaic landline resting on the bedside table, its dial tone beckoning for attention.

"Wait," she interrupted. "We can use this phone, but calling Nathan's phone is out of the question since it's connected to the Command Center."

Recognizing the wisdom in her words, I left the phone untouched. "Then how do we alert everyone?"

A glimmer of determination sparkled in Nicole's eyes as her resolve held strong. "Nathan and Madison are in route to her family's house in Chattanooga for Christmas. We'll reach out to Madison's Aunt Becky." She handed me the contact details. "Dial this number. Let her know Nathan needs to contact us through this landline, bypassing the Command Center."

We dialed Madison's Aunt Becky and conveyed the urgency of Nathan's need to make an immediate call to this specific landline, free from any routing through the Command Center.

ALL THE ROOMS IN THE estate enveloped us with an air of grandeur. Nicole's room boasted an enormous bed that seemed to stretch out endlessly. To reach the mattress, we had to take a small leap, landing with a slight bounce upon its plush surface. Between the window and the room's cozy fireplace, ancient metal mattress heaters hung on the wall. Thankfully, the estate used modern heating systems now, dispelling any chill that dared to permeate the room.

As we awaited Nathan's call, we found solace in lighthearted conversation, discussing topics that brought laughter and ease to our hearts. "Can you believe how much our lives have transformed? Three months ago, Corey was determined to be a loner and fight everything on his own, and now we have house improvements, a dog, an impending baby, and our upcoming marriage."

The whirlwind of events had indeed swept us off our feet. "It has been an extraordinary holiday season for all of us. By the way, was that dog as large as it appeared?"

Nicole's eyes twinkled as she recalled the delightful surprise. "It doesn't matter. Druids despise people owning pets, and he treats all animals as wild. I accepted the idea of never having a dog. Valkyrie is a wonderful addition. Plus, it seemed friendly."

I hesitated, recalling the imposing presence of the dog. "Well, let's just say it will be friendly to anyone Corey asks it to be." Memories of dogs trained for fighting stirred unease within me, and I couldn't help but notice Valkyrie possessed a similar aura. "But the burning question remains: how did a daughter of a store employee convince Corey to rescue a dog?"

Nicole paused, deep in thought. "With Corey, there's no need to worry. Isabella won't be fifteen for a few more months, and Corey didn't give me a second glance until I turned twenty-one."

Nicole's jealousy caused her to miss a detail. "Nicole, how often do people approach Corey without one of us there to soften his demeanor?"

She fell silent, pondering my question for what seemed like an eternity.

"Exactly," I said. "Corey's Realized powers attract those who possess a spark, individuals on the verge of their own realization."

"Isabella has the spark," said Nicole, mirroring my thoughts.

The shrill ring of the landline interrupted our thoughts. I picked it up, bringing the old-fashioned handset close to my ear so that Nicole could join me, her ear pressed against it.

"Nathan, we received an alarming message," Nicole said. "Have you heard of someone named Marrianna, spelled with two 'r's?"

Nathan's surprise was apparent in his response. "No, I haven't. Why all this secrecy?"

Nicole explained her encounter with a mysterious link in the church, which prompted her to unplug everything. The situation had escalated, prompting caution.

Nathan's advice was clear. "Keep using the current phones, but refrain from sharing any sensitive information through them. I hope I don't need to tell you to stay off the church network."

Nicole's expression shifted, and she shared a revelation. "Oh, and by the way, Isabella is Realized or is on the brink of it."

"Corey informed me about it. He's handling the situation. He had told me it sounded like another person was talking to animals last week and it turned out to be her, which is why she trusted animals others didn't."

"Great," Nicole said. "So, aside from all this intrigue, what else has been happening?"

He gave the news of Wesley's father's imminent retirement after the school year. "It's remarkable, considering he's been the principal there for what feels like an eternity."

Nicole's eyes widened in astonishment. "Wow, that's a significant transition."

I had my ear pressed to the receiver as well, and Nathan changed the subject. "And while we're on relationships, we should give Rachel a gentle nudge. I caught her practicing how to write her name as 'Rachel Matice' and 'Mr. and Mrs. Wesley and Rachel Matice.'"

"Nathan, that's normal. As long as she knows to dispose of any incriminating evidence." I couldn't help but recall how I had practiced writing my name as 'Rebecca Norwood' even before I mustered the courage to ask Corey out.

Nicole laughed. "I've been practicing 'Nicole Norwood' since tenth grade. It'll be six years from when I started practicing to when I'll marry him."

Madison's laughter echoed in the background, and a playful remark slipped from her lips. "With the way you two carry on, I would have thought you had him practicing Corey Hendrix."

Everyone erupted in laughter, and I almost tumbled off the poster bed, saved by the tall column on the footboard.

Nicole glared at me and ended the call with a final quip. "We'll let you go since we need to prepare Rebecca for her lunch date tomorrow."

"That was a secret," I said.

"Nathan told Madison in confidence. You know she couldn't keep it to herself, so she confided in me."

I nodded, grateful that at least Nicole was aware of the need for discretion. "Alright, as long as you know who mustn't find out."

Nicole's smile widened, her eyes dancing with mischief. "Rachel, Wesley, and Corey are off-limits." She then turned her attention to me, curiosity piqued. "Now, tell me more about Lance, the hunk."

"Foremost, he's not a hunk. He's pursuing a Ph.D. in Theology from Georgetown's philosophy department."

Nicole raised an eyebrow, her interest piqued. "Oh, the exact opposite of Corey? So, apart from being a brainiac, does Lance have any other fascinating aspects?"

"He spent four out of five years serving as an intelligence officer in Afghanistan," I said. "The position is required to be fluent in at least two languages."

Nicole's gaze lingered, contemplating the extraordinary experiences Lance had encountered. "War zones and weapons training. That's something. Is he a looker?"

I hesitated. "It's difficult to say. The camera angle could have been flattering, or he might not have paid much attention to it."

Just then, a knock echoed from the adjacent room and a man's voice called through the door. "The heating is being turned off for the night." The warning repeated as the footsteps advanced, each knock warning others on our floor.

"We should get beneath the covers," I said, aware of the impending chill that would soon seep into the room. "It grows cold."

Nicole's eyes pleaded, "Will you stay here with me? I feel uneasy being alone in an unfamiliar place."

I felt a rush of warmth in my heart at her request. Without hesitation, we nestled under the thick quilts, seeking solace and comfort in each other's presence.

Chapter 11—Madison

Madison and Nathan strolled back to their car, the conversation with Nicole and Rebecca lingering in their minds like a fleeting respite from the weight of Chattanooga's memories. The ache of Madison's bullet wound seemed insignificant compared to the deeper pain resurfacing within her.

While arriving here, Madison noticed the familiar landmarks that held great significance in her life and reminded her of how unwanted she was for several years. A couple of the roads leading to foster homes where she stayed, her old school, and the park where'd she hide.

When they passed by the entrance to the woods, where she once lived after aging out of foster care, her stomach stayed in her mouth. However, the Lookouts baseball stadium that her entire existence changed, calmed her and reminded her she had a new life.

And then there was the Mellow Mushroom, a place she worked at feeling normal after her Aunt Becky led a team of witches to imprison Madison's grandparents, liberating her parents and great-grandparents from a time prison. Ten years wasn't a long time, but those ten years were when she was eight until she was eighteen.

Nathan tugged at Madison's hand, pulling her towards the house. "You, okay?" he asked.

"Sorry, reminiscing." The last time she had set foot in that house, they gave her books, preparing her to lead the Chattanooga coven. However, the immense surge of Earth energy from Corey had altered her Realized powers, transforming her into a Realized hunter instead of a witch suppressing her need for acceptance within a closed coven.

Now, she had friends and a loving boyfriend. Everything felt new and exhilarating, though beneath the surface, she struggled to contain the whirlwind of emotions threatening to overwhelm her. The Southeast Territory was where she could prove her worth and stay happy. It was time to collect herself to keep baggage from accumulating. People didn't like those with baggage.

Nathan's hand trembled as he fumbled with the trunk of the car, but on his second attempt, he opened it, revealing their luggage and collection of presents. Madison took hold of the gifts, her gaze fixed on the doorway, bracing herself for the impending onslaught of questions. The inquiry she expected most was whether her team trusted her as a hunter or if they were sidelining her.

If she could provide a satisfying answer, the rest would fall into place. That Nathan led the Southeastern area under Preacher Jon, only strengthened her position. Preacher Jon's decision to entrust the team's operations to Nathan during his vacation spoke volumes about Nathan's capability and the trust the team placed in him. This trip could be baggage-free, and things would stay great in Atlanta.

However, as they made their way inside, the impending discussion about the Marrianna name and the complexities of the Shared Supernatural System loomed on the horizon.

Aunt Becky offered a helping hand, guiding Madison up the stairs when an alarm blared, filling the stairwell with a crimson hue. Aunt Becky unfurled her cape, conjuring a cloud of mystical purple smoke from prepared powder from a hidden pocket, silencing the alarm. "Did either of you bring a magical item?" Aunt Becky asked, her appearance betraying a youthful readiness that would not seem out of place at a dance club, save for the cascading purple witch's cape trailing behind her.

Madison retraced her steps in her mind. "No."

Nathan sounded concerned. "I have a device, but I declared it on the list."

As Aunt Becky deliberated, her grin betrayed a mischievous undertone. "It's not that. Let's go through everything one by one."

Several minutes passed as they handed over their luggage and exchanged presents. Among the wrapped gifts was a pair from Corey—one for Madison and one for Nathan. These were the culprits.

"Apologies, but we can't wait until tomorrow to inspect an undeclared magical item," Aunt Becky said with amusement. Though the possibility of a trap seemed unlikely, adhering to safety rules took precedence.

One by one, they unwrapped their Christmas gifts from Corey. Nathan's eyes widened in delight as he revealed a beautiful set of handcrafted grilling tools imbued with enchantments. Handcrafted wooden tools with metal inset by hand. Corey had noted Nathan's joy whenever he had the chance to showcase his culinary skills during team meetings on the patio.

Madison's heart swelled with gratitude as she unwrapped her gift, revealing a collection of crafted wooden arrows, each one infused with an enchantment. It was these very arrows that had triggered the alarm, setting off a cascade of crimson warnings.

Aunt Becky's gaze locked onto the exquisite weaponry. "An enchanted weapon. These arrows are magnificent."

Fingers delicately caressing one arrow, Madison marveled at its perfect balance and enchanting craftsmanship. Not only were they aesthetically pleasing, but their enchantments ensured they would never deteriorate—never warp, break, dull, or become unusable.

Madison's uncle emerged from within the house, adding another layer of magic to the scene. "Earth magic, too," he said. "It seems the druid intends to fight alongside you for the foreseeable future."

In that moment, all doubts about her team's trust in Madison melted away. There would be no questions. Corey's thoughtful and kind gesture, coupled with the practicality of his gift, had stopped questions about whether he wanted her on the team.

Aunt Becky assumed the role of hostess, gesturing for them to follow. "Allow me to show you to your room. We can discuss your two business matters over dinner. You'll have an hour to freshen up and unwind from the journey," Her gaze shifted to Nathan; her concern clear. "And Nathan, as diligent as you are, don't forget to take it easy. Remember, you both still bear bullet wounds."

Madison's uncle Kenneth, the one who brought her to Korea as a child, added accolades. "And let's not downplay your remarkable feat of sensing the shooter and shielding our girl from harm. Since the thirteenth century, you're the first two non-witches to become a part of our family."

Moments later, they found themselves in a guest bedroom on the upper floor. The room boasted a grand king-size bed and an array of elegant furnishings, creating an atmosphere of comfort and serenity. Aunt Becky had informed her that her parents would indeed show up to dinner but not expect much. They were out of a magical coma, and their minds were healing.

It was heavy. The reminder that her parent's last action was to save her and Aunt Becky from her grandparents and that had them mind tortured in a time prison for ten years was daunting. Not only had Aunt Beck freed them, she now worked to recover their minds.

Nathan put his arm around Madison and lightened the mood. "Of all the possibilities I pondered regarding how our introductions would unfold, I didn't expect triggering an alarm with magical weaponry."

A smile played at Madison's lips, her heart brimming with affection. "I told you my family would adore you." She relaxed. This holiday with her family had already surpassed her expectations, weaving a tapestry of warmth and acceptance.

Now, as they prepared for a well-deserved day off, Madison couldn't help but feel a glimmer of hope for the future. Corey's gifts, both intended and accidental, had given upon her a renewed sense of purpose. In this moment, as she embraced the joys of family, the greatest gift of all was the reminder that she was not alone—she was here with Nathan, and for the first time, he was a person who would stay with her even if she proved nothing to him.

On the way to dinner the two walked through the hallway covered with paintings of famous family members from history. The stairs provided a spectral hand guiding their descent, and they entered the Foyer and proceeded down the hallway adorned with sculptures from the family during the Hellenistic and Roman eras.

"Nathan and Madison, could I borrow a moment of your time?" her uncle, Kenneth, asked. He led them to a room flanked by paintings of two priestesses from farming cults. "I need this contraption to function to identify the faulty component."

"No problem." Nathan rarely used his powers around others. He had a touch capable of reanimating any piece of technology. In fact, on their first pseudo date, the two escape a gargoyle by Nathan stealing a car.

He extended his hand towards the sprawling device occupying the room. The machinery roared to life and the room's walls became a vibrant depiction of the multiverse. Eight Outer Realms, the inner Fey and Darkness Realms, and Earth were all depicted, each colored to reflect their respective alliances.

Her uncle cast a spell with some prepared powder and the puff of smoke gathered around one section of the contraption. "Here it is." Her uncle unscrewed the fourth plate in the sixth cabinet and extracted a piece of machinery replete with vacuum tubes and archaic circuits. The vibrant images vanished. "You've just saved me months of troubleshooting."

Madison couldn't contain her elation. Nathan's act would endear him to her family, and any concerns from their journey now seemed inconsequential. However, it was a reminder Nathan was out of his element. He kept the Command Center devoid of frivolous magic and didn't use his magic unless he had to.

She clasped his hand. The house they now occupied was an embodiment of a magical reality. Just the remainder of the stroll to the dining area was filled with magic.

Torches cast an Autumn Fey fire, their flickering glow creating an ethereal ambiance. Unseen servants floated, presenting dishes that appeared to dance in the air. Doorways shifted and transformed under an invisible force, ensuring the shortest routes to desired destinations. Even the floor adapted beneath their feet, providing a comforting parquet surface tailored to their steps. Others walked on carpet, cherry wood, or even stone, depending on their desired sensation while traversing the house. Normal here was not normal in the Southeast Command Center.

Returning home felt like reverting to her magical childhood, with the magic returned in full swing and the years between now an interruption. Seeing Nathan using his technological magic reminded her of the dual worlds she inhabited. She would pull Nathan aside later to help him adjust to the house.

Madison and Nathan found themselves seated side by side at a magnificent twenty-foot-long medieval trestle table adorned with intricate gothic carvings. Plush padded benches lined each side instead of conventional chairs, offering a comfortable yet regal seating arrangement.

Madison's voice resonated with excitement as she shared the table's intriguing history. "They rescued this table from the Palace of Fontainebleau after the passing of Charles IV during the onset of the

Hundred Years' War. And it's enchanted with Fey Autumn Court magic."

Nathan's eyes widened in wonder as his fingers traced the table's intricate carvings. "It's exquisite."

Becky, now seated beside Madison and Nathan, removed her cape and joined the conversation. More family members filled the table, a dozen or more, their cheerful chatter and laughter blending with the enchanting ambiance of the room.

With Aunt Becky serving as the family's matriarch, the meal began with lively conversations and shared jokes across generations. Madison's parents, however, remained silent, still grappling with the treatment. Ten years of torture meant the treatment would take a decade. It started off in a magical coma, which they released them from last year. Now, without constant pain, they were relearning how to use their minds.

Aunt Becky informed them that Madison's parents had recently rejoined family meals. It was a marvel but surreal to see them again after fifteen years, as they hadn't aged a day. The experience of beholding them, as they remained gaunt and frail, filled Madison with a mix of emotions. She followed her aunt's advice not to stare.

Instead, Madison marveled at the seamless coordination of the unseen servants, fulfilling every guest's desires. Nathan, she noticed, had his colored food preparation done seamlessly in beige. The invisible attendants crafted his dishes, discerning his preferences. Aunt Becky recounted a past lover—an heks from Belgium—who shared Nathan's obsession with the aesthetics of his food.

But tonight was a time for celebration and camaraderie. Madison's great-grandfather, his voice aged yet lively, captured everyone's attention. Just past his two hundredth year, he spoke with the wisdom accumulated over his lifetime. Leah, a young woman a few years younger than Madison and Nathan, received a lighthearted commendation for being the youngest family member present.

"You two," her great-grandfather said, turning his gaze toward Madison and Nathan, "have made quite an impression. All admire your relationship."

Leah directed her words to Madison and Nathan, "As for me, I'm boyfriend-less. His last social media post read, 'Thank goodness that's over. I'm glad I'm still human after Leah happened to me.'"

The single word "happened" spoke volumes about the turbulent nature of their relationship. It was strange to find Leah single and sad. As the 'pretty one' in the family, boys always had flocked to her.

Aunt Becky joined the playful banter. "Most witches require magic to evoke such a reaction. Leah, you accomplished it effort-lessly, by being yourself," she teased, provoking laughter around the table.

Aunt Becky redirected the conversation, suggesting they post-pone discussing the tome they had encountered the previous day un-til after the holidays. She commended their efforts to safeguard it, as-suring them of their commendable actions.

"Bow," her father's voice resonated through the room. The table fell silent, every eye turning towards him. Madison understood it was her moment to step forward, offering support. Memories of their shared experiences flooded her mind, and she spoke with heartfelt sincerity, "Do you remember, Dad, when you used to take me bow hunting as a little girl? Those moments kept me going, and my love for archery became my primary Realized power."

Tears welled up in both of her parents' eyes, a mixture of emo-tions coursing through them. Her mother said, "Videos." Madison caught a whispered "wow" emanating from beneath the table, real-izing that the videos from the Atlanta Command Center had capti-vated her parents. They had witnessed her marksmanship, her battles against the Dark Fey and their counterparts from alternate universes.

Uncertain about how to respond to the unexpected attention, Madison hesitated for a moment before continuing, "Remember how we used to shoot bugs off the paling at our hunting cabin?"

Emotions surged within her parents, their hands trembling. Aunt Becky, sensing them overwhelmed, suggested, "Why don't you take your dinner to your room? Tonight has been overwhelming." Invisible servants lifted Madison's parents, guiding them upstairs while the plates and glasses floated along, following their path. Aunt Becky reassured Madison that everything would be fine, emphasizing their plan to restore her parents to their former selves. With centuries ahead of them, there was no need to rush the process.

Her great-grandfather's voice filled the air once more. "They both spoke a word, recognized their daughter, recovered memories from before their imprisonment, and showed genuine emotion."

Seated beside him, his wife added, "Consider me humbled. I was mistaken in my skepticism."

Aunt Becky fixed her gaze upon Madison, catching her off guard with a direct question. "How are you addressing your own healing, Madison? Changing your name and appearance, entering a healthy relationship—those are important steps. But what about the internal healing?"

Surprised, Madison stumbled for a response, realizing that avoiding the question would impede her desire for a baggage free trip.

Nathan offered her a hint. "Mare and Melinda are not confidential."

Gathering her thoughts, she mustered the courage to answer, "It's not therapy, per se. I've been helping two girls who've had a rough time in foster care, guiding them towards reclaiming their lives after a traumatic event."

Aunt Becky's eyes sparkled with admiration. "You're helping other girls who have gone through experiences similar to your own. That's wonderful."

Leah added, "Your boyfriend helps you out of jams instead of putting you in them?"

Madison's smile grew, warmth spreading through her heart. "He not only saved my life and supported me through difficult times, but he also trusts me to make my own decisions." She patted Nathan's leg.

It was a pleasant end to all the tough questions. She felt like she aced a test.

As the table resumed its chatter, Nathan's preoccupied expression caught Madison's attention. Curiosity piqued; she leaned closer. "What's on your mind?"

"I've been thinking about Corey and his concern over the lineage book and an unknown enemy," Nathan confessed, his eyes reflecting a mix of concern and worry. "When I received Nicole and Rebecca's phone call earlier, it seemed innocuous, but now it is coming together. And I'm feeling a sense of unease."

Determined to ease his worries, Madison reassured him, "Let's set those thoughts aside for now. It's Christmas Eve, after all." Turning to Aunt Becky, she posed the question. "This will put Nathan's mind at ease. Do you know anyone powerful whose name starts with 'March'?"

Aunt Becky's eyes widened, and a sudden silence descended upon the room. "Why do you ask?" Her confident tone wavering, revealing a crack in her composure.

This was not the response she expected or wanted. Now, Madison was catching up to Nathan and beginning to suspect what scared Corey.

Nathan spoke up, surprising Madison with his assertiveness. "It's a significant clue related to a problem that has Corey concerned. It led us to uncover an information gap."

Aunt Becky retrieved a quill from her cloak and produced a puff of smoke, writing the words in the air in front of her and Nathan—a spell to avoid scrying. "Marchosias is a fallen angel, one of a handful found deceased in recent years." Then the smoke dissipated.

Aunt Becky's gaze shifted between Nathan and Madison, her expression betraying vulnerability. "This is not a conversation for open ears. We'll need a silence spell or a scrambler to ensure privacy. Let's change the topic for now."

Madison's mind raced, contemplating the implications of their conversation. If their suspicions were true, Old Donnie and Marchosias had a baby—Marrianne. This could explain her motive for eradicating other angels and concealing her identity within the church's computer system... or impersonate the AI within the Shared Supernatural System.

She knew it in her heart to be true. Corey's actions, the unexplained attacks, the unreliable computer system, powers that were unknown until now, the Outer Realm's war—it all made sense. The human Nephilim had become an unstoppable force, drawing power from every realm—a creature of immense strength and unparalleled evil. If that were the case, then... Madison struggled to fathom the depths of the impending danger.

As the dinner drew to a close, Madison and Nathan retreated to their room, their thoughts consumed by the secrets that now burdened them.

"The thing we discovered tonight, let's not discuss it outside of magic. I'll tell Corey within one of his magic circles." Nathan cuddled next to her.

As they settled into their cozy bed, they held each other, finding solace in their shared commitment to face whatever lay beyond the veil of uncertainty.

Nathan was right, but Madison found a true inspiration in her Aunt Becky—the person who exemplified the strength and compassion needed to navigate their challenges. Aunt Becky had rescued their family, run the household, taken care of Madison's parents while working towards their recovery, and gathered invaluable information about the realms to save Earth. That was the person Madison aspired to become.

Chapter 12—Rebecca

Nicole and I wrapped ourselves in the plush embrace of our thick bathrobes, seeking refuge from the chill as the fireplace crackled and emanated a comforting heat. The grand hall glowed; its majestic staircase adorned with the flickering glow. Gentle murmurs of servants and the enticing scent of breakfast created a serene ambiance that enveloped the room for informal breakfast.

By the fireside, the Addkinson foxhounds nestled cozily, basking in the toasty embrace of the flames. The hall exuded elegance, a testament to the diligent efforts of the army of servants. As we strolled towards the food, we ventured through a corridor adorned with columns of Grecian marble, intricately embellished with golden patterns. Carved statues and illuminated paintings adorned the walls, capturing the eye with their artistic allure.

At the far end of the hall, towering close to the vaulted ceiling, stood a magnificent twenty-foot Christmas tree, resplendent with shimmering baubles and twinkling lights. It beckoned us to gather around its towering presence as we prepared to savor the morning feast.

"Pig out at breakfast," I said. "This is the meal where you can relax and indulge without fear of judgment."

A familiar voice caused us to turn. It was none other than grandmother, whose presence graced the room. "Thank heavens for the informal breakfasts," she said. "It's my favorite part of the holiday festivities."

The double doors leading to the courtyard bathed the hall in a luminous green light. The room fell silent as the attention of both family members and servants turned as the radiant illumination filled the hall. And then, in a magnificent display, Corey emerged through the doors, his commanding presence filling the room.

Corey waved to them and strode in with a majestic Great Dane, its massive frame painted in hues of beige with delicate black stripes adorning its noble figure. The duo moved with an undeniable sense of purpose and confidence, captivating all in their wake.

Corey sported his dressed-up look, an ensemble of jeans and an untucked forest green button-down shirt, accompanied by his boat shoes. His hair flowed past his shoulders, catching the gentle breeze that blew through the open doors. His large smile captured attention and an undeniable charm radiated from him, drawing eyes towards him like moths to a flame.

Corey grabbed the doors to shut them, but a wave from the servants urged him to let them handle such matters. Nicole rushed towards Corey. He reciprocated her ardor, setting down his presents and sweeping her up into his arms, their passion flowing through every embrace and every kiss.

"They are a passionate couple," I said.

"We better join the spectacle," grandmother said. "Otherwise, we might have to wait in line for that handsome man."

We hastened to Corey's side, each of us greeting him in our own way. I extended the back of my hand to Valkyrie, and she nestled herself beside me. What a friendly and endearing creature she was.

As Corey set Nicole down, she, too, turned her attention towards Valkyrie, showering her with affectionate gestures and heartfelt words. And like a loyal guardian, Valkyrie made her way to the fireside.

The Addkinson foxhounds stood and barked.

Corey whistled, the sound echoing through the grand hall and commanding everyone's attention. "No. Everyone gets along while we are here. No disagreements among the animals," he asserted.

The foxhounds grew quiet and settled by the fire, and Valkyrie lay down beside them.

"Did Corey just order my foxhounds as if it were nothing?" grandmother asked.

"Corey doesn't recognize pets or ownership," I answered with a grimace. Corey assumed any place with animals was under his domain. "At least he is just ordering animals." Her grandmother did not look mad she looked hopeful.

"Come, Corey, you're allowed to indulge in breakfast," Nicole said.

"Well, it would honor me to witness Ms. Addkinson's choice of breakfast fare before I dare take such liberties." Corey's charming smile never wavered.

"Ah, a grand entrance and a charming demeanor. How delightful. I'm curious to see what a man like Young Corey can devour." The ordering of the foxhounds already past.

"I am hungry," Corey said with a grin.

The servants had arranged a fifty-foot-long table, adorned with an array of self-service breakfast items, all presented with elegance, using a casual set of china and silver settings. The tantalizing aromas wafted through the air.

Without hesitation, Corey and Nicole each grabbed two plates, their hunger urging them to seize the delectable offerings before them. Corey, in particular, displayed an insatiable appetite as he sat beside Nicole, relishing three of the four plates. And then, with nonchalant confidence, he sauntered back for seconds, filling his plate to the brim.

"Indeed, Young Corey can eat," grandmother said, her eyes twinkling with amusement.

The hall reverberated with the playful laughter of children, their youthful energy contagious as parents tried to get them to finish eating. Excitement permeated the air as they tore through their presents, their infectious joy creating a symphony of delight.

Corey looked around and asked, "Where is your artist friend?"

Grandmother chuckled. "Oh, my Corey. He told everyone how you were the only person to wake him up at first sunlight."

Rebecca remembered during a restroom call in the middle of the night, she had seen a light in the courtyard and the painter was on his phone.

A little girl with innocent eyes filled with curiosity approached Corey, her gaze filled with wonder. "Are you the killer who lives in an enchanted tree?" she asked.

Corey's laughter rang out. "Who told you about me?"

I couldn't help but stifle a giggle, pressing my hand against my lips, as the girl's mother scooped her up with a mix of surprise and apologies. Corey's striking presence and his aura of strength made him stand out.

"Speaking of my reputation," Corey said. "Khalil has returned from the army. He joined a few months after high school, completed a four-year stint in the military, and arrived home yesterday. I introduced him to Clive, and we've kept our promise to Clive by finding someone reliable who understands weapons. Khalil will start working for Clive after the holidays."

Curious, I asked, "How is that part of your reputation? I haven't heard of Khalil before."

"You probably heard him called by his nickname Dawg. They still talk about the fight between Corey and Dawg in high school," Nicole exclaimed with excitement. "Wesley and I were more popular because... I won't spoil the story," she added, bouncing up and down, capturing the attention of the entire room.

Corey had alluded to that fight but said it wasn't that big of a deal.

"That's not a story we share during Christmas," Corey said. "Just know that it has a happy ending, and Khalil is a friend."

A young boy exclaimed, "If it has a happy ending, it's a Christmas story!"

"Exactly," agreed grandmother. "Now, let's hear the story that isn't a Christmas story, but is."

"Yes Corey, it seems you downplayed the story when you mentioned it before," I taunted.

Corey relented and shared the following tale.

My friends Miles and Trish had a breakup, but it wasn't like their usual breakups; it was significant. Trish was acting strangely, and she was close to a bad decision. One she would regret for a long time. Things came to a head in the hallway leading to the gymnasium.

I stood in front of her, telling everyone to leave her alone until she regained her composure. Well, one guy thought I would back down. I was fighting him when Dawg blindsided me.

Me beating his friend enraged him, and I was furious that he broke the rule of not interfering in a fight. We clashed like two eighteen-year-olds brimming with testosterone, adrenaline, and rage.

Nobody could separate us, and two people who tried ended up in the hospital. Finally, they had to cancel football practice to break us apart. Coach Kennedy ordered four players on each of us, and then ten players each, to keep us separated.

We both received a standard three-day suspension, but we had to meet with Principal Matice before being allowed back. Three police officers escorted me, just as they did with Dawg.

"Holy crap," I exclaimed. I knew Corey must have had a history of fighting, but six police officers for two high school kids?

"Corey was already big from his warehouse job," Nicole said. "It's the same Principal Matice that's Wesley's father."

Yeah, well, both of us were at risk of not graduating, mainly because of English class. Haley, bless her heart, was doing everything she could to ensure Rachel and I graduated, but Ms. Bate's composition class required me to write essays in class. I had a fifty-nine average.

Our punishment required us to write a long paper together after school. Khalil, Latisha, Haley, and I worked together three evenings a week. Latisha was Khalil's girlfriend. We ended up becoming friends, graduating high school, and staying in touch while the army stationed him overseas. He's back, and we're still friends.

"Ms. Addkinson," Corey paused the story. "Here's something you can learn about me. The lesson I learned is that sometimes your enemy can become your friend. I live my life by that principle."

"This is how you trusted the gargoyle, Strumath," said grandmother. Her eyes widened like a light went off.

Corey agreed. "Despite spending my whole adult life fighting gargoyles, I trusted Strumath from the beginning. He sought peace, and I agreed during our first meeting. This was a life-changing lesson for me I've kept. I'll become friends with anyone."

This was significant news just a few weeks ago. Corey had found an alliance within a faction of his greatest enemy, forging a path towards peace. I always wondered how Corey, the kind-hearted yet fierce fighter, negotiated with his adversaries while still combating them.

"I dare say that is an apt story," grandmother said. "A mistake made in youth, a compassionate adult offering support, a life lesson that benefits everyone, and six years later, two young adults remain great friends."

As the children finished unwrapping their gifts, anticipation hung in the air, akin to a delicate veil ready to be lifted.

With a mischievous sparkle in his eyes, Corey stepped forward, bypassing Nicole, and presented me with a wrapped gift. A surge of anticipation coursed through me as I untied the ribbon and unveiled the contents beneath the paper.

In my hands, I discovered a masterpiece of craftsmanship—a breathtaking handcrafted leather belt. Its supple texture beckoned me, and as I secured it around my waist, the wide custom cinch belt embraced me. Intricate engravings of the one tree adorned the belt's ends, sending a tingling sensation through my fingertips.

Gasps of admiration resounded throughout the room. Corey leaned in. "It's enchanted," he confessed. "Just two days ago, after all they made the custom items, I infused them with enchantments."

Intrigued, I turned to Corey, my eyes wide with wonder. "But how did you choose this style?" I asked. The belt was a handcrafted work of art, its quality rivaling that of a high-end accessory worth a small fortune.

Corey's voice remained steady as he answered. "I once saw your grandmother wearing a similar style, and I knew that if anyone deserved such elegance, it was you. So, I borrowed a touch of her taste and wove it into this gift."

Grandmother's voice filled with warmth. "Oh, young man, you have an impeccable sense of style," she exclaimed, her eyes twinkling with admiration.

I embraced Corey, expressing my heartfelt thanks. "Thank you."

Grandmother's gaze shifted toward Corey, a playful smile gracing her lips. "Truly a beautiful belt, young Corey. Your taste is remarkable," she praised.

With a mischievous glimmer in his eyes, Corey moved on to the next gift, his gaze speaking volumes of affection and mischief. Turning his attention to Nicole, his voice infused with sincerity, he said, "I knew you'd probably get practical baby gifts, like cribs and stuff. But I remembered what happened with Trish and Miles, and I didn't want us to forget why we are a great couple. So, I picked something to remind us that we're a passionate couple before everything else."

Intrigued, Nicole accepted the two small boxes, and the wrapped clothing box from Corey's outstretched hands. Her nimble fingers untied the ribbons, revealing the contents of each box, each harboring its own secret.

With a delighted gasp, Nicole unveiled the small boxes, revealing two anklets. "One for everyday wear and one for our camping adventures," she exclaimed, her eyes shining with nostalgia. Memories of dating Corey and his frequent gifts of ankle bracelets flooded my mind. Perhaps I should start wearing them again.

Nicole wasted no time putting the golden anklet on.

Corey's mischievous grin widened. "You may want to save the bigger box for later. It's not appropriate for this gathering."

Eager to unveil the mystery, Nicole wasted no time. Her fingers trembled with anticipation as she opened the larger box, revealing a delicate powder-blue strapless baby doll negligee. Its sheer fabric whispered promises of romance and intimacy.

Grandmother, with a mischievous gleam in her eye, clapped her hands in delight. "Let's see what young Corey deems 'inappropriate,'" she encouraged, her words sending ripples of laughter through the room. Even the servants observing from the sidelines seemed to take mental notes of this scandalous display.

Nicole, her cheeks flushed with a mix of embarrassment and excitement, held up the sheer, see-through baby doll negligee. Its daring design left little to the imagination, and the room buzzed with whispers of admiration and awe. Nicole couldn't help but blush as she folded it. "Corey," she stammered, her voice a breathless murmur, "where on earth did you find something like this?"

Corey described how while he was working with the members of The Tribe who sold hand crafted goods for a living, Meat, a warrior Corey knew, had mentioned where he could get the style of dress he was looking for, to duplicate with leather for Rachel. It was at this 'establishment' that Corey also found the negligee.

This was excellent news for the relationship between Nicole and Corey. He gave me a practical gift that he could give to any woman. He gave Nicole things to spark their intimacy. Nicole's eyes saw she picked up on it as well. That was the genuine part of his gift. He told Nicole with his actions that she was the lover in his life.

Meanwhile, Corey's voice resonated once again, this time loud enough for all to hear. "I also sent friends a framed picture of our engagement. I believe Nathan sent it to other territories as well."

Nicole, her eyes brimming with excitement, held up Corey's phone. "Look at this!" she exclaimed. Displayed on the screen was a photograph of Corey, down on one knee, presenting the engagement ring to Nicole, whose hands covered her mouth in utter astonishment. It was a snapshot that captured the essence of that magical moment.

Overwhelmed with emotion, Nicole leaped into Corey's waiting lap, her lips seeking his in a passionate embrace.

Meanwhile, the parents, their hearts filled with joy, allowed the children to cause a small ruckus.

"Well, Corey, Rebecca and I made our gifts work together," said Nicole. They each handed Corey a box. "Your idea for Rachel inspired us."

Corey pulled out a wool kilt and a leather vest. With a touch of playfulness, he removed his shirt and donned the vest, followed by donning the kilt. "How do I look?"

"Cool tattoos," said two boys.

"He has two bullet scars," said the girl who asked him if he was a killer who lived in a tree. "He must even more than the stories say he is."

Corey protested his demeanor, but even with my agreement the children didn't buy it, faced with his battle proven torso exposed.

Nicole adjusted the kilt, ensuring that everything fit. "There. No more undressed Corey in fights, and you can expose all four points to Earth Power."

"Are you the most wounded person?" asked one boy.

"No," said Corey, pointing at me. "Rebecca had a wound from here to here." He traced his finger along his side.

"How could you see that?" asked a girl. "It goes past her privates."

"She saved my life on the battlefield, and I'm the one who bound her wounds and carried her to the doctor."

The kids all turned to me, and I gave a slight nod. This was not an appropriate topic for a Christmas gathering.

The children fired questions at Corey, their curiosity uncontainable. "What's your favorite weapon?" "How hard can you punch?" "Is it cold in the tree?"

Corey laughed at the questions and pointed to each child, answering their queries one by one. "Tonfa. The other day, I punched a bad guy so hard he lifted a foot off the ground. I have a bunch of rocks around my tree, and I light a fire."

I couldn't believe Corey answered the questions truthfully—except for the living in a tree part. The parents gathered their kids, and soon we wrapped up the festivities. Corey left to visit with Rachel and Wesley at Wesley's parents' house, while I prepared myself for a lunch date with Lance.

Chapter 13—Rebecca

I sat on the edge of my bed, my attention on the trio of dresses laid out before me. The first one, a deep maroon ensemble, had exuded elegance during last night's videoconference. However, I dismissed it, knowing I couldn't wear the same outfit on two dates in a row. My gaze then wandered to the blue floral dress with its plunging neckline.

"Nicole, is this neckline too much?" I called out to the room next to mine, hoping for her reassuring answer.

"Ah! Don't come in!" came her startled response. I brushed off the uncertainty and put on the dress.

While waiting for Nicole, I busied myself with a delicate touch-up of my makeup and hair, seated at the makeup station adorned with an oval mirror. Moments later, her voice echoed through the door, breaking the silence.

"Are you ready?" she asked.

"Come on in. What happened earlier?" I asked.

Nicole emerged, draped in a tulip-sleeved, blush pink V-neck dress, a shade lighter than her own radiant skin." A pair of flesh-colored kitten heels graced her feet and showed off her delicate new anklet. "I was planning to send Corey a selfie wearing that blue thing, and it embarrassed me.

Nicole adjusted my V-neckline, her touch conveying reassurance. "You look stunning. I'll have a hard time feeling comfortable in that blue thing. It barely holds together and creates an illusion of coverage."

I wore my belt from Corey. "Oh. You'll get to meet Baron today and grandmother arranged a shopping trip for the three of us tomorrow. He was my third video date, and he is a hoot."

"Should Lance worry?" teased Nicole.

"If Corey meets Baron, maybe you should worry." I teased back.

A siren wailed throughout the estate, shattering the calm. With urgency, I slipped into my heels, joined by Nicole as we made our way to the grand staircase. A man dashed past us, ascending the steps at a frantic pace. We stepped aside, granting him passage as he gasped for breath, his voice projecting a message of assurance.

"Hi. There's no need to panic. We've raised the alert to orange status because of an unauthorized entry into the Chesapeake Bay Territory," he conveyed, each word punctuated by a labored breath. His reassurance did not instill a sense of calm when he sprinted about.

I thanked him, but his silence regarding the incursion spoke volumes. This warning could only be a Realized invasion—the kind Nathan predicted would follow us here.

"I'm putting Corey on alert." Nicole said.

"It's happening," I said, my fear looming closer.

"What's happening?" Nicole asked, dialing Corey's number.

"Corey, there may be trouble here. We might need Hero Corey," she said into the phone before hanging up.

She turned back to our conversation. "He's doing presents with Rachel and Wesley, but he's getting ready. What do you think is going to happen?"

"They'll delay for too long, and Corey will emerge, armed with death. His hair will dance in the wind, and he'll become our hero." It was this very dependence that had deterred me from embracing the idea of dating.

"At least you've saved his life multiple times, not just in the battles," Nicole said.

"It's not that," I said. "It's hard to explain. How can you date someone when you know the words 'don't worry, my ex will save us' might escape your lips?"

Her face mirrored confusion as she tried to process my dilemma. "I hadn't considered that. But perhaps this will be nothing. I hope so because the last thing I want to witness is Hero Corey in action again. How much more can he endure?"

As we descended the staircase, our hands intertwined for support, our surroundings transformed into a bustling corridor. A man in uniform approached us, and reminded us they did not list us Chesapeake Bay Territory defense. The Southeast Territory could only defend if Chesapeake Bay could not fend off the attack.

He marched away, having used a peculiar method to communicate the rule. But the rule was correct. My relationship would cause political harm if I were to call the defense team incompetent—even if through my actions.

"What was that about?" asked Nicole.

"My grandmother hired the defense team. They follow the standard Realized rule that unless there is a pre-approved exception, a Realized cannot practice magic in another territory." I wondered why the person reminded me just now, though.

"Given how Corey put two people to death from here for doing that in the Southeast, is it worse?"

"Not really, because of our circumstances. Corey and I are pre-approved to protect you since we know the Delta Vampires still list you as a target. But if I join in, my involvement is political by my insinuation that I didn't trust the people my grandmother put in charge. It's worse since I'll lead the territory one day."

"If they fail, please jump in and worry about politics later."

I chuckled. "Don't worry. If Corey needs help, I'll be in the fight before they get to you."

We saw the grand ballroom had a bar setup for the dinner to help people socialize before the meal started.

"A drink would be nice, but as a Scion, I'm immune to alcohol." At the bar, I ordered water for Nicole and a drink, so we'd fit in. "I'd like a Barolo, served in a burgundy glass."

"Certainly, ma'am," the bartender said.

Nicole looked perplexed by my specific request and questioned my choice.

"It's just a wine from my grandmother's favorite region in Italy," I said. "I've always preferred the wider glasses."

The bartender reached for a burgundy glass, uncorking a fresh bottle of Barolo. He offered me the cork to sniff, pouring a small amount into the glass. I swirled the wine to simulate, testing its viscosity and aroma before taking a sip. "This is perfect." I savored the rich flavor.

Chuckling, Baron leaned in toward the bartender. "You see that enchanting woman? She's the fantasy of every eligible bachelor and an impeccable sommelier." A playful wink accompanied his words, as if sharing a secret known only to the two of us.

Baron greeted us with a splash of flamboyance in his pink cummerbund and navy-blue suit. The open collar revealed a glistening gold chain adorned with a dazzling diamond pendant. His charm was undeniable as he commanded the attention of the bartender, who handed him a glass of wine.

Nicole's laughter tinkled like wind chimes in the background, intermingling with the symphony of the bustling waitstaff. Baron extended his hand, grabbing the zucchini fritters from the waiter and offering one to me and one to Nicole. "To prepare yourself for a four-course meal," he urged. "One must savor every course."

"Thank you." Nicole's laughter infused with delight as she accepted the offered fritter.

"I'm supposed to leave you alone for Lance. He's been regaling us with his chilling tales of his time in the army. Gives me goosebumps, I tell you." With a confident saunter, Baron departed, acknowledging the familiar faces that gravitated towards him.

"I hope it's a false alarm," Nicole said. "I can't wait to shop with him tomorrow."

Just as her words dissipated into the air, Lance materialized before us, a vision of traditional elegance. His classic blue suit, crisp white shirt, and gold-trimmed blue tie exuded a timeless charm. "My mother made me dress conservatively."

"A shame," I lamented, a playful grin tugging at my lips. It was important to project my best self and not dampen the mood. Lance seemed like a genuinely nice person.

Introductions followed, with Nicole playing the role of intermediary. "Lance Tilson, ex-army and a PhD student in philosophy," she said. "I'm thrilled to hear your stories."

Meanwhile, my gaze locked with Lance's as I handed him my glass. "Can I refill your drinks? Ice water and a Barolo?" he asked. A momentary pause clouded his features. "The Scion is immune to alcohol."

Lance's voice held a hint of apology as he explained his unusual affliction. "My Realized power compels me to blurt out facts whenever I'm around religious or historically significant items or people. I have no control over it."

Before I could stop myself, a giggle escaped my lips. "We didn't even notice because you're nothing like Rachel."

Nicole stifled a laugh and added. "Rachel never met a comment she didn't blurt out."

Lance's smile broadened, and he turned to the bartender. "Hello, another round of these and a Schneider Weisse in a stemmed Teku glass, please."

As the drinks arrived, Lance shared about his passion for fine beers, just like Corey.

A man, acting as today's majordomo, ushered us to our seats. Lance guided our path, ensuring Nicole settled on my left.

As we settled into our seats, waiters presented plates of stuffed mushrooms, tantalizing our palates with their appetizing aroma. My attention shifted as Nicole lifted her hand after the prayer and I took her hand.

Rising from her seat, my grandmother's commanding presence enveloped the room. "Thank you all for joining us on this joyous Christmas feast. Let us relish this celebration."

With a gentle squeeze, I released Nicole's hand. "Dig in," I whispered.

"Thank you."

The mushroom yielded to the knife, and I seized the opportunity to engage Lance in conversation. "Lance, did your love for German beers blossom during your army days?"

A flicker of nostalgia sparked in his eyes. "Indeed, it did. My first taste of German beer came during my preparations for deployment in Germany. I stumbled upon a beer tasting event."

A sudden alarm pierced the air, causing me to grasp Nicole's leg, oblivious to the disruption. Ignoring the commotion, I focused on the conversation at hand, diverting attention from the encroaching chaos. "The Romano in these mushrooms stands out."

A man donning a military uniform, his insignia marking him as a colonel, leaned in, whispering urgent words to my grandmother.

Fifty diners seated became quiet with only the whispers of a handful of well-behaved children blending with clinking silverware. Grandmother's voice cut through the mounting tension. "There's no cause for alarm. Some intruders approach, but our security is well-equipped to handle the situation."

In an orchestrated display of seamless precision, the waitstaff presented the main course—a medley of venison medallions encrusted with spiced crumbs. Gunshots echoed in the distance, and the atmosphere grew fraught with apprehension. The time for enjoyment waned as the looming threat seeped into our midst.

Nicole leaned to me needing a diversion. "Now that you and Corey told me your secret, is the Delta Territory targetting me because I am pregnant with the next druid or because of the end of the world thing?"

"Both," I said.

The large double glass doors swung open, allowing a rush of cool Christmas air to spill in from the courtyard. Figures, cloaked in darkness, fell bleeding through the entrance. But it was not just mortal men who arrived; the preternatural figures of vampires, graceful and deadly, soared above, their lithe forms casting eerie shadows against the darkened sky. Vampires, the ones who intended to kidnap Nicole!

The dinner guests erupted into panicked screams, their voices mingling with the chaos unfolding before them

Nicole rose from her seat, her eyes closed as she focused on her empath power. "Corey, now!" she exclaimed.

She didn't need to say it out loud since it was using the powers of her mind, but I think people forgave her.

Thoughts of the previous warning gnawed at me. I couldn't help the defense without calling my home's defenders incompetent. What could I do? The children.

In an abrupt motion, I reached out and grasped a terrified young girl, my grip firm yet reassuring. "What are you supposed to do?" I needed to get the little girl to think of her drills.

The girl paused, her eyes wide with fear, searching for an answer. "Hide... under the table," she stammered, her voice a whisper.

I called out, filled with urgency and strength. "All children, take shelter beneath the tables, just as they have taught you!" I commanded, my words resonating through the hall. "Those with medical skills line up against the wall near the doors. The rest of you remain here and be prepared to assist the children. Remain calm. Soon, you will witness a signal, and safety will be mere minutes away." In my head, I knew what the signal was. Corey's green magic.

"Will it be him? The enchanted killer?" asked the girl from this morning.

Before I could answer, it happened. They bathed the besieged courtyard in a green Fey glow, a radiant signal that shifted the very tone of the battle. Corey arrived defending Nicole. I made my way toward the double glass doors. Nicole could call for defense with a minor insult. If I joined, the repercussions to grandmother would be severe. However, I could be ready, just in case.

"Take cover!" Nicole shouted, her voice carrying over the chaos that engulfed the courtyard. Her eyes darted around, assessing the situation with a keen awareness.

"Baron, prepare a triage area! I will bring in the wounded!" Christopher, the painter, announced as Lance and he assisted Nicole in guiding the injured towards safety.

Next to her, the guard from the front gate, Samson, looked gravely wounded on a stretcher. "He won't make it," said Baron with a tear.

I cast *Healing Touch*. Saving a life shouldn't count as defense. The spell wasn't as strong outside of my *Angelic Form*, but Samson would live.

The sky above bore an unnatural darkness and gnawed at my senses. With determined strides, I stepped through the door and into the edge of the battle, the enchantment of my new belt casting an Earth powered hue upon me.

Corey, Valkyrie, and Rachel had become an unstoppable force, battling vampires with lethal grace. Corey, armed with his weapons, moved with elegant ferocity, while Valkyrie's jowls emanated a green luminescence from Corey's druidic bond. They were a formidable trio, leaving a trail of fallen vampires in their wake.

"Lance, do you see that sky?" I asked, my gaze fixed upon the ominous darkness that shrouded the heavens.

Lance lifted his eyes, his face reflecting fear and unease. "The darkened sky is the harbinger of a fallen angel," he shouted back, the tremor in his voice betraying his dread.

Feeling the urgency of the situation, I kicked off my heels and ran into the courtyard, driven by the need to protect. The local defense had failed!

"Druid, we witnessed you in Atlanta!" A woman, clad in black, her aura suffused with black smoke, descended upon the scene, filling the courtyard like it was under a black light. Her black and gray wings unfurled with a chilling grace, reminiscent of my own *Angelic Form*.

"Stand back, Corey!" I bellowed, my voice carrying a sense of urgency. Corey, Rachel, and Valkyrie lunged at the flying female, weapons poised for battle, but derisive laughter met them. The fallen angel unleashed a corrupted light, suffused with gray smoke that carried the scent of sulfur. It engulfed the valiant trio, throwing them backward.

I took my *Angelic Form* and floated twenty feet high with wings outstretched, sword and shield in hand. Golden light from the heavens filled the courtyard.

"***Fidei meae tegmine munitus es!***" I yelled, shielded the three with a *Celestial Sanctuary* spell surrounding them in protective spheres. Once safe, I released them from the spell. I flapped my wings and soared towards the fallen angel.

"Careful," Corey warned. "That cute goth girl packs a wallop."

I summoned a *Healing Deva*, its form radiating ethereal beauty. I commanded, "***Me servum regni caelestis adjunge!***" The words resonated with a powerful enchantment.

"Oh, how amusing that a mere mortal should attempt to embody a superior being," said the fallen angel, her angelic features twisted into a mask of disgust. She floated; her two-handed sword of smoky gray light pointed at my chest. "Since you've chosen the sword of Celestial Light instead of Creation Light, I shall match your choice." Her voice dripped with disdain.

My deva weaved its healing magic, golden light caressing wounded soldiers, dissipating their pain. I assumed the stance Corey said I could perform correctly, adopting a square stance. My sword found its rightful place in my grip, while my shield remained steadfast, poised to intercept any incoming assault.

The fallen angel paused. "Hmm, it seems you possess more training than I presumed," she said, betraying a hint of surprise. "Surrender the ancient evil and the girl the vampires desire, and I shall spare everyone else. We shall meet again on a different battlefield."

Corey's words echoed in my mind. "Appear strong, even in weakness." My response was resolute. "First, Nicole is going nowhere. And as for the ancient evil you seek, I would have already vanquished such a threat." A breeze rustled my angel wings, causing a momentary falter.

"Oopsie, seems your divine form is not as flawless as you pretend," taunted the fallen angel, seizing the opportunity to strike. She swung her sword with mighty force, knocking my shield from my grasp. I lunged forward with a riposte that she countered effortlessly, throwing me off balance.

Corey launched his assault from one side, while Valkyrie pounced from the other. Rachel's surujin became a blur of motion, ensnaring the fallen angel's vulnerable foot. The coordinated attack of the Fey-powered warriors secured the fallen angel allowing Corey's knife and Valkyrie's teeth to inflict deep wounds.

Baron's presence ignited. He released a sunbeam piercing through the darkness. The vampires, disoriented and scorched by his radiance, faltered and retreated.

Corey slid down the angel's form, his movements ripping a hole with that magic black blade similar to the wound I had experienced. The courtyard became awash in brilliant sunlight, and the vampires, weakened by Corey, Rachel, and Valkyrie's relentless onslaught, shrieked in agony as they succumbed to the burning rays.

"Insolent fools!" the fallen angel hissed, her anger palpable as she dissipated into a cloud of gray smoke, vanishing from sight.

I descended clumsily from the heights, my *Angelic Form* fading away. Disappointment weighed on my shoulders as I had failed my third straight battle. Gritting my teeth, I gathered my shattered confidence and focused on aiding in the post-battle cleanup.

"Wow, Rebecca! Three days of training, and you paused a sword master with just a single stance," exclaimed Corey.

A rush of warmth enveloped me as Rachel approached, wrapping her arms around me in a tight embrace. "I couldn't be prouder of you, Rebecca." Her voice brimmed with admiration. "You faced her like a seasoned warrior, as though you've been training for years."

Tears welled up in my eyes. "But I failed—again." There were no sugar-coated words that could mask my defeat.

"Failed?" Lance exclaimed. "You halted a master swordsman with centuries of battle-hardened experience. That was Onoskelis! However, her departure will rouse the attention of nearby Nephilim beasts."

"Baron!" Nicole exclaimed; her voice filled with awe. "Your use of sunlight was flawless!"

"I—I've done nothing like that before," the young man stammered, taken aback by his own abilities.

Corey slung his arm around Baron. "Welcome to the Realized. Your contribution saved lives." Corey then turned to Nicole and embraced her, a silent acknowledgment of their shared triumph. "Things get trickier now. This was a worst-case scenario in my and Nathan's planning. Please call him."

Meanwhile, the grand hall, once a grandeur-filled space, had transformed into a makeshift infirmary for the unprepared fighters. Christopher, Baron, and Lance stood out amongst the chaos, their triage and medical skills proving invaluable. They did not list them on the combat rosters for Chesapeake or New England, yet the three exhibited unrivaled effectiveness within our local Realized community.

Nicole spoke into her phone with urgency. "Nathan, Corey says it worked. They attacked up here, but there was a fallen angel accompanying them." She glanced at Corey, her eyes pleading for guidance. "Nathan reports a reading near Bottomless Ravine."

"Tell him we'll proceed with the two-team's strategy," he said. "And inform him we have another containment issue at my house, involving the Matice family."

Corey turned to Baron, a mischievous glint in his eyes. "Who are you? I can't call you *Ray of Sunshine*."

A giggle escaped Baron's lips, transforming his once solemn expression. "You most certainly can," he chuckled. "I am Baron."

Corey then directed his attention to our grandmother. "We need to borrow Baron, as he will fill out the second team. Rebecca will be the point of contact for the Nephilim beast team, and Nicole will handle communication with the vampire team."

With a tight embrace, Corey assured Nicole, "We cannot fight together, but I promise we have a strategy in place to keep you safe while we battle."

"Corey, we'll also need Lance," I spoke up, my voice filled with urgency. Although this day had taken a turn for the worse, Lance possessed religious knowledge that none of us had.

"The Torc of Awareness, created in the early twelfth century by Merlin and Morgan Le Fay." Lance pointed to Corey's neckwear.

Corey arched an eyebrow at me. "Are you certain?" He patted Valkyrie, reassuring the animal who stood by his side.

"He possesses knowledge we don't," I said.

Corey approached me, his voice lowered to a whisper. "Are you absolutely sure?" he asked, a flicker of concern in his eyes.

"Just because he was my date doesn't mean he lacks the skills we need. Get over yourself," I whispered with annoyance.

Corey's eyes widened with realization, a smirk forming on his face. He glanced at Lance before turning to our grandmother. "It seems we'll also require Lance's help."

Stepping back, Corey commanded attention, his voice resonating with authority. "Rachel, take Valkyrie and wait with Wesley and his family at my house until Nathan, Wesley, and Miles arrive. Nicole and Rebecca, pack your essentials. You two, Baron, Lance, and I, will depart immediately. Once we're on the road, the Chesapeake Territory should be free from any further attacks. Ms. Addkinson, if anyone targets the estate, reach out to Nicole, as I have a contingency plan ready to provide support." He clapped his hands and injected urgency into his tone. "Let's move, people!"

As Corey busied himself with the aftermath of battle, I followed grandmother to the estate's situation room, on the other side of the sprawling grounds. I marveled at the transformation in her demeanor. Gone was the jovial grandmother I knew, replaced by a figure of authority.

With Corey preoccupied, I took a moment to confide in our grandmother. "He's not diplomatic, but that's why we elected him as

Tactical Leader. He expects his orders to be followed without question."

A glimmer of pride danced in grandmother's eyes. "Oh dear, he's more than fine. Such assertiveness is what a wartime leader should embody. For the first time, I feel confident that we are in excellent hands."

Curiosity tugged at my thoughts. Why did Corey mention he would ride back with us? He could travel back instantly using trees.

"Battle Leader Norwood," our grandmother addressed Corey, her voice carrying a tone of formality.

Maintaining his battle-hardened expression, Corey strode towards our grandmother, his bare feet echoing on the marble floor with every sharp step. "Yes, of course, Ms. Addkinson."

"I have dispatched messages to summon my current military leaders. I request you keep Rebecca here for an hour to accommodate this schedule," our grandmother said.

Corey contemplated the request, weighing the options in his mind. "To gather the supplies, pack, and prepare for the journey, it will take at least thirty minutes. An hour is reasonable."

"Thank you, Battle Leader Norwood. I'll ensure the car is ready."

Observing the exchange between our grandmother and Corey, I marveled at the unexpected formality that permeated the air. They had forged a new level of partnership, a synergy I had yet to witness. When had Corey learned to navigate the military-like protocols of interacting with leaders?

I couldn't help but recall the lighthearted mockery I had directed at him during his encounter with Preacher Jon when he had acted in a similar manner.

I STOOD AT PARADE REST, my luncheon dress clinging to my form, as I positioned myself behind my grandmother. The room ex-

uded an air of authority, housing twelve individuals who commanded respect. Full bird Colonels, adorned in their dignified military
uniforms, sat with unwavering discipline, while the suited men displayed a sharpness that matched their attire. Grandmother, a towering figure at the podium, held everyone's attention as she unveiled
the report Nathan and Corey prepared for her.

Before she could even finish her sentence, a Colonel interrupted
with a dismissive tone. "That's not really a good—"

"Silence!" Grandmother's voice thundered, harsh and uncom-
promising.

Surrounded by military regalia, embarrassment crept over me in
my luncheon date dress, and I forced myself to swallow my feelings,
projecting an image of stoicism. The desire to transform into my
Scion form seemed appealing, as it would provide some respite from
this uncomfortable situation.

Grandmother's anger reverberated through the room. "Never in
my life have I been so embarrassed. I had to call upon another territory for defense. And what did they send? An army? A company?
No, just a platoon? Not even close. They sent two people. Two individuals and a dog. These were the same people my most trusted
military minds deemed unfit for battle, advising me against granting
them swift entry to our estate."

The Colonel who had dared to argue, persisted. "Ma'am, with all
due respect, those were supernatural beings."

"And that is precisely what we deal with," grandmother retorted.
"I suspected you were no longer up for your role when the Southeast
warned us ahead of time about the attempt on my life. Luckily, I am
Realized and used my power to escape from the attack without help
from our military!"

Grandmother could explain any used Realized power. She must
have seen someone and knew what power they used to break in to
give her escape an advantage.

Grandmother was still furious. "Colonel Hanscomb, I relieve you of your command. Vampires are the second most populous Realized beings on Earth, and yet you failed to neutralize a platoon of fifty. Baron killed the ones slain by someone other than fighters from outside our territory—the same man you labeled as unworthy. He is now chosen as one of two individuals accompanying the Southeast Battle Leader."

The men remained defiant, their expressions reflecting an astonishing level of incompetence. Disbelief flooded my senses as I witnessed this display of ineptitude within these walls.

Grandmother's anger continued to surge. "I would love to hear the solution your team had concocted for the fallen angel, had the Southeast team not arrived. Oh, wait. Not the entire Southeast team, just two members of it."

A tense silence enveloped the room as grandmother's gaze swept across the attendees. "Anyone? Shall I remind you that the Southeast team explicitly mentioned this in their warning report, yet you advised me to stand down? I expect a satisfactory answer."

One man, dressed in a suit, stood up with trepidation. "The Southeast team has proven their skills. Under our guidance, they could—"

"Oh, enough," grandmother interrupted, her words cutting through the air like a well-sharpened blade. "If Battle Leader Norwood were here, and he tore out your throat for uttering something so ludicrous, I would grant him that privilege."

She positioned herself in front of the defiant men. "In case your manicures preoccupied your time, let me enlighten you. My granddaughter stood face to face with a fallen angel. I witnessed her *Angelic Form* and bravery in battle. And where were any of you?"

Grandmother's fury was palpable, near spitting mad. "In battle, she proved she is the Scion. She isn't ready to take the lead of the

Territory yet, but I am promoting her to Tactical Leader and Battle Leader."

I maintained a blank expression, masking my internal turmoil. The position overwhelmed me. How on earth could I handle this?

Grandmother never hesitated; her voice unwavering. "Our new Tactical Leader now has her own office here, but I stationed her in the Southeast, at the very frontline of the Realized war." She paused, her gaze drilling into each individual. "Her orders are to continue studying Military Tactics of the Realized Training, alongside those who have been fighting for three years."

Grandmother returned to the podium, her presence commanding the attention of everyone present.

"Colonel," she addressed a particular individual, her voice ice-cold, "I expect your resignation on my desk before the day's end. As for the rest of you, prepare summary reports of your positions for Battle Leader Adams. She will have to handle the repercussions of a Nephilim beast." A hint of venom coated her final words. "Unless any of you believe your skills prepare you for that fight?"

They exchanged uncomfortable shifting and uneasy glances throughout the room.

"Our new Battle Leader has already reported that we should expect two, possibly three, incursions before the year's end. It is our duty to support her and evaluate our readiness by January 2nd. Battle Leader Adams, I grant you permission to accompany Battle Leader Norwood from the Southeast. Until your training is complete, you are to defer to his command."

"Yes, ma'am." I turned smartly and exited.

The door closed behind me. I wasn't ready for this, but I would not argue in public. All I knew was grandmother respected the way Corey handled the interrogation and the way he delivered orders.

I could help Corey, and I would watch him and learn from him.

Chapter 14—Madison and Nicole

Madison's eyes widened with amazement as she observed Nathan in action. The man she knew as her boyfriend, who had always seemed reserved and introverted, now stood at the helm of yet another meeting. It wasn't the first time he had taken charge this week, but each instance had a profound effect on how she felt about him.

Pausing for a moment to check her vibrating phone, Madison relayed the status to everyone present. "I just received word from Nicole. They're on their way, about to turn onto Holcomb Bridge."

Sarah, seated next to Wesley on Corey's patio, shifted her gaze from Madison to him and asked, "What about the pizza?" With Rachel cradled in Wesley's arms and Tiberius perched beside them, Sarah's expression hinted at playful frustration. "Wesley, wouldn't it have been a better power to know when pizza deliveries arrive, rather than knowing when everyone dies?"

The number of people gathered here was a testament to how many lives Corey, Rebecca, and the team had affected in their battle against evil. Madison knew half of the people present, but she intended to learn the rest.

Haley, seatedon the other side of Wesley and Rachel, sighed as her toddler, Corrinne, worn out from chasing faeries from the Spring Fey Court in the backyard, nestled against her side. Nearby, Haley's mother, Anne, engaged in a quiet conversation with Trish.

Mare and Melinda had sat next to Isabella, Ada, and Sarah. They did not act comfortable around the others, but that was to be expected. They got thrust into a new environment in the worst possible way.

"I'll get it," Isabella exclaimed at the sound of a knock on the door. Ada and Sarah joined her, the trio of teenagers on the brink of starvation. Perhaps not famished enough to indulge in a Poke Salad, but on the verge of becoming hangry.

Curiosity piqued, Jennifer, Wesley's mother asked Madison quietly. "How long have you known Nathan?"

"Six weeks. We're not as swift-moving as these other couples. We prefer taking our time to nurture our relationship," Madison didn't mention that she was going to prove herself invaluable in making this her home first. No sense in demonstrating baggage.

Jennifer's smile was tinged with a hint of reminiscence. "This is all so strange. Nathan was the president of the Matheletes for three years. The pinnacle of excitement in their lives was when they secured third place in a Southeastern math championship during his senior year. It's a wonder you all haven't given up with all that's going on."

Madison chuckled, her laughter filling the air. "I apologize," she said, her eyes meeting those of everyone on the patio. "Soon, you'll understand why no one gives up and why we all believe we'll triumph."

The three teenagers reappeared; their arms laden with eight large pizzas. People passed out plates of food. Rachel opened a big bag of dog food and placed a can of wet food on top. Isabella sat next to the giant dog as it ate. Madison couldn't help but wonder why a fourteen-year-old girl would be here without her parents.

"Corey wants a plate with two slices, loaded with the meatiest toppings," Isabella called out. It must be true that she communicated with animals like Corey.

Miles offered to fetch the plate for the "druid boy," taking on the task with a lighthearted demeanor.

Approaching Madison, Nathan arrived with a plate holding a slice of vegetarian pizza. As he handed it to her, their lips met in a gentle kiss. "How are you doing?" he asked.

"Just anxious," Madison admitted. "I'm waiting to hear the plan."

"We'll share as much of the plan as we can," Nathan said. Empaths remained a cause for concern, as did the persistent hacking issue. Nathan and Corey were privy to details unknown to others.

Isabella skipped over to Nathan and Madison. "Corey is going to call his team the B-team. Don't correct him. I don't know why, but he said it's important."

Valkyrie barked, coinciding with the sound of car doors slamming shut in the driveway. With an air of purpose, Corey strode through the door.

"Hello, everyone," Corey greeted, offering a friendly wave as he collected his plate from Miles. "Nicole and Rebecca will be back." His gaze drifted to the orange paint and construction tape on his lawn. "Construction has already begun?" Corey's voice trailed off.

"Relax, Corey. They're just getting things set up. Nothing starts until January," Nathan said.

Corey, known for his prowess in battling devils, Dark Fey, and gargoyles without hesitation, found himself entangled in a web of uncertainty and apprehension when preparing for a baby.

"Monster!" cried the toddler, her voice playful, as if using a nickname from a game.

"Corey," he corrected in a playful demeanor hinting at the shared game.

Rebecca and Nicole returned, their expressions tense as they remained standing. Lance, one newcomer, had excused himself to use the restroom.

"I apologize for the urgency, but we must act. There's a Nephilim beast on the loose, and Team Bravo is heading out to intercept it. I'll be leading that team, with Rebecca handling communications.

Nathan will lead Team Alpha with Nicole as their communications specialist."

"Corey, I appreciate your conciseness, but some of us here are unfamiliar with the prerequisites of your orders," said Principal Matice.

"Thank you," acknowledged Corey.

"Welcome to the Southeast Territory of the Realized, which now finds itself in the heart of a supernatural war zone. I've been on the front lines for several years, protecting civilians. In the past two months alone, we've thwarted a devil summoned by vampires, battled a dozen gargoyles, encountered a deer woman, a snake hunter, a different Nephilim beast, ex special forces led by the Curia, and over a hundred Dark Fey."

"For those of you who need clarification on any of the terms mentioned, please consult the communications member of your assigned team. I apologize for the time constraints, but eleven hours ago, a fallen angel named Onoskelis released a Nephilim beast. We drove her back, and defeated her cadre of vampires, but the repercussions are dire. We tracked the beast and it's trapped in Bottomless Ravine, but if it escapes, it will reach Asheville within a few hours. It could devastate the city. Fueled by human life force, it would move on, wreaking havoc."

Some light hearted commentary from the others filled the patio. It was common when faced with the unbelievable made real for light-hearted conversation to happen.

"Team Bravo, gather your supplies and be ready to depart in fifteen minutes. Alongside me, Rebecca, Valkyrie, Rachel, and Lance will form Team Bravo. Nathan, you'll need Baron with the vampires. He's our Ray of Sunshine."

"He insisted on that nickname," Nicole said.

Miles asked, "Did you defeat a fallen angel?"

"Rebecca faced her head-on, empowering us all to work together. She was the true superstar." Corey gave her a big smile.

"I was so proud of her," said Rachel.

Observing Nathan's hand placed on Rebecca's arm to quiet any potential protest, Madison wished Rebecca would take charge. Corey and Nathan needed Rebecca to become a leader.

"As Team Bravo sets off, we expect another attack from the Delta Vampires aimed at capturing Nicole. While Team Bravo cannot help Team Alpha fight. Nathan will lead Team Alpha. Just as they have kept us scant on details regarding their mission, we shall do the same for them. Our enemy employs a combination of modern spy technology and magic, including the use of empaths."

Soon, Team Bravo embarked, armed with most of the team's combat prowess, leaving Nathan to re-assume control of the meeting. Sensing Jennifer's curiosity, Madison leaned in. "That's why we believe we can triumph." Building confidence in the assembled group was a way to support Nathan.

NICOLE STOOD AT THE threshold, her gaze fixed on her fiancé as he departed, venturing into the heart of danger. A wave of unease washed over her, mingling with the undercurrent of determination that fueled her resolve. She had gained the ability to sense when someone cloaked their emotions with magic, a skill she had learned from Corey's demonstration when he removed his earring. Lance was adept at concealing his thoughts and feelings behind an impenetrable magical barrier.

She had grabbed Corey, who informed her how Valkyrie had sensed Lance's supernatural presence and how he had known about Lance from the start. That explained why Corey traveled with Rebecca instead of using trees to come home hours sooner.

Meanwhile, Nathan grappled with maintaining order on the patio. Nicole put her fingers in her mouth and created a whistle which pierced the air. "My life is the one in danger, and Nathan needs everyone's attention."

Nicole maneuvered herself to sit beside Haley and Anne, a flicker of understanding present within her as she recalled glimpses from Corey's mind—vivid images of squirrels being dispatched to Nathan, a precursor to this momentous meeting. While she couldn't grasp all the specific details, she comprehended they would sow seeds of information and orchestrating an ambush against the vampires. And she, herself, would play the role of the bait.

"Now that Corey and Valkyrie have departed, let us retreat indoors.

The warm living room, a welcome respite from the chill of the approaching night fit everyone. Nicole made a mental note to find a solution for the next winter. She couldn't bear to spend another winter huddled around a firepit. However, given the recent discussions surrounding patio changes, she dared not bring up the topic again.

"Please treat Wesley kindly," Nathan said. "He has visions of the death of those closest to him. He endures the agony of experiencing our deaths, often in the most gruesome ways. We use this knowledge to save lives. Miles and Trish, you will soon receive information regarding your upcoming New Year's Eve party. However, do not make any changes based on this knowledge. We possess the ability to manipulate the surrounding circumstances, an advantage civilians lack."

Wesley delved into a trance-like state, his mind entering a realm far beyond their immediate reality. Every individual in the room hung onto his every word as he began his revelation. "Let me start with Team Bravo. Corey's fate remains unchanged; he faces two deaths, while Rebecca has countless possibilities. As for Rachel, she either meets her demise in a cavern alongside a hawk-spider hybrid, or both she and Nicole fall victim to an invisible Dark Fey, transforming into an old-time gangster during... a peculiar scene at the party."

Nicole found herself awestruck by Wesley's ability to maintain composure. He had grown in the past three months.

"Now, let us shift our focus to ourselves, Nicole. No communication with Rebecca. Silence is our greatest asset," Nathan said.

Nicole's heart clenched with worry for her fiancé, thrust into the dangerous mission of protecting Rebecca from an ancient evil that had infiltrated their team. Yet, she scarcely had time to ponder over his well-being, for her own safety was precarious.

"Our plan appears grim," Wesley said. "The entire Team Alpha meets their end at two o'clock tomorrow."

"Damn," Nathan exclaimed, taken aback by the grim revelation.

Wesley, still immersed in his trance-like state, continued with his revelations. "Even if we run, two days from now, Nathan, you succumb to Dark Fey, killing Madison, Trish, and me. We all perish."

"But wait." Wesley gave a glimmer of hope. "I have a viable option. Nathan let Trish take charge of the Team Alpha. This team comprises Nicole, myself, Baron, Miles, Madison, and you."

"Trish?" Miles asked, directing his gaze towards her.

Nathan ignored Miles' inquiry. "Trish, would you be willing to lead the team for this ambush?"

"If it means saving lives, I am more than willing." Trish approached Wesley, a hint of confusion crossing her features.

"With Trish in charge, we can all survive until the New Year's Eve party," he said, still in his trance.

Sarah's comment broke through the tension. "I want to go to the party."

Nicole winced. Teenagers could ignore stress, but their comments were ill timed.

Wesley, still entranced, provided a chilling prediction. "An ornate gargoyle tears off Ada's head, while her blood cascades down the creature's throat. And Sarah, you meet your end at the hands of a Roman Legionnaire's gladius."

"Cool," said the two teenagers.

Luckily, the room ignored the comments.

Nathan rose from his seat, a glimmer of determination sparkling in his eyes. "That's perfect," he said. A brief pause followed before he continued, "If you are not part of the Team Alpha, it is imperative that you leave. This house is now a danger zone without Corey able to return to defend it."

The others made their way towards the exit while Trish stood up, assuming her new role. "Miles, remove those pictures from the wall and shift the chairs to the other side. Nicole, fetch me paper and tape. We'll create a makeshift whiteboard to work from. I need everyone's information, our gathered intelligence, and explanations of powers to plan a comprehensive plan."

"Dude, do you realize what you've signed us up for?" Miles asked in disbelief. "Trish will extract every ounce of information from us, examining all our options to select the best course of action. She will leave no stone unturned. I dated her for six years, and we've been married for two. We are about to be wrung dry of information."

Nicole, aware of the task ahead, hurried to retrieve the supplies Corey had used to mark up his wall for beer brewing. She marveled at how Wesley's choice of Trish, with her innate sense of control and planning, had saved lives.

Chapter 15—Rebecca and Nicole

The SUV's engine roared as I maneuvered it along the winding road, heading towards Asheville. The rhythmic hum of the tires on the pavement filled the air, accompanied by faint laughter and whispers emanating from the backseat. Lance sat beside me in the passenger seat, his gaze fixed on the passing scenery.

In the rearview mirror, I caught sight of Corey, Rachel, and Valkyrie huddled together, their bodies pressed close, yet an air of tension surrounded them. Corey pretended to be asleep, his eyelids flickering with curiosity as he observed Lance. I knew Corey well enough to sense that something was amiss.

"He's engaged to her sister, and yet they're so intimate?" Lance asked.

The topic was an easy one for me to broach. "They share a unique bond, born out of co-dependency," I said. "They crave physical touch and need it every few days. Nicole watched their unusual connection for eight years, so it no longer surprises her. They've never crossed the line into romance, and the mere thought of dating sends them spiraling into chaos."

Lance's eyes widened in disbelief. "Wow. I've seen soldiers in Afghanistan become close and seek comfort in each other's arms, but I always assumed it was behavior confined to war zones... Oh." His expression shifted. "But we're at war too."

"They've been at war since the Curia killed their parents in high school." The realization of us in a full-blown war had struck me two days prior, but now it sank in. We had an Outer Realm's war, a war with an unknown enemy, war with the Curia, and war with the Delta Territory. Believing it was all orchestrated by one enemy was too terrifying to consider.

Lance remained silent, his thoughts swirling in the newfound understanding. As the Battle Leader of the Chesapeake Bay Territory, my role had evolved into something unfamiliar, a responsibility I struggled to comprehend. I vowed to keep this secret until I uncovered the reason Corey rode with us. I know he had a tree where he could travel instantly and prepare the area for us. But since he was keeping it quiet, so would I. Plus, why did he call us Team Bravo? He, Rachel, and I made up most of the power in the Southeast.

With his head against the headrest, Lance stared at the ceiling of the SUV, lost in contemplation. Corey had stowed away my new hiking boots and socks in the back, showing the wilderness that lay ahead. The untouched packages containing my new clothes remained arranged among our supplies.

The hours stretched on, and the moon shone high in the night sky as I continued to navigate the road. "How much longer until we reach our destination?"

Corey leaned forward, handing me his phone. "I found an address for a tent camping site. I've secured a spot for us. Do you think you can get us there?"

"Lance, could you please input this address into the navigation?" I requested, passing the phone to him.

He complied, tapping the screen with his fingers. "Three hours and three minutes," he said before returning the device to Corey.

"We can make it, but it'll exhaust me," I said. "We'll need to rest once we arrive."

A gentle rain patted against the windshield, distorting the outside world. Corey's voice cut through the soft symphony of droplets. "Since it's raining, I'll set up the campsite while you take shelter in the SUV."

Corey reclined in his seat, his eyes fixed on the road ahead, vigilant and alert.

We pulled into the campsite; the gravel crunching beneath the tires echoing through the air. As the vehicle came to a stop, Corey wasted no time, leaping out before the engine's growl had even settled. His energy was palpable as he turned to us, his eyes glimmering in the dark early morning. "Wait here. I'll set up."

Corey gathered the gear, organizing four distinct areas within the campsite. My tent found its place on the left side. Corey arranged tents for himself, Rachel, and even one for Valkyrie, positioning them at the heart of the campsite. Last, he erected a tent on the opposite side, reserved for Lance.

Corey's voice pierced the silence. "Guys, I hate to be a stickler for security, but a fallen angel is tracking at least one of us," he informed us, his tone laced with caution. "Rebecca and Rachel, I suggest you make use of the women's facilities. It's the brown building at the end of the road. Once you're back, Lance and I will take our turn."

Rachel and I found ourselves out of earshot, missing the rest of their conversation. Entering the dilapidated bathroom, a pungent odor of urine gone sour assaulted our senses. Torn paper towels littered the grimy floor, painting a picture of neglect and disarray.

"Rachel, what's going on?" I asked.

"Hold on," Rachel retrieved a crumpled note from Corey. "Corey wants us to abide by a 'need-to-know only' protocol," she said, a grin spreading across her face. "Sometimes, I feel like 'need-to-know' rules govern my whole life."

I couldn't help but chuckle, appreciating the shared sentiment. Together, we read through the cryptic messaged.

"I'm about to say some things that might sound insane. Promise me you'll agree with everything, no matter how crazy it sounds."

"Anything else?" I mumbled through the minty freshness of brushed teeth, exhaustion tugging at my weary bones. All I could deduce was Corey felt the need to lie to Lance. I'd go along based on trusting Corey.

"Nope. For me, nothing changes," Rachel said then grinned.

Settling into the sanctuary of my tent, my body cocooned in the warmth of a dry sleeping bag atop a thin pad, I succumbed to the embrace of sleep. Meanwhile, Corey and Lance ventured toward the men's facilities, their footsteps fading into the night. The world outside faded away as fatigue took hold, enveloping me in a dreamscape before my eyes could glimpse another fragment of reality.

THE MORNING SUN CAST a warm glow over the campsite as I emerged from my tent. A sense of adventure filled the air, accompanied by the tantalizing aroma of a delicious meal cooking over the fire. Corey, Rachel, and Valkyrie were already up and about, preparing for the day ahead. Lance's tent had movement as well.

"Restrooms?" I asked, rubbing the sleep from my eyes.

Rachel flashed a mischievous grin, holding up a toiletry kit and a towel. "Let's go freshen up and change before lunch."

Still groggy, I asked about the beast, "How close is it?"

Corey reassured me, "the canyon still traps the beast. We can intercept it if it escapes, but I don't think it can escape before nightfall. Though its progress is surprising, considering it relies on vibrations and sound."

Feeling relieved, I followed Rachel to the shower area. The light rain from the evening was gone and the ground dried quickly in the frozen air. The shower building was in much better shape. The staff had cleaned it while we slept. Rachel set up an array of cleaning supplies. I unwrapped the items she laid out, grateful for this small luxury on our journey.

I reminded myself that Corey was going to say lies, and I was to agree with him. As the warm water cascaded over me, I couldn't help but reflect on the odd shirt Corey had given me to wear. "Who is the Rossington Collin's band?"

Rachel chuckled, spitting out some water. "The guitarists from Lynyrd Skynyrd had a band with a female singer for a while. It's the girliest shirt Corey could find."

Despite the shirt's awkwardness, I couldn't help but laugh. "Well, at least it's not as bad as Nicole's pink Taylor Swift t-shirt. Do you think composers like Mahler had custom shirts made for them?"

Rachel chuckled. "I'm not that well-versed in modern music. My tastes are more old-school, thanks to Old Donnie."

The comment made me chuckle. "We should explore some new bands once we get back. At least Corey tried."

Back at camp, Corey greeted us with plates of meat, rice, and beans. He and Lance excused themselves to the restroom while we ate.

When everyone reconvened, I was astonished to find that Rachel and I had devoured our entire meal. Corey then handed each of us a bag of his homemade trail mix, with an extra addition of jerky. Lance and I wore waist packs, while Corey and Rachel carried full backpacks. I found it amusing that Rachel filled her pack with dog food for Valkyrie.

"Is this all the gear we're taking for weapons?" Lance asked.

Corey smirked. "The A-team always gets first pick of the gear. That's why we're team Bravo."

I couldn't help but smile at Corey's response. He came out and said we were the B-team. It was no longer implied. This was the first lie. If we had team designations, we were clearly the A-team.

He packed up the gear, placing a pass on the SUV's dashboard. With a confident stride, he led us onto the mountain path.

As we climbed, Rachel and Valkyrie brought up the rear. Corey and I walked together, enjoying the breathtaking views.

Corey broke the silence when Rachel picked up Valkyrie and carried her over some rocks. "Rachel, how come you're Valkyrie's favorite?"

Rachel beamed with affection at the Great Dane. "Oh, Corey, I love Valkyrie!" she exclaimed, patting the dog's back. "I'm so happy you rescued her from those terrible people who trained her to fight."

He kept hiking at a brisk pace and answered, "It wasn't a rescue. I told her about our adventures, and she wanted to use her skills to help people. Plus, the idea of being part of a loving family intrigued her. I formed bonds with her, both beast and Fey."

The mention of the bond excited Rachel. "Can we bring her to the Fey Spring Court? She would love running through the Fertile Fields!"

Corey's eyes lit up. "I think she'll enjoy the Cloven Hills even more!"

Lance asked, "Why did you both decide to join the Fey Spring Court?"

Corey pondered for a moment before replying, "We had a lengthy discussion about it. Considering Rachel and I were so close and embodied the ideals of the court, it made perfect sense. But Preacher Jon emphasized the importance of strengthening us to level the playing field with the other team."

That was a significant fabrication, and I suspected Corey had doubts about Lance. It explained everything. He didn't want Lance to come, and Corey hadn't stopped watching Lance since then. Plus, now all these lies. Nothing else made sense. Suppressing my concerns; I played along. "I suppose, with some improvement in the coming years, we might even give the Hunter team a run for their money." My lie made sense since Miles and Madison were both hunters and the only combatants we didn't bring.

Corey seemed impressed by my remark. "I hope so. The Fey Spring Court has been incredible. Rachel and I have been studying the next ritual together. With my kilt and Rachel's dress, we make quite the pair," he said.

Corey extended a helping hand as we tackled a challenging part of the climb.

The climb continued, testing our stamina. Even Rachel, usually energetic, was panting.

Lance panted out a sentence. "How do you have such stamina, despite your size?"

Rachel answered, out of breath. "He's barefoot and uses Earth Power."

With a reassuring smile, Corey gave us the standard line given to tired compatriots. "There's a plateau just up ahead. We'll take a long break there and then descend to the ledge, surprising the creature in the darkness."

Lance then asked between pants, "Why did they send such a small group to take down the Nephilim?"

"Let's keep it clear," said Rachel. "I get confused a lot. This is a Nephilim beast. I hope there are no more Nephilim giants or a human Nephilim, but we should be careful with the words."

"Sorry, you're right," said Lance.

Corey spun his web of intrigue. "We weren't strong enough to join the team against the three Nephilim beasts that escaped from the Raccoon Caves in Chattanooga. However, this time, there's only one. They trust us with one."

Rachel spoke up. "We aren't going to the bottom of Bottomless Ravine, are we?"

"No." Corey shuddered and fear crossed his face. He picked up his lies again, but either he had learned to act or the thought of the ravine terrified him. "They wouldn't allow us to go down there, although I could join a more seasoned group."

Corey was the only one who could lead a group, so that was a crazy big lie, so I added another lie on top so no one would think on it. "I didn't see any vampires or werewolves yesterday. Were they out somewhere? I remember traveling with them to the Okefenokee Swamp during the Raccoon Cave incident."

Corey continued to build on my fabrication. "They didn't allow me to talk about team three or even tell me their location."

Since Coach White and Clive weren't technically on our team, there was no one left from our discussions for the team three we just made up.

As we continued our ascent, our conversation shifted to lighter topics, providing some respite from the physical exertion. I hoped that the plateau Corey had mentioned, always just "up ahead," would soon come into view.

NICOLE WATCHED WITH rapt attention as Tricia crafted the plan, her fingers gliding across the parchment, documenting every detail. Tricia's methodical approach stood in stark contrast to Corey's impulsive tactics, highlighting the difference between them.

It wasn't military knowledge that made the plan compelling. Nicole, with her limited expertise, could appreciate its soundness and organization. The plan showcased a harmony that poised every team member to complement one another.

Hours of dedication had left Nicole and Tricia fatigued. When team members had relinquished their information, they slept.

Tricia's sleep-deprived eyes, with dark circles etched beneath them, were a testament to her unwavering commitment. Nicole couldn't help but sympathize, knowing that she mirrored Tricia's weary countenance.

In this game of deception, Nicole played the role of a retired witch, concealing her true identity as she ventured into Chattanooga. Tricia had positioned the team at the ambush site well in advance. Now Tricia chauffeured Nicole, both aware of the dangers that awaited them. Madison and Miles, with their keen instincts as hunters, positioned the team with the precision for the impending assault. Baron would unleash his radiant beam of sunlight, aiming to shock the vampires into submission. Nicole had provided Fey-powered bullets entrusted to Wesley, Baron, and Nathan.

To fortify their defenses, Miles and Madison had set up two remote fire guns. Corey's Fey Earth powers he embedded throughout the southeast at his territory pole combined with Baron's sunlight would give the Southeast team a favorable advantage. The vampires, experts at manipulating natural abilities, had to decide to either safeguard themselves from the Baron's rays or the Earth Power from Corey's Territory spell. They couldn't withstand both without weakening.

Tricia and Nicole clasped their Ruger 22/45 suppressed handguns, each armed with three clips containing ten Fey rounds. These silent instruments of destruction had the lowest decibel output among the arsenal. Since it was Trish and Nicole in the SUV and they were both pregnant, they selected the quietest weapon. They made the weapons effective by infusing Fey magic into the bullets.

Tricia maneuvered the vehicle along I-75 as they approached the Tennessee border. A palpable tension hung in the air, causing Nicole's heart to flutter within her chest. Tricia's voice trembled as she asked, "Do you always feel this way before a battle?"

Nicole let out a soft sigh, her nerves fraying at the edges. "Even after eight years as a spy, fear still clings to me whenever I embark on an operation. It was when Corey joined me on a mission that I felt calm." She tried to steady her trembling hands, fearing they would betray her anxiety.

As they crossed the juncture where I-75 and I-24 intertwined, the world transformed into a monochromatic palette of black and white—the Realm of Shadow. The enemy thrust the team into a fierce battle, their senses heightened, and their instincts honed. Tricia pointed out four vampires attempting to regroup under the relentless onslaught of sunlight, their resistance futile. Undeterred, she surged forward, navigating the vehicle over the four bodies.

The SUV screeched to a halt, and without hesitation, Nicole flung open the rear compartment, retrieving four wooden stakes and a hammer. She wielded the heavy hammer with determination, driving each stake through the undead hearts. The vampires dissolved under the unforgiving illumination of Baron's sunlight.

Once they discovered they had fallen into an orchestrated ambush, the vampires writhed in agony, their desperation palpable. Every member of the Southeast team had cover, positioning themselves for lethal attacks. Miles and his colossal sword met those foolish enough to venture close.

In their agony, the vampires sought an escape, but their lack of foresight left them trapped. They fell prey to the chaos that surrounded them. The team cut them off from the south and a relentless barrage of remote fire automatic weapons barred their east and north routes. The team combined Fey bullets and Madison's unerring arrows, bombarding their western retreat. There would be no regrouping allowed.

Nicole delivered a box of stakes to her comrades, ensuring the swift demise of any wounded vampires before replenishing her supply. Each stake driven home was a testament to her unwavering resolve to halt the undead menace in its tracks.

Returning to the SUV according to Tricia's meticulous plan, they had finished their part. The team executed their orders, permitting a select number of vampires to retreat. Tricia had set a clear aim for the team—to secure victory with minimal casualties and prevent postbattle skirmishes. This level of precision planning stood in stark contrast to Corey's looser approach.

Nicole viewed the aftermath—a hundred lifeless vampires strewn across the battlefield, with fifty more fleeing in disarray. Tricia and Nicole departed the scene, their journey taking them on a circuitous route back home.

An hour passed before Nathan's message arrived, breaking the silence that enveloped the vehicle. "Team secured, injuries treated, heading back. One hundred and twenty-three enemy vampires confirmed dead."

Nicole's voice brimmed with triumph. "These numbers prove that the Delta Territory is lying about their total numbers."

Tricia's eyes sparkled with determination. "We must collect magical signatures and compare them to registered ones. But for now, let us press on to phase two of our plan."

Nicole's hopes soared as she envisioned Corey executing his plan with equal finesse.

Chapter 16—Corey

Corey surveyed the terrain, his gaze sweeping over the area. He approached a fallen log and moved it aside, creating a seating area for his companions. "Alright, let's take a moment to rest and have a quick meal. I sense the beast. After we eat, everyone rest while I scout out the ambush spot."

As the others plopped to the ground, their exhaustion clear in their grumbling, Corey wasted no time. While they complained, he set to work digging a fire pit and kindling a fire. The flickering flames danced in the chilly air, casting an orange glow on their surroundings. He prepared a large, hearty stew. "Hey, Rebecca, could you do me a favor and take charge of heating and distributing the stew?" Despite her grimace, she nodded in agreement. He disliked burdening his companions, but it was the most practical choice. The Nephilim beast moved fast.

The disheveled campsite and scattered backpacks testified to Corey's plan. He had pushed the team to their limits, and their weariness gave him hope. His plan revolved on exhausting Lance physically. Lance was an ancient evil housed in a human's body and he bet the entity did not understand the limitations of flesh. Once they killed Lance, he could then plan for the beast. He was about to face two enemies and he had to have help to fight each one. To make things easier on his mind, he used the monikers of Lance and ancient evil in place of each other. He couldn't afford to waste time thinking about what to call the entity.

Determined, Corey removed his shirt, exposing his solar plexus to channel more Earth power, and maneuvered through the dense underbrush towards the path leading to the ledge.

The distance measured ten miles from the spot where Suit and Red Shirt had pushed Haley and Corrinne off the cliff. The supernatural beast lurked closer than ideal. Undeterred, he remained confident that they were within an acceptable range. His plan involved blocking the entire ledge with a magical circle, trapping Lance, the ancient evil. Navigating the treacherous path, a mere foot wide and composed of loose dirt and crumbling rocks, he would need to assist or carry each member of his team.

Skidding down the precarious path, Corey landed on a patch of light gray rock adorned with thin, scraggly bushes clinging to the cracks. Debris from above littered the ground. After venturing half a mile towards the path leading to a lower level, he discovered a straight ten-foot section extending for twenty feet. The sporadic patches of scrub did little to impede his progress, but he cleared rocks from the area, creating a circle spanning the entire width. Behind a rock located ten feet ahead, he arranged a honeysuckle bush and extracted eleven twigs from it.

Once placed within the circle, Corey concealed the twigs beneath a layer of debris, using his druidic vision granted by the torc. Within the confines of the ravine, darkness descended earlier because of the imposing tree line to the west. Between the Animal Domain and Earth Power, he learned the beast noticed his presence, but remained oblivious to any workable means of ascending the ledge. The nearest climbing area between the levels lay five miles away. But the beast moved fast, fueled by a hatred of druids, the ones who trapped all them in the caves.

Time was of the essence, and Corey ran back to the campsite, signaling his comrades to prepare for departure. "Guys, it's approaching. We must hurry. We can return here to rest once the task is done," he said before dropping his waist pack and grabbing his weapons.

The ancient evil, still known as Lance, had deteriorated. His gaze fixated on Rebecca with a mix of fear and fascination. Corey paid little attention to the ancient evil's infatuation; it would be its downfall.

Rachel spoke, "Oh man, at least we ate. Valkyrie was smart, finishing her food." Corey extended a helping hand to Rebecca, assisting her in standing, while Rachel attended to a groaning Lance. So far, his plan had yielded the desired results. "There's a descent route up ahead. We'll go down one at a time, and I'll carry each of you. The path is treacherous even during the day, and I'm the only one with clear night vision."

The team proceeded toward the path to the next level, positioning themselves alongside a scrubby growth where the wind had left a delicate layer of snow on the leaves. Corey took on the responsibility of carrying Rebecca first, mindful of her delicate frame. This order guaranteed Rebecca and Lance would never be alone together. Valkyrie required constant support throughout the descent, her weight distributed between Corey and Rachel, who navigated the challenging terrain with Corey's help. Finally, Corey carried Lance downward, who quipped, "Thought you forgot about me."

"No way," Corey said. "I bet you'll have crucial information about this creature once you see it."

"Fingers crossed." Lance's eyes flickered in anticipation.

As they moved, a faint vibration traveled through the ledge, signaling the beast's impending arrival. Corey quickened his pace, leading the group towards the selected ambush spot. "That noise—it sounds close," Rebecca said, her voice laced with unease.

"Yes, why we need to hurry," Corey confirmed. "I've chosen the location for our ambush." The beast's swiftness allowed for Corey's haste, concealing his true intentions as he positioned his comrades.

With stealth, he used his Animal Domain, connecting with Valkyrie. "When I start the attack, you grab its ankle until I can bind it." There was no time to prepare for the Nephilim beast. He'd have to react if it arrived too soon.

Valkyrie remained silent, acknowledging the telepathic communication through their shared Animal Domain. Her positive response resonated within Corey's mind.

"Lance, once you see the creature, shout out any knowledge you possess and retreat. If anyone gets injured, pull them back for triage," Corey ordered. HE needed to keep Lance unaware by lying about the plan.

"Got it." Lance's gaze still fixated on Rebecca. He moved into the circle.

With a firm grip on his tonfa, Corey tripped Lance, then initiated the magical circle. He yanked Rebecca and Rachel backward, ensuring their safety. In an instant, Valkyrie lunged, seizing Lance's foot as he screamed in pain. Rebecca and Rachel kept a safe distance, witnessing the unfolding spectacle while Corey began the binding ritual. It was apparent that Valkyrie had been trained to kill because if Lance were human, he'd already be dead.

"***Bho àm immemorial, cumhachd an t-seanairginn a 'gairm thugad. A bhith ceangailte ris a' phortal agam agus fo smachd mo thoil***," Corey intoned, his voice resonating with ancient power.

Rachel called out to Valkyrie, who returned leaving Lance alone. "You knew something was amiss all this time, and you waited until now?" Rebecca's voice rang out, filled with a mix of anger and frustration.

As Lance's body contorted and hurled itself against the barrier of Corey's enchanted circle, the magical focal points within amplified the containment. The circle, comprising eleven focal points, now pulsated with even greater strength. Rachel chanted the saga of "The Battle of Chattanooga", her melodious voice weaving through the air, infusing the circle with a vibrant green glow, showcasing her bardic power. Valkyrie howled in unison with Rachel, though her contribution did not add to the circle's power like Rachel.

Lance's human facade crumbled, revealing a visage devoid of humanity. His once familiar face dissolved into a grotesque, gelatinous mass, undulating in mid-air. Snarling and growling in guttural tones through one of its stalk-like protrusions, the creature battered against the barrier, futile attempts against the circle.

A celestial light bathed the area as Rebecca's celestial form unveiled itself, radiating her brilliance. The creature recoiled, howling in agony as the celestial light further weakened its essence.

He continued the binding ritual, harnessing its power to the fullest during the ten-minute duration. Once he achieved maximum strength, he initiated the banishment phase. "***Tha Rìoghachd dorchadas a 'gairm agus le mo chumhachd rìoghachdan ceangailte tha mi a 'cuir casg ort gu dorchadas!***" he commanded, his voice exuding authority.

The first attempt proved ineffective, yet the creature convulsed and howled in response. Its complexion shifted from its initial hue to a sickly green, then transformed into a menacing black. Corey persisted, repeating the banishment incantation twice more. On the third repetition, a remarkable phenomenon occurred. Golden streaks intertwined with the vibrant green of the circle. That had never happened before.

The amorphous mass of the creature splattered against the confines of the circle's barrier, fracturing into five fragments of light. A brilliant green blast struck Corey's chest, while a golden flash smacked Rebecca. A pink surge of light pulsed into Rachel, and a second green blast surged towards Valkyrie. The fifth light, tinted with darkness, darted down the ravine, disappearing from sight.

Corey counted the fragments. Earth took part of the ancient evil's essence and granted it to Corey with the green blast. Celestia grabbed part of the essence and gave the power to Rebecca in the gold flash. The Spring Fey court awarded Valkyrie and Rachel with their share of the ancient evil's power with the second green blast and the pink blast.

Part of the ancient evil escaped. That black ball that shot down the ravine meant the entity still had some life force left.

This was the first thing to ever break one of his circles and he had held devils in it.

Whatever remained of the body Lance had taken over, had absorbed into the oozing substance that flowed down the side of Corey's invisible circle. Assisting each other to their feet, the group reestablished the protective barrier. Rachel ceased her singing, and Valkyrie fell silent. Rebecca stood in her original human form.

"I powered up again, like with the Snake-Hunter," said Rebecca.

A resounding howl of anger reverberated through the air, jolting the quartet and sending them crashing to the ground. The ground quivered beneath their weight as the beast materialized from the shadows, its immense horned head assaulting the barrier of the circle. The corrupted celestial power from the Nephilim beast surged, ripping through the fragile confines of the protective ring. Though the creature couldn't breach the circle to launch its attack, it unleashed a celestial force that threatened to shatter the weakened barrier.

A creature colored a dismal and mottled shade of grey, loomed before them. Its head bore a resemblance to that of an elephant, with prominent ears but devoid of a trunk. Instead, a row of wicked six-inch horns adorned its head, running in a menacing mohawk-like fashion down its neck and face. Its body stretched ten feet wide, and along each side, five appendages with razor-sharp claws and menacing spikes protruded from its ten-foot-long form.

The consequences were dire; should the circle fall, a cataclysmic magical backlash would annihilate all four of them. Corey faced a pivotal choice: to fortify the circle and reinforce its protective properties or to dismantle it altogether and confront the beast head-on. As he turned to instruct Rachel to unleash her singing prowess, her finger pointed skyward, directing his attention.

Onoskelis, the once-injured fallen angel, ascended above them, restored to full strength. The lighter shades of Corey's kilt, Rebecca's shirt, and Rachel's leather dress glowed like luminescent beacons, as if under the influence of a black light. With wings unfurled, the fallen angel hovered in mid-air, her ebony toga billowing. The wind gusted, causing her black hair to dance, while her obsidian eyes radiated an otherworldly luminescence. Wisps of grey smoke wafted from her form as she extended her palms towards the group, hands empty of any weapon.

The Nephilim beast froze in its tracks, immobilized by Onoskelis' commanding presence. "Druid," she hissed contemptuously. "You have proven to possess an unexpected level of competence." Pausing with disdain, she directed her gaze towards the three humans and their canine companion. "With the power you four have absorbed from the forces of evil, you have weakened this ancient malevolence to where I can eradicate it." She sighed. "With your help, that is."

Engaging her in combat under these conditions would lead to their demise. Thus, Corey held his tongue and allowed Onoskelis to convey her proposition.

"Here's the deal. I shall escort Barnisfer back to the very location where the ancient druid first sealed him. In return, you will refrain from inflicting harm upon him. Once daylight breaks, I will visit you under the banner of a truce, and we shall discuss the terms of another agreement."

The gravity of the situation left them with no choice but to accept the fallen angel's offer. "I agree," Corey agreed. "He felt lucky for the offer was exactly what he would have wanted."

"Onward, Barnisfer," Onoskelis commanded, landing beside the Nephilim beast like it was her pet. Together, they retreated from the group, their figures fading into the shadows.

Corey released the binding spell, removing the protective circle that had shielded them. "You knew he was evil at the bottom of the mountain. Why didn't you kill him, then?" Rebecca asked.

"I knew in Virginia thanks to Valkyrie. However, I lacked the confidence that I could contain him and wanted a buffer zone in case I failed," he said. "That's why I kept watch over you."

Rebecca countered. "But it wasn't only me."

"He feared you. That's why I told the lies about us as the 'B team,' in order to keep him underestimating me, Rachel, and Valkyrie."

"So, my first in person date turned out to be an ancient evil who feared and sought to kill me?" Rebecca shook her head as Corey scooped her up, ascending the treacherous ravine.

He knew that Ms. Addkinson, Rebecca's grandmother, had given her the promotion and requested his support. He had pledged to do whatever it took for Rebecca's benefit.

Valkyrie followed, with Rachel leading the way, cradling the dog in her arms. Corey lent his strength, providing support when needed, until they reached the summit.

Seated on a moss-covered tree stump, Rebecca erupted in fits of laughter.

Rachel acted perplexed by her friend's mad mirth. "Have you lost your mind?"

"No," Rebecca managed to get out. "Listen to this. I was worried that my worst-case scenario for dating would involve saying, 'Don't worry, my ex will come and save us because your weak ass can't handle it.' But guess what? It turns out my date was an ancient evil that wants me dead. My ex had to save me, and now we have to join forces with a fallen angel to finish the job!" She dissolved into laughter once more, tears of amusement streaming down her face. "It turns out, it wasn't so bad."

Rachel joked along. "Girls going to frat parties in college experience worse dates than this."

Rebecca, still convulsing with laughter, composed herself. "Want to know what's awful?" Her laughter waned, replaced by a hint of melancholy. "That meeting my grandmother summoned me for? She relieved the battle leader of the Chesapeake Bay Territory of his duties."

"Your grandmother is a wise woman, and I trust her judgment," he said, concealing the fact that he had already been privy to the news.

She leaned forward. "She named me battle leader of the Chesapeake Bay Territory."

He encouraged her as best he could. "From what I saw, you'll do great. Fitz delivered some company and platoon training. I'll share these with you, and we can study them together."

Rachel grinned and patted Valkyrie. "You did so well!"

Rebecca used Corey's hand to stand. "We learned you won't fight anyone, anytime, anyplace, or anywhere." She laughed again, and Rachel joined in. Valkyrie barked, too.

Her remarking about the old southern saying brought him joy after the fight. It was like old times.

He led the crazy little group back to the campsite and finished setting it up. Lance's section got cleared out, and he moved a fallen tree trunk for Onoskelis to sit on when everyone talked in the morning. "Let's get a good night's sleep."

Rebecca stepped over and kissed him on the cheek. "Thank you, Corey. I don't say that enough to you. I am glad to have you as a friend and someone who will help me."

She laid down and slept. He crawled under his makeshift shelter and went to sleep since Rachel and Valkyrie were already asleep by the fire.

Chapter 17—Rebecca

The morning dawned upon me, a heavy weight clinging to my weary limbs and impeding movement. I remained cocooned within the warmth of my sleeping bag, observing Corey as he prepared breakfast before the rest of us stirred. Valkyrie bounded to him, and Corey attended to her meal. Rachel had brought an abundance of food for her.

Rachel stumbled to the crackling fire; her gaze fixed upon the dancing flames. Her voice cut through the serene morning air. "What is an ancient evil? It sounds like a term someone uses when they're guessing."

Corey shook his head, his expression etched with sorrow. "I'm afraid we lost the druidic definitions. Many of the Abernathy family perished within the depths of the caves below. I've even been using the name Lance and ancient evil synonymously."

I sat up, wincing as my tired muscles protested the motion. With determination, I slipped my feet into my shoes, ready to join the discussion. "I've heard a couple of theories. The teachings in Virginia say when the finger of God ignited the spark of creation, it tore through the void, causing small ruptures. Some of these ruptures, feeling abandoned by the creator, turned against the intended creation. These renegade entities are now known as ancient evils. Their sole purpose is to unravel the fabric of creation and absorb all the creative energy to fortify themselves."

Corey's voice carried a hint of skepticism. "Sounds far-fetched, doesn't it?"

I couldn't help but agree, though I knew he wouldn't be too keen on the alternative. "Well, according to the witch definition, our universe is a bubble within a vaster universe. It emerged because of the rapid inflation after the big bang, but now the still-expanding part of the universe seeks to harness the power of all bubble universes. Powers in the wider universe sometimes possess the ability to enter our bubble. These incursions can distort the natural order and create a malevolent life force."

A chuckle escaped Corey's lips. "The finger of God, huh?"

Rachel joined in the laughter. "Consider my question retracted. I quite like the concept of ancient evil."

We were all in agreement. "We could always consult Wesley for a more in-depth explanation. He talked to the outer world entities and I about bubble universes, and I had to pretend liked I followed along."

Corey changed the subject. "While we wait, Rachel, perhaps we should focus on studying the next Fey ritual. I believe we are close to a breakthrough."

The Fey rituals demanded a joint effort between Rachel and Corey, as druids comprehended half of the spells while bards held the knowledge of the remaining half.

"Awesome idea," Rachel agreed. "We'll study the ritual once we've spoken to Onoskelis."

"My legs are still sore," I confessed with a grimace.

Corey's voice carried remorse. "I apologize for my plan. I had hoped that Lance, unaware of the limitations of a human body, would be easier to trap when exhausted."

"Geez, Corey, that was clever," I said, taking a gulp of water. My phone showed a message from my grandmother. "She says that Commander Goseling and Lieutenant Shevski are the two individuals I can trust in this new group. I should be cautious of everyone else."

Corey nodded. "That's a good starting point. Two trustworthy people in a brand-new group is no small feat."

"Corey, you used to have few people around you. How did you work like that?" I figured this was as good a time as any to learn something.

"I tried to be a loner. When Trish got pregnant after Old Donnie's death, I tried to be a loner. I failed, but you remember that."

"How are you stopping from being a hero all the time?" The dehydrated camping food was plain but edible.

"I try to include everyone, but sometimes, I'm the strongest and I'm the leader, and I have to step up." He sat down to eat. "You call it a hero complex, but I call it accepting responsibility for using the gifts given to me by the Earth."

With an insatiable hunger, I tore into my breakfast. The weight of being a Battle Leader felt heavy upon me. Perhaps it was a temporary position, caused by the turmoil plaguing the territory, and I would train for the role once my grandmother replaced me.

"Since we pushed your muscles to their limits, let's spend the night and head back to the car tomorrow. We can return home in time for lunch," Corey said.

"I have my prayer book I can study. Let's do that." Relieved at the prospect of immersing myself in familiar and comforting words while resting sounded heavenly. When I went through my pack, I saw Corey thought ahead and packed the things I'd need to study spells.

As Corey cleaned the dishes and gathered firewood, a gentle gust of wind accompanied by a swirl of gray smoke announced Onoskelis. Gracefully folding her wings, she sauntered into our campsite and settled onto the log that had once been Lance's usual spot.

Onoskelis observed us for a few seconds. "When I witness scenes like this, I am reminded of a time when your kind was pure and unspoiled. There were moments when I questioned my choice. However, witnessing the love for material possessions and the unquenchable greed that consumes many, I am reassured that my decision was the correct one. One day, I shall return home and they will reward my unwavering conviction."

My instinct urged me to contradict her, but Corey cut me off, diverting the course of the conversation. "Let us make the most of this temporary truce and use this time productively."

Recognizing the wisdom in his words, I remained silent, allowing Corey to take the lead. Onoskelis nodded, acknowledging the shift in our approach.

"Excellent. I am attempting to be diplomatic with humans. You three have showed that you are extraordinary beings, committed to preserving the Earth and standing against any malevolence."

"Both those statements hold true," Corey affirmed, his tone steady.

"The evil you sought to contain has escaped and now seeks to hide and recover its strength over several centuries, devising a new plan. But with your help," she paused, drawing a deep breath, "I can eradicate this weakened evil once and for all."

Corey stretched his legs before responding, "What do we need to do to make this alliance possible?"

"Hold on," said Rebecca. "Why do you need us?"

"I like Corey's term for you, Fantasy Girl," said the fallen angel, but then she answered. "Fine. The entity you call Lance comes from outside our universe. It can control the Nephilim beasts and giants in the caves. I cannot deal with him while fighting the beasts I've cared for the past dozen millennia."

"Thank you for your answer," said Corey with more diplomacy than I felt.

"Convince me you can form a temporary alliance, and then we will embark on a journey together. We shall venture into the nearby caves, tracking down this malevolence and ensuring its ultimate demise," Onoskelis said, her gaze fixed upon Corey.

With a sense of purpose, Corey leaned back, contemplating her proposal. "I can commit to this. Rebecca, could you please check on the status of the other team?"

I reached for my phone and sent a text to Nicole. "We're ready for an update. We have an important meeting here."

Nicole's prompt reply appeared on my screen. "Did Lance die? We won and won decisively. Let Corey know I'm unharmed. Wesley sustained minor injuries—a sprained wrist and a cut—but he's fine and eating with us."

Relief washed over me as I read Nicole's words, and I let Corey and Rachel know of the team's success and health. Then I asked, "How did Nicole know about Lance?" I typed out a reply. "We defeated Lance but did not finish him off, yet. Hold on for further news."

Corey smiled. "She tried to read his mind and warned me he could shield his mind before we left. I told her how Valkyrie warned me so she'd focus on her own safety and not me."

"Another checkbox for Corey trying hard in his relationship with Nicole," I said and smiled at him.

Corey settled beside me, ready to share a story with Onoskelis. "Here's a tale that'll prove my flexibility." Corey recounted the story of his encounter with Khalil, detailing the lesson he had learned and how it had shaped his alliance with Strumath. When Corey told grandmother he would befriend anyone, he told the truth.

"I'll be damned," Onoskelis exclaimed, captivated by Corey's account. "I believe you. Let us form this alliance. How do you propose we proceed?"

Corey's unwavering faith that had paved the way for us to stand before Onoskelis. Was this blind trust a virtue or a potential flaw? I had been wrong before, doubting the prisoners, but I still harbored reservations. *Would I have believed Strumath?*

Corey continued in charge. "We need to spend a day and a night here. Rachel and I must continue studying the Fey ritual. Tomorrow, during lunchtime, we will meet with the team. Rebecca, please relay this message."

"Okay." Accepting my role as the messenger, I prepared to type.

"Type this, please," Corey smiled, dictating his words. "Nicole, inform Nathan to organize a mandatory meeting tomorrow at lunch. I have crucial information to share with everyone. There will be no vote, but attendance is mandatory."

I typed out Corey's message, transmitting it to Nicole. Moments later, her response appeared on my screen. "What is the meeting about?" she asked.

I hesitated before replying, realizing the gravity of our revelation. "Don't divulge this to anyone. It may cause unnecessary alarm. We are forming an alliance with a fallen angel."

Nicole's immediate response mirrored my initial reaction. "What in the world? Don't worry, I'll pretend I know nothing. Nathan said he will arrange the meeting and provide the details."

"Nicole shared my initial thoughts. Nathan assured us he will take care of the arrangements and furnish us with the details later today," I said.

"Perfect. Thank you," Corey acknowledged, rising from his spot alongside the fallen angel. "We will receive the details tonight, and tomorrow, during lunch, we ensure everyone is on the same page."

Onoskelis nodded in agreement. "I shall return at sundown," she said before soaring away.

"Corey, have you lost your mind?" I mustered the courage to voice my concerns. My eyes locked with his as I stood, determined to meet him on equal footing. "That's a fallen angel."

"A fallen angel who recognizes us as the best chance to eradicate evil," Corey said with conviction. "Eradicating evil is kind of our thing."

Rachel perked up and said, "I may be slow, but why does a fallen angel want to eradicate an ancient evil?"

Corey opened his mouth to answer, and nothing came out. "All I can say is I believe her."

"You're right Rachel, we should have asked, but let's move on." I wish we had asked that. "You're saying that we would kill traitors who wished to harm us, but now we're willing to work with her, someone who also wanted to kill us?"

Corey's eyes softened, filled with understanding. "That's not quite true, is it?" he countered. "She tried to negotiate with us. She had a goal, and we stood in her way. The traitors had one goal—to end our lives."

He had a point. The situation felt unnerving. "But five people are serving life sentences while she becomes our ally." I struggled to reconcile the complexities of our predicament.

Corey sighed, his expression grave. "They transferred Sheila to the Cascadia Territory for possible rehabilitation. They confined the other four in a prison far away from others because of the Dark Fey influence. The traitors will spend their days in perpetual darkness, trapped with each other until the end. In some ways, death might have been a more merciful fate for them."

The weight of his words crashed upon me, causing me to collapse onto a nearby log. The mere thought of enduring a fate worse than death sent shivers down my spine, the darkness of their confinement echoing the despair within my heart.

Corey attempted to ease my shock, his voice gentle. "Look, none of this is black and white," he said. "You may be right, and history might mock me for this decision. All I can do is share what I believe and provide you with the details from the Chesapeake interrogations."

I nodded, accepting his explanation, and distanced myself to seek solace within the pages of my prayer book. The situation we found ourselves in was complex, and now I stood alongside Corey. The weight of the world rested upon our shoulders, and it left me grappling with the question of what I would do. Would I allow evil to stay and fester over time? The answer eluded me, hidden within the depths of uncertainty. "I'm going to read my prayer book."

Rachel and Corey joined me in quiet study, pausing once to satiate their hunger with dehydrated food—a makeshift late lunch. It was nice and peaceful. Corey and Rachel studying a Fey ritual and me studying my spells in my prayer book with information on Celestia, where I tried to make sense of my life.

As the sun began its descent, casting long shadows upon our campsite, I received a text from Nicole, providing the address for our meeting. Nathan had rallied everyone together, even with the short notice.

"I have the address and time," I relayed to my two companions.

Corey grinned. "It's a dozen people, and we can convene on my patio. But if Nathan prefers a different location, that's fine, too." He was reflective. "Though it is an important topic, I'll need to be ready."

With dinner drawing near, Rachel stood up, a triumphant smile adorning her face. "I've got it!" she exclaimed, her voice brimming with excitement.

It sounded like she figured out the last part of the ritual those two had been working on.

She displayed her newfound ability, and to my astonishment, delicate butterfly wings sprouted from her back. A mesmerizing fusion of light green, pink, and purple. Their Fey beauty brought cheerfulness to a tough day. As Rachel moved, the wings guided her, releasing delicate streams of pink in their wake.

"Your turn!" she urged, her voice dancing with anticipation from her elevated position in the air.

Valkyrie barked, mirroring Rachel's enthusiasm.

Corey's expression didn't mirror the same exhilaration as mine and Rachel's, but he obliged and cast his own wings. Four wings emerged, elongated and slender, like those of a dragonfly. The edges donned a mesmerizing dark green hue, cradling gossamer-like light green interiors that exuded a pulsating Fey Power, glimmering in shades of iridescent green. As Corey arranged his wings, they resembled a flexible hang glider, spanning an impressive twenty feet. Though he required ample space to test their capabilities, the immediate test appeared promising.

Embracing my *Angelic Form*, I ascended into the sky, joining my companions in the air. "Now you'll be able to train me," I said with a hint of excitement, a sense of wonder at being tutored by a butterfly and a dragonfly.

New wings caught our attention. "How nice," a voice taunted, dripping with disdain. "A false angel and two faeries."

Corey's wings retracted as he touched down on the ground, his attempt to appear strong and unaffected. Meanwhile, I landed beside him, unable to suppress my amusement at his fleeting embarrassment. Onoskelis, the fallen angel, descended and fixed Corey with a mischievous grin and a sly wink.

Rachel soared above us, her voice carrying on the wind. "Come on, Corey! Show everyone the beauty of your wings!"

"My wings are not just beautiful, but also a precious gift from the Fey Spring Court," Corey said diplomatically. "They will enable me to train you, Rebecca, and unlock a tremendous range of functionality."

Rachel landed, folding her wings behind her. "Oh, come on! You must show everyone," she insisted, her eyes sparkling with a mix of playfulness and challenge.

Corey showed the address to Onoskelis, our unexpected ally. "This is the location," he said. "The venue opens tomorrow at noon, and Nathan assures me that everyone will be present by one pm. I suspect he might have enticed them with the promise of a free lunch to ensure full attendance."

Onoskelis accepted the information, her gaze meeting Rachel's, as if an unspoken understanding passed between them. Then the fallen angel departed. That was the least weird thing that had happened in the past two days.

"Corey, I wish I knew how you choose who to trust," I said.

"I wish I could say I trust everyone until I can't. But that isn't true. I will say I'm willing to trust everyone."

That would have to do for now. I needed to refine the question.

"Guys, I'm going to take a nap and depart at midnight," Corey informed us with weariness. "With my tree spell speed, I can travel from here to my house within moments. Rachel, I trust you and Valkyrie to protect Rebecca. Make your way to the car and drive to the house to prepare for the meeting. Rachel, please come to pick me up at noon."

Corey retired early while I immersed myself in my prayer book, illuminated by the waning light. Tomorrow held unknown challenges, and I knew I had to face them with strength and resolve. With every page turned, I sought guidance and clarity, preparing myself for the trials that awaited us.

Chapter 18—Rebecca

We had a slow and uneventful walk back, and the drive was pleasant, allowing us to stop for breakfast and still arrive on time. While Rachel went to wake Corey, Valkyrie and I parked in front of the theater, bathed in the harsh light of noon. We joined Nathan, my heart pounding with anticipation. We all waited for Corey, knowing that our unity was paramount for the upcoming meeting.

Grandmother had made the same journey, underscoring the significance of this gathering. Nathan reached out to every territory in North America.

A ripple of excitement surged through me as Rachel and Corey arrived together. The soldier in him took measured steps and as he stepped up the curb toward the glass doors. "A movie theater?" he asked.

"Do you have any idea how many people we've gained? So many individuals have awakened with new powers, and we're also dealing with many containment issues." Nathan checked off a clipboard with a woman in a red vest, who verified the room and the meals.

I whispered to Corey, "I stand by your side because I know you would do the same for me. Just remember, you're not alone in this decision."

A smile tugged at Corey's lips, gratitude radiating from his eyes. "Thank you. I have a good feeling about what lies ahead."

With a flutter of wings, Onoskelis, the fallen angel, descended upon the theater's entrance. She folded her wings, a cloud of corrupted gray smoke dissipating beneath her feet. Her ebony hair cascaded down, and I couldn't help but agree with Corey's earlier assessment—she possessed stunning beauty, which would be heightened by a smile. Though lacking a sword, her presence emanated power. Dressed in a black toga, complemented by pants and leather boots, she didn't hide the wings on her back or the Outer Realms gray smoke that trailed her.

Corey's voice broke the silence. "How will we ensure Valkyrie's entry?" he asked, concern furrowing his brow.

A touch of exasperation danced in Nathan's eyes as he came out from behind the door. "You're worried about your dog while we have a fallen angel among us?" he said. "Never mind, I've secured permission for Valkyrie to join us, but we'll be responsible for any messes," he added, his gaze never straying from Onoskelis.

Onoskelis spoke up, her deep voice resonating without an echo, and her corrupted light no longer shedding its dark aura. She appeared like a normal person who favored the color black. "Stoic Nathan Abernathy. Are my wings concealed?" Her inquiry was direct, her eyes piercing.

Nathan paled at the sound of his name.

Corey's voice brightened. "That's awesome. You still look stunning with your whole black ensemble. People might stare, though," he complimented her with a wink.

Corey had a flirting problem, but a fallen angel?!

A soft, melodious laugh escaped Onoskelis's lips just as Nicole rushed out to embrace Corey, her love for him clear in the passionate kiss they shared. Then her gaze shifted to Onoskelis. The timing couldn't have been worse.

"Onoskelis, this is Nicole, my fiancé," Corey introduced them, oblivious to the undertones of jealousy that had festered within Nicole. "Nicole, meet Onoskelis. She's here as our ally and the reason behind this gathering."

Nicole's forced smile masked the simmering envy that threatened to consume her.

"Your fiancé is with child, druid," Onoskelis taunted, her tone betraying a touch of mischief.

Corey winked playfully. "Yep, I did that," he said.

"Shall we proceed?" Nathan sounded eager to steer the conversation back on track.

Corey scooped up Nicole gently, his protectiveness shining through. "Let me carry you, baby. Save your energy for later," he said.

Perhaps Corey sensed the tendrils of jealousy creeping within Nicole, for he diffused the situation. There was something different about Corey now—a newfound intelligence.

He astounded me before with his dealings with a gargoyle, long before factions became common knowledge. He had advocated for vampires and werewolves to join the Southeast Territory, but now I understood that his friendship had no boundaries. Conversely, his wrath held no limits for those who crossed him, endangered his friends, or threatened his loved ones. He was the remorseless killer he always claimed to be. The question lingered—how did he make these decisions, and could I harness that skill as the Scion?

Together, we passed through the double glass doors, leaving behind the outside world. The deserted bar on the left caught our attention—a solitary figure eagerly awaiting the morning movie. With Nathan leading the way and an escort guiding us, we advanced past the ticket taker, taking a right after passing four theaters and the restrooms.

Our destination was theater eleven, where the theater labeled "Corey's Mandatory Talk" awaited us. The name drew a chuckle from Corey as we approached, his senses heightened and alert, attuned to every nuance.

Nathan positioned himself at the center of the lit stage, emanating an air of authority that commanded attention. Corey paused, his gaze sweeping across the rows of seats before us.

"Keep moving, hotshot." I urged him forward.

He whispered to me. "Someone here has been near a gargoyle, but I can't discern who."

"Stay focused, everyone. The stairs leading to the podium are straight ahead," Nathan directed, gesturing towards a set of temporary wooden stairs.

"Honey, could you take Valkyrie and sit near Rachel?" Corey asked Nicole, his voice filled with tenderness, as he released her from his embrace.

Nicole pressed her lips to Corey's, their connection palpable in its intensity, before taking the imposing Great Dane towards the stadium-style seating. I remained close to Corey, following him up the stairs. Corey carried a stool and positioned it front and center at the podium.

In the middle of the stage, Nathan addressed the expectant crowd. "I'm unaware of the exact topic. Corey emphasized two things—he implored everyone to listen to him and said that this was not a matter for voting. Judging by the tremendous turnout, it's clear that the response has been overwhelming. I want to acknowledge and appreciate all the representatives present here, as well as those joining remotely."

As Nathan glanced down at a note card, the door swung open, causing him to halt. Preacher Jon, accompanied by a woman, entered the room, creating an air of anticipation. "Please, continue. I may be on vacation, but Corey insisted I listen," Preacher Jon quipped, eliciting a ripple of amusement. As leader of the Southeast Territory, it was unusual seeing him take a spectator seat, but his vacation was deserved and it helped proved the rest of the team could run the territory in his absence.

"The Southwest Territory is represented with the addition of May. And now, we have representatives from the following territories are physically present—New England, Ohio River Valley, Chesapeake Bay Territories, the Southeast Territory with its sub-regions of Charleston and The Tribe. We have remote participants from Key West, Canadian Atlantic, Great Lakes, Canadian Shield, Rockies, Great Plains, Cascadia, Canadian Cordillera, New York, and Southern California. Without further delay, let me introduce Corey, who has requested to address us all for the first time."

I half expected Corey to falter, considering he couldn't have expected addressing such a monumental gathering. But to my astonishment, he rose to the occasion, taking a simple stool and seating himself at the front of the stage, his gaze steady and unwavering.

Corey's elegant voice resonated through the opulent auditorium, filling the air with a graceful cadence. As the room fell into a hushed silence, he began, a playful glimmer in his eyes, "Oh, this is funny for so many reasons. I only expected a handful of familiar faces among our team members. But with this newfound knowledge, Nathan has once again saved me from making the wrong communication choice. The irony, though, is that as much as stage fright grips me, I have an overwhelming desire to embrace every one of you here, but alas, the sheer number of people present escapes my count."

Onoskelis, the fallen angel, stepped forward, her authoritative presence casting a spellbinding aura. She listed the attendees according to threats. "We have eight individuals classified as tier-one threats, two Daoine, an Empyrean, an Ellyll, and an Elpys, plus an additional ten tier-two threats, fifty-nine tier-three threats, and seven civilians."

Corey chuckled at the pragmatic listing. "So, we have eighty-nine individuals present on-site, with more joining us remotely."

In the excitement, I felt a sense of pride, understanding the significance of the moment we were experiencing. I picked out the same outer realm beings from the fight at the second chance school, except Fionnestra also brought her friend Verenioulla.

Corey directed his attention towards me, his voice filled with anticipation. "Now, let's cut straight to the chase. Rebecca," he said, turning to me and pointing with a flourish, "has been reborn as the Scion of the New Church. And might I add, she made the announcement in the Archdiocese of Atlanta at the Basilica of the Sacred Heart."

Laughter rippled through the room as I marveled at how Corey had convinced me to make such a bold move. However, today his eloquence and quick-witted nature were out of place, and I couldn't help but wonder what changed.

"But there's more," Corey continued, mischief lacing his voice. "Rebecca has sacrificed a great deal and, in her quest for companionship, found herself on a first date with none other than an ancient evil harboring plans of destroying the world."

A chorus of questions erupted from the audience, their curiosity demanding answers. Corey, however, raised his hands to regain control. "I didn't catch all the questions, but it turned out better than her dating me, from what she experienced."

Polite laughter filled the room, and I couldn't help but appreciate Corey's lightheartedness, despite the gravity of the situation.

Corey told how their team had discovered and defeated the ancient evil entity. This triumph not only forged an alliance with the fallen angel, but also showed their strength and unwavering resolve.

The room buzzed with excitement, but Corey reestablished order. "Please hold your comments," he commanded, his voice firm and authoritative. "I want to clarify that I didn't come here seeking your approval or conducting a vote. My purpose is to inform you."

Corey's assertiveness silenced the room, capturing the attention of all present, allowing Onoskelis to step forward and share her thoughts. Her voice projected with haunting clarity, commanding the room's focus. "Rebecca, I request you assume your *Angelic Form.*"

With a mix of anticipation and trepidation, I rose from my seat, calling upon My *Angelic Form.* My angelic wings unfurled and draped me in a flowing white robe, emanating a celestial glow. There was no need for my armor, shield, or sword—I hoped. I encapsulated the room in a golden glow, and Peridot reflected the celestial light in the audience.

"Corey, it's your turn," she directed, fixing her gaze upon Corey.

Bemused by the unexpected turn of events, I watched as Corey suppressed any embarrassment and rose to his feet. With a resolute expression, he extended his arms, releasing a shimmering display of Fey magic that lifted him from the ground. Delicate gossamer wings adorned his back, contrasting with his manly physique.

Onoskelis shed her facade, revealing her true form. The corrupted light that clung to her body dissipated, and her black and gray wings unfurled, exuding a sinister yet captivating aura. It dimmed the golden glow in the theater. Many in the theater gasped at the appearance of a fallen angel in recognizable form.

"I requested this for a few reasons." Her voice carried an air of authority. "First, it was Rachel's fervent desire to witness Corey in this state before a larger audience, and as much as it pains me to admit it, she is remarkably likable. Corey's discomfort serves as a counterbalance to her endearing charm. Second, I witnessed them taking life force from the ancient evil and becoming stronger, but no druid or bard has had the gift of flight in thousands of years. And last, it serves as a reminder that while I may possess superior power, this alliance is not one-sided. Corey, Rebecca, and Rachel each wield extraordinary abilities that surpass the limits of human potential."

Valkyrie barked in agreement, prompting a few amused chuckles from the audience. Onoskelis rolled her eyes at the dog's antics. "Together, we possess the prowess to combat the ancient evil that now lies weakened before us. Corey, on behalf of humanity, has accepted my offer of an alliance, solidifying our united front against this malevolent force."

A wave of excitement rippled through the room, sparking discussions and contemplation about the future. Onoskelis regained control of the situation. "However, before we proceed with further discussions, it is imperative that Corey relinquishes his death wish and Rebecca embraces her role."

Corey and I exchanged a brief glance, understanding the weight of the fallen angel's words. Though Corey tried to hide his vulnerability, I shook my head, conveying my support. I hoped he had caught my gesture, reassuring him I stood by his side. We could ignore the quip about me since she didn't realize the promotion I was holding and eventually train into.

Corey stood tall once again, his gaze scanning the room. "Nathan, it appears we are ready to address the questions now that the humorous interlude has subsided." He kept his voice firm and commanding.

Nathan, quick to respond, leaped up the stairs and took his position. "Our new ally has studied our group for some time and it is a legitimate question. Rather than evading the question or allowing someone else to pose it, Corey, please answer: Do you harbor a death wish?"

Corey, embodying the resilience he often encouraged in me, stood and walked forward. "This is easy. Rachel, please join me up here," he said.

With a spirited bound, Rachel ascended the stairs, accompanied by the enthusiastic Valkyrie. Corey embraced her, his affection clear to all. "They better be lying."

Corey spoke with confidence and introduced some of the newer team members and making a lighthearted joke before tackling the question. "Onoskelis, what are the chances of anything swaying Rachel toward evil or turning her against me?"

"If she is your excuse, know many of us see through it. But I feel Rebecca will get with you once you convince those who don't know you," she said, audible to those on stage. Out loud, she said, "Nearly none. The amount of force magic to apply would be noticeable and not worth doing."

"Thank you for that confirmation. Unwavering purity, love, and loyalty guides Rachel. Nothing could never sway her toward the path of evil," Corey affirmed, his words carrying an air of certainty. "Rachel, tell our friends, with no input from me. What's the one promise I made to you that stands above all other promises?"

Rachel, her eyes shining with unwavering devotion, answered, "He promised me one thing above all else: that he would never leave me."

"Exactly," Corey said. "If I were to turn to evil, would I be leaving you? If I die?"

"Duh," Rachel said without hesitation.

Corey's tone grew resolute as he locked eyes with Rachel. "Do you believe me when I say I would never leave you?" he asked.

"Of course!" Rachel exclaimed, her certainty echoing through the room. She embraced Corey, gratitude and trust radiating from her.

I weighed the emotional exchange that had just taken place, recognizing its importance, yet aware that it didn't address the underlying concern. Corey's unwavering loyalty to Rachel was undeniable, but his lack of self-preservation troubled me.

He threw himself into every battle without a second thought for his own safety, risking his life without hesitation. While he didn't seek death, the dangers he faced in the line of duty meant that if he were to fall, he wouldn't be breaking his promise to Rachel. I'd take Onoskelis' issue up to help her.

I took a step forward and redirected the conversation. My voice carried authority as I addressed the group. "Thank you, Corey, for your response to a tough question. While you take a moment to collect yourself, CJ, Fitz, Nathan, Nicole, Trish, Onoskelis, and I request your presence for a follow-up discussion on an unrelated matter once this meeting concludes."

Corey believed his answer, which is why it was honest, but the fallen angel's meaning was his self-preservation. With my declaration, I solidified my commitment to this pact, forging an alliance with the fallen angel. I even brought my friends into this pact.

Nathan surveyed the assembled council members and took charge. "Let's table that discussion for now, as Corey's response seems comprehensive. Leander, do you have a question?"

A voice emerged from the depths of darkness, belonging to Leander. "Hello again, Corey. As the head of the Coven in Chicago and the Ohio Valley Territory, I pose this question from the council. Corey, we're not here to debate or question your decision, but to understand the thought process behind this alliance. We acknowledge your right to establish a short-term alliance. We seek clarity."

Corey took a moment to absorb the softened question. "That's a fair inquiry. Many of you know this story, but those from outside the region do not. The lesson I'm about to share stems from my days in high school, under the guidance of Principal Matice." Corey relayed the story for the third time in as many days and then extended his hand, pointing toward the fallen angel. "Now, Onoskelis and I had our initial skirmish, which escalated into a full-blown fight. It took Rebecca and her hero complex to swoop in and save me." Corey turned, grinning at me.

Corey resumed his explanation with a newfound confidence. "Now, we have the opportunity for a deal. Will it lead to friendship? Perhaps it will be a short-term agreement aimed at eradicating a specific evil from the world. More likely, it will fall somewhere in the middle. But what I learned from that high school experience is that just because someone starts as your enemy, it doesn't mean they have to remain that way. That's the logic behind my decision."

Nathan glanced at Corey with genuine admiration. "Wow, Corey, you're on fire today. Let's move on to the next question."

"One second Nathan," interrupted Corey. "It occurs to me a valid question is why would I be using this story now. I'd like to explain that until August, I was still in training with the great man, Old Donnie. You know him as the druid, Donald Abernathy. I never had to make these levels of decisions before, as he used his wisdom to train me to make them. I hope that answers your question." He nodded to Nathan to continue.

Corey continued to impress me, he even answered unasked questions.

In a composed manner, Nathan announced, "We have a remote question from the Rockies."

A voice resonated from the speaker, inquiring about the report Corey's team had run on the Shared Supernatural System that raised concerns.

Corey took a deep breath before answering, aware of the impact his response would have on me. "They briefed me on the report, but I read a summary paragraph. They swore me to secrecy, and they did not prepare the report in my territory. Hence, I'm not well-versed in the protocol. I cannot provide any further information on that question."

Corey's answers were alert and concise. I couldn't help but wonder where he had been the previous night and what arrangements he had made with Rachel. His sudden display of intelligence left me intrigued.

Nathan proceeded with the meeting. "We have a remote question from the Key West Territory."

A voice emanated from the speaker, seeking insights into the situation between the Southeast and the Delta Territory.

"I can offer you speculation since all our actions have been defensive." Corey spoke carefully on the tricky subject. "A century ago, the US government enlisted the help of the Realized to eradicate vampires from the panhandle. My mentor, Old Donnie, accomplished this task, leading to the birth of the Delta vampires. Naturally, they held a grudge. However, their numbers are dwindling. They listed two hundred and fifty-one Realized, yet they've lost over two hundred documented vampires in Virginia, Tennessee, and Georgia."

Corey gathered his thoughts, taking a moment to catch his breath. "The chaos ensuing from the Alpharetta attack hindered precise readings of vampire casualties. It would be wise for an ally to check on them because I doubt they can maintain their functionality much longer."

Impressed by Corey's eloquence and political insight, I marveled at his ability to persuade. I considered the implications of his words, contemplating Corey's dangerous tendencies and the urgent need for a conversation among the concerned individuals.

Nathan announced, "Last question from May of the Southwest Territory."

"Young druid, what is your stance regarding being submitted at North American War Leader by Chesapeake Bay?" The woman spoke with a lisp like she had a forked tongue and I saw a tail underneath her dress yet she held onto Preacher Jon's hands like they were lovers.

Corey stood, ready to address the inquiry. "First, congratulations. This is the first question that has caught me off guard. I imagine they put forth my name because I led a team to take down the ancient evil. Since the Delta Territory also attacked us while our team was out, we were on communications lockdown by my order. Last night, I needed to renew my connection with the Fey Spring Court and returned just in time for this meeting. Nathan and I will discuss this topic further, taking everyone's input into consideration. We will discuss responsibilities, time, politics, and anything else that a simple druid such as myself could not contemplate. I wish I could provide more information, but I have none."

I couldn't help but wonder about Corey's recent activities and the toll they had taken on him. Then it hit me. He ignored our warnings and went to Serene Pond in the Fey Spring Court. That's why he was so alert. I told him not to travel to that spot. This was another example of his reckless behavior.

However, with the formal meeting concluded, I scanned the room, identifying the individuals I needed to confer with regarding Corey's well-being and his risky behavior. We would find a secluded place to discuss these matters while Corey enjoyed the company of his friends, hugging and catching up with them. The concerns surrounding him demanded immediate attention, and I intended to address them.

Nathan stood up, signaling the end of the meeting. "Thank you, everyone. I understand side meetings will be necessary, and we have this room at our disposal for the rest of the day."

Madison broke away from Nathan and said something to Corey and ran out, and that was unlike her. Curiously, Corey made a quick sprint to Miles, said something, and Miles chased after Madison.

I wanted to know what was happening, but my focus shifted to the task ahead. With mental notes of the individuals I needed to confer with, I searched out our conference room, determined to ensure Corey's well-being and temper his dangerous tendencies.

I NESTLED INTO THE spacious conference room that Nathan had added to his account. The attendees were a gathering from Corey's past—the people I knew could assist me in helping Corey.

The room exuded an air of comfort, furnished with a long table that seated twelve individuals. Positioned near a window, I caught glimpses of the bustling parking lot and the main road beyond. It was in that very parking lot that the trajectory of my life took an unexpected turn—a pivotal moment etched in my memory.

By the roadside stood the donut shop, the site where Corey banished a gargoyle—the first time I witnessed the magical side of the world. It was the day that rumors and hints became real in a very personal way. The memory of that event lingered in my mind as I joined the rest of our group in the conference room, ready for an important discussion.

Peridot walked into the conference room, bathing it in a golden light that touched everything except Onoskelis. "Greetings honorable Fennimore ally," he said to Onoskelis.

The Outer Realm's war must be large for an Empyrean from Celestia and a fallen angel to be allies.

He continued. "The Scion has undertaken a quest for destruction of Lance, the ancient evil. Your destruction of him will help end the Outer Realm's war, and we have noticed your contributions. Thank you."

This was unanticipated, but the Empyrean smiled and waved at me and then the five elf-like beings all disappeared.

"You know things are not going well when everyone works together," said Onoskelis. "But, slick response, Fantasy Girl. Inform Corey that you caught him, and let the rest of the group know. By the way, does anyone have any clue where Corey got those new brains?"

"He was on fire," CJ said. CJ and Fitz represented The Tribe, the location where Old Donnie had trained Corey. CJ and Fitz were giants of men, hardened through years of survival in the Appalachians and in their camouflage, looked every bit of the type of trainers who worked with Old Donnie and had honed Corey into the fighter he was.

"It's a Fey trick," I said. "He retreats to a place known as the Serene Pond in the Fey Spring Court for twelve hours. Time loses all meaning for him there, passing in an instant. But after those hours, he gains increased intelligence for a handful of hours, similar to his experience in the Fey Realm."

"Dangerous," muttered Onoskelis.

"A costly trade," Fitz, another senior member of the tribe, said.

"Not today," Nicole said in Corey's defense. "He left a message for me with Rachel, instructing her to wake him up. I can make my way to the Serene Pond as well, though I don't traverse the Fey Realm like those two do."

There was no time to waste, and the discussion shifted gears. "Alright, let's delve into Corey's self-destructive tendencies. He doesn't desire death, but he's willing to risk anything to prevent others from getting hurt, even while nursing his own injuries. He enters battles wounded and yet takes the lead," I said.

"The young man already exhausted the most potent spell a witch can conjure," Samantha added, as she and Morgan entered the room, closing the door behind them. The two witches were the ones who cast the spell and resurrected a long-dead druid bloodline to create Corey. Samantha was Corey's birth mother.

"Morgan, what a pleasant surprise," Onoskelis greeted her warily. "Has it been three hundred, or perhaps four hundred years?" she asked, her gaze fixed on the timeless figure with long, sleek black hair cascading down her back and her ever-present purple coat.

"I believe it's been quite a while." Morgan had a touch of caution coloring her voice. "Trish, did I hear you led the team to repel the vampire invasion?"

Trish leaned back in her chair, a smug smile gracing her face—a testament to her well-deserved pride. "I think the Realized folk rely on their magical powers and forget the importance of hard work and organization."

CJ erupted into laughter, a sound I hadn't heard from him since our days at the firing range before I met Corey. The joviality was a welcome respite from the weighty matters at hand.

"So, why does Corey seem to harbor a death wish?" Samantha asked.

Nicole, quick to respond, jumped in. "First, as an amateur psychologist with empathic powers, he has never overcome his abandonment issues from his family's disappearance. He devoted one hundred percent of his time to taking care of Rachel and me, neglecting his own emotional well-being. He convinced himself that his purpose was to stay alive to protect Rachel, and he never delved beyond that."

"Well said," Fitz added. "Your theory has lots of evidence."

Nicole continued with a wavering voice. "It intensified after the last major battle when he spoke with Old Donnie."

"He visited the Earth Power Creation? Crossing the line of death and visiting the location for dead druids?" Samantha asked, her eyes widening in astonishment. Earth Power Creation was where deceased druid's spirits went to distribute Earth Power and love around the world.

"Is that where Corey harnessed a pure artery of Earth Power?" Morgan asked.

"That's the place," Onoskelis confirmed.

"I can vouch for it. Corey met his father, and I can assure you, it was all too real," Morgan said. "His openness to the Realms must be frightening."

I kept us on track. "Old Donnie informed Corey that he had surpassed all expectations and helped undo a significant portion of his own troubled life. However, he had one last request, a plea borne out of acknowledging his own failures as a father. Old Donnie implored Corey to put an end to the cycle of his flawed fatherhood, both legitimate and illegitimate," I added, leaning back in my chair. "This revelation reawakened all his dormant fears."

The name "March" held an inexplicable dread for Corey, even though he couldn't quite articulate the reason behind it. "Corey fears an incomplete name, the name 'March,'" I shared, watching for any reaction from the fallen angel among us. I even hoped for someone to brooch the name of Marrianna.

Onoskelis shifted, her expression blank before returning to its usual stoic facade.

"Whom does he trust?" Morgan's gaze focused on each one of us.

"Rachel, above all," Nicole said. "Then there's a tier of individuals led by Rebecca, followed by me, Fitz, CJ, Carol, Richard, and Miles. He rarely questions us unless it's something outlandish. The next tier includes those he holds in high regard, though he exercises caution and fact-checks their information. Trish, Nathan, Preacher Jon, Wesley, Samantha, and Morgan."

"What are the odds of Rachel reaching out to him?" Onoskelis asked.

"Zero," Nicole and I said simultaneously.

"Hold on. I understand Corey better than most people, and I've started unraveling some crucial insights about him. First, he believes that excuse he gave about Rachel," I said. "He forms friendships with anyone he can. However, as some of us have learned firsthand, he can be ruthlessly protective of those he cares about. I say this because I no longer view this as a simple issue with him."

"I've already attempted to give him a direct order to stay out of harm's way, but his argument that there's no one else to take the frontline is solid," CJ said.

"The vision," Morgan interrupted.

"That must be the key," Samantha agreed.

"What vision are you referring to?" Trish asked.

"The bigger boobs vision," Nicole said. "Corey envisioned Rebecca as an angel in battle attire even before she became the Scion. Rachel remains unchanged in his eyes, and he sees me adorned with feathers on my shoulders, wearing armor with a unique plant-like motif, while Madison wields her bow. Everyone but Rachel had bigger boobs, though."

"Hold up," said CJ with a chuckle.

We needed to explain this so I took over. "Corey had a post death vision of myself, Nicole, Rachel, and Madison geared up for battle. When he showed it to Nicole with his thoughts, we all had larger breasts. We've been calling it the bigger boobs vison for lack of a better term. However, Nicole and I are untrained, so we're at least two years away from the warrior intent of the vision becoming a reality."

"Five or six years of training more likely," Onoskelis said. "But you still have time before all hell breaks loose—ten to twenty years. Most predictions will start crumbling beyond the ten-year mark, signifying that the battle draws near."

"In that case, we must ensure Corey remains alive for the next six years," Fitz proposed, determination etched on his face.

"We need to help him confront his fatherhood issues," Nicole added.

"Uncover the driving forces behind his actions," I continued, my thoughts veering toward my own requirements.

"We need to guide him in addressing his abandonment issues," Trish contributed, her voice laced with empathy.

"And, if possible, make him fall in love with me before the babies make me lose my figure," Nicole said.

Ouch. I thought I saw Nicole's face contort when she said Corey trusted me before her.

"We must combat the greatest evil plaguing our world, prepare for the big battle, and ensure my Nephilim charges remain unharmed," Onoskelis concluded, a weighty task laid before us. "Plus,

I believe we are days away from discovering the hidden enemy. Portents are aligning."

The room fell silent as we absorbed the magnitude of our responsibilities, aware that the fate of our intertwined destinies rested on our shoulders.

Chapter 19—Rebecca and Madison

The sun began its descent, casting a warm golden glow over Corey's patio. It was a precious moment, a chance for respite in the chaos that had consumed our lives. Nestled on a cushioned seat, I delved into a weighty report. Corey, his features softened by sleep, cradled Valkyrie beside him. On his other shoulder, Nicole slumbered, her breathing rhythmic and serene.

Meanwhile, Nathan manned the grill, conjuring aromas that wafted through the air. Assisted by a gleaming set of grilling tools, a Christmas gift from Corey, he cooked with expertise. Madison stood by his side, offering both support and a mischievous squeeze to his rear end.

Wesley and Rachel were the absentees among us. Corey's patio, adorned with cherished memories from our past, now served as the gathering place for our tight-knit group. Each moment was a testament to the indelible bonds we had formed.

As I allowed my thoughts to wander, I reflected on the gathering at the theater. It was a rarity to see so many Realized individuals congregated in one place, a phenomenon acknowledged even by my grandmother. When I posed the question to her, she chuckled and said, "Not in my lifetime."

Meanwhile, my grandmother and a diverse group of companions enjoyed a lavish evening at a posh restaurant. Leander, Onoskelis, Morgan, Samantha, Preacher Jon, and Mayven accompanied her.

Valkyrie lifted her head and surveyed her surroundings. Her senses detected a faint sound that escaped our notice. After a moment, she settled back down, her calm demeanor reassuring us. Nathan distributed plates, and I tore my gaze away from the report, frustration simmering within me. It provided a comprehensive listing of our comrades and their unique abilities, yet its convoluted nature only obscured the information I sought.

Exasperated, I couldn't help but voice my frustration to the group. "Does anyone possess the expertise to decipher these capabilities reports?"

Corey gave a reassuring response. "I can assist, though it's not my forte. Let me fetch an old one I created with The Tribe." His suggestion carried a hint of nostalgia, a remnant of his training days.

Madison exuded confidence as she volunteered her expertise. With a hamburger in hand, she inspected the report displayed on my computer screen, munching. "This isn't a proper report; it's nothing more than busywork," she concluded with a wry smile.

My frustration grew, and I admitted defeat. "I can't make sense of this," I confessed, feeling the weight of confusion bearing down on me.

Corey's response offered a glimmer of hope. "Here's one I compiled during my training, tailored for a team of sixty. It contains rows, columns, and codes that convey crucial information such as morale, readiness, and other pertinent details."

Madison nodded in agreement. "This is the capabilities report you need. I'll transfer it onto my laptop and make it more presentable."

Excitement coursed through my veins as the potential held within this newfound clarity. It wasn't just the report itself that invigorated me; it was the understanding it provided. Perusing its contents, I marveled at the organized wealth of information, from conventional weapons to specialized gear, battle readiness to the intricate complexities of Realized power and battle-tested ratings.

The prospect of capturing our capabilities in a tangible format stirred a sense of purpose within me. "But let's not stop there. We should create a tailored report for our own group. We may store the knowledge within Corey and Nathan's minds for now, but it's time to transform it into something tangible, something we can share," I resolved, a newfound determination taking root.

Corey tended to Valkyrie's needs, ensuring she was well-fed. The cost of her upkeep was significant, but her unwavering loyalty made every penny worthwhile. "When you talk to your team in Virginia, do not ask for the report. Tell."

Curiosity piqued, I probed further. "What do you mean?" I asked.

With a skillful imitation of Old Donnie's voice, Corey donned an air of wisdom. "Corey, people are funny. They rebel against being told what to do but need someone in charge who is competent. If you ask for something, you won't get it. When you are in charge, give orders with confidence."

Nathan emphasized Corey's point. "Grandpa Jon has mastered the art of turning orders into persuasive requests, making obedience a seamless choice."

Corey and Nathan's shared laughter rippled through the gathering. With newfound determination, I transcribed the order to compile the summary list of the report, incorporating Madison's input.

Seated beside Nicole, Corey leaned toward Nathan, catching his attention. "Nathan, did you consider verifying the intention of the word 'everyone' in that text message?"

Nathan's grin widened. "Oh, I thought about it. But then it would require a day's worth of work and countless behind-the-scenes conversations. Besides, I wanted to witness how many Realized would show at your request."

A shared chuckle rippled through the group. "All the conversations taking place and the growth of our community seen country-wide turned out to be incredible," said Nicole. "My baby showed us at our finest."

"Corey, you surpassed all expectations, silencing the arguments of those who doubted your communication skills and casting aside any doubts about your ability to wield your power," Nathan praised, patting the inside of Madison's leg. "With all of us on the same page, our command structure remains unassailable."

Madison joined in, her laughter blending with the gentle evening breeze. "And let's not forget how the enchanted arrows you gifted me silenced any lingering doubts about trust within the team," she exclaimed, her eyes sparkling with gratitude. "They served as a perfect testament to our unity."

"Alright, while we have some time, Corey, create a secrecy circle for the four of us. Rebecca, Madison, please join Corey and me in the circle," said Nathan.

Finally, we'd be all on the same page. Plus, we'd find out why Madison charged out of the meeting.

"So, those of us who can't shield our thoughts will sit on the patio... alone," Nicole teased. Corey patted her on the backside as she passed, causing her to smile.

We settled on the grass, and nothing changed, except Corey appeared more relaxed. "Alright," he said.

Madison started us off. "First, let's ensure everyone is on the same page. Marrianna is a human Nephilim, created by a now-deceased fallen angel named Marchosias and Old Donnie. She has been posing as the AI in the Shared Supernatural System."

I tried to hold it together, but a human Nephilim was an aberration to the universal laws. Some laws seemed silly, like angels must trade their services for equal value, but if anyone broke the rules, our universe would cease to exist. She could destroy our universe.

"But she was also in the church system," I argued. Maybe they were wrong about her, but I knew in my heart this problem was worse than Lance.

"Yes, she moves between the two. Aaron discovered the connection between the systems by following Corey's lead," said Nathan. "But let's focus on the new information."

"When I became Realized and gained helpful powers, I didn't take any additional bow abilities," said Madison. "One power I gained is *Permanent Tracking*."

Wow, that sounded impressive.

"At the meeting, something invisible bumped into me, and I felt a smooth exoskeleton, like that of a crab. I informed Corey and tracked it while the magic stayed active," Madison continued.

"All hunters can track allies, but Madison's ability allows her to track prey she has seen or touched without flaw," Corey clarified. "I sent Miles to ensure her safety."

"Well, he saved my life. Listen to this. I tracked it for a few miles, and then a boy—around fifteen—appeared and confronted it. It was still invisible, but he didn't notice. He didn't use any powers. Corey, that kid, would out fight you. He killed that Dark Fey and a gargoyle with just a knife and a tire iron. Miles agreed that the kid was a scary good fighter and made sure I stayed hid from him."

"What?" Corey looked incredulous. "I'm about to help train people in The Tribe. There's no one like that in the Southeast."

"He doesn't register as having the spark," said Nathan. "I checked the sensors."

"It gets even stranger. As I chased the older boy, a seven or eight-year-old boy saw me, and he disappeared in a swirl of gold, silver, green, red, purple, black, and brown magic that sent out a wave toward me. Miles tackled me and shielded us with his Fey shield, but the little boy still tossed us about."

"That's a Nephilim. Is Marrianna eight years old?" asked Corey.

"No," said Nathan. "You're right. He did leave a signature, but when I entered it into the Shared Supernatural System, the AI deleted it. Long story short, this afternoon Aaron and I went through off-loaded sensor logs. We discovered another Nephilim signature from the sixties, erased from the system."

"The nineteen-sixties?" I asked.

He nodded. "We have no further information, but as Battle Leader, you need to be informed about what's happening. Rebecca, you're the first person in Chesapeake Bay to know."

"I think the little boy prevented me from following the older boy, but I don't know why," said Madison, shrugging.

A teenager with no magic, who was a better fighter than Corey? Two human Nephilim, one of them a small child, and now a dead Dark Fey and a gargoyle. We had one thing to connect the pieces. "Onoskelis said we were close to finding our unknown enemy and we have. Marrianna has been pulling the strings behind the scenes for decades."

Madison frowned and stated her knowledge to calm herself. "An angel and a person with the spark will produce a beast like in the caves. A shaman and an angel will produce a giant. However, a druid and an angel produce the greatest evil. The Nephilim will appear to us as a human but it uses all the magic of all the realms and is not bound by our universal laws."

"They can take control of our universal bubble and remake it," added Corey.

"Or steal the power of our bubble universe to go into the greater universe" He paused. "Or coordinate and start an Outer Realm's war."

The circle became quiet. We had marching orders to take out Lance, but this news became our largest concern.

Stepping out of the circle, I absorbed everything. Knowing the enemy did not make me feel better. A human Nephilim could kill angels, take over a continent-wide AI system, coordinate with other bubble universes, and bring ancient evils into play as needed. How could we fight it?

The sliding door glided open, revealing Rachel and Wesley, their faces flushed. Nicole, not knowing our heavy conversation, sprang to her feet playfully. "Hold on, I have just the remedy for your dehydration," she exclaimed. With a playful wink, she retrieved two large bottles of water from the cooler's icy depths.

Nicole's playful banter continued, drawing laughter from everyone present. "Luckily, no one thought to call the police," she teased. It was a pleasant break from the weightiness of the situation.

Rachel dismissed any hint of embarrassment. "I'm thirsty, but I'm not embarrassed." She wasted no time in quenching her thirst, guzzled half a liter. Meanwhile, Wesley busied himself preparing plates with care. As they settled by the fire, Valkyrie approached Rachel and rested her head in her lap, offering silent comfort.

Nicole seized the moment and couldn't resist a playful remark. "Now that Rachel has her water, I can claim my rightful place on my husband's—or should I say, fiancé's—lap," she said, a twinkle of mischief dancing in her eyes.

"The Fey Spring Court acknowledged you as the Consort to the Druid of the Fey Spring Court. You could call me 'druid,'" Corey teased her. His ability to move from universe ending information to playful banter was wonderful. The patio seemed to hold its breath, basking in the beauty of our connections.

Wings fluttered through the air as Onoskelis descended from the heavens, exuding an air of mystique. Adorned in a breathtaking black evening gown, she landed in a scene of enchantment—a cozy setting illuminated by the warm glow of a crackling fire and embraced by the joyful laughter of couples.

The fallen angel kicked off the meeting with a taunt, her voice dripping with sardonic amusement. "Isn't this cozy? Roaring fire, happy couples. Wait, fantasy girl, you're alone? There must be a quarter of a million men in this city alone who want to hold you."

A concerned furrow etched across Corey's brow as he approached Rebecca. "Whoa," said Corey. "Rebecca has a lot to overcome. She's going to lead the Chesapeake Bay Territory, and her last date turned out to be an ancient evil."

Eager to defend my honor, I couldn't help but interject. "Hey, hero!" I called out, a mixture of frustration and determination lacing my words. "I am more than capable of fighting my own battles. Given the chance, I will find someone who appreciates me for more than the trials we face."

"You shouldn't be too quick to dismiss Corey's role as your hero, considering how often you've been his," taunted Onoskelis.

Heat rose to my cheeks as I rebuffed the notion. "Just because he verbalized it doesn't make it true."

Unyielding, the fallen angel continued her appraisal. "Corey, Rachel, and Valkyrie would still be confined to their vulnerable states if it weren't for your intervention with your *Celestial Sanctuary*," she said. "I hear you made a perfect shot, taking down a Snake Hunter. Preacher Jon even mentioned how you never hesitated to protect Corey."

My ankle adorned with the marks of my triumphs; I couldn't help but question the comparison. "But those accomplishments are not the same," I argued, frustration threading through my voice.

Corey intervened once more; his voice filled with newfound self-awareness. "Let's not bicker," he proposed, a glimmer of understanding in his eyes. "It has taken me time to acknowledge my hero complex. Every time someone threatened Rachel, Rebecca, or Nicole, I charged in, driven by an inherent need to protect. I'm embracing who I am."

Nicole leaned back, her eyes filled with concern, seeking reassurance. "Are you okay?" she asked, giving him a playful wink.

A pang of vulnerability pierced Corey's facade. "No," he confessed, his voice laced with raw honesty. "The thought of becoming a father terrifies me. The mere idea of putting our loved ones in danger fills me with dread. Even our marriage brings a wave of worry. I fear losing those who surround us. But I am learning to take things one step at a time, and right now, I need to confront the perception that I have a hero complex."

Onoskelis spoke with authority. "Shed that burden. You are far too valuable to lose."

Corey's voice brimmed with self-assurance. "I wouldn't possess any value if I weren't the person I am."

Stepping forward, Madison steered the conversation toward a different path. "Hello, I'm Madison," she introduced herself with a warm smile, her presence commanding attention. "We haven't had the chance to meet until now. Why do you want to take out the ancient evil?"

Thank you, Madison. I'd meant to ask this earlier, but her thorough answer to my first question allowed her to move on.

"Well, Madison." She drew a breath. "You, with your destiny to restore the glory of the Appalachian witches before fate and druid magic intervened—I have a deep-rooted desire for the Earth to endure long after humans cease to exist. Most fallen angels are arrogant, convinced that the destruction of the Earth will somehow guarantee their return home. But I hold no such belief. You and your friends possess the potential to aid in the battle to save Earth."

Lost in contemplation, I pondered the significance of this revelation. What if Corey had remained ensnared by his prejudices and refused to work alongside a fallen angel, as I would have?

Corey's voice broke the silence. "On that rather cheery note, we depart in the morning. Our team will comprise me—"

"Hold on," Wesley said. "I have one job and have to see everyone's gory deaths over and over. I'll tell you who is going tomorrow morning."

"Huh, that's fair." Corey conceded and pulled Nicole closer to him in his chair.

Inside his trance, Wesley spoke aloud. "Corey, Rachel, Rebecca, and Onoskelis... No, let's add Valkyrie. Ah, even worse, Madison joins the ranks too. Whoa, that's bad. Nathan's life depends on her presence tomorrow," Wesley relayed, his tone heavy with the weight of his gift—seeing the deaths of his friends.

Curiosity piqued, Onoskelis leaned forward, her eyes gleaming with interest. "He possesses the ability to glimpse into the future?" she asked.

Rachel turned around, detaching herself from her boyfriend's embrace. "He sees when and how people will meet their end. Every detail," she confirmed, a mix of awe and trepidation threading through her words.

Approval escaped Onoskelis' lips. "He would make an exceptional fallen angel."

He spoke with a command. "Nicole, you must join them. Madison, Miles, Trish, and I need to venture to <u>Miles Away from Town</u> tomorrow."

"I'll meet the lovebirds and the fantasy girl at the campsite during lunchtime," Onoskelis added, a playful note creeping into her words.

I hated to complain, but I needed to. "Make it a late lunch. Last time, Corey worked our legs, and my thighs have yet to recover."

MADISON LUXURIATED in the tranquil embrace of the patio, reminiscing about the bygone days of blissful family gatherings before her grandparents' time. Tonight, as the troubles that plagued them faded into the background, she found solace in Nathan's company. His arm cradled her, offering a comforting presence.

"Corey, Madison and I will stay here tonight," Nathan said. "I'll research what Wesley witnessed about our team."

Corey probably didn't hear how Nathan would be on his laptop, researching the new information in the Shared Supernatural System. The druid had already scooped up Nicole and headed for the tree covered with sap from the woodpecker. His ability to give a thumbs-up surprised Madison, considering the intensity of their gaze, hinting at their plans for the night.

Rebecca broke the silence. "I've changed the sheets in the back bedroom. You two can take that one." She pointed towards the cleaned room. "As for these two, they can keep the room they've been using."

Madison couldn't witness Rachel's mischievous grin, but she could sense it in the air. Despite the girl's earlier apprehension about her relationship with Wesley, they seemed to do just fine.

At the dining room table, laptop at the ready, the throbbing ache stole Madison's attention in her leg—the lingering reminder of the bullet wound. The small team's workload had placed an immense burden on Nathan, and in her desire to prove she belonged, she accepted on additional responsibilities.

"Honey, you're perspiring. Let me fetch something to ease our pain," Madison poured two glasses of with glasses of water and pain medication, she handed one to Nathan.

Madison scooted closer to him. "Now, what will expedite our journey to bed?"

Nathan swallowed the medicine. "Could you please summarize the Chesapeake Bay and Key West territories for the next three days? Focus on identifying tier one and tier two threats."

"I'll search from can see to can't see," she said.

"What in the world?" Nathan exclaimed. His email was open and showed a formal letter from Chesapeake Bay.

Rising from his seat, he swung open the sliding screen door, prompting Madison to follow suit. It was rare to witness Nathan's sudden movements, and it piqued her intrigue.

"Rebecca, are you the Battle Leader of the Chesapeake Bay Territory, assigned to the Southeast Territory, with deference to Battle Leader Norwood for training?" His portable printer churned out pages on the table behind Madison, yet the unfolding conversation held far more intrigue.

Apologies tumbled from Rebecca's lips, mingling with a sigh of resignation. "Nathan, I had forgotten the proper protocols." She continued, her resolve wavering. "I, Rebecca Adams, heir to the Addkinson Family Estate and appointed heir to the leadership of the Chesapeake Bay Territory, have been assigned as Battle Leader. Grandmother instructed me to continue my work here until..." Rebecca's voice trailed off, her struggle to maintain composure clear.

Without hesitation, Madison rushed forward, enfolding Rebecca in a comforting embrace. "It's alright. That's quite a mouthful, and you don't have to have all the answers right now," she said.

Rebecca's sniffles mingled with her heartfelt embrace. "I meant to tell everyone."

Nathan's tone softened as he inquired further. "Does Corey know?" His concern reverberated through the air, softening the atmosphere.

Rebecca nodded, her eyes glistening with unshed tears.

Rachel rose from Wesley's lap and joined in the embrace, enveloping Madison and Rebecca in a shared moment of support. "And I knew as well. You can yell at me—I haven't had my turn yet." Even Valkyrie leaned against her hip.

"No worries. Congratulations are in order," Nathan said leaving the door open. "I got the formal document so everything is legal.

"Could you join us inside? I'll show both you and Madison how to navigate the Shared Supernatural System with a joint territory search."

Guiding Rebecca, Madison led her towards the inviting sanctuary of the indoors, settling her in front of her computer. Rebecca retrieved her phone, her fingers tapping away at the screen. "I have the logins, but I'll need to call Kim for activation."

"Rebecca, Kim works late. She's more of a noon-to-ten person," Nathan said.

Rebecca dialed the number, her fingers inputting the login information on Madison's laptop. The speaker crackled to life, and a melodious Virginian accent resonated through the room. "Hi, Rebecca! We adored your dating app profile."

Rebecca laughed, a lightness to her voice. "I did not intend the main picture to be provocative, but Nicole insisted it was the best choice."

"Well, it worked! So, what can I assist you with?" Kim's voice oozed enthusiasm.

"I'm calling to activate my ID. I'm reading the email containing the information," Rebecca said.

Kim didn't know Rebecca had her on speaker. "One moment, please. While we wait, could you put in a good word for me with Nathan?" Kim's request floated through the air; anticipation woven into her words.

Nathan perked up, intrigued yet silent, waiting for the outcome.

"Of course. What is it for?" Rebecca asked.

Kim's voice crackled through the speaker once more. "My boyfriend has a regular job, and he's up for a promotion in Atlanta. He's asked me to join him, and considering the growth you all are experiencing, I'm guessing there will be IT positions opening up. I would love to apply."

Nathan's fingers danced across his phone's screen, his text conveying his response to Rebecca. She glanced at her phone and shared the news. "Nathan mentioned earlier that there will be official positions available in January. Send me your resume."

"Thank you so much! There, the system has verified you. You'll notice several new icons. Whenever you have time, let me know if you need a walkthrough or help with anything," Kim concluded.

"Appreciate your help. Good night," Rebecca bid her farewell, ending the call.

Nathan chuckled, a ripple of amusement coursing through the room. "Preacher Jon is away for just a couple of weeks, and upon his return, it seems we will double our ranks. We are so desperate for IT support that CJ warned me against poaching his personnel. I can call Aaron for help."

"Virginia and Atlanta may soon become kissing cousins at this rate." Madison settled into a chair beside Rebecca.

"Look at this. The Council of the Realized has censured the Delta Territory. Of all the dead vampires, not a single one was on the official Delta Territory roster," Nathan said.

"What does that mean?" asked Madison, curious about the implications.

"It means everyone knows something is going on there, and it's documented. No actions yet, but at least everyone is monitoring them, and it's not just the Southeast Territory complaining," Nathan said. "Now, when I put in the report that our sensors picked up that none of the vampires in the attack had the spark, others will research it, too."

That didn't seem like much, but if Nathan thought it was important, it must be.

Rebecca yawned but spoke up. "Nathan, I've been scatterbrained, but you have another out of territory person here because of me. He's an artist named Christopher Murphy who claims I'm next on his list. He's been lurking around and even had Corey throw a knife at him."

Nathan rolled his eyes. "If he deigns to paint you. Sometimes he shows up just to insult people who commission him. Let's focus on something more likely to happen."

Rachel had entered and grabbed some paper towels. "Don't worry about him leaving. Nicole said Christopher has a crush on Rebecca."

"He doesn't have a crush on me. He sees paintings with me in them," said Rebecca. "His first painting is a mural of Corey and me. Grandmother is working out the details now."

Rebecca wouldn't notice how many men had crushes on her, her and Leah had the same kind of beauty men wanted. The three of them searched much longer than it should have taken since searches were slower without using the built in AI took. But they had better confidence in the answers. Hours passed with obscured information; barriers found at every turn. Then Madison had a breakthrough. An idea struck her—an Outer Realms being wouldn't understand well: weather. She found the missing piece that tied everything else together.

"Look at this," Madison exclaimed after a while.

"The weather?" Rebecca asked. Weariness half closed her eyes.

"The sudden temperature shift creates an ethereal atmosphere, and there's an unexpected skrift. Combine that with the surge in Gullah activity." Madison's voice brimmed with excitement.

"Hold on, I think you're onto something," Nathan said. "When casters exert significant magical energy, it depletes the surrounding area's energy, creating a low-pressure weather system."

Madison nodded in agreement. "Exactly. The Delta vampires shattered a magical barrier, unleashing Boo Hags, while reports show that the Gullah lost control of a spell."

Rebecca's exhaustion made it difficult for her to process more at the moment. "I can't handle any more right now. I need some rest."

"Let me help you to bed, and I'll be back," Madison offered. With a gentle guiding hand, she led Rebecca towards Corey's bed—a place where Rebecca seemed to find solace more often than Corey himself.

Chapter 20—Rebecca and Madison

Under the gentle morning light, Corey and I stood before Nathan, anticipation filling the air as we awaited the crucial briefing. The good night of sleep certainly helped, but the weight of responsibility pressed upon me. "I don't know what to do. There are too many variables in motion, and I'm unsure of the resources at my disposal."

Corey met my gaze with understanding. "You possess more knowledge than you realize. I'll help guide you through it."

Relief washed over me, "Please. I can't afford to make mistakes in the first battle as leader."

"Of course," Corey said. He delved into his notes from an Army training manual, seeking clarity as he posed a question to Nathan. "Do we have documented immediate actions for a known attack in our Territory?"

Nathan shook his head.

"Very well," Corey said. "Could you compile a list of necessary documentation and create immediate action plans for suspected attacks, validated attacks, and surprise attacks?"

"I'll start the list," Madison said.

"Excellent. Thank you." Corey nodded to me to read Chesapeake Bay's immediate action plans.

I read the attack preparation actions from the Chesapeake Bay manual aloud. "Step one, alert the Territory leader and assemble the on-call battle team. Step two, activate the emergency response team and start round-the-clock monitoring of territory incursions, with reports required every six hours. Step three, determine the nature of the attack. And finally, step four, develop a comprehensive defense plan."

Corey nodded approvingly. "That's an excellent plan. Before you make the calls, run your actions by me."

Once again, Corey's presence became a shield, protecting me from the doubts that gnawed at my resolve. "Let me make some notes," he said, transitioning into the confidant I desired.

"Let's discuss this in the car." Then he called out through the house. "Say your goodbyes, Rachel. It's time to go."

Nicole jumped inside with a flourish. "The car's packed and overloaded."

"Nathan, let's establish two points of communication," Corey proposed, his mind already focused on the next steps. "I suggest Rebecca handles the communications for Chesapeake Bay, while Nicole oversees communications for the Southeast defense and the Lance mission."

"Very well," Nathan agreed. Turning to Madison, he assigned her a critical role. "Will you maintain communication with Rebecca?"

Madison flashed a thumbs-up.

"No one?" asked Nicole still holding her flourish.

Just as Rachel and Wesley appeared, the scene brimming with purpose, Nathan assumed command once more. "Wesley, you'll be in communication with Nicole. You'll serve as the liaison for the Southeast defense and the Lance destruction mission."

"Understood," Wesley acknowledged.

"If you're willing to hold a joke that long, I'll help you," said Rachel taking her sister's hand.

The notes from the territory plan gave me enough of a start. "I'll arrange a conference call for one hour from now, ensuring everyone in Virginia is present. I'll review the report you provided, and then we'll activate the emergency response team, requiring regular reports from both teams every six hours for the next thirty-six hours. After that, we'll increase the frequency to every two hours. I'll request the teams to share their most up-to-date defense strategies against Boo Hags or Gullah threats." I looked for support.

Corey held up one finger to me, then opened the door of the waiting SUV. "Nicole, would you mind taking the wheel?" Corey asked, sprinting around his house. "I'll be right back."

"I'm going to say it. He didn't hear a word I said." Nicole joked as she carried items.

I sat in the rear seat, burdened by the weight of responsibility that settled on my shoulders. There was reading to do while Nicole and Rachel cleaned out items from the trunk into the carport.

After the last load into the carport, I glanced up and glimpsed Corey's running approach. Determination etched his features with as he slid into the passenger seat beside Nicole, commanding attention with his presence.

"Rebecca, your plan is excellent." Corey kept his voice steady. "But remember, if anyone dares to question you, do not negotiate. They will attempt to undermine your authority. Tell them your orders are not requests and that they should document their comments in official reports. Second, label all your reports with B2312-27."

I nodded, absorbing Corey's advice. He had a way of instilling confidence in me like no one else. I turned my gaze towards him, searching for answers. "Corey, that's a code my grandmother uses." *How did he get a security breach code?*

"Yeah, where'd you go?" asked Nicole.

Corey met my gaze, a knowing smile playing at the corners of his lips. "I used the tree we setup to see your grandmother face to face to get the code." "Nicole, Nathan, and I have agreed to use the same designation, but with an 'S' for Southeast."

"So, it's like the year, the month, the twenty seventh, and 'S'?" Nicole had forgotten her joke as she typed into her phone.

"Exactly." Corey sat in the front passenger seat.

"Corey, that's an internal investigation number," I said. A knot of apprehension forming in my stomach as realization dawned on me. I shifted my gaze to the window to find that Nicole had already maneuvered the SUV onto the main road, propelling us forward into the unknown. In my mind, I listed the names of the few individuals my grandmother had deemed trustworthy—Goseling and Shevski.

"Alright, everyone, from this moment onward, secrecy is paramount," Corey said. "Spellcasters unleash Boo Hags with specific targets in mind. That they have struck both Atlanta and DC with the same spell leads Nathan and Madison to believe that we in the Southeast are nothing more than a diversion, meant to draw attention away from Chesapeake. Someone intends to exploit our team being out of contact while we deal with Lance."

The gravity of Corey's words weighed upon me. "But why? They would kill my grand..." I paused, the realization dawning on me. "Unless their true motive is to discredit me. They're after my grandmother because I'm not yet ready to assume leadership, and we have no succession plan in place. If you, I, Rachel, and Nicole are dealing with Lance, no one is there to protect my grandmother." The gravity of my promotion sunk in.

Corey agreed. "It hit me this was the perfect opportunity to take her out along with Nathan. We have to use our resources to protect Nathan, leaving your grandmother unprotected. The spell's intensity doubled at five o'clock this morning for DC," Corey said. "Rebecca, you'll be sitting in the back seat of the car, appearing alone to the outside world. No one must utter a word, and you ensure that everyone else stays off camera."

I took a deep breath as the enormity of my position sank in fully. Grandmother wouldn't leave Virginia for her safety. Doubts gnawed at the edges of my confidence, threatening to consume me. It was then that Corey's unwavering support resurfaced, his words a lifeline in the tempestuous sea of uncertainty.

"You can do this," Corey said. "Remember, we trusted the other team to defend Nicole. We can trust them to defend Nathan and your grandmother."

He trusted others to protect Nicole. Now his sacrifice was so much more significant to me. "It's all so much. Every decision I make has multiple implications." It was so easy before I had other responsibilities.

"Remember, there's more than one way to establish a stable line of succession. Nathan doesn't need to marry because they know he has my unwavering support. No one will dare challenge me. Prove to them you can handle this dilemma, and you'll find yourself in a far stronger position."

Corey's words stirred something deep within me. If I led the defense, proved I could deal with exceptional threats, and commanded the loyalty of the military, I wouldn't need to rely on finding a husband until I was ready. The realization surged through me, igniting a fierce determination to seize control of my destiny.

"So, I can take a nap then?" Rachel asked with her trademark grin.

"Sure, rest up." A soft chuckle escaped Corey's lips as he transitioned between his two personas—hard Corey and playful Corey—a skill that never failed to amaze me. But now was not the time to dwell on such details. I had help, and I would do whatever it took to fulfill my duty.

As I observed Corey, a sense of gratitude washed over me. In this world of uncertainties, he was a steady presence, a pillar of strength upon which I could lean. With his unwavering support and guidance, I felt empowered to face the challenges ahead.

With renewed determination burning in my eyes, I cast a last glance at Corey. "Thank you."

Corey nodded, a silent understanding passing between us. "You have what it takes. You're stronger than you realize."

With an unwavering expression on my face and a voice brimming with confidence, I took dialed up the phone and took charge of the video meeting. "Let us begin. We are about to face a flurry of hectic days," I said, determined to embody the resolute nature of hard Corey. These were the same individuals who had argued with grandmother in the previous meeting, but this time, I would not allow them.

As the meeting started, two figures appeared on the camera while the rest avoided sitting on camera. My eyes scanned the ranks of the two I could see, identifying a commander and a lieutenant. Ah, those must be the two individuals my grandmother spoke of—those whom I could trust.

"The first piece of information concerns the attack in the Chesapeake Bay Territory. We verified this as tier one," I said.

A masculine voice, coming from somewhere off-screen, spoke with a hint of skepticism. "Shouldn't we verify the information ourselves before reconvening? We need our own intelligence. Let's end this meeting and I'll reschedule."

In that moment, I swallowed my anger. What would Corey do? "Who said that?" I demanded.

Silence permeated the room as no one dared to speak up.

"Speak up, now!" I maintained Corey's stern countenance.

Finally, a voice broke the silence, belonging to Major MacKinnon, the Head of Information. However, he did not deem it necessary to show his face on camera to address me.

I pressed on, undeterred. "Is Commander Goseling present?" I demanded. I'd make a statement. They'd learn there was a hard Rebecca like hard Corey.

"Relieve Major MacKinnon of his duties until further notice. Did his second-in-command attend?" I controlled my anger, having learned from past battles the importance of restraint.

"Ma'am, may I know the charges against him?" Commander Goseling asked.

"Certainly. He displayed a lack of immediate action knowledge in the face of an active threat, failed to comprehend the chain of command, and crucially—failed to provide the ordered summary report prior to the attack. Send me the paperwork for his reassignment. I'll add the codes and signatures. Now, unless anyone else intends to hinder this meeting, I'd like to proceed."

Silence continued to prevail.

"Very well. Boo Hags are a targeted group that feeds off the breath of their victims, rendering them helpless. They possess the ability to don the skin of their chosen victim and assume their guise. However, the defense against Gullah magic is missing from our action plans. Include the plan in the initial report. We require validation of information and a status report on both the emergency response team and the ongoing operations team. This will be a thirty-six-hour period, with reports submitted every six hours, after which we will transition to a two-hour interval."

Rebecca opened the floor to questions. "Questions?"

"Yes, ma'am," a voice said. "Lieutenant Commander Shevski, from the Communications division. If the Southeast Territory is also under attack, do we have a designated point of contact?"

"Yes," I said, locating the contact details within the meeting invite. "I will provide you with the information in one hour. They will have a single point of contact, so will we."

"Ma'am, do we know if we can expect help from the Southeast Territory?" Lieutenant Commander Shevski asked.

"The Southeast Territory is under lockdown, and as I am engaged in a mission alongside them, it falls within our operational status. However, the Chesapeake Bay Territory possesses ample resources and should not require help from other territories for a singular attack."

The room fell into a hushed silence, the weight of the situation settling upon us all.

"Thank you for attending this meeting. I would like to remind everyone that if you choose to be present in the meeting room but opt to remain off-camera, submit your resignation to me prior to the start of the meeting. This will allow me to arrange for a suitable replacement. I await your first report at thirteen-thirty." With those last words, I concluded the call.

Turning off the phone, Corey's gaze reassured me. "You did great! I understand the pain of those calls, and I am proud of you. My first call, where Old Donnie made me lead a search and rescue mission, fell apart."

As exhaustion threatened to overtake me, my inbox flooded with messages demanding attention. I knew I had to connect Madison and Shevski to ensure the seamless coordination of efforts.

MADISON, ACCOMPANIED by Nathan and Wesley, arrived at Miles Away from Town. The store gave a welcoming and freeing atmosphere. They approached the entrance, ready to assist Miles and Trish in establishing a Command Center away from the connections to the Shared Supernatural System.

To their surprise, Clive, a vampire, awaited their arrival, accompanied by a handful of his nocturnal brethren. Just days ago, she had fought against vampires, their fangs bared in ferocity. Yet, today, she worked with friends who happened to be vampires. It was a strange twist of fate, a testament to the ever-shifting nature of her reality.

Pulling her phone from her pocket, Madison prepared to assume her role in the Mobile Command Center. She understood the gravity of the situation, the need for professionalism and formality in their interactions. With a composed demeanor, she raised the device to her ear and spoke, her voice steady and commanding. This new responsibility felt familiar to her; she had manned phones for a crisis hotline in high school.

"Mobile Command Center," Madison answered, her tone imbued with authority and confidence. Though Nathan had not provided specific instructions on the exact words to use, she knew the importance of maintaining a formal approach.

On the other end of the line was Rebecca, whose voice echoed through the phone, introducing Lieutenant Command Shevski as their point of contact for inter-territory communications. Madison acknowledged the information.

"Excellent," Madison said with gratitude. "Thank you for the introduction, Battle Leader Adams. Our status is 'Prepared,' and we have deployed our defense groups on site."

Rebecca conveyed her well wishes before the call ended. The line fell silent, leaving Madison poised and eager to connect with Lieutenant Command Shevski, who remained on the other end of the line.

"Hello, Mobile Command Center," the male voice called out, seeking reassurance of her presence.

"Yes, I'm still here," Madison said, her voice carrying a hint of relief, infusing reassurance into its fabric.

"How formal should we be?" he asked. "When it's just the two of us versus a group, informality may be more appropriate. However, in a group setting, I understand the need for titles such as 'Southeast Mobile Command Center' and 'Chesapeake Emergency Response Team.'"

"I'm Madison," she introduced herself, injecting warmth into her voice. It was essential to bridge the gap between formality and familiarity, forging connections in the face of impending danger.

"Great. I'm Dave." Relief seeped into his words. Madison's presence seemed to reassure him, dispelling any lingering apprehension.

"Are you Dave Shevski?" Madison asked.

"That's me," he confirmed. They laid the foundation for a fruitful partnership, and Madison sensed the burgeoning camaraderie. "Are you Madison Roane?" Dave asked.

"That's me." This was her moment to shine, to prove she was multi-faceted and could fill many roles and fit in.

"Great, I'll add you to our status updates. They will remain confidential," Dave informed her, emphasizing the gravity of the information they would exchange. Trust was paramount in their line of work.

"I'll gather as much information as I can and ensure its approval," she said, her mind already brimming with plans and strategies. "Good luck."

"Thank you. You too." The weight of their responsibilities hung in the air, but the knowledge that they had each other's support fortified their resolve.

As Madison returned to Nathan's side, she couldn't help but ponder the strange encounter she had just experienced. Dave's apprehension in the presence of Rebecca had caught her attention. With her mind teeming with questions, she sought solace in the familiar task at hand—compiling the information they needed to share with their newfound allies.

Observing Nathan, she noticed a slight quiver in his demeanor. His unease was palpable, his eyes darting around as if expecting an unseen threat.

Together, they delved into their research, determined to uncover every detail about the Boo Hags. Madison's fingertips danced across the keyboard. She would find the answers they sought.

Chapter 21—Rebecca and Madison

The team gathered at the foot of a steep hill, basking in the warm, golden glow of the sun. Corey, his eyes filled with genuine concern, addressed the group with a touch of tenderness in his voice.

"Lance was a little black ball when he floated away," said Rachel. "Why is he a worry?"

"It's funny that everything about Lance is gone and all that's left is a small ball of ancient evil, but we still think of it as Lance." He became serious again. "He'll heal up in a couple of centuries. As a bard, you live as long as I do and will be around. Do you want to fight him at full strength again?"

Rachel stuck her tongue out at him. "I've been ignoring my lifespan change."

After he chuckled, Corey continued. "Okay, team, we're about to embark on a hike up this mountain. This will allow Rebecca to attend her meeting at seventeen-thirty."

A surge of resistance welled up within me. "You don't have to treat me with kid gloves. I can handle myself."

"You've accepted on additional responsibilities, and I understand the challenges that come with the decisions you've made. You're traveling with a natural enemy, facing adversaries who seek to undermine you, and you're pursuing an ancient evil who disguised himself as your date, intending to kill you. It's only right that you receive some support."

Nicole's voice filled with empathy. "That first phone call you made was intense. You spent two hours typing afterwards, and you were none too happy with the one you just finished."

My second call at the six-hour mark was mainly between my grandmother and me, saying the team needed more time. This was not promising.

Rachel, leading Valkyrie by her side, exclaimed, "it's my turn to play the mean one! Let's see... You're beautiful, sexy, and an amazing friend. You help everyone so much that I can't find a single flaw in you." She paused, mischievousness dancing in her eyes. "And well, that makes it hard on me."

I laughed, a sense of gratitude wash over me. "Thank you, Rachel. Now I have a semblance of normality."

Her grin widened, and mischief sparkled in her eyes.

"Trust me," her sister said, "she can do better."

"Really? Like this?" Rachel and Nicole's sister rivalry must have sparked by something I didn't understand. "Corey, only women with the spark attract you. What about angels?"

Corey stumbled at the question. "I'm engaged to the only woman I'll ever need, so while I find her attractive, I can focus on Nicole."

It wasn't a bad answer, but I needed to help Nicole because Rachel just pushed one of her sister's buttons. "We all know Corey can ignore women with the spark romantically," I teased Rachel. "He's done it with you for a decade!"

"Oh, no!" Rachel busted out laughing. "I must have been too mean since Rebecca jumped in to protect Nicole!"

We engaged in playful banter to keep the mood light. However, our banter had to end as we prepared to embark on our hike. I laced up my hiking boots, shouldered my pack, and followed Corey up the incline, with Nicole following Valkyrie and Rachel by her side.

As we made our way partway up the hill, Corey paused and cast a spell on Valkyrie. "I'm sorry I didn't take the time to heal you last time, girl," Corey said. "But from now on, let me know whenever you need it, and I'll tend to you as often as necessary."

Valkyrie barked in response, her tail wagging with approval.

Corey chuckled, translating her barks. "She says I'm back in second place behind Rachel now. Apparently, your fight in the courtyard impressed her, Rebecca." Corey kept his tone light. "I tied Rachel for first, but after she witnessed me getting my butt kicked one day, blammo—Rachel became her favorite."

We shared a lighthearted moment, laughter filling the air. Yet, beneath the surface, I couldn't shake the growing concern for Corey. So much had transpired in our lives, especially in the past day. And through it all, Corey had been my unwavering pillar of support. What had started as my intention to assist him had transformed into a dynamic where he was now training me, guiding me as the Battle Leader, and showing me unwavering compassion. But I could sense that he was taking on more than he could bear.

"Help me understand your threshold for determining whether someone is a potential ally or irredeemable." It was a question that had been gnawing at me. Considering I had dismissed the most senior officer during our drive here, it seemed likely that my role as Battle Leader would be a long-term commitment, and I would need to rely on Corey's guidance until I could assist him in return.

A contemplative expression crossed Corey's face as he considered his response. "I wish I could give you a definitive answer, but it's more like a set of guidelines," he said. "First, anyone who aligns themselves with Dark Fey has had their mind altered. While there may be a sliver of hope for their redemption, I'd err on the side of caution and lean towards viewing them as irredeemable. Second, everyone else falls into the potential ally category. Sometimes that alliance may be short-lived, contingent on the circumstances. Even Lance, for example, became an ally during the fight because Onoskelis was targeting him."

"Lance?"

"Remember in the battle with the vampires? He told you the clouds were the sign of a fallen angel, then helped triage and heal fighters? He was playing a role so he could hide from fighting Onoskelis and you at the same time—but that made him an ally in that fight."

"That's a loose definition. A temporary ally of convenience." My argument sounded good.

"Sometimes that is all we have. That's why I was ready to believe Onoskelis. We need allies for what we are up against."

His words sparked a new perspective within me, but I wasn't done. "But fallen angels are associated with inherent evil."

Corey shook his head, his expression thoughtful. "That sounds like propaganda. Dissatisfied because they believed their father ranked humans higher than them in the divine order, they asked legitimate questions and became exiled. From my standpoint, as someone defending Earth, it doesn't sound evil."

Arguing religion with the living embodiment of a pagan religion who attended Catholic church with Nicole would not work, so I let that drop.

My mind grappled with the complexity of Corey's perspective, yet I couldn't ignore the implications of his unwavering loyalty. "But you show no mercy to certain enemies," I pointed out, acknowledging the darker side of his judgment.

A hint of intensity flickered in his eyes. "True. No one may harm any of you. The team is my family, and if anyone dares to lay a finger on you all, they are gambling with their own life. They're saying that their life is the price they're willing to pay for crossing me... or perhaps even an eternity of torment confined within one of my Jars of Bliss."

I couldn't help but shudder at the weight of Corey's words, the gravity of his protectiveness sinking in. "I choose not to dwell on those implications," I said. "Now, help me navigate my next steps with Major McKinnon. What would make him redeemable, or would his actions warrant his demise?"

Corey's gaze turned serious. "First, nothing in him seems redeemable. If his arrogance were the only issue, then I'd say you should relieve him of his duties. However, if he was concealing something that jeopardized the safety of this area, if he had been recruiting others or was the one behind the attack on us—then death would be the consequence."

His words hung in the air, and I couldn't deny the weight of the responsibility that lay ahead of me. Could I become the arbiter of such judgments?

Deep within, I found a flicker of resolve. "Thank you, Corey. I will need to find the strength to make those decisions."

Corey nodded, a mixture of pride and concern etched on his face. "You're stronger than you think. Lean on me until you can stand on your own. We'll face whatever challenges come our way together."

The team trudged through dense undergrowth, reaching our campsite. Feeling the weight of exhaustion settling upon me, I sank down onto a moss-covered log, allowing my body to rest. Corey took charge of our meal, cooking over an open flame. It would be our last decent meal for a day or two.

Nicole's voice broke through the camp's stillness. "We've established an information-sharing agreement with the Chesapeake Bay Territory regarding the impending threat."

She approached Corey, anticipation in her eyes. "Madison has sent a report that requires your review. It seems we are being all official-like."

"Could you show it to me?" Corey flipped the precooked meats and vegetables sizzling in the pan.

"Of course." Nicole handed him the report, and together they delved into its contents. Corey's brow furrowed as he absorbed the information, contemplating his next move. "Send my approval and inform them I will take responsibility for informing the Chesapeake Bay Battle Leader."

A groan escaped my lips, despite my best efforts to stifle it. The news did not bode well.

"Rebecca, your report will not be good—"

I interrupted him. "I'm too overwhelmed for beating around the bush. Give me the bad new bluntly." I steeled myself.

He put the spoon down and looked at me. "The corrupted military leadership erased all the information on fighting the supernatural creatures in the Chesapeake Bay archives. The Southeast is helping refill it. Someone destroyed the sensor network in Chesapeake Bay years ago and kept it hidden. There are no military funds because they embezzled them all. The Southeast has taken over scanning Chesapeake Bay on your grandmother's order."

I took a deep breath. I could deal with this. "If things were in good shape, grandmother wouldn't have been quick to fire a full bird colonel and put me in his position." I opened my phone to gather the report.

"Hold on," said Corey. "The man you called out is being held for treason and embezzlement. The Dark Fey have influenced him like those who came to Atlanta."

Setting my phone aside, I leaned forward, my head finding solace in the embrace of my knees. Corey, sensing my distress, drew me into a comforting hug.

"I'm fine," I said. I'd have to interrogate him like Corey had done the others.

"No, you're not," Corey said, giving me a stronger hug. "You need support. Old Donnie trained me for situations like this during my time with The Tribe. Just because I didn't complete the full training doesn't discount the four years I completed. They have thrust you into this role with minimal preparation, and that's an unfair burden." Valkyrie approached and rested her head on my lap, offering silent comfort.

"Did Old Donnie teach you the art of interrogation?" I asked. I knew Old Donnie taught Corey not to murder.

"Old Donnie may not have always been the saint I've painted him as," Corey confessed, his voice laced with sorrow. "He had his darker moments, especially before Preacher Jon returned. There was a time when he took lives—many lives. But the path to a territory founded on love demanded a change. He taught me how to kill, what to expect when faced with death, and why it should always be a last resort. He guided me through my first encounters with Dark Fey and my first gargoyles, ensuring I understood the weight of those experiences. And if you wish to hear about those who sought to infiltrate The Tribe, I can share that with you as well. I didn't end their lives, but I witnessed their demise." Corey's voice was heavy with the memories he carried.

This stunned me into silence, my hand covering my mouth in disbelief. "You've carried all of that within you?"

"In his defense," Rachel joked, "Corey's mind has a tendency to misplace things often."

A surprised laugh bubbled from my lips, surprised by the unexpected joke. "Okay, that's funny," I acknowledged. "Thank you, guys. I will lean on you when I need it."

With a sense of determination, I turned her attention to my phone, discovering two new emails awaiting me. The first, from grandmother, expressed pride in my handling of the earlier meeting. "Guys, my grandmother commended me for how I handled the situation. Corey, thank you for preparing me." My reply to the report contained a clear directive to keep the traitors detained until I could address them. This was my duty, my responsibility.

As Corey distributed plates of lunch to everyone, I turned my focus to the second email. The report was deplorable—lacking readiness and comprehension of the situation at hand. As Corey told me, they had been required to seek support from the Southeast, with grandmother's permission, and were collaborating with Madison and Nathan in their efforts.

Interrupting the silence, the figure of Onoskelis, the fallen angel, descended to the ground. "You guys lose your cuddly charm when preparing for battle."

"We would have brought more men, but Corey is all we got." Rachel joked, eliciting a chuckle from the group.

"Preacher Jon told me Corey alone has been enough," Onoskelis said.

"We had joked about Corey often enough in front of Preacher Jon that he may have the wrong impression." My comment brought out another chuckle from everyone.

I sent a message to the Virginia Emergency Response Team, my text carrying a weight of seriousness. "Our group is leaving to combat the Nephilim beast. If you receive no response from me, stick to the plan."

Rachel tended to Valkyrie's needs. Soon, our team of five stood ready, poised for what lay ahead.

"Empath, can your strength read an angel's mind?" Onoskelis said, her gaze piercing through Nicole.

"I didn't sense you assessing our combat readiness," Nicole said, pasting an innocent look on her face.

Nicole acted playful with the fallen angel. Was I the only one dealing with Onoskelis correctly?

"Alright, team." Corey took charge once more, his voice commanding attention. "The first part of the ravine is off-limits to climbers, and it grows more treacherous as we descend. The ledges are perilous, and the passes are few. We cannot afford to take unnecessary risks, for at the bottom lies true terror."

Onoskelis nodded. "Let's begin our descent. We shall approach near the crevice known as the Bottomless Ravine. Be cautious and do not use wings in that vicinity."

"I'll carry Valkyrie and tether the three of you to me." Corey assumed his leadership role. "Onoskelis, you have the option of joining the tether with us or remain independent. But for the rest, you will wear harnesses. I have traversed that ledge twice in the company of Old Donnie and Miles, and on both occasions, fear gripped me." He handed out harnesses, securing each member of the team to ensure their safety.

I understood the gravity of Corey's words and the seriousness in his eyes. This was the Corey I knew not to argue with, the Corey whose experience and knowledge demanded their unwavering trust. With a renewed sense of purpose, I vowed to heed his guidance as we embarked on the next leg of our perilous journey.

THE WEIGHT OF NATHAN'S intense gaze fell upon Madison, his eyes locked onto her with unwavering intensity. A gentle smile curled at the corners of her lips as she turned to face him, her voice soft and inviting.

"Yes, dear?" she said with a touch of warmth.

Nathan's eyes flickered with admiration as he continued to stare, his voice filled with a mixture of awe and genuine appreciation. "You are remarkable in this role," he complimented, his words laced with a genuine sense of admiration.

Heat surged into her cheeks. She tucked a strand of hair behind her ear, feeling a mixture of self-consciousness and pleasure at his kind words. "After observing you these past two weeks, I see you possess something extraordinary as well."

A radiant smile spread across Nathan's face. "Ms. Addkinson was so impressed with our situational reports that she requested we share our process. I've included it in Corey's list of things we need to document, and I've been working on compiling a comprehensive guide. With Corey's training book as a reference, I incorporated insights from Dave, You, Clive, and Trish."

Madison nodded, a sense of purpose filling her. She recalled the detailed report she had read from Virginia, realizing the significance of providing more comprehensive information, especially given the recent nationwide meeting and the increased scrutiny of the Southeast. Maintaining the independence Preacher Jon secured was crucial, and she knew she could play a role in achieving that. Fitting in overwhelmed her with happiness and relief.

Wesley followed Trish into the room, his presence injecting a touch of urgency. He read from his phone. "This will be our final report before it becomes too dangerous to speak freely. Corey is leading with confidence. Onoskelis also has a quiet certainty. The journey fills Rachel with joy, while Rebecca appears contemplative. And Nicole…" He paused, a chuckle escaping his lips. "Nicole is scared out of her mind. She just typed, 'Don't tell anyone how scared I am, but holy crap.'"

Madison leaned back, her mind racing with questions. She couldn't help but wonder if there were any updates from Clive, but she stopped herself, realizing it had been forty-five minutes since he mentioned a two-hour timeframe. Her stomach rumbled, a reminder of her own needs.

Trish noticed Madison's hunger and offered a solution. "Good idea, Madison," she said. "I'll go fetch us some food from <u>JennyF's Burgers</u>."

Madison turned to Nathan, a playful glint in her eyes. "Caramel beige, honey. Let's match your coffee to the color of the burger's outside." With a smile, she retrieved the creamer she always carried in her purse, knowing it would change the color of the coffee for his single-color meal.

Trish stared at Madison with surprise on her face. "Wow," she exclaimed, shaking her head in amusement. "If Miles sees the two of you, he'll get ideas. Although, if he snuggles me like Corey and Rachel, I won't mind keeping up with his eating habits." She stood up, determination in her stride. "I'll be back."

Madison pondered Trish's reaction for a moment, a subtle realization dawning on her. Carrying something that made her boyfriend's life easier wasn't a mere triviality; it was a testament to the bond they shared. It was a minor act of love and care, a reflection of the nurturing nature of women who always seemed to have everything they needed tucked away in their purses. She also wouldn't point out that Miles would have his special triple burger delivered without asking for it.

I REACHED OUT, SEARCHING for something to hold on to, but the sheer wall offered no handholds. Jagged rocks protruded like snapped fangs, and relentless gusts of wind taunted my futile attempts. Corey cradled the Great Dane in his arms. The dog glanced back at me with a mix of concern and pleading in his eyes. The dog's gaze seemed to implore me to understand, to heed the unspoken warning. A whirlwind of voices echoed in my mind, cautioning me to reconsider if Corey appeared frightened and insisted on extra safety precautions.

Every nook and cranny, every rock, shrub, and speck of dirt, had vanished into the insatiable void known as Bottomless Ravine. From the ledge above, I had thought the howling winds were severe, but as they descended into the ravine's depths, Corey's demeanor shifted, as the howling grew severe. He double-checked everyone's harness, ensuring each strap was secure, before tugging on the rope to verify its tightness.

"Rebecca, I need to feel your hand on me at all times," Corey ordered. "Rachel, you're responsible for Nicole. This is my third descent into this abyss, and I'm terrified."

"He's not exaggerating, kids," added Onoskelis.

"No one except me will carry a pack beyond this point—only weapons." Corey conjured his druid berry spell and distributed the enchanted fruit to everyone except the fallen angel, who sneered.

That had been thirty agonizing minutes ago, and tears threatened to escape my eyes throughout the entire descent. My fingers ached for something to hold on to—even the cutting crevices above would provide some relief. I could attribute the moisture on my cheeks to the relentless wind, masking the true terror coursing through my veins. The slate-gray walls of the cliff gave no solace, only a frigid surface against which I could brace myself. Occasionally, small rocks, twigs, or dust would descend, to be snatched away by the ravine's unforgiving gusts. Nothing remained still in this place of perpetual motion.

The rock face exuded an icy coldness, intensifying the discomfort of its lack of handholds. It was a stark reminder of our vulnerability, as if the very cliff conspired against us.

We exchanged no words. The wind's deafening howl drowned out any semblance of conversation. Corey distributed ear protection, but Nicole and I had already equipped ourselves with our own, though the shrill whistling noise still pierced our defenses.

Guided by Onoskelis, even the fallen angel moved with deliberate steps, pausing whenever the wind unleashed its wrath. Corey forged ahead. My left hand grasped his harness and mirrored his every step.

Corey's training encompassed far more than just druidic magic and combat skills—it included search and rescue techniques, stealth, and the qualities of a battle leader. Meanwhile, my knowledge extended to politics, territories, and a degree in classics. Corey had been engaged in physical battles and rigorous training long before his formal instruction began. I would have to rely on him, yet in doing so, I knew I had a responsibility to help him overcome his own challenges and navigate the intricate web of politics that awaited us.

Rocks cascaded down the cliff face, whipped by the relentless wind, until Corey halted, his eyes fixed on the tumbling projectiles until they no longer posed a threat.

A part of me yearned to turn and assist Nicole, but all I could manage was the reassurance of her hand nestled within my harness. The wind assaulted my face, leaving my skin chapped and raw. Even in the warmth surrounding me, my trembling form betrayed the grip of fear that held me captive, mingling with my tears.

Seeking stability, my right hand groped for purchase against the frozen cliff wall. It provided no respite, its icy touch intensifying the discomfort. An inexplicable temperature shift sent shivers down my spine.

After an eternity, the wind's tone changed, signaling a shift. Onoskelis, her wings concealed, settled against a wall, a rare moment of respite. Corey placed Valkyrie on the ground and embraced me. "You made it," he said. He turned to Nicole with concern etched across his features. "Are you alright?"

Nicole nodded, her grip on me still in place until Corey hugged her.

What had Wesley seen to ensure Nicole came on the trip? A pregnant woman wearing a harness and scaling cliff walls was insane.

"Rachel, once again, you've been incredible," Corey commended, a smile gracing his face. "The support I gained from you bracing me from behind gave me the strength to press onward. You're all true champions."

I didn't feel like a champion, but in that moment, the celebration of surviving seemed like cause enough for jubilation. We had not succumbed, and though our journey was far from complete, we had achieved something remarkable by surviving.

Rachel's smile wavered, but she joined the group, stumbling toward the wall where a collective hug awaited them. Valkyrie, the faithful companion, joined in, adding a touch of canine camaraderie.

Rachel beckoned to Onoskelis, her grin now radiating with new-found confidence. "Will you join our celebration, Onoskelis?"

The fallen angel's initial sneer transformed into a perplexed expression. "You're serious. Who are you, Rachel Pureheart?" Her voice held a mixture of confusion and intrigue.

This time, Rachel unleashed a full, uninhibited grin.

"Keep your harnesses on, but I'm removing the rope," Corey said. "What's the next step from here?"

Onoskelis rose to her feet. "I would like to believe it's a straight-forward path, but I can't detect any readings from those under my care. We must pass through the druid gate, navigate past three slumbering Nephilim beasts, proceed through the first cabin, cross a stone bridge, and then, I sense him in the second cavern."

"Well then, let's proceed. I'm excited to make our way back across that ravine," Corey said.

I checked my phone to find no signal in this rocky abyss. Distance and rock severed cellular and satellite connections. This isolated our team until we climbed back out.

Chapter 22—Madison and Rebecca

"Sixteen forty-four marks the precise moment when we lost contact with the team," said Nathan, his face etched with worry. Although his intention was for Madison to record them in the report and send an update to Chesapeake, he sounded like he was uttering them like a mantra, trying to calm himself.

Madison unplugged her phone from the charger, her heart pounding with anticipation. She dialed the number, and after a few rings, Dave's familiar voice answered on the other end.

"Hey, Dave, I have an intermediate update. Let me know when you're ready," she said. Dave had always been a reliable ally, and he had shared with her the unvarnished truth about the situation in Chesapeake. She was determined not to jeopardize his position or let his honesty go to waste.

"Go ahead, Southeast Mobile Command Center. You're on speaker with the extended team," came the resounding voice, crisp and clear, as if it enveloped the room. That was Dave's warning to her to be professional. She had established camaraderie with Dave, and she sensed he was trying to prove himself, and she would help him.

"Chesapeake Emergency Response Team, this is Southeast Mobile Command Center," Madison's words resonated with resolve. "The ancient evil team has reached their first milestone. They lost communication at sixteen forty-four Eastern Standard Time. We expect their next communication in twelve hours, with a mandatory update due in twenty-four hours." She transcribed the need for more procedures, adding it to the growing list of emergency protocols they needed to establish.

"Southeast Mobile Command Center, who has assumed the role of tactical leader?" asked a voice, as authoritative as it was grandmotherly.

Madison gathered her thoughts, choosing her words. "At sixteen hundred, the Strategic Leader designated Patricia Einer, known as Trish, to assume the responsibilities of Tactical Leader until team one returns and is combat-ready."

Trish, surprised, shot Madison a bewildered look, as if she had sprouted a second head. Madison returned the gaze with a confident smile.

"Trish and Nathan. My Realized power is to understand and explain all Realized powers once someone casts them. Major McKinnon's Realized power is to transfer information to supernatural creatures. The Boo Hags have the location of your Mobile Command Center."

Trish stood up. "Alerting the others!" She ran out.

"We've made contact!" Wesley's voice rang out, interrupting the tense atmosphere.

"Considering this development, we are transitioning to combat communications mode only. Ending call." Madison ended the call with relief.

Speaker calls were always precarious, and she had no intention of leaving anything to chance. She awaited further updates from Wesley or Trish, using the brief respite to jot down a few additional notes on tactical leader turnover and communication protocols. She placed the terms 'black out' and 'combat only' in parentheses for clarity.

Nathan rubbed her back, providing a comforting gesture that sent a wave of relief coursing through her. She knew it was not appropriate to find solace now, but at that moment, she couldn't help feeling grateful for his presence.

"We've contained one Boo Hag. Baron, Clive, and Miles emerged unscathed from the encounter," Wesley said. He went back to his phone call.

Before anyone could react, Isabella barged in, panic etched on her face. "The animals say something evil is near!" Then she screamed, her voice laced with terror.

In an instant, the world seemed to lose its color, plunging into a monochromatic realm of black and white. Madison had battled before, but never against an invisible foe. She had taken easy shots in the Command Center earlier, but this was where her skills would shine. This was where she could prove her worth.

The knowledge of Boo Hags raced through Madison's mind. These insidious creatures would drain the life force from their victims, assuming their identities and perpetuating their insatiable hunger. Lethargy and eventual demise awaited those unfortunate enough to fall into their clutches. They did this by sucking the breath from a person, but they had to be close enough to kiss.

With calm determination, Madison summoned her magical bow, feeling its Fey energy coursing through her fingertips. With unwavering focus, she notched an arrow made of pure Fey magic and let it fly, guiding it to land two inches to the left of Isabella's trembling mouth. The arrow hovered in midair, a testament to her mastery over the bow.

Isabella stumbled backward, then crawled, seeking refuge behind Madison, her fear quelled by the display of accuracy.

Her magical arrow remained suspended in the air as Madison aimed at her floating arrow and unleashed her lethal precision once more.

An earth-shattering roar reverberated through the hallways. Coach White transformed before their eyes, his human form twisting and contorting until he emerged as a towering werewolf. His fur, a majestic shade of gray, stretched to accommodate his immense size within the narrow confines of the corridor. With ferocious paws armed with razor-sharp claws, he snatched the air and ran out like he carried something. The arrows went with whatever the werewolf carried.

Without hesitation, Madison pursued the transformed Coach White, her heart pounding in synchrony with each step. They emerged into the open, bathed in sunlight, as Coach White flung his captive into the radiant beams. The creature, a grotesque figure standing at five feet tall, possessed a spindly, white frame and hands adorned with thin claws. It screeched in agony as the sunlight seared its unnatural flesh.

Madison unleashed a barrage of arrows, each finding its mark with unerring accuracy. The creature's tortured screams ceased as it burned away, vanishing into nothingness. Satisfied with the result, Madison secured her bow, her gaze unwavering as she observed Coach White approach the charred remains. Without hesitation, he reached down and ripped out the creature's still-beating heart, bashing it to the ground in a display of triumph. In an instant, Coach White reverted to his human form, his demeanor returning to one of stoic normalcy.

In a minute, the world reemerged from its monochromatic stupor, the sounds of traffic and bustling commerce flooding Madison's senses. She turned to walk back alongside Coach White, her every movement exuding a quiet confidence. Nathan, his gaze fixed upon her, was a curious blend of awe and desire. It was an inappropriate mix of emotions, but Madison couldn't help but revel in the appreciation.

"As the acting Tactical Leader," Trish teased with a chuckle, her eyes dancing with mirth, "perhaps you two should save the goo-goo eyes for a more opportune time and focus on the task at hand."

Madison chuckled as the team reentered the room, their strides purposeful and confident. As she stepped inside, her attention brushed past the mundane surroundings. This place was her sanctuary, where she felt a deep sense of belonging both as teammate and as a seasoned hunter. Nathan, her teammate and lover, acknowledged her presence, his approving gaze affirming her worth. She knew she belonged and that no one would question her place. This was her home, and she was content.

Putting his hand over the phone, Wesley's voice pierced the air, announcing their latest victory. "Team one, second Boo Hag neutralized," he said, his tone resonating with triumph.

Trish's voice carried a hint of excitement. "Looks like we've discovered two distinct methods to detect and handle these Boo Hags. Our animal allies will act as early warnings, while the strength of werewolves can overpower them."

Nathan added, "And let's not forget the effectiveness of our hunter arrows. They've proven their worth once again."

Nathan addressed the team with unwavering authority. "We've cleared the Southeast territory. Team one, you're now released to Chesapeake. Team two, stay put."

Wesley signaled Madison to stand down, acknowledging her contribution. She watched as he relayed the instructions to team one. "Team one, you're cleared to proceed to Chesapeake. Report to the Emergency Response team at Addkinson Estate. Copy that."

One of the team members responded, "In route now. Estimated arrival in four hours."

Wesley spoke on another line. "Go ahead, Charleston," he prompted, his focus unwavering. He focused. "How certain are we about that?" he asked.

Wesley concluded the call, his words brimming with assurance. "With high confidence, the Gullah interrogation revealed that Nathan was the primary target in the Southeast. The second Boo Hag was a catalyst for chaos."

Madison's mind replayed the events that had unfolded—the moment she had saved Isabella's life, she saved Nathan's.

Nathan's voice broke through her reverie. "Understood. Do we have any intel on the Chesapeake Bay target?"

Wesley paused, his expression grave. "Major Mackinnon was the mastermind behind the Gullah's employment. While Grace Addkinson is the listed target, two others are conspiring to seize control of the military and sow chaos."

Leaning back in his chair, Wesley looked at Madison. "Can you draft a detailed report of this information? Wesley, reach out to Chesapeake as our alternate communications contact."

Madison watched Nathan's gaze. She already understood him well enough to know he was testing Wesley's ability to handle additional responsibilities. How many capable individuals did he have to shoulder the burden?

Isabella's voice trembled with fear. "So, should I be panicking?" Her anxiety was palpable.

Trish guided the young girl back to the couch. "Come, sit with me. We'll navigate this mess together. Perhaps someone can explain it all to us."

Nathan turned his attention towards Trish and Isabella., his voice carrying a mix of reassurance and solemnity. "The Boo Hag targeted me and had my location because of the traitors. But Isabella's connection with animals enabled her to detect its presence, marking her as a threat to be subdued. Madison interrupted its murderous intent. Coach White, attuned to the supernatural, then witnessed its true form and dispatched it into the sun. In the end, it was the combined efforts of Madison and Coach White that brought it down."

Coach White looking more like a volunteer football coach and less of a season warrior spoke. "Never encountered a white vampire before, but the wolf knew its heart had to be removed. And what better opportunity than when it was fending off those arrows?"

Nathan nodded, a glimmer of relief in his eyes. "It worked," he affirmed.

Coach White's rugged features softened, and a nostalgic grin crept across his face. "Glad this old wolf still has a howl left."

Isabella's voice quivered with uncertainty. "So, because I told you what the animals said, something invisible wanted to kill me?"

Coach White posed a friendly question to the young girl. "Do you still wish to follow in Corey's footsteps?"

Nathan, his voice gentle yet firm, explained. "Each of us takes turns being targeted. Corey, unfortunately, bears the brunt more often. Today, it was our turn."

Isabella, her smile breaking through the fear, spoke up. "That arrow came awfully close, didn't it?"

Madison assured her with a reassuring grin. "I've got you. Placing an arrow next to your lips is a piece of cake."

"Speaking of cake, my quinceañera is coming up. Is the territory going to help me celebrate?" The young girl grinned.

"I think so," said Nathan, laughing at how quickly the teen recovered.

"Trish, do you have a security camera in here?" Madison asked. She remembered how her parents' first two words spoken were 'bow' and 'video' because they had watched her shooting in the Command Center. Aunt Becky might use the tape to help her parents.

"We do." Trish pointed to a corner to her left. "I'll send you a login and timestamp to view the encounter."

Wesley's voice resonated once more, cutting through the tension. "Chesapeake Emergency Response Team, this is the Southeast Mobile Command Center."

"Southeast, go ahead." Dave's voice sounded concerned.

"Two Boo Hags neutralized. Our Strategic Leader, Nathan Abernathy, was the primary target, while the other served as a diversion. Team one is in route. Three Realized individuals—one from Chesapeake and two from the Southeast will cross the border."

Dave asked over the speaker, "Southeast, did you experience casualties causing changes in roles?"

That was sweet. Dave was asking about her. It reminded her, now that the immediate tasks were done, she should walk out and check on Mare and Melinda. Someone needed to keep them in the loop.

Wesley shrugged. "No casualties. Our Standard Command Center Operating Procedure has the backup team ensconced in the Command Center. Today that paid off, as the second attack was on the mobile Command Center."

Dave's astonishment seeped into his response. "Whoa."

Undeterred, Wesley proceeded. "Major Mackinnon orchestrated the Gullah's involvement. Grace Addkinson is the listed target, but two others Boo Hags aim to seize control of the military and sow chaos. This information comes with high certainty."

"Understood. Any estimated time of arrival?" Dave asked.

"Still twenty-four to seventy-two hours," Wesley said.

Dave expressed his gratitude, and the call concluded. Madison jotted down vital information, updating the process lists. Command Center Protection, backup teams, and the handover of communications. She marveled at the efficiency of the Southeast's operations without procedures. Three months ago, their team comprised six members.

"The next update will be from the Ancient Evil team," said Nathan. He plopped into the chair next to the desk. "Not only are Corey and Rebecca on the team with the fallen angel, but my two sisters are, too."

COREY AND ONOSKELIS led, Rachel protected our rear flank. I walked alongside Nicole, our footsteps echoing through the lit cave.

Her grip on the staff with its peculiar hooks at the top was so tight that it drained the color from her fingers. Concerned, I touched her hand, urging her to loosen her hold, allowing her to endure the strain for longer periods. Nicole glanced at her pale hand and grimaced, the weight of her unease clear in her eyes.

"Don't worry." I hoped to offer comfort. "We're a team, and we'll watch out for each other." It was crazy she was here. What did Wesley see?

Nicole's face revealed a mixture of fear and uncertainty, showing how she felt out of her depth in this dangerous venture. Unlike me, she lacked magical combat abilities, her powers of empathy proving less useful in this perilous situation. Her sister and fiancé accompanied us, and their presence would increase her chances of survival.

As our group ventured deeper into the cave, we discovered a peculiar absence of stalagmites and stalactites. "There was a fight here that destroyed the natural formations," said Onoskelis.

The monotonous dripping of water and the occasional gust of wind broke the eerie silence. Rachel, holding a light carried by her bardic spell of a servant, illuminated our path with a welcoming radiance. The light extended in a generous one-hundred-foot radius, unveiling a vast cavern of weathered gray stone tainted with the odor of decay.

"This is getting weirder by the second," said Onoskelis with unease. "There should be at least one slumbering beast here. The druidic barrier is intact, and finding suitable hiding spots for them is no easy task."

"I can hear their whispers," Corey spoke matter-of-factly, his tone downplaying the severity to avoid alarming the rest of us. "They're aware of our presence. In just reaching out to find them, I've fueled their animosity towards druids. In their minds, they believe they only have each other. Be prepared to engage airborne foes."

Corey's words amplified my anxiety. The realization that the focus would be on him, to pay back the druids who cast and trapped them in here, instilled a deep sense of fear within me.

"The bridge up ahead seems like a probable spot for an ambush," Onoskelis said, her demeanor shifting into battle mode. "They shouldn't be aware that we have four individuals capable of flight. It seems the ancient evil has a significant impact on their loyalty or perception of angels."

That's when I figured out Lance released Barnisfer. A portal of sorts inside my head started filling with facts of all Nephilim. Celestia was rewarding me for something I couldn't figure out yet.

"Is there enough space after the bridge for us to launch a counter-ambush?" Corey asked.

The fallen angel scrutinized him. "Yes, there is. Two of us will need to take to the air."

"You can stare all you want," Corey said. "Their hatred for druids overrides any other considerations. They're coming after me, regardless. But I wouldn't mind some help when facing one."

"Is Corey the primary target?" I asked. "Can I take pressure off of him?"

Onoskelis wanted to argue but finally agreed. "I would place my bets on Corey being correct, that their hatred for him will supersede all other considerations. As the one who has been their point of contact for the past century, I might become their next target if they lack any memory of my intentions. Let us proceed across the bridge and complete our strategy."

Despite it all, my confidence grew. Battling Nephilim was my realm of expertise. I couldn't explain the source of this newfound assurance; it felt like fulfilling my destined purpose. Observing the seamless cooperation between Corey and Onoskelis provided further reassurance. Corey's training had prepared him to align with a fallen angel boasting millennia of experience.

Nicole uncovered her nose, her voice muffled. "Rachel, can you do something about the stench?"

"Absolutely," Rachel said. "But I'll need a circle drawn by Corey, and it can't follow us. However, it will create a warm and cozy space, perfect for a bard to sing songs, tell stories, and entertain us all." Her grin let us all know she wanted to cast it for her sister.

"Could we take a moment before engaging in battle to make ourselves more comfortable?" Nicole asked.

"Of course," Corey said. "I'll create the circle, and Rachel can work her magic before I start the lure of the creatures. Keeping us all in top fighting conditions is appropriate before a fight."

Nicole covered her mouth and nose, the one among us without a specific class. I possessed immunity to diseases and poisons, while the immunity of the druid and bard classes remained a mystery to me.

We moved forward until we reached a stone bridge. To my relief, it wasn't the precarious, two-foot-wide arc one might expect from movies. Instead, it spanned about thirty feet and was over ten feet wide. Both the bridge and the ledges on either side comprised solid gray stone, mirroring the rest of the cavern. While a few cracks and fragments marred its surface, it appeared sturdy enough. The opposite end of the bridge led through a rocky opening flanked by platforms on either side.

"Alright, I'll create a circle right in the middle of the bridge," Corey said, outlining our battle plan. "Rachel and Nicole, I need you to stand on the right side. Nicole, focus on long-range strikes and employ the defensive capabilities of Nunti-bo. Avoid getting too close to the creature. Rebecca, take the left side in your *Angelic Form*. I'll position myself in front of the circle, ready to retreat and activate my transformative binding if things take a turn for the worse. Onoskelis, can you launch aerial attacks from above?"

I assumed my *Angelic Form*, crossing the bridge in a straight line. Corey had mentioned that we would incorporate flying skills into our training schedule. I needed it.

Rachel positioned herself in front of Nicole, who adjusted her stance, widening her grip and adopting a forward foot position. I assumed a square stance, casting a *Healing Deva* over the central portion of the bridge. "***Me servum regni caelestis adjunge***," I chanted.

Rachel summoned Valkyrie, who stood by my side.

"The malevolent presence awaits us in the next chamber, and it trembles with fear," Onoskelis said, her eyes fixed on me. "It senses your ability to wield the blade of creation magic—the power it fears."

Before I could inquire further about her words, the ground beneath us quaked, and the resounding roars and howls of enraged Nephilim beasts reverberated through the cavern walls.

"They're in a frenzy," Corey alerted us, his voice filled with urgency. "Here they come."

The air crackled with anticipation as the ominous horde of beasts surged toward us, their wrath palpable.

The ground trembled beneath our feet, and the reverberations echoing through the lit cavern. Corey stood in the middle of the bridge, and I positioned myself to his left, anticipation coursing through my veins. The formidable wall that separated us from the imminent danger quaked as if the forces of darkness sought to breach it.

"They tried to all come through," Corey spoke with urgency. "Only one can fit, and their hatred of me has stripped them of any plan they had."

With a swift motion, Corey unsheathed his tonfa, the cold wood gleaming in the faint glow of the cavern. I brandished my sword and shield. With my blade held high, a golden celestial light emanated from it, illuminating the entire battlefield, except for Onoskelis.

Celestia granted me new powers! My sword could take on three distinct forms: Celestial colored gold, Creation colored white, and Angelic steel. They rewarded me for taking on the Nephilim. They made the Creation blade of the force used to create all things, meaning it can annihilate!

Corey made his circle, and Rachel cast her spell. The area lit up green.

The ground beneath the others quivered again, causing Nicole to lose her footing, sliding toward the treacherous edge. Rachel grabbed her and pulled her back.

Rachel's dress and Nicole's ankles glowed with green Fey Magic. Inhaling, Nicole uncovered her nose. Corey stood in the middle of the holding two tonfa.

The floor rumbled, and a menacing creature emerged from the abyss. Its monstrous form bore a smooth orb for a head devoid of any discernible features. A pristine, white sphere sat atop its body, without eyes or a mouth. Darting with surprising agility, it hurtled toward Corey, its two python-like appendages dripping with venom.

My newly granted knowledge was accessible in my *Angelic Form*. The beasts defied the laws that held the universe together, making them outcasts. These creatures drew power from all realms, making Earth's magic ineffective against them. Celestia designed my *Angelic Form* for combating Nephilim. When I saved Corey's life, Celestia knew it would lead me here. That's when I became Realized as the Scion.

Fueled by newfound confidence, I switched to my white sword blade, which bathed the area in a bright white light, illuminating the approaching Onoskelis. With a mighty swing, I cleaved through one of the python appendages, reducing it to nothingness. The white blade annihilated the entire appendage!

A shrill, ear-splitting hum resonated from the smooth orb atop the creature, vibrating the very stones beneath their feet and causing a searing pain in my ears.

As the appendage disintegrated, another snake-like form emerged from the wound left by my strike. Onoskelis, her dark and corrupted aura swirling around her, sliced through the black serpent being that emanated from the creature, sending it hurtling into the deep crevice below.

Valkyrie displayed remarkable agility, leaping over the beast and seizing the other python-like appendage. Rachel and Nicole, undeterred, launched a coordinated attack against the thrashing serpent.

Corey had transformed into the Green Man he fought with in the data center, his giant frame focused on the creature's head. I took in our surroundings. From above, a spider-like creature with hawk-like talons descended upon Onoskelis' back. Sensing the imminent danger to our ally, I used my wings to get there and sliced through the creature's feet just before they touched her. A follow up swift stab dispatched the spider-like menace, its body dissolving into nothingness.

Empowered by the white blade's awe-inspiring strength, I couldn't bear to part with it.

With the lifeless spider tumbling into the gaping crevice, Onoskelis glanced at me before returning her attention to the fierce battle. A golden beam of light struck me, sending a jolt through my chest. It was just like with the Snake-Hunter.

Corey transformed into the Green Man, a towering figure composed of interwoven sticks and leaves, standing at a formidable twelve feet. With astonishing strength, he seized the three-ton beast and hurled it into the crevice, its smooth orb-like head leading the way.

Corey, Rachel, and I each received balls of light that matched the color of their aura, impacting their chests with an otherworldly force.

Unbeknownst to them, a second spider-like creature approached Corey from above, behind her head. No one could get to it in time—except Nicole!

Nicole missed the creature but ensnared its thread with the hook on her staff, causing the creature to flail and struggle. It had to stop its attack on Corey, but it dragged her to the edge.

Rachel caught Nicole and hurled the heavy chain of her weapon, knocking the spider-like menace away. Meanwhile, I conjured a *Sanctuary of Light*, a protective barrier of sunlight around Corey.

He recovered, and with a powerful punch, he sent the flailing spider flying away. Nicole clung to her staff, snapping the thread of the spider-like Nephilim beast and severing the connection, watching as the spider plummeted into the abyss below.

Nicole had saved Corey's life and without Corey in the center with his druid circle, we would have all died. Wesley has foreseen it all.

The beasts had been dying to our attack, and every death, either Earth or Celestia, granted us the power of the creature by shooting the beams of light that hit our chest. A brilliant green beam emerged from the abyss, splitting into two, arcing toward Nicole's abdomen. *Did they penetrate her womb instead of her chest?*

"We've awakened a Nephilim giant," said Onoskelis.

Was she crying from killing Nephilim beasts?

In that moment, a white light as pure as my sword blade created a rift, crackling with white lightning, and a man and woman stepped forth, accompanied by a young boy. The other Nephilim beasts reared at the light and retreated into the shadows, their thunderous footsteps fading away.

"Green Man," spoke the young boy with a touch of antiquity in his voice, a mixture of modernized old English and Greek. "We seek your counsel, for our need is great."

Corey, holding the mantle of the Green Man, looked down upon the boy with a deep sense of contemplation. His voice resonated with wisdom as he replied. "Speak."

The boy's eyes darted between the group gathered before him as he continued, "The Curia from our universe has suffered a devastating blow at the hands of a potential ally in this world. Someone dispatched a Cardinal from our version of Earth, and we must intervene. But we lack knowledge of when and where this encounter will take place." As the boy's companions, clad in modern armor, scanned their surroundings, shock washed over their faces.

My angel form could see a strange signature on something I intrinsically knew was an anchor. These were humans from the other bubble universe!

In the role of the Green Man, Corey gave a response that sounded less like a wise forest guardian, and more like Corey. "In Buford, a city northeast of Atlanta, Georgia, in the United States, there is a camping store. A New Year's celebration will take place there, but hidden beneath the festivities, a battle awaits. Seek the allies you require, but travel incognito. When you arrive, request that the band play the song 'Rocking into the Night' to announce your presence."

It was lucky they asked Corey a question about the attack on New Year's Eve. He had that information.

Gratitude filled the young boy's voice as he repeated the city's name and the song's name, then thanked the Green Man. With determination, the woman carrying a bolt-action sniper rifle pulled the boy back toward the shimmering white portal. The man with the assault rifle grasped his companion's collar, leading them backward until they disappeared into the portal, which sealed shut, leaving behind a lingering sense of possibility and uncertainty.

Corey released his hold on the Green Man's mantle, reverting to his true form.

I scanned the surroundings, my gaze lingering on the gore upon the rock. The aftermath of the battle hung heavy in the air, a palpable tension whispering of both triumph and impending challenges.

Silence settled around us as Corey's eyes met mine, an unspoken understanding passing between us. There was much more to come, and we would face it together.

In that pause, my mind returned to the white blade, its radiant glow etched into memory. Its power was indescribable, connecting me to greatness.

"That team used the power of creation in great quantities. The beasts will be scared for some time," said the fallen angel. That white light of creation can annihilate even them, as Rebecca has shown.

"Let's continue," said Corey. He had already taken steps through the tunnel that the other beasts had retreated through.

Rachel grabbed Corey's arm and pointed to Nicole lying on the ground.

Wanting to keep the moment from overwhelming us, I kept things light. "Corey, with all those Greeks standing there, you communicated using music, and you didn't choose Vangelis?" I shook my head at him, a mischievous grin spreading across my face. The presence of Nephilim didn't unnerve me as much as it should have. Celestia made this form for combating them and it gave me confidence like I never experienced before.

Nicole's demeanor lightened as she looked up from her sprawled position on the ground, peering over the edge. "Really, Corey? Didn't the Kefefs, the HK33, or even the Greek flag on their military uniforms give them away?"

Corey glanced down at his fiancé; concern etched on his face. "Are you alright?"

"Could someone help me?" Nicole gestured toward something under the ledge that emitted a vibrant green glow, much like her anklet.

Rachel rolled up her surujin and grasped her sister's feet while Nicole lowered her weapon and maneuvered it. "I've got it, but I could use some help. It's heavy."

Corey positioned himself beside her, and without hesitation, I vaulted over and seized hold of his feet. Together, the four of us hauled up a cocoon that had seen better days. Within the cocoon, a book and a vambrace peeked out. *Someone wearing armor?*

Corey split open the cocoon, revealing a sight that left Nicole's eyes wide with astonishment. "Oh my God, the title of the book says <u>Abernathy Lineage</u>."

Each time Nicole contacted the cocoon, its interior illuminated with a vivid green light. A memory of the green light splitting hit me and I remembered only classes could power up with defeating powerful beings. Regular Realized, like empaths, only got stronger through practice. "Corey, Nicole is pregnant with twins and they're going to come out stronger because of this fight."

"What?" Corey looked at me like I was crazy.

Nicole fell back from the cocoon. "Twins run in my family. I was wondering why the green lights went into my stomach."

"It's a druid in armor," said Rachel, staying on task.

Onoskelis spoke next, her gaze drifting away from the cocoon, fixated on the bottom of the ravine where they had disposed of the lifeless creatures. "The Abernathy druids lost a dozen druids while trying to trap the Nephilim in these caves. The giants were the primary culprits, as the beasts initially trusted the druids because of their ability to communicate."

Onoskelis displayed no sign of sorrow or anger. Instead, she looked away from the cocoon and directed her attention toward us.

"This isn't the setting for discussions or to open this," Corey said. "Let's gather everything, including the remains. I'll ensure the druid receives a proper burial, and we can examine this further later." Retrieving his telescoping poles, Corey fashioned a wrapped stretcher, cocooning the artifact within it.

Nicole and Rachel shouldered the burden while Onoskelis surveyed the party. "Are we ready, kids?"

With determination, we traversed the ten-foot-long entranceway, our footsteps echoing through the lit passage.

In an opening of a cavern between jagged rocks, a mysterious black orb pulsated on the floor. The ancient evil in a weakened state.

Onoskelis strode toward the dark sphere and placed her hand upon it.

Something was wrong. The fallen angel let out a piercing scream, flickering in and out of existence.

Corey lunged towards the fallen angel, tracing a circle on the ground. He placed three white and red honeysuckle plants within the circle's boundary, then pressed his hand against the fallen angel's hand, clasping the malevolent orb. His other hand remained within the confines of the circle.

Onoskelis regained her composure, and then an extraordinary event unfolded before us. Another pair materialized, mirroring Corey and the fallen angel. With the black orb clasped in their outstretched hands, they embraced one another, swaying in an ethereal dance. And then the ethereal copies of Corey and Onoskelis shared a passionate kiss.

I glanced towards the writhing bodies on the ground, their forms contorted in agony, while Corey's hand glowed with a brilliant green radiance where it touched the earth.

In the next moment, the floating couple underwent a profound transformation. Onoskelis radiated a resplendent golden light, her celestial wings and halo glistening with golden celestial luminescence. It was a scene of incomparable beauty, and tears of joy welled up in my eyes.

Corey collapsed onto the ground, tears streaming down his face. As the ethereal apparitions dissipated, Corey and Onoskelis rose, their gazes locked, their chests heaving with exertion.

Unable to contain herself any longer, Onoskelis fell backwards. She screamed, her anguish reverberating through the chamber. With that, she turned and fled.

Confusion gripped Corey, his mind struggling to grasp his surroundings. He spun in circles, disoriented.

"Is it gone?" Rachel shouted, breaking through the chaos. Guiding Corey in the right direction, she pointed him towards the exit.

Corey's voice rang out, a mix of bewilderment and alarm. His words came out in perfect German. He had never spoken another language before. But he asked who we were!

A roar that sounded human echoed through the cave, accompanied by heavy thumps that shook the cavern. It was a Nephilim giant!

The black orb vanished from sight, Corey was confused, and a giant was trying to squeeze into the cavern. "It's done, and we need to leave," I cried out.

Grasping Corey's hand, I led him out, while Rachel shouldered the burden of the stretcher, and Nicole took hold of Corey's other hand.

Chapter 23—Rebecca

Beyond the druid barrier shimmering with Earth power, we emerged from the cave into the welcoming embrace of the outside world. We sought solace against the weathered stone wall, hiding from the relentless winds that threatened to consume us near the gaping crevasse. Corey's expression betrayed his confusion, his haunted eyes revealing the unseen horrors that plagued his thoughts.

He did not recognize us!

Night had descended as we emerged from the treacherous depths of the cave. Guiding Corey to the left, I urged him to rest against the jagged edge. Our companions settled beside him, their watchful eyes scanning the surroundings for any sign of Onoskelis. However, her elusive presence remained swallowed by the darkness. Tension hung heavy in the air, and Nicole's voice pierced the stillness, her frustration echoing through the rugged terrain. "What happened in there, Corey?"

Seated on the cold ground, Corey's trembling form cradled by his own arms, tears streamed down his face. Corey mumbled, but I understood him. He still spoke German!

"You've blocked everything out!" Nicole was close to losing control.

She must be talking about hiding his thoughts and emotions with his earring. I pulled Nicole into a comforting embrace. "Nicole, this is not the place or time to demand answers. Give him some time." If Corey blocked all of his thoughts and emotions from Nicole, something major happened.

Gradually, Nicole's trembling subsided, and she found the strength to speak again. "I'm sorry, Corey. This scared me. Please, tell me what happened."

I kneeled next to Corey. "Sprich Englisch," I whispered. My degree in Classics finally had a use.

"I," he pointed at himself and struggled with words, "practice the King's English," he fumbled out in a German accent. He looked at me curiously.

This was a start.

Minutes stretched into what felt like an eternity, but Corey raised his tear-stained face and wiped away the remnants of his anguish. He spoke in German and wanted to know where we were. My linguistic skills were rusty, but I could pick out of enough of simple sentences.

"They kissed!" cried Nicole.

Now, more than ever, we needed to regain control over our tumultuous hearts. "Let's all calm down. Nicole, what you witnessed was an apparition. Some power locked Corey and Onoskelis in a struggle, writhing in pain on the cave floor." Turning to Corey, I said in German, "dangerous cliffs," since I couldn't remember the word for ravine.

Rachel put her hand on her sister's shoulder. "Exactly! It was like a scene from a movie. Corey never even left the ground—I watched his every move. You know I wouldn't stop watching him."

Nicole nodded and Rachel had calmed her.

A fluttering of wings broke the silence. "The universal laws require me to make even trades like it does you." She handed me a Prayer Book of Celestia.

Corey interrupted, "Onoskelis."

She spoke in German to him. I picked up 'This is the real,' in her response. I didn't understand the rest.

"Thank you." I accepted the book of sacred prayers from the fallen angel. It was nearly a duplicate of the one I carried in my purse. My connection to Celestia calculated the balanced required of all angel trades and I had saved her life.

With a grumble, the fallen angel continued, "Your white sword blade possesses the essence of creation—the primordial power that predates everything and holds the ability to shape or annihilate anything. It is the same power the other universe's humans used that instilled fear in the hearts of the beasts. Exercise caution in wielding it, for its influence can transform you. That is what the forces of evil dread. This fulfills the universe's law requiring angels to make fair trades."

The fallen angel addressed Rachel. "Rachel Pureheart, from this moment forth, no one shall berate Corey for knowledge of what happened." As if to emphasize her point, Onoskelis opened a box, shielding her eyes from its luminous contents. "No one, not even his fiancé or wife, shall demean him for the information. I offer these weapons to help protect his fragile mind."

"Guys, if you don't agree, you'll break a universal law and things could go badly," I said.

"Very well, Corey. Your secret shall forever remain between us, as you wish," Rachel said, her gaze fixed on Nicole.

Nicole's eyes locked with Corey's pained expression, and after a moment of internal struggle, she agreed. "Fine. But it's because you said it's protecting his mind."

Why would a fallen angel give gifts to protect Corey?

Rachel handed Nicole a glowing nunti-bo, while she herself received a luminous surujin. Both weapons shimmered with celestial power, and Onoskelis could not bear to look at them.

"This concludes the fair trades required to balance the laws of our universe. I will be absent for some time, but when the forces of evil rear their heads once more, we shall unite again."

Onoskelis put her arms on Corey's shoulder and he stared into her eyes. She spoke to him in German and her last word was English.

"I try," said Corey.

Onoskelis turned to me, and tears filled her eyes. "His mind isn't ready for this. He'll need help. Treat him like he has amnesia. I've been alive for dozens of millennia and two centuries is nothing to me, but to him…" Onoskelis had tears in her eyes. She didn't finish. Onoskelis' wings propelled her upward as a swirling cloud of corrupted gray smoke ascended with her.

Corey's eyes teared again.

Valkyrie nestled against Corey, seeking solace in his presence. Corey hugged the large dog.

"Valkyrie still recognizes him as Corey," Rachel said. "But we need to go. It's growing darker, and the stories of what lurks in the shadows down here frighten me."

Corey patted Valkyrie, then rose to his feet. He yanked on my harness, then his harness, and shrugged.

"Bottomless Ravine," I said and pretended everything was normal. I tried to get as much German as I can remember and tried to say "your skill is needed to lead us out."

It was enough because he started securing us. He got to Rachel and placed his hands on her shoulders. "Rachel? Rachel?"

Rachel hugged him, then he lifted the muscle-bound Rachel like she was my weight and yelled, "Rachel!" His excitement was palpable. He hugged her.

This was a start. He looked at me. "Rebecca," I told him.

"Rebecca," he repeated.

"Okay. Do you remember Valkyrie?"

He hugged the dog. "Bond," he answered.

Nicole was crying. "Why did I get a weapon? What can't I ask Corey about what happened? How do I know what going on?" Her emotions scared Corey and he ignored her. Nicole needed consoling.

I hugged her. "Let's get safe first. Remember, you have my promise to help you two as a couple." She wasn't quite ready to move on. "Look, this is super complicated. Let's not risk making things worse."

"That makes sense," she agreed.

I turned my attention to the daunting ravine, its unforgiving edges disappearing into an abyss of darkness. The wind, laden with moisture and sand, whirled into its depths with dizzying velocity. We would need to navigate its treacherous expanse with the help of the relentless gusts. An overwhelming sense of dread seized me as we found ourselves bereft of the fallen angel's guidance, the comforting embrace of daylight, and confronted with a changed and confused Corey.

I pointed to the treacherous area. "Bottomless Ravine."

"Licht?" he asked. He secured us together with our harnesses.

"Rachel, we need light," I translated.

Rachel cast a spell and her bardic light lit up the area.

"Leader," he said and pointed to himself. It wasn't a question, and that was a relief. He handed the pack to Rachel, Secured the cocoon to his back and picked up Valkyrie.

He was competent and confident. That, at least, was something to hold on to. I pointed the direction we needed to go and translated as much as I could to say, "we turn up when we get to our packs."

We started our perilous trek once again, braving the treacherous winds that threatened to sweep us away with every step. Communication became impossible in the deafening howls, leaving us to face the relentless gusts in silence.

As we ventured further, a surge of fear coursed through me, causing my confidence in Corey to waver. Doubt gnawed at my core. How could I carry him if he faltered? Worst-case scenarios made me ready to unleash my *Angelic Form* and envelop us all in protective sanctuary bubbles. We would find ourselves alive in the depths of the ravine. There must be a bottom to this abyss.

The maelstrom of swirling winds and clutter continued unabated and whipped at me, but nothing hurt like remembering the pain in Corey's face. I had counted on him for so long.

I pressed my left shoulder against the icy rock face, seeking refuge from the elements. In a position behind Corey, fear tightened its grip on me, threatening to unravel my concentration on the spell preparations that held our lives in balance. The wind whined and howled, mirroring its previous torment, but the darkness obscured the forms that swirled around us until they came into Rachel's servant's light. Corey quickened his pace, and our group left behind a trail of determination.

Out of breath, we reached the first stopping point, a ledge leading to higher ground. Corey remained silent while we retrieved our packs, yet we remained tethered together, climbing the safer path along the ravine. Tears of relief welled up in my eyes, replacing the sting of the biting wind. The hardest physical part of the journey was over.

With control of my terror, I contemplated the disparity between Corey's power and mine. His transformation had altered him, and now it fell upon me to rise to the occasion. It was no longer fair to rely on him to carry our burdens. This would not be an overnight metamorphosis, but he had shouldered too great a weight, and it was time for me to step up. It was time for me to take charge of our destinies like he had done for so long. The encounter between him and the fallen angel had shaken them both.

Had she ascended to heaven, only to return to our realm? Why did she choose to come back? What did she mean that two centuries were nothing to her, but it hurt Corey's mind? There was nothing positive to think about, so I focused on staying alive and making alternate plans should Corey falter.

Two arduous hours later, we arrived at our campsite. Though he had driven us hard, Corey wasted no time in tending to the essentials—a fire and a comfortable resting place.

Corey must have summoned Earth power, as he was the sole individual capable of physical movement. He remained resolute in his unwavering determination, the embodiment of hard Corey. Instead of cooking, he conjured druidic berries, offering one to each of us. With a touch of his healing power, he tended to Valkyrie's wounds.

Corey laid down and hugged himself.

Nicole responded without hesitation, drawing him close and lay beside him, while Rachel positioned herself on his other side. As if following an unspoken cue, I nestled beside Nicole, extending my arm over her in a display of support. Nicole grasped my arm and guided it towards Corey, creating a reassuring connection. Soon, exhaustion overwhelmed me, and I succumbed to sleep, finding solace in the warmth and unity of our shared slumber.

SUNLIGHT HAD NOT ARRIVED when Corey's movement to find a place to relieve himself stirred all of us awake.

I stayed awake while Nicole and Rachel fell back asleep. When he returned, his eyes reflecting compassion, Corey called me to the side and kept his voice so only the two of us heard, "Rebecca. Deutsch?"

"A little," I whispered back in German. I had my phone with me to cheat.

We communicated in broken English and broken German until he knew why we were here, what was going on, and what our statuses were. I caught him up on Lance, the bubble, the vampires, the Gullah spell, and the Boo Hags. He got it, but things were not good with Corey. This was an enormous burden, but one I would not let down.

He smiled, and asked me a question I had to translate a couple of times. He wanted to know if the name Austrian Empire stuck or if we were still the Holy Roman Empire.

"I wrote a paper on the decline of the Hapsburg Monarchies. That's over two hundred years ago," I said in German.

His face saddened and he nodded. He stumbled back to the sleeping area; we could figure things out later when our minds rested more.

I mustered my remaining strength, despite my numbed fingers and foggy mind. Physical exhaustion intertwined with the weight of fear, the knowledge I had come to terms with about the Nephilim and creation power, and Corey's deteriorating state, all colliding to bring tears to my weary eyes as I struggled to type out a coherent message. Dispatching brief texts of our success to Chesapeake and including Madison in the correspondence, I promised more comprehensive updates come daylight. The all-encompassing fatigue left no room for coherent thought, and I needed rest.

As the darkness re-embraced me, sleep claimed my senses, drawing me into a realm of dreams alongside my steadfast companions. This time, movement would not wake me.

At the break of dawn, Corey attempted to slip away, to find all four of us wakened by his movements. "Fire," he said.

Despite my exhaustion, I resisted the urge to curl up, took care of my needs, and settled beside the crackling flames, joining Corey in heating water and preparing the dehydrated eggs. I gestured toward the phone nearby, a symbol of our connection to the outside world.

He shrugged.

"I sent a simple status last night. We need to update the Command Center."

Corey pointed to himself and then pointed to me. "English."

"Yes?" I wasn't sure what he said.

"Show." He stood and snapped to attention then saluted like he had a practiced ritual. "Captain, notify your command under King George of readiness. Our troops are in good health and morale is high. Please provide instructions."

This was a clue and before I updated everyone, I wanted to clear something up. In German, I asked him what his name and title were.

"Freiherr Reiser, retired Wachtmeister." His eyes picked up, and he asked me something with a lot of words I didn't grasp.

That was such a huge clue. I knew his training and location.

"Let me report first," I said in German. With my phone in hand, the weight on my shoulders lightened as I cycled through my messages and summarized the information. I translated into German using my phone's translation app to help.

"Let's start with Atlanta. No injuries reported, and we have dealt both Boo Hags with," I said. "Nathan was the primary target, but Miles, Clive, and Baron took down the first Boo Hag. Isabella, Coach White, and Madison handled the one that sneaked into the Command Center."

Corey mumbled "vampire der neuen welt," and I understood it

I nodded. "Yes. Boo Hags are vampires from the new world."

"I have a lot on my plate because of treason and embezzlement," I confessed, weariness slipping into my voice. "The Southeast has provided resources for detection and pursuit. Boo Hag Team One has deployed to Virginia, and we expected the incursion within twelve to sixty hours."

Corey's frown deepened, reflecting the gravity of the situation. I intervened, cutting off his concerns before they could spiral. He pointed to himself. "Keep secret." Then in German he said he graduated from the Theresianum.

With his title and that statement, I had enough information to know he was discussing the seventeenth or eighteenth century. I had to know when.

His answer shocked me. "Seventeen-fifty"

"Twenty-twenty-three." I put this to the side until I finished my duties. The revised message got sent to all relevant parties. My previous night's text message caused me to chuckle, and I hoped it didn't alarm anyone. Three words all ran together because of my exhaustion.

As the morning progressed, the hanging water container doubled as a makeshift wash area, adorned with a couple of towels for the much-needed sponge baths we each embarked upon. Corey served plates of dehydrated breakfast and a druidic berry, ensuring we were all nourished. Rachel had carried enough dog food for Valkyrie, who devoured her meal.

Rachel's voice held a touch of excitement as she addressed Corey. "Can you create a large circle? Nicole and I will be inside it, along with the items nestled within the cocoon," she requested, a radiant smile gracing her face. "With my bardic lore skills in one of your circles, we'll be able to get a lot done." She had to pantomime a circle.

While they did that, I consoled Nicole. "He thinks he's an Austrian from Vienna in the eighteenth century."

"What am I supposed to do with that?" She did not improve with the news.

"Please trust me. Like I trusted your computer knowledge when spying, trust my knowledge to find something we can work with."

She wasn't happy but agreed to work with her sister,

Corey drew a circle, and it differed from he used to make. He made the area between his two circles larger and put a honeysuckle bush where he used to put honeysuckle twigs.

Meanwhile, the lingering questions posed in my recent messages drew my attention. "Corey, they're inquiring about how to include different troop types in the report," I informed him, seeking his guidance. He looked at my phone and I showed him the report.

"Paper and quill?" he asked.

He wrote out a beautiful report for four hundred men with proper statuses. I studied the diagram he sketched out while enjoying my meal. It made perfect sense, although I noted I would need to familiarize myself with some of the troop types mentioned. I transcribed the details into my phone and sent out the revised report to the concerned parties.

With the cooking supplies now clean and stowed away, Corey stumbled to his sleeping area. He needed a break.

In need of recovery and solace, I planned to study the prayer book from Onoskelis. Corey laid down, but instead of surrendering to rest, he retrieved a folder from his pack and perused its contents. Valkyrie nestled beside him.

I couldn't help but watch Corey for a while, my eyes tracing the lines of exhaustion etched upon his features. Yet, in the weariness, there was something resilient about him. My gaze shifted to the prayer book in my hands, a tangible reminder of the weight we carried and the power we possessed.

Studying the new prayers for Onoskelis could really help calm my mind. As I perused its pages, I discovered Onoskelis hadn't rewarded me lightly. The words within promised the acquisition of four new spells by day's end—four potent spells that could turn the tide in our favor. Grateful for the opportunity, I relished the anticipation of unlocking this newfound magic. My energy surged with this knowledge, and I buried myself in the words from Celestia.

Chapter 24—Madison and Rebecca

Madison stood in Corey's spacious living room with her gaze fixed on Nathan's restless pacing. Wesley, filled with nervous energy, bustled around the room, tidying up after breakfast and cleaning every sheet and towel in the house. They had been waiting all night and into the morning, anticipation building as they expected communication from their team.

Madison's laptop emitted a soft ding, signaling an incoming email. "It's Rebecca!" she called out, breaking the tense silence that hung in the air. Relief washed over her, grateful that it wasn't another text riddled with a single giant typo. Nathan sank down beside her, and Wesley settled on the other side, their collective attention focused on the screen.

Madison's eyes scanned the email, absorbing its contents. "It's a genuine message from her, but she sent it to everyone," she informed her companions. Doubt gnawed at her, for this wasn't typical of Rebecca's usual behavior. She read aloud the check-in report. "They were successful, and Onoskelis has confirmed their triumph. She will return as planned, rendezvousing with the Territory Leaders. The team is resting because of both physical and emotional exhaustion. They'll be monitoring communications, ready to assist us if needed. Otherwise, we should expect them tomorrow morning."

Nathan pondered the email, a perplexed expression on his face. "At least this seems official. But why mention emotional exhaustion?"

"Rachel confided Corey has a fear of Bottomless Ravine," Wesley said.

She considered the implications before suggesting, "Should we call Miles? He's been there before. Maybe he can shed some light on it."

Nathan nodded in agreement. "Yes, that's a good idea. We know Virginia will ask about our thoughts on this matter." He reclined and dialed Miles' number, the phone's soft ringing filling the room.

"Good morning, Miles," Nathan greeted as the call connected. "We've got a couple of things to discuss. I'll put you on speaker with Madison, Wesley, and myself."

"Hey, guys," Miles' voice boomed over the speakerphone. "We're here munching on junk food, and it's doing wonders for our spirits."

"That's great," Nathan said. "We received an update from the team. They're all safe, but they mentioned being physically and emotionally exhausted."

Miles swallowed his food, then continued, his tone serious. "The last time Corey used those words was after he, Old Donnie, and I ventured to Bottomless Ravine. Trust me, if I had to take Trish there, I'd ask for a month to recover if we made it back alive."

Madison's mind connected the dots. "Corey had Valkyrie, Nicole, Rachel, and Rebecca with him. Corey was the only experienced climber." A shiver ran down her spine.

Miles continued, his voice filled with a mix of caution and trepidation. "Bottomless Ravine spans a narrow ledge, stretching from six to fifteen feet wide. Winds howl at speeds ranging from sixty to over a hundred miles per hour. One wrong step, and you're lost forever. It's impossible to measure the depth because of the relentless winds and the peculiar nature of the rock formations. Certain death awaits anyone who dares to venture too close."

"Rebecca typed out the message, but her previous text was a single typo, meant to read 'success,' 'exhausted,' and 'sleeping,'" Madison said, hoping to provide some context.

"I can do more than track Corey since I've tracked him for years. Let me search for him," said Miles. After a pause the man responded. "Huh, he's changed."

"What do you mean changed?" asked Nathan.

"It's him. He's still an ally, but his power signature is off the charts," he said.

"I'll check it out," said Nathan. "The team is alive but Corey is much stronger. That's not an emergency."

While they had him on the line, Miles shared some vital information. "By the way, we're heading toward the Pentagon, but something feels off. My instincts are tingling for an airbase near Virginia Beach. Baron says it's called NAS Oceana."

"Thanks, Miles. We'll get back to you soon." A faint smile graced Nathan's face. "I feel better now that I'm no longer worried about the team. We can deal with a stronger druid when we have more time. I'm celebrating everyone is alive."

Turning to Madison his face turned serious. "Can you send an official message to Rebecca?"

She leaned into him, finding solace in his comforting presence. "What should I write?"

"Let her know the Chesapeake team has deployed team one to the Pentagon. Also, include this part in quotes, tell her, Miles said, 'My senses are tingling for NAS Oceana.'"

Madison slumped into her chair, her anxiety subsiding. "Message sent. Now you and Wesley should get some rest. There won't be any immediate developments, and I'll wake you if we receive any updates. Take a nap while I handle the communication."

"Good idea," Nathan agreed. Wesley had already succumbed to slumber on the nearby couch. Wesley's peaceful smile hinted at the relief he felt upon hearing Rachel's safety.

THE ANCIENT PRAYER book engrossed me in its delicate pages adorned with symbols of power, with Rachel and Nicole's conversation serving as a soothing backdrop to my secluded study. The fragrance of incense hung in the air, creating a comforting ambiance. Spells etched their way into my mind throughout the day.

Just as this book of power gave me its wisdom, my phone vibrated, bringing me back to the present. Madison's name and picture flashed on the screen, and I reached for it, my fingers trembling with anticipation. I read the text and I needed to take charge of my team again.

They were ignoring the senses of someone trained to hunt prey with magical abilities. I'd need to remove everyone from the leadership team who was not Realized. My first message was polite to see if they understood their mistake. "Ensuring team one from the Southeast has everything they need to be at Naval Air Station Oceana."

A reply returned, originating from an unfamiliar number. "We feel the Pentagon is a more appropriate location," it read.

Furrowing my brow, I contemplated the implications of this. There may be another traitor in the response team. The next message I received would hold immense significance, determining the fate of our mission and the safety of all involved. I demanded the sender make the change Miles expected, threatening interrogation if they resisted.

"The team is on the way. We apologize for any inconvenience caused and will make the changes," the text came, relieving the tension that had coiled within me.

The unfamiliar number on my screen caused a wave of unease to wash over me. I tainted my first encounter with a recruit using a touch of intimidation. Maybe more than a touch. In that moment, I resolved to find a middle ground, balancing compassion and unwavering leadership. I needed to forge my path.

The atmosphere in our camp settled into a tranquil rhythm, broken by the rustling of pages as I immersed myself in my studies. Corey prepared a late lunch for us.

Lost in the world of ancient spells and arcane knowledge, dusk had already cast its velvety cloak over the land. Spells had entered my mind and my power had increased with the knowledge. Corey's sudden exclamation shattered the serenity, and I turned to face him, my heart quickening with anticipation.

"Down!" he warned.

"Freund!" exclaimed Christopher. He had shouted friend in German.

What was he doing here?

Curiosity piqued, I followed Corey's gaze and found myself face to face with an unexpected visitor—a man with disheveled dark hair, cradling a portfolio in his hands. Recognition flickered in my mind.

"It's okay Corey," I said, running over.

He nodded and laid back down.

Undeterred by Corey's doubt, the artist unfolded his portfolio, moving through our camp with a graceful purpose. Despite his unkempt appearance, his attire exuded an air of sophistication, and every step he took seemed focused on his artistic pursuit. There was something captivating about his unwavering dedication to his craft, reminiscent of Corey's unwavering resolve.

"It is a pleasure, Rebecca," said the artist. He smiled at me then he studied Corey, as if envisioning a potential painting. "Wow! I wouldn't risk angering a fallen angel to paint this story, let alone discuss it. Although I must admit, traveling with you holds a certain appeal."

A bemused smile danced upon my lips as Corey's confusion played out before me. It was a welcome respite from the weight of our recent trials. Rachel and Valkyrie joined us, their infectious energy filling the air with excitement.

The two of them started conversing in fluent German. They talked too fast for me to keep up, so I went back to my new spells in the new Prayer book after Corey looked at me with a huge grin. At least he and Christopher weren't enemies. They were having a jolly time talking in German.

After I secured this new knowledge, Rachel called out for us all to hear. "Look at Nicole," Rachel called out, her voice brimming with anticipation. "She's the Abernathy Legacy Warrior."

I turned my gaze to Nicole, the embodiment of strength, adorned in the resplendent armor of the revered warrior druid, Charis Abernathy. The sight stirred awe within me, and I couldn't help but share in Rachel's exhilaration. One of Christopher's paintings drawn from the stories of her exploits adorned the grand hall in Virginia.

"The armor of the last great warrior druid," Christopher exclaimed, unable to contain his enthusiasm. "How utterly exciting!" The painter, sensing the significance of the moment, sketched notes in his notebook.

"Nicole is a direct legacy to Charis Abernathy." Rachel's eyes sparkled with pride as she clutched a book. "The lineage is from both sides of her parents, making her closer related than me!" Valkyrie joined in with a playful bark.

History unfolded before us, and I marveled at the convergence of past and present. The painter's fascination was clear as he approached Nicole, his eyes alight with curiosity. His gaze roamed over her, capturing every detail as though he were painting with his mind's eye. Then he walked over to the circle where the remains of the druid were lying.

"I promise not to touch—just reading the aura," the painter said.

I overheard Corey mutter, "Wait!" he yelled. He had a huge smile.

He took my hand and said, "angel." When he placed me in my *Angelic Form* next to Nicole, he placed Rachel on the other side of Nicole. Then he pointed to my other side.

"He's putting us in his vision order," said Nicole, getting excited. She pointed to the empty spot and pantomimed a bow. "Madison is back in Atlanta. With her red hair and bow."

Corey hugged Nicole.

"The darn bigger boobs vision is how he remembered me." Hey happiness streamed through her voice and face.

Corey stepped back and incanted a spell. A red light shone from under his kilt and then Nicole's jeans lit up red. "Fey! Consort." After yelling, Corey stepped backwards and leaned against the tree his mouth agape.

Christopher ignored us, engrossed in the circle with the body. "Inside a druid circle, no less! This is truly fabulous," he exclaimed, his voice brimming with genuine fascination.

I reveled in the chaotic beauty that surrounded us. Laughter cascaded from my lips as Corey wavered between laughter, shock, and a desire to maintain control over the unfolding situation. Rachel and Valkyrie rushed over to join me, their infectious enthusiasm spreading like wildfire.

"This is going to work out," Rachel said with a huge grin. "Corey saw Nicole in this armor long before he knew of Lance or knew a fallen angel."

Her words resonated within me, the significance of Corey's vision striking like lightning. With a newfound understanding, I called out to him, looking up the words on my phone. My voice filled with excitement. "Corey! You saw Nicole wearing this armor before the world changed," I said in German.

Corey lifted Nicole and kissed her while spinning her around. "I'm remembering!"

"Stop that! I'm a legacy warrior!" Nicole protested, laughter mingling with her words. The kiss that followed, once a source of pain, now held the promise of a brighter future. It was a testament to the restoration of normalcy and the strength of their bond, as well as my acceptance of Corey as a friend, rather than a lover.

A jarring ringtone pierced through the jubilant atmosphere, interrupting our celebration. My phone demanded immediate attention. Nathan's number appeared.

"Rebecca, it's Nathan. The team has encountered one of the three Boo Hags at the airbase. We're tracking another one that has materialized near your grandmother's mansion. She's the target."

Every fiber of my being snapped to attention, the weight of responsibility settling upon my shoulders. There was no time to waste, no luxury for hesitation. The newly gained spells whispered promises of power and protection, and I resolved to put them to the test. I didn't need Corey; this was my duty.

"Hey, everyone, I'll be heading to Virginia. Christopher, provide translation. Rachel, take charge of Corey." I embraced my true nature—the Scion, a force to be reckoned with. Summoning the celestial light, its golden glow enveloped me in a shimmering embrace.

With unwavering focus, I envisioned the Emergency Response Team Situation Room, the very heart of our operations. Corey's voice broke the silence. "What—"

But there was no time for explanations. The mission beckoned, and as I stepped into the newfound realm of my abilities. The world outside blurred as the celestial light transferred me. In an instant, the room shimmered into existence—a nexus of power and coordination, the epicenter of our operations.

Chapter 25—Rebecca

My arrival bathed every corner in a resplendent celestial glow. The once somber space, draped in the shades of black and white from the Realm of Shadows, now radiated with golden light, penetrating every nook and cranny demonstrating the power of Celestial light. A figure, craven in mottled white, hovered close to my kneeling grandmother, its power holding her head aloft. Their proximity was reminiscent of an impending kiss.

With a clenched fist, I summoned a newly mastered spell, the *Celestial Beam*. As I unleashed its power, a torrent of luminous energy surged downward from the heavens, propelling the spindly, pale-white being across the room as if it were a marionette severed from its strings.

A flap of my wings assisted in a jump over a nearby desk. I executed a precise maneuver, my blade slicing through the creature's limb with a decisive stroke. Mindful of my teachings of form and stance, I slowed my movements, seeking to harness every ounce of power. With Onoskelis' solemn warning in mind, I envisioned the golden celestial blade, its essence pulsating within me.

The spindly white creature, a macabre tapestry of bones, lunged toward my defenseless grandmother. From a steadfast square stance, I swung my golden celestial blade with unwavering determination, cleaving deep into the creature's skeletal chest.

Men cowered in the shadows, their terrified pleas urging me to aid her. "Help her!" I bellowed, pointing at my grandmother's prone form.

With a firm grip, I seized the creature, its spine severed, and threw it through the window into the sunlight.

As grandmother was helped up to one knee, I closed the distance, my wings unfurling to carry me towards the entity. With wings tucked, I breached the shattered window, hurtling into the sunlit beyond. The radiant rays of the sun cast an incandescent spotlight upon the writhing creature, its emaciated flesh concealing its human-like skeletal frame. It possessed clawed extremities, both hands and feet, while its mouth mirrored the chilling visage of a vampire, emitting a guttural, snarling symphony.

I strode towards the convulsing, smoke-shrouded creature. Corey had ripped the hearts out of enemies and I would too on such an evil being. My sword pierced the creature's chest, carving a circle, before I grasped the pulsating heart and cast it to the ground.

Thick tendrils of smoke billowed forth from the creature's fading form, its very essence dissipating into the air. My foot crushed the pulsating heart, a grotesque act necessary to ensure its ultimate demise.

As the smoldering heart disintegrated into the earth, the world regained its familiar semblance. I leaned into the shattered window, inquiring about the state of affairs. "Status!" I called out, concern lacing my voice. Grandmother lay motionless, her frail figure now a testament to the trials we had faced.

Without hesitation, I leaped into the room, invoking an *Angelic Heal* to mend her wounds. "Oh my," grandmother gasped, her voice laced with weariness. "Rebecca? You're just like Corey. You are a hero."

Grandmother comparing me to Corey was strange, so I helped her to a chair.

"I'm fine after the magical healing spell. Let me gather my wits," said grandmother.

I had my wits and gave orders. "I need a status and I need someone to report to Atlanta. This Boo hag is dead and Grandmother is safe."

"Thanks to your heroism," she said. "If I had known you could heal the pain in my joints, I would have asked you for a heal at Christmas."

"The team killed the first Boo Hag at the base, but they say they may lose the second!" shouted Lt. Shevski.

Grandmother joking showed the heal had done its job. I turned to my next duty. "I'll head there. Assemble everyone and compile detailed reports." Then, with a gathering of celestial light around me, my attention focused on Miles, his figure standing out against the commotion. Gathering my thoughts, I tapped into the power within me, feeling the celestial light envelop my form, resonating with the deafening whine of a jet engine.

"Rebecca?" Baron's voice cut through the din, laced with concern. I was on a runway with fighter jets.

"He's in the plane!" Clive shouted, pointing at the roaring jet with twin exhaust jets ablaze. Its dual tail stabilizers vibrated with untamed energy. It had not left the ground but moved away with the engines winding up.

Setting my gaze on a specific point ahead, I encased myself in a radiant halo of celestial light and teleported in front of the plane. With my golden blade leading the charge and shield in place, I pierced through the air, focused and determined.

Although I wasn't a skilled fighter or flyer, I knew I could fly straight and strike someone strapped in a seat. With my plan set, I soared forward with my sword and shield guiding the way. Panic flashed across the face of the man in the cockpit, his feeble attempts at control futile in the face of my impending approach.

The shattering of the transparent cockpit cover unleashed a torrent of debris, scattering fragments of the plane in a chaotic dance.

The pilot's seat ejected, and the shattered cover draped over me like a mantle. Illuminated by my celestial glow, the Boo Hag revealed its true form—an abominable entity disguised as a man. Without hesitation, I sliced through the restraints, binding the captive soul, wrenching the imposter from his seat and tossing him to the ground below.

I floated above the plane as it passed underneath me and wore the canopy around my waist. Both hands pressed down on the twisted metal and plastic wreckage, freeing me from the shattered cover. I landed on the ground, surveying the aftermath of our confrontation. Miles had already begun his grisly work, carving into the man's flesh, while Baron unleashed a searing ray of sunlight upon the disfigured creature.

As I flew down, a man I didn't recognize in a uniform ran to me. "Angel, can you help me reach the plane? Please, angel, ma'am," pleaded the man, his chest adorned with a small pin bearing golden wings. The plane hurtled, picking up speed toward a populated area of the base, a disaster waiting to happen.

Without hesitation, I grabbed hold of him, surrounding us in a radiant cocoon of celestial light, teleported in front of the plane, waited for it to pass under us, and lowered him into the decimated cockpit from above. The engines fell silent as he took control.

As the crowd on the runway exchanged bewildered glances, the pilot who had stopped the rogue plane emerged, his trembling form collapsing to the ground, his head cradled in his hands.

Exhaustion seeped into my bones; a tangible reminder of the energy spent during our battle. Soon, I would have to learn the art of flight, as teleporting as I had been doing demanded fortitude. With awkward flaps of my wings, I approached my team.

"Is that all?" I asked, a smile curving my lips as I surveyed their weary yet triumphant faces.

"If you killed the one within the estate, then yes," Clive said. "Other than the containment issue." He gestured towards the on-lookers who witnessed an angel, a vampire, and a massive man with a sword emitting green light fighting together with a man radiating sunlight.

"Contact Nathan and confirm," I said.

Miles dialed the required numbers. "All clear, Rebecca—uh, I mean, Corey, I mean Rebecca. Man, I'll never tell you two apart now," he grinned, the remnants of the battle fading from his eyes.

I brushed aside the jest, my focus shifting to the well-being of my companions. Assessing their physical states, I exhaled a contented breath.

Miles beamed. His weariness forgotten in the light of triumph. "Today was a good day!"

A soft chuckle escaped my lips as I shared in Miles' mirth. Turning to Baron, I noticed a subtle shadow cast across his expression. "Are you ready to depart, Baron?" I asked.

Baron, the lone contributor from Chesapeake Bay, his smile lacking its usual radiance, said, "Yes, I no longer feel like a Ray of Sunshine." He looked exhausted, just like a man who'd never fought before would after his first few days of battle.

"Dude, you better come to our party." Miles fist-bumped the smaller man. "You rocked it."

Moved by a surge of affection, I enveloped Baron in an embrace, a celestial aura enveloping us both. With a gentle surge of power, I transported us to the Emergency Response Team Situation Room, where we stood in the heart of a bustling chamber encircled by Grandmother and four members of the leadership team.

"I want to go home," Baron's voice quivered, revealing a hint of vulnerability.

Grandmother's weathered hands settled on the shoulder of the man who had seen better days, her touch conveying both reassurance and authority. The room fell into a hushed silence in response.

With a swift motion, I shed my *Angelic Form*, the ethereal glow fading into the mundane reality of jeans, rugged hiking boots, and a plaid flannel jacket, concealing two layers of t-shirts. This transformation marked a transition from the extraordinary to the ordinary, a reminder of the human beneath the supernatural.

"Baron, your bravery deserves a grand dinner party," Grandmother's voice resonated with pride and excitement. "I've just received a message from Nathan, and he spoke about how Corey himself bestowed upon you an official designation. You've played a pivotal role in three out of the five formidable adversaries we've faced."

"Rebecca was the superstar. I was part of a team." Baron's modesty echoed in the room as he found solace at an untouched desk, free from the chaos that had unfolded earlier.

"They placed you on team one, working alongside a vampire and our Lead Hunter, both of whom sing praises of your accomplishments," I said in, aware that the respect shown by Miles and Clive spoke volumes. "Earning accolades on that team is no small feat. Plus, this is my assigned duty. You joined and risked your life because it was the right thing to do. That puts you in rarefied air."

Grandmother added to the argument. "Baron, your acts of heroism deserve recognition. They have come when our territory faces unprecedented challenges. Your story will not bring joy to people's hearts, but also establish you as a legend, the toast of every gathering for years to come."

A spark of enthusiasm ignited within Baron's eyes, dispelling his weariness. "Well, I ordered a dress for Rebecca. Could she wear the one I picked out instead of looking like a lumberjack?"

Laughter erupted from within me. "Corey's fashion sense is better suited for treacherous mountain expeditions—unless you know the Rossington-Collins band."

"Dear you should rest. I'll arrange a light dinner for you. Tomorrow, we shall gather to honor Baron's triumphs with a celebratory feast."

"Wait," I said. "I need to deal with Major McKinnon."

Grandmother's eyes softened, understanding the weight I carried. "I'll bring you before the presence of the five."

I ACCEPTED THE STEAMING cup of coffee handed to me by Lieutenant Shevski. As the warmth seeped into my hands, the aroma of brewed beans enveloped the hallway. The room we peered into was unlike any ordinary chamber; They equipped it with state-of-the-art lie detection technology—just like the room I witnessed Corey interrogate the traitors. However, Lt. Dave Shevski had more surprises in store for me.

With a confident gesture, Lt. Shevski directed my attention to a set of adjacent rooms, six all soundproofed. It was a unique addition, setting this facility apart from others of its kind. Each door stood as a silent sentinel, keeping the prison from hearing the interrogation. Anticipation mingled with the remnants of caffeine coursing through my veins, quickening my heart.

My eyes swept across the room, settling on a large table that dominated the space. Twelve chairs surrounded it, but that arrangement wouldn't suffice for my plan. "We must remove the table and chairs," I said, my gaze fixed on Lt. Shevski. "And we'll need a protective covering for the floor—a large, white drop cloth will suffice."

My mind raced, processing the fragments of information I had gleaned from the five individuals involved. But it was not enough; I needed to see the previous interrogations.

Lt. Shevski wasted no time. He dialed a number on his phone, ordering action as he mobilized workers to fulfill our needs.

After he gave me a folder of the interrogations, a team of six workers jogged past me, moving the table and chairs. In their wake, they lay a thick white sheet on the floor. Was I ready for what lay ahead? Corey could do it, but I would not ask him to be a part of this.

The essence of my celestial being came to me as I stepped through the small doorway, feeling a surge of power electrify the air. My wings unfurled, expanding until they brushed against the walls. A radiant display of celestial beauty. Clad in a flowing white robe, adorned with a halo that emanated celestial light, I filled the room with an otherworldly presence. Two guards stood nearby, their presence a reminder that they would help restrain our elusive subjects.

Over my shoulder through a crystal ball, the witch, Leander, watched from afar per interrogation requirements.

As I perused the notes from the previous interrogations, flaws in their accounts came into focus, amplified by the additional information I possessed. Major McKinnon, whom I had dismissed from the call, had claimed authority, yet lacked sufficient knowledge.

He may have held the highest military rank, but his authority remained in question. Each questioned individuals had flaws in their knowledge for their position save one, Commander Tsia. Even without experience or formal training, I recognized the significance of this revelation.

Turning my attention to the guards, I requested the most junior individual, my voice carrying a sense of purpose. "Bring me Lieutenant Bradish," I ordered.

The guards unlocked the door to the young man's confinement, guiding him toward me with a gentle firmness. "Look at me and do not turn around," I commanded. "I do not wish to assume my battle form today—again."

"Y-yes, ma'am," he stammered, his trembling frame a reflection of remorse etched upon his face.

"You hold the position of financial officer." I kept my voice steady and measured. "I have discovered that Major McKinnon was not in charge. You admitted to concealing the funds, but you have not revealed how you tracked them. Who approved your budgets, and where did you balance this ledger?"

"It was Major McKinnon," he said. The room blazed red. He lied to me.

At that moment, my transformation begun. I assumed the attire for battle, the halo fading from existence. My sword, its form shifting, transformed into traditional steel, a dormant power awaiting its destined moment.

"This blade possesses three forms," I said. "The steel form holds untapped potential for the future, but today, it shall remain sheathed." With a flick of my wrist, the sword burst into a radiant, golden light. "Celestial light, a blade of grace and might, shall guide my hand." A thought ignited the sword to transmute into a pure white light. "This blade harnesses the essence of creation itself, capable of annihilation upon contact."

"The spell," he pleaded, his body convulsing, blood streaming from his mouth, staining the floor with a crimson hue.

I channeled the healing power given upon me and cast *Angelic Heal* upon him. As the golden light enveloped his trembling form, the violent convulsions ceased, and the blood-streaked floor bore no trace of his affliction. "Place him in the cell," I commanded, a flicker of realization sparking within me. This was but a piece of the puzzle. The truth would have killed him without my gifts from Celestia.

"Bring forth Christina Tsia," I ordered, preparing a healing spell to counter any potential threat. My sword gleamed in anticipation, an extension of my resolve to uphold justice, even in the face of darkness. Just in case, I choose the blade of creation light and pointed it at her.

The woman sneered, her tone dripping with scorn. "Aren't you the clever one?" she taunted, her once-pristine flesh peeling away. "You may have won today, but this is but a bump that could have happened any time in the past decade!"

Sensing the imminent danger, I readied my shield, my grip tightening around the hilt of my creation sword. Christina's physical form disintegrated, revealing a new being—blonde, flawless, with an ageless countenance that could have belonged to someone anywhere between thirty and fifty. Clad in a resplendent golden toga, her eyes radiated a potent aura of creation power. "Revel in your minor win and my delay knowing I am inevitable!" she mocked, her voice resonating with a chilling confidence.

A surge of white light, tinted with an unsettling crimson hue, emanated from the woman. In an instant, I recognized the need to protect all those present, both friend and foe alike. As green stripes materialized, forming a barrier around the glowing figure, I cast my sanctuary spell, enveloping Lt. Shevski, the guards, and myself in a cocoon of safety.

Before I could protect the prisoners, the room erupted into a blinding display of light. My protective sphere collided with the walls, the force reverberating through the chamber. The ball of *Celestial Sanctuary* blew me and the others high into the air.

When the brilliance subsided, no smoke or debris remained. The room stood in ruins, as if caught in the aftermath of a cataclysmic event. The other three spheres of golden light, dispatched to shield the innocents, ascended into the air, soaring a hundred feet above before descending back to the ground. Relief washed over me as everyone within those radiant orbs was unscathed. Yet, the destruction was undeniable—other prisoners and the very structure that housed them—gone without rubble. I scanned the surroundings, searching for any trace of the being who had unleashed such power. Had she vanished into the heavens?

I ascended into the air after ridding the protective sphere, my wings propelling me to a vantage point high above. But there was nothing—no sign of her ethereal form against the backdrop of the ever-expanding sky. My heart sank.

The blaring sirens and flashing lights of emergency response units pierced the chaotic aftermath, signaling their arrival at the decimated building. Knowing that time was of the essence, I released the remaining three spheres, allowing Lt. Shevski and the guards to regain their composure. Their wide-eyed terror mirrored the devastation that lay before them. However, I needed Lt. Shevski to take charge, to lead in the face of calamity.

"Lt. Shevski," I called, my voice steady and commanding as I descended to the ground, my feet finding purchase on the shattered remnants of the once-sturdy floor. "Take charge of this area," I ordered. "Triage any casualties. Attend to those in need."

His eyes widened, mirroring the weight of responsibility that now rested upon his shoulders. Yet, a glimmer of determination shone through his gaze as he rallied himself to the task at hand. The wailing sirens harmonized with the urgency in his voice as he barked orders to his team, orchestrating a synchronized effort to bring order to the chaos.

While Lt. Shevski marshaled his forces, I stepped back, my heart heavy, knowing that the battle was far from over. This encounter had revealed but a fraction of the truths concealed. With every fiber of my being, I vowed to uncover the answers that lay dormant, to wield justice as a shield against the encroaching darkness.

It was time to take care of the living and I began with the two guards quaking before me. I issued clear instructions, my voice authoritative. "Take up positions on the lawn just outside the building. No one gains entry unless Lt. Shevski approves them."

The guards snapped to attention, their salutes crisp, their trembling bodies stilled. With unwavering resolve, they sprinted toward the designated positions. Meanwhile, I remained in my *Angelic Form*, radiant wings unfurling behind me. I took flight to survey the area.

Hovering in the air, my eyes surveyed the aftermath. The first circle I beheld showcased the devastating effects of the blast, spanning a hundred feet in all directions. Despite being within a secured facility, surrounded by impenetrable steel walls, the explosion had obliterated the protective barriers. Fortunately, the destruction hadn't spread beyond the prison estate itself. Emergency responders from far and wide converged upon the scene, their sirens blaring as they raced against time.

It hit me. I had come face to face with our adversary and survived. Marrianna had a face, and I had driven her back and exposed her role in the Chesapeake Bay troubles. I landed beside Lt. Shevski, transitioning back into my ordinary attire.

Grandmother approached me with determined strides, her presence demanding attention. We'd need to stem the impending flood of inquiries. "I need to brief you in private before our next meeting. However, the immediate threat is gone," I addressed her. Turning to Lt. Shevski, I ordered. "Prepare for a pre-meeting with Commander Goseling in one hour, once the situation is under control. I shall provide you with the location."

"Yes, Ma'am," Lt. Shevski said, resuming his duties of coordinating the influx of emergency vehicles.

"Belay that," said grandmother. "Six hours. Clear everything up and gather all the information."

"Yes, Ma'am," Lt. Shevski said again.

The day had been long and arduous, the strain of my angelic teleportation taking its toll. Although my body yearned for a proper respite, I followed grandmother to the conference room where I collapsed into a chair.

Grandmother's voice carried understanding and empathy. "It has indeed been that kind of day. Now, let us gather our thoughts. What do we know?"

Feeling the weight of exhaustion pressing upon me, I endeavored to organize my swirling thoughts. "Major McKinnon was not in command. It was Commander Christina Tsai, though a human Nephilim, Marrianna, had overtaken her," I said.

Grandmother acknowledged the impending tasks at hand. "It will take a few hours to gather all the information. In moments like these, the roles of grandmother and Territory Leader intersect. Go, get some rest, and be prepared for our next meeting," she advised, her voice holding a gentle concern. "After your heal upon me and protection of our men, you now need rest more than anyone."

With a nod of gratitude, I mustered the remaining strength within myself and made my way to the bedroom.

Chapter 26—Rebecca

I descended the grand staircase, my fingers brushing against the cool, polished wood handrails. The grand hall sprawled out before me, its high ceilings adorned with intricate tapestries and marble statues. A scent of lavender, lingering from my recent shower, mingled with the air, calming me as much as the long nap. Our Christmas tree was partway taken apart. The events must have disrupted normal activities.

Clad in a delicate chiffon dress chosen by Baron, I felt the whisper-soft fabric caress my skin. Though not ideal for the meeting, it was still a step up from my recent attire.

As I made my way towards the center of the room, I spotted Nicole passing by, dressed in an unexpected ensemble—blue camouflage pants and a matching t-shirt. Unable to resist, I asked, "Are you dressing down today?" Before she could respond, I noticed the glistening tears in her eyes. "What's wrong?"

Nicole's voice trembled as she spoke, her words muffled against my shoulder as she hugged me. "I can't stay in the briefing... and...and they're talking about Corey."

"Nicole, trust me. Whatever it is, I will make sure..." I said, my reassurances cut short as a sudden burst of vivid green light demanded my attention. Startled, I turned towards its source and found myself face-to-face with Fionnestra, a Daoine from the Fey Spring Court.

"Fear not, Consort," Fionnestra said. "They have dispatched me to stand on your behalf. I am honored to represent you."

Surprised by the unexpected arrival, my confusion deepened. However, before I could gather my thoughts, another shimmering burst of light illuminated the room. This time, a golden glow surrounded Peridot, the Empyrean, from the outer realm of Celestia.

"Well met, Scion!" Peridot exclaimed, bowing before me. "I am here to assist you."

Overwhelmed by the sudden reunion of these extraordinary beings, I couldn't help but admit, "It's great to see everyone, but I don't know what's going on."

"Corey and Onoskelis are discussing what happened in the cave, and I am not allowed to be there." Nicole sniffed and wiped away a tear.

"Nicole, rest. I promise I'll catch you up. With Fionnestra advocating for you and myself standing by your side, even if I don't yet understand why, I assure you everything will be fine," I said.

Grateful, she embraced me. "Thank you."

Watching her depart with a heavy heart, I turned my attention back to the conference room and addressed Peridot. "Do we have any idea what's happening in this meeting? I thought it was an after-action report."

"I apologize, Scion, but nothing can be said outside that room, away from its scrying protections," Peridot said, emphasizing the gravity of the situation.

Peridot, Fionnestra, and I hastened toward the conference room.

At the head of the grand table sat my grandmother, exuding an air of authority that demanded respect. Commander Goseling and Lieutenant Shevski stood behind her, their dress uniforms exuding a dignified presence. On the opposite side of the table, Nathan, Corey, and Onoskelis stood, their expressions wearied and burdened. Peridot, Fionnestra, and I claimed chairs on the near side of the conference room, preparing ourselves for what lay ahead.

Lieutenant Shevski guarded the door, ensuring our privacy and security. Commander Goseling, focused and determined, flipped switches on the wall behind my grandmother. "Room defenses are active," he said then the two soldiers then left and took positions outside the door, sealing it with a thud.

Grandmother wasted no time and introduced each individual in the room, assuming that we were already familiar with one another.

Corey wore a translation device over his mouth and right ear. His weary eyes belied the youth in his face, bearing the weight of sorrow and experiences far beyond his years.

"Who would like to summarize the information and bring everyone up to speed before we proceed?" Grandmother asked.

Onoskelis, the fallen angel, rose from her seat, projecting an air of calm authority. "I'm known for being concise," she stated. "When we defeated the ancient evil, Corey and I landed in an alternate timeline."

"It also sealed the rift and stopped the attack on our flanks. You saved thousands of us," added Peridot.

Corey continued the account. "This alternate timeline differed from our own in a crucial aspect. The result was the disappearance of all beings from the outer and inner realms, including every human with the spark of magic. Onoskelis and I remained as the sole magical beings."

Onoskelis took over. "In the first century, we went our own way, but in the second century, we fell in love, got married, and discovered that love alone couldn't overcome the evil within our child, a human Nephilim. We ended our child's life at thirty."

Unable to contain my astonishment, I stood, unable to process the weight of their words. "Holy... holy crap," My thoughts whirling. I gathered myself and held up one finger as I sat down. "Sorry," I said. "That caught me off guard. I'll process that part later."

Onoskelis' voice resonated with solemnity. "The reason this is crucial is that Marrianna, created by Donald Abernathy and Marchosias, has been orchestrating events for over seventy years. She has taken control of the Shared Supernatural System, disguising herself as its artificial intelligence, and was manipulating events to reshape our universe according to her desires."

"Since she can move through bubbles, she watched us defeat..." Corey cried and couldn't continue.

"She watched us defeat our child and now has defended herself from the one known method of killing her," added Onoskelis, who comforted Corey.

They had made a good call. Nicole could not be in this meeting.

"The Outer Realms were unsure if she could be beaten," added Peridot.

"Until you exposed her and threatened her with the power of creation," said Corey, now in better control of himself.

"However, the situation is worse now. There are two human Nephilim, but one is a child," Nathan said. "We must focus on gathering information to identify the areas that demand our attention."

Curiosity danced in Onoskelis's eyes as she turned to me, her gaze filled with intrigue. "Two questions. How did you survive her blast? And how were you able to expose her?" Her inquiry hung in the air.

I took a deep breath, collecting my thoughts before answering. "I shielded myself, the guards, and Lieutenant Shevski with a protective aura of sanctuary."

Grandmother spoke up next, her voice filled with wisdom. "She shouldn't have survived, but I can explain any Realized power. Rebecca and Corey share a unique bond of love, connecting them as heroes driven by an overwhelming confidence in their abilities. In dire situations, they can even borrow each other's power. Rebecca enveloped Marrianna in Earth Power just before the explosion. She combined this with her unique *Angelic Form*. Celestia granted her a form that gives focused strength in battling Nephilim."

"That explains how Corey's circle held Lance, initially," said Onoskelis. "He must have also had Celestial power in his circle.

"To the second question," I answered, "I discovered inconsistencies in the knowledge of those being interrogated. However, one person answered flawlessly for her position. That was my key."

Nathan spoke with a slight sneer, "Well, the 'artificial intelligence' in the Shared Supernatural System 'broke' when you drove her away."

"And Marrianna has gone into hiding," added Peridot. "She damaged herself trying to kill you."

Grandmother's voice cut through. "How dire is the situation in the Outer Realms?"

Peridot rose from his seat, his celestial form shimmering. "a blood-soaked war with the opposing universe has consumed the Outer Realms. However, as the conflict is winding down, we have uncovered evidence of ninety-three permanent deaths among angels, devils, demons, aeons, and other powerful beings in the Outer Realms, not attributable to the war. We suspect that Marrianna is responsible for these murders."

Nathan stood, holding a scroll case, radiating a vibrant purple glow. "You're mistaken by fifty percent. Here is a list that witches have tracked." He extended the scroll to Peridot, who unfurled it. As he read the contents, his eyes shimmered with an otherworldly brilliance that I sensed was a mix of sorrow, anger, and surprise.

"But we know we have new resources to fight her with," said Grandmother.

"That's not important," Peridot interrupted. "She's gone into hiding and retreated from Earth. Celestia has stopped granting new founts of Celestial Nectar, so unless she exposes herself, she cannot heal quickly."

The information about how nectar worked wasn't important now. I added, to help with the conversation. "She told me to 'revel in the delay because she is inevitable.'"

"So, we have time to plan," Grandmother said.

This was the moment for me to step up. While they looked to Corey for leadership, he needed time. This was my fight, and it was time for me to take charge. "I will lead the Nephilim plan," I declared.

All eyes turned to me, and I continued with conviction. "Celestia has granted me power over all Nephilim, and the choice is between Corey and me. I've relied on Corey's leadership for too long, and now it's my turn to step up and be the leader Chesapeake Bay needs me to be."

"I support Rebecca taking that position," Corey said.

"Before I support this request, explain how you will solve this dilemma," Grandmother said.

I paused, uncertain why Grandmother would question me.

"A few miles from here is the estate owned by the Cassidy family," she said. "Corey placed Masterston's and his sisters' hearts in Bliss Jars. Masterson's wife chose suicide instead of riding to Georgia in the van."

I knew there would be a price for this, considering the power of that family.

Grandmother presented the issue at hand. "There is a girl who survived this ordeal and had reported her family. It turns out she kept reporting it to a corrupted faction within our leadership. Now at sixteen, she has developed Realized powers related to realms and gained immunity to Fey magic. That's how she survived, though it couldn't explain everything."

"I'm following," I said.

"My leadership team suggests bulldozing the Cassidy property, erasing their name, changing hers, and relocating her. The reason being, she has provided us with valuable information. If we keep Hannah within our ranks, Marrianna will know we possess this information, and we lose a crucial advantage. How will you handle this?"

Here was my chance to find a middle ground, offering a solution that would not come without its challenges. "Without seeing the information, I'll assume it gives us a tactical advantage. However, discarding a girl of such resilience is unacceptable. Instead, we will cleanse the estate instead of eradicating it. We bring this girl to the Southeast and describe her as bait to trap Dark Fey."

I knew I should explain this. "By doing so, we can both protect her and exploit her knowledge, since the enemy will not approach someone who is bait. We'll keep her at arm's length, discrediting her within the territory, but still make her attend meetings and school. If she survived ten years surrounded by Dark Fey, I believe she'll emerge—resentful of me—but alive and salvageable."

Grandmother retrieved a pack from her bag on the floor. "Her name is Hannah Cassidy. I approve of Rebecca leading the Nephilim initiative."

Peridot rose from his seat, his celestial form shimmering. "Onoskelis and Scion Adams, assume your *Angelic Form* and open the primary angelic channel."

Onoskelis hesitated. She spoke with incredulity. "No one has accessed this channel in over a hundred thousand years. Fallen angels only use the fallen channels or their realm channel. Regular angels act similarly. All angels have not talked together since the fall."

I took the form and opened the channel. First, I had a direct contact from Onoskelis. "I saw your eyes. The reason I returned to my status of fallen was I could not abandon my responsibility, nor could I leave Corey alone in his state. Fallen angels are the responsible angels. We will sacrifice our home to make things right."

Peridot contact me as well, his words filled with urgency. "Kimarisa, the fallen angel who trained all angels in combat, is from Archeron. We have chosen you as the arbiter of his proposal since you have no preconceived notions because of prior interactions with him."

Putting these comments to the side—I had a lot to deal with later—I connected to the main channel of all angels. A surge of celestial energy enveloped me, connecting me to angels in Celestia, the aeons in Albios, and all domains. The darker realms of Hades, Gehenna, and Archeron merged with devils, fallen angels, and demons. The magnitude of the situation overwhelmed me; I felt like a minor star in a vast galaxy.

"I shall speak," a voice boomed from Archeron, resonating in a deep, thunderous timbre. It carried an undercurrent of fear, embodying the essence of terror itself. "Decades ago, I foresaw this very problem and crafted a contingency plan. I have created the purest warrior in the universe, honed for combat. I shall provide no further details except that I can persuade him to believe he is running away from me. He is the best chance to defeat her."

A voice from Celestia spoke, its tone laced with wisdom. "Scion, you possess limited knowledge of the realms and those involved. The decision rests with you."

The weight of the moment pressed upon me, and I knew my answer had to be a resounding yes, even as logistical concerns swirled within me. This is where lessons from Corey took hold in me. Marrianna was by far the more dangerous situation. "Kimarisa, I heard your words, and though I lack knowledge of how to recognize him or where we could work with him, I will accept this warrior's aid."

A haughty, confident laughter filled the air, exuding both pride and arrogance. "Tell me who you are to say anything to me!" he ordered.

When weak, appear strong. Corey's mantra echoed in my mind. "I am the designated leader of the Nephilim team. I am the one who outed her and gave us this delay. And I am the one who will lead the team to see her dead."

The channel went quiet. His deep voice resounding with darkness spoke softer. "Fallen angels are the ones with the sense of duty, yet I sense responsibility in Celestia's representative. Some of your associates have seen him fight. To your senses, he will appear as a human. In his weaker form, he is a human of his own age—sixteen years since his conception. He is only in his first days upon Earth, he knows nothing except the art of combat. He has a battle form, though he no longer likes to use it."

With resolute determination, I voiced my agreement, aware that there was no alternative and recognizing the immense value of having the greatest warrior in the universe on our side. "We agree, but we will need him here on Earth." The gravity of the situation settled within me, casting a shadow of both hope and uncertainty.

"Onoskelis," Kimarisa's voice commanded, "I trust you and respect your sense of duty. You shall be his first contact."

The channel closed, and a profound silence enveloped my mind. The weight of the decision weighed upon me, mingling with doubt. I turned to Onoskelis, who had shed her fallen angel form and now sat beside Corey.

"Big brass ones, fantasy girl," said Onoskelis.

Peridot looked at me with open eyes that glowed brightly. "You did that," was all he said. His eyes were wide open and shock painted his face.

I took my normal form. "Nathan, I know who the teenager Madison witnessed is, why he is the universe's strongest fighter, and we need to make him an ally. We will work together on that." I then updated the table with the decision I made. Everyone was shocked, except Corey, who looked at me with pride.

Grandmother stood up to gather the table's attention. "Well, this is a promising turn of events. What shall be our immediate actions?"

Fionnestra, her voice carrying a sense of urgency, broke the silence. "What is the current status of the Consort and the Druid?" She attacked her duty before we moved on.

A heaviness settled upon Onoskelis as she spoke. "The portents are clear. Without the next generation of druids, surviving this cataclysmic event means the real challenge will obliterate the universe in two decades. I have a newfound respect for you, Rebecca, and I am giving Nicole the same deal you gave her. I relinquish my claim to Corey for Nicole's natural life span. However, her lifespan is two hundred years, while Corey's spans a millennium. I intend to rekindle our relationship upon Nicole's natural demise."

Fionnestra nodded with a smile. Nicole had her work cut out for her—again, but she had Corey.

Nathan stepped forward, his voice brimming with confidence. "Allow me to outline the tasks at hand."

"Please do." Grandmother granted him permission to take charge.

"We must proceed with our plans as usual for the final two encounters, the dinner for Baron, as it is the expected point of attack. We must establish communication channels with the Nephilim team without convening in one location to avoid arousing suspicion. Last, the events of New Year's Eve looms larger than it did a day ago."

Grandmother's admiration shone through her words. "Excellent. You have proven to be the ideal choice as the Southeast Strategic Leader. And let us not forget the importance of maintaining a semblance of normalcy. Rebecca, tomorrow, take Nicole and Baron shopping. We shall keep the dinner engagement intact."

I saw a way to take advantage of this plan for another necessary task. "Corey, plan to train tomorrow morning in the courtyard. I need to set an example that it's okay to train from nothing and work towards where we need to be."

Poor Corey was never good with relationship talks and now he was dumbfounded, confused, out of time and even needed magic to understand our language. I was going to help him and if he wanted Onoskelis, and him to be married after two hundred years with Nicole, then I'd help him with that, too. I was all in on helping Corey the same way he was all in on helping me.

Corey smiled at me. "You don't know how good of a fighter I am now."

"Please turn the dinner into a ball," asked Onoskelis. "Before I surrender Corey for two centuries, I wish to dance one more waltz with him."

Corey smiled at the word waltz. It seemed he wanted to as well, but did he know how?

I had three buckets of information to deal with. I had the Nicole bucket, the Nephilim bucket, and the Corey bucket. With the meeting adjourned, I needed to focus on Nicole next. What would I share with her?

Chapter 27—Rebecca

Nicole had cried herself to sleep, and I kept her busy getting ready for training first off in the morning. We had averted disaster during Nicole and Corey's training session. I requested she refrain from confronting Corey until we talked. She agreed, and while Rachel trained Nicole, Corey took on training me.

It was a challenging experience, as I stumbled and failed to grasp certain moves, but our determination was clear to the many onlookers observing Nicole and me. This was going to be my life. I'd have heavy decisions and still needed to perform. I needed to learn to train with the weight of everything around me.

Despite lacking the required strength and skills, we persisted, knowing our efforts would pay off. The rumor that I had assumed a proper stance, causing an opponent to hesitate, had taken on a life of its own. It was more a result of Onoskelis' overconfidence and a fortunate reset, but I chose not to question this stroke of luck. It achieved the desired effect.

During a brief break, I stole a moment alone with Corey.

He held up a finger and put the device on his head that covered his right ear and mouth. "I'll be fine with English in some days, but I still need the translator."

"Before I talk to Nicole, I need to clear some things up. I'm planning to use the story that you waited a hundred years before seeking someone other than her to talk her down. How accurate is that?"

Corey met my gaze with sadness. "Violence consumed me. I am only attracted to people with the spark, so no woman was worth a look by me. After a century, Onoskelis foresaw imminent disaster and was lonely. She brought me back to Vienna and helped me attain a title of a free noble. It was a bond of friendship. We were friends for twenty years, and then it happened."

"You didn't cause the end of the world." There was another problem for the Corey and Nicole bucket. Corey proved his claim that he caused the end of the world alone false. Nicole was back to being the most dangerous person on Earth... most dangerous human.

He looked at me and nodded. He knew exactly what I referenced. "But there's something you don't know," Corey continued. "It's not Rachel's love that keeps me on the right path. It's any form of unconditional love. The love of my troops kept me grounded, but it was Onoskelis' love that restored me to my true self. How do I convey to Nicole that the love of Onoskelis and I is as potent as the combined love between her and Rachel?"

"You don't have to do that. I will tell her about the decades you spent together as friends before love blossomed. It's not fair to compare a few months to decades. No one can predict where you'll end up with Nicole. You keep that in mind."

He rambled a bit. "Morgan is helping me deal with this change and has been urging me to stop hiding the centuries I lived and learn to confront those memories. If I'm to live for a long time, I need to embrace that knowledge and face it head-on, rather than hiding from it."

Morgan, who possessed centuries of life experience, understood what Corey was going through. "Corey, it's time for you to rely on others. I'm here for you, and you can lean on me."

Corey gathered our staffs and put them away. "I should head to the Southeast celebration before it ends, or else you might miss your chance to reach Nicole before she confronts me."

"Where is everyone going?" I had enough to discuss with Nicole and felt that minimizing distractions would be helpful.

"We're going to a location called Frenco's for an all-you-can-eat brunch," Corey said with a chuckle. "I hope it's better than camp stew."

There was one burning question I had for tonight. "Enjoy yourself. But Corey, do you know how to waltz? I mean, do you know?"

"You'll find out tonight." He grinned and took off his headset. With that, he took a few steps towards a tree, his entire demeanor changing as he moved with a lightness and grace I had never witnessed before. He twirled and disappeared back to Atlanta, leaving me bewildered.

"What just happened?" Nicole asked.

I dared not say he just performed a flawless fleckeris on the spur of the moment.

"He left for the all-you-can-eat brunch before me," Rachel said. "That's all."

"While we're out today, Baron will teach you how to waltz," I informed Nicole.

"Pardon me," Christopher interrupted. "I know how to waltz. May I join you on this shopping trip and help teach?"

"That would be delightful, Christopher. Meet us down here in an hour, and we'll depart together," I accepted his offer.

"I'm looking forward to it." Christopher sauntered off while Nicole and I made our way up the grand staircase to our rooms.

NICOLE'S WEARIED EXPRESSION brightened, and a smile graced her lips as she posed an important question. "Before you deliver the news, tell me, did you make the first move on Christopher, or is he making the first move on you?"

At least she wasn't melodramatic. "You're crazy. Plus, I have good news."

We walked inside the grand hall and started up the stairs to our room.

Nicole's curiosity piqued, and she pressed, "I might be crazy, but I know when a man's gaze lingers on the person beside me, ignoring me. But please tell me the news."

We entered the room and settled onto her spacious bed. "Foremost, Corey's distant look and disoriented state resulted from experiencing two hundred years' worth of life in those sixteen seconds because of an alternate timeline."

"What?!" she exclaimed.

"Morgan is assisting him in navigating through these centuries of memories, urging him not to skip any. It's an overwhelming ordeal he's facing. That's also the reason you weren't part of the meeting. You'd have wanted to comfort him."

"Holy crap. What is he dealing with? There must be a big reason," Nicole fretted, her hands wringing and her eyes welling up with tears. "Two centuries. Wow. I mean. Wow. I can't handle it. What happened to him?"

"Well, during the first hundred years, he found himself on a dark path and ended up joining an army. He excelled in his endeavors."

"Which army? The US?" she asked through sniffles.

"They existed in the seventeenth-and eighteenth centuries. While I don't have all the details, it seems to resemble the Holy Roman Empire under the Hapsburgs. My knowledge in classics proved useful, as I'm well-acquainted with that time period."

Nicole shrugged, her expression showing her lack of familiarity with the topic. "That doesn't mean much to me."

"During that time, he searched and waited for you, but he had no means to return. He didn't realize he was still bound to his own circle," I said. "I cannot tell you the reason he waited over one hundred years due to church empaths, but I one-hundred percent believe him. He didn't even consider another woman." It was sad we left Nicole out of information, since she couldn't hide her thoughts without muting her power.

"One hundred years?" she gasped, her eyes widening in disbelief.

"I've confirmed it. No women for a whole century," I affirmed.

"Okay, then what happened?" Nicole stared at me, ready to hear the rest.

"I cannot disclose the reasons, but Onoskelis and he spent twenty years together in Vienna. They were friends during that time," I continued, preparing myself to deliver the difficult news.

"But the way they looked at each other... It was more than friendship." Nicole's voice trembled as fresh tears cascaded down her cheeks.

"Not during those initial twenty years. Nicole, he waited for one hundred and twenty years, and then he and a fallen angel fell in love."

"So, it's not his fault, but I'm still a single mother," she sobbed.

"No, Onoskelis has extended the same agreement to you I did. Corey will be yours for your entire natural life."

"What? Why?" A blend of hope and sadness played across Nicole's face.

"Because while your natural life spans twice as long as that of an average human, Corey can live for over a thousand years. Onoskelis has told him she'll wait." I hoped my words would provide solace.

"I always wondered if you felt the same," Nicole confessed.

"No, these past few days have shown me I need someone who aligns better with me and can support me during challenging decisions. Corey is tender and supporting, but he deals with the same issues I do. I need someone who doesn't have to perform these actions. Someone who isn't looking for me to be a better fighter or better leader."

"I—that makes sense," she said.

"Corey and I will always remain close, but our romantic relationship has ended. It's a truth I accept." I knew I had come to that conclusion, but the weight lifted as I said it out loud.

"What should I do then?"

This part was simple. "Today, you'll learn to waltz, so you can share a dance with Corey after Onoskelis has her final dance with him. Then you'll resume your role as the fiancé of a man who's going through a lot." It resembled her previous arrangement.

Nicole embraced me. "Thank you. I believe I can handle it. Can you give me an idea of how terrible those first one hundred years were for him?"

A sadness washed over me. "I talked to him a little before we started training, and he mentioned I would struggle to comprehend the extent of the violence. Somehow, he channeled that energy into accumulating enough wealth to secure an officer's commission. He was an officer over Grenzers for a century."

"I'm going to need your help learning about the words you used, like Grenzers, Hapsburg, and others," she said.

"You help me with computer stuff and I'll help you with history."

We hugged and concluded this conversation. It was time for us to prepare ourselves, and Nicole had much to think about.

THE SHOPPING EXCURSION had been an unequivocal triumph, leaving us filled with joy and carefree spirits. Over a delightful lunch, we indulged in the pleasures of spending money and forgot our troubles—for at least a short time. Later, we found an open club, empty of patrons, and practiced the waltz. Before long, our attention turned to the impending night's events. Before I dressed, I toured the troops on duty for the night and make sure they knew my orders—no one shoots a weapon at a gargoyle and we rely upon Corey for the foe. However, the two Dark Fey were to be ours.

As the hours passed, while I prepared for the evening, I found myself attuned to the faintest sounds emerging from the adjacent room. I don't think Corey joined her yet. They had their fair share of challenges as a couple, but in a world where alternate timelines were a possibility, they needed to adapt to the extraordinary.

Summering in Virginia allowed me to attend ballroom dancing classes. I felt confident in my ability to glide across the floor. Nicole possessed a natural talent, having received training in dance and cheerleading during her formative years. Christopher and Baron worked with both of us, ensuring we felt confident in our steps for the upcoming ball. Christopher was elegant and dancing with him gave me peace of mind.

I had envisioned wearing a gown of my own choosing, a selected ensemble awaiting the skillful hands of a tailor. However, circumstances had conspired against me, leaving me with no choice but to opt for a dress recommended by my grandmother's trusted seamstress. While appropriate, it bordered on excessive in its ornate details. The strapless lace ball gown in shimmering gold felt overwhelming, unnecessary for my physique and personal taste.

In hindsight, I questioned my decision to have Christopher Murphy accompany me to the ball and sit by my side. It seemed akin to a date, the closest approximation to a romantic rendezvous one could expect.

I arranged our adjacent seats to exude an air of intimidation, akin to Corey's presence, yet with a distinct charm. Christopher possessed undeniable charisma, an appreciation for music, and fluency in multiple languages. In this world, a man of such refined tastes was a refreshing change. I wondered if I was afraid of his presence because it felt like a date—a real date.

My luminescent golden gown struggled to maintain its position, frequently slipping downwards. With my left hand, I upheld the delicate upper portion of her garment, all the while keeping an ear out for any unexpected sounds from the adjacent room. Knocking on the connecting door, I asked to enter. She said to come in, but I didn't know if Corey was there or not.

"No, I'm afraid I can't," I said. "Do you have any fashion tape or safety pins? I can't afford any wardrobe malfunctions with Corey present."

"He's not here, but I'm coming over," Nicole said.

The door creaked open, and Nicole snuck through holding her gown with the same issue as I, but she hands her hands full of supplies.

Nicole scattered an assortment of fashion essentials onto my bed. With six strips of fashion tape securing my strapless bra and two safety pins attaching the dress's lining to my brassiere, I could savor the assurance of uninterrupted dancing.

"Goodness, your grandmother's seamstress seems determined to dress you as lavishly as they have me," Nicole said. "The backless gold lace creation makes a statement."

"The vibrant red of your gown is breathtaking," I said.

Nicole responded with a mischievous giggle. "Earlier today, most people saw us in workout sweats. We transition from workout sweats to ball gowns."

Her playful tone elicited a reciprocal jest from me. "Indeed, find a woman who can do both."

Nicole raised her eyebrows in a playful glance. "Your charming boyfriend will be amazed at your transition."

"He's not my boyfriend," I clarified, eager to dispel any misconceptions. "I designated him as my companion for the evening because of his delightful company and the joy I find in his presence." Wild rumors propagating about us would spread everywhere. While I couldn't deny that spending an evening with such a charismatic gentleman would be enjoyable, rumors of my potential boyfriend as the Scion would spread quickly.

"Baron agrees with me," Nicole continued, her tone brimming with amusement. "He thinks the two of you engaged in flirtation which societal standards call excessive. Not 'proper' at all."

Our laughter mingled, accompanied by the mispronunciation of the word 'proper.' "Let's strive to maintain composure. Besides, our team lives in life and death and we bond faster than normal people. We shouldn't expect that speed in normal relationships."

"You may not realize it, but you live in life and death situations, too. Don't you think you bond as fast as the rest of us?"

Before I could respond, Corey's knock resonated through the door. "Are you two ready?"

"Please, come in," I said.

Corey walked in and stared at the two of us. "In this esteemed gathering, I must remark that the both of you appear truly resplendent, and your choice of formal attire is most befitting the occasion."

We both ignored that he was not talking like Corey, the country boy from North Georgia.

"Those eyes of yours," Nicole accused Corey, her hands resting on her hips, "were they only upon your fiancée, or did they wander towards Rebecca?"

"The sight of the two of you together, adorned in such resplendent attire, proved overwhelming. You both radiate an undeniable beauty, and it would be unjust to judge anyone for their reactions upon witnessing your joint appearance," Corey said, flashing that charming smile. His headset was on and I was wondering when he would take it off. Pre-alternate timeline Corey did not talk like that.

"In that case," Nicole conceded, sashaying over to him and pretending to give a kiss upon his cheek, "I suppose you get a pass."

"As per tradition, I should clasp Nicole's left hand, designating her as my date, and extend my right arm to Rebecca as her accompanying partner," Corey recollected, sharing the customary etiquette.

"A little outdated, but it will work at the estate. Lead the way down the grand staircase and towards the bar they set up again. I'll join Christopher should he approach before we reach our destination." I took Corey's elbow.

Corey, dressed in a classic tuxedo, exuded refined elegance. I couldn't help but notice his subtle looseness and perfect posture, a testament to his readiness for any situation—probably with hidden weapons.

Taking his arm in mine, we descended the majestic staircase. The air was thick with anticipation, mingling murmurs of the guests and soft strains of music from the ballroom. Crystal chandeliers cast a warm radiance, reflecting off the polished marble floor and illuminating the intricate details of our crafted attire.

Our journey to the bar begun, our synchronized steps captivating the gazes of all we encountered. Each whisper and admiring glance served as a testament to the breathtaking impact of our transformed appearances. The cascading layers of lace on my golden gown shimmered, intertwining with the delicate strands of light filtering through the grand windows, casting a celestial glow upon my figure.

Nicole's scarlet gown exuded vibrant allure, its fabric rippling and dancing with her graceful steps. She emanated confidence, her radiant smile mirroring the woman she had become.

"Presenting Strategic Leader Rebecca Adams escorted by Southeast Battle Leader Coire Norwood and his fiancée, the Southeast Operations Officer Nicole Hendrix." Polite applause followed, and Christopher approached me, his charismatic smile filled with admiration.

"Mr. Murphy, would you escort me to the table, please?"

STEPPING INTO THE OPULENT dining hall, my gaze swept across the scene before me. Candlelight danced upon the polished silverware, lending an air of elegance to the room. I pondered the juxtaposition of partaking in a meal while an impending attack loomed overhead. Yet, it was the nature of the event that held significance and, therefore, a chance to lure the attack where they know where we will be—hopefully unaware.

Christopher offered me his arm, guiding me to my rightful place at the table. As I settled into my seat to the right of my grandmother, I observed the orchestrated arrangement. My grandmother occupied the seat at the head of the table. Three to her left, after a placesfor Onoskelis sat Corey and Nicole. Christopher took his place to my right.

Baron occupied the next seat, accompanied by a woman unfamiliar to me, whose quiet demeanor and modest attire seemed out of place.

The anticipation in the air was palpable as the first course was served. Having indulged in a large lunch, I found my appetite lessened. Nicole's animated chatter filled the air, informing others of Corey's planned attendance at various classes—marriage, childbirth, and the art of raising children. Corey's masked reactions, his suppressed comments swallowed by a smile and a nod, spoke volumes. The headset was off and I wonder if he did that on purpose.

The next course arrived—a vibrant green apple and walnut salad. My grandmother, the matriarch of our family, motioned for me to rise, her crystal wine glass emitting a soft, melodic chime. As the other guests followed suit, a hush fell over the room, attention focused on me.

I stood and addressed the assembly. My voice resonated with sincerity. "Thank you all for joining us tonight. We dedicate this dinner and ball to Baron Mills, a man whose journey to becoming Realized began with aiding in the defense against vampire attacks. Since then, he has fought alongside us. The team slaying one hundred and twenty-five vampires, two Boo Hags, and two Dark Fey. The Southeast team, recognizing his unwavering bravery and commitment, has spoken of him with high regard. Allow me to quote one of them: 'The dude rocked. He better join us at the party.'" With a nod of appreciation, I directed their attention to Baron, whose acknowledgment elicited a round of applause. Satisfied, we resumed our seats, and the celebration continued.

Nicole's voice rang out, infused with good humor. "Miles always gives the best recommendations."

"Baron's name wasn't the only one mentioned. His recommendation stood out, painted with vibrant strokes," I added.

A question lingered in Nicole's voice. "Was Dave the second person they spoke of? I overheard Madison and Wesley discussing him."

I'd call out Lt. Shevski when he was present. "Yes. Our communications were exceptional."

With the serving of the next course, cooked steak medallions accompanied by a medley of savory potatoes, my attention shifted to the flavors dancing upon my palate.

The atmosphere underwent a subtle transformation as the dining hall turned into a dance floor. An ensemble of two dozen musicians dressed in formal attire, emerged from the shadows, their instruments poised. The sweet melodies of minor notes and gentle tuning accompanied the crescendo of flavors in our mouths, heightening the senses as we savored our meal.

The lingering desire for dessert wove its way through my thoughts, eclipsing the impending threat of the gargoyle. But time pressed on, and duty called.

Chapter 28—Rebecca

Commander Goseling burst into the room, his eyes ablaze with urgency, his every movement exuding palpable energy that hinted at an impending storm. Though he seemed on the verge of shouting, he instead strode to the front of the table and delivered his message with calculated restraint.

"A gargoyle approaches at breakneck speed," he announced, his voice cutting through the air. "Two priests are being held for questioning."

Corey, a stoic figure among the gathering, stood up, shedding his jacket. His gaze sharpened, revealing a determination that matched his every movement. With practiced ease, he reached into his pants, retrieving a tonfa, its sturdy grip fitting in his hand. From a leather sheath concealed at the small of his back, he withdrew his long-handled knife—an obsidian blade. Corey possessed a talent for concealing his arsenal.

"You stay here," he told Nicole, his voice carrying a hint of protectiveness. In one fluid motion, he slipped a crimson trumpet into his torc, a decorative necklace that radiated an aura of Earth power. Alongside his weapons, he clutched a handful of honeysuckle twigs.

With resolute steps, Corey ventured out into the courtyard, his footfalls echoing with purpose. I discarded my gold pumps and called out to Baron, beckoning him to join me in this impending confrontation.

"If I may, Rebecca," Christopher said. "I possess the means to defend myself."

I nodded.

As we stepped into the courtyard, the world shifted to the Realm of Shadows. Even the sounds became muffled, as if nature itself held its breath.

Corey placed his headset back on. "I'm supposed to wear the translator for emergencies and recover my English." He grinned sheepishly. "I'm still a slow learner."

Snarls and howls joined screams as a whirl of blue tore around the corner on all fours. The fierce creature moved toward us, and I took my defensive stance.

"Hey, it's marble," said Corey. "Let me bring it down a notch, and we'll use it for training. Transform into your *Angel Form*." Was he that confident in fighting? This was the same size Gargoyle that wounded him and Miles two months ago. The two of them needed Rachel's help to kill it. He and Miles both needed immediate medical care.

The gargoyle, crafted from blue marble, emerged before us, its colossal frame standing ten feet tall. Thick torso and limbs, hewn from the stone it embodied, commanded both awe and trepidation. Its hands and feet bore foot-long claws, while its oversized head resembled that of a alligator, complete with three sets of menacing fangs. One elongated horn adorned its crown, and with a guttural yell, it unleashed a snarling declaration: "I've awaited this moment for six hundred years, longing for the chance to confront a druid."

"Your wait is over, cutie," Corey taunted, his voice exuding confidence as he advanced towards the towering gargoyle. Corey was always confident, but there was something different about him now. His actions bordered on boredom.

In that moment, I embraced my *Angelic Form* enveloped in a golden light that permeated the courtyard. I planted my feet on the ground, adopting a square stance.

The gargoyle, propelled by an unstoppable force, charged forward. Corey cast a spell and caused the grass beneath its feet to erupt, growing six inches in an instant. Corey proved his mettle, striking the attacking appendage with the back of his knife, his blow transforming the creature's left arm into solid stone. In one fluid motion, he pivoted, delivering a powerful backhand strike with his tonfa, preventing the gargoyle from regaining its footing.

Undeterred, the creature lunged at Corey, but he evaded the assault and struck the gargoyle's right leg. Stone encased the appendage, rendering it nearly immobile, transforming its marble surface into a stunning, albeit unintended, work of art.

Corey stood up straight, like he would taunt the fearsome supernatural beast. Instead, he backed up to me while the gargoyle struggle with an arm and leg unusable.

"Okay," Corey said while stepping back. "He's still dangerous, but hobbled. Close in on him while he's recovering. Use your stances and execute a swing from the upper right downward."

With unwavering determination, I, now attuned to my newfound power, landed and assumed a squared stance. The gargoyle, its ferocity undiminished, lunged forward, to be met by my shield, executing a mid-block. Sliding across the grass, I absorbed the force of the blow, numbing my arm. I retreated a couple of steps, my mind racing to devise a countermeasure.

"Excellent!" Corey's voice rang out, brimming with pride. "Now you understand its strength. How will you counter that?"

The answer eluded me, but within me, a newfound resolve took hold. I knew what to do. I transformed my sword, its blade shimmering with the power of creation. A surge of confidence coursed through my veins as I poised myself, the weight of the weapon feeling just right in my hands. The white blade of creation was part of me, and I controlled my fate.

The gargoyle, its left leg dragging, its every movement tearing up the grass beneath it, fell prey to me. I feinted a jab, goading the creature into lunging forward with its remaining arm. I brought my blade down in a swift arc, cleaving through the arm. The appendage vanished, leaving a sense of exhilaration coursing through my veins.

A resounding howl escaped the gargoyle's maw, even in the muted realm that enveloped us. Unfazed, I turned, maintaining my shield position to defend against the creature's menacing jaws. In one swift motion, I swiped my sword, targeting its remaining leg. With each strike, the empowering energy coursed through my being. Stepping back, I adopted a long stance, my sword poised for another formidable swing.

"Okay, okay," Corey said. "You've got this. Holy crap."

The gargoyle, now missing an arm and a leg, its remaining appendages reduced to solid marble, writhed on the ground, emitting anguished wails. Corey wasted no time, plunging his obsidian blade into the creature's vulnerable form, securing its demise. As he withdrew his hand, the Earth would tattoo a new gargoyle name on his chest. How many such marks adorned his body remained a mystery.

With the gargoyle's impending threat subdued, attention turned to the approaching priests. A man sprinted towards the grand hall, announcing their imminent arrival, filling the air with a renewed sense of urgency.

"Behind me, Corey," I commanded. "Commander, gather the team. Hand Baron the fourth weapon."

Corey, his battle-honed instincts kicking in, positioned himself behind me. Though still the unyielding hard Corey, his military bearing took on a more formal aura, elevating the gravity of the situation. It was a subtle change, one only those who understood the intricacies of battle could perceive. His position behind me gave me the confidence I needed to test my team.

"Baron, the safety is off," Commander Goseling instructed. "We need sunlight to illuminate our adversaries, then unleash the full force of two-seventy-seven rounds until they cease their twitching."

Commander Goseling assumed control just as I had hoped, embodying the authority and assertiveness I expected from him.

My *Angelic Form* wings unfurled, ascending into the air, my eyes fixed on the impending clash. With a resounding call, I summoned the *Celestial Light*, a force that bathed the courtyard in its gentle glow. Baron conjured his *Ray of Sunshine*, his power intermingling with my light. The weakening of the creatures sent by the Unseelie were weaker for the light.

Two Dark Fey emerged from the remnants of the priests; their malevolence palpable in the air. The first resembled a centipede, its slender mandible protruding four feet, and its armored body adorned with a menacing array of horns. Its elongated form stretched ten feet. The second was a crab-like creature with an unsettling dozen claws, scuttling forward with clear intent.

Without hesitation, our united team focused their fire on the centipede-like Dark Fey, the collective click of clips being switched reverberating through the courtyard. Meanwhile, the crab-like creature, propelled by unnatural agility, leaped towards me, determined to confront the one burdened with destiny.

Bracing myself, I prepared to receive its assault, but a bolt from Christopher collided with the creature, causing it to freeze in its tracks. It frosted over, its movement arrested, providing me with an opportunity I couldn't resist. My date... errr the artist... had a hand crossbow that shot a bolt with magical powers.

Christopher's voice yelled. "Five to ten seconds, that's all it lasts," he warned. "Usually, I use that time to retreat."

I suppressed the innate desire to step forward and eradicate the remaining threat. The temptation that beckoned from within me which screamed to unleash the power of creation. My white blade, an instrument of creation and destruction, called to me. But I had learned to exercise caution, to resist the addictive pull of unrestrained power. The lingering temptation released me. I refocused my attention on the battle at hand.

Taking stock of our team's ammunition, we were on our third clip, having already spent a staggering one hundred rounds per member. Time seemed to stretch, the weight of the battle bearing down upon us. A small twang resonated through the air, followed by Baron's exclamation of pain.

"Something bit my ankle!" he exclaimed, surprise lacing his voice.

The second Dark Fey perish with another bolt from Christopher and three clips from my troops who had proven they were up to the task.

"Something bit my ankle as well. Is there another creature here?" asked Christopher.

"No," Corey said. "You, and Baron, have been blessed with the honeysuckle tattoo." His gesture towards the tattoo adorning my ankle provided tangible confirmation. The tattoos were rewards from the Earth. It marked those who defended it and while our Earth based tattoos didn't match Corey's, we all had honeysuckle tattoos with red trumpets for each Dark Fey the Earth credited us for killing.

Color flooded back into existence. The resplendent wings of Onoskelis cast a surreal shadow as she landed before us. In a flurry of black and corrupted light, the fallen angel transformed, assuming the form of a woman clad in a breathtaking black ball gown. In her left hand, she held a pair of obsidian pumps.

"Good evening," she greeted, her voice a melodic blend of warmth and darkness. "Creation magic, a siren's call that beckons. Are you addicted to its intoxicating embrace? Even angels find themselves ensnared by its allure." Onoskelis, her fingers intertwining with Corey's.

The desire to swing the white blade of creation power was gone. The fallen angel was telling the truth, and I'd have to avoid the blade.

Christopher guided me through the door Baron opened for us with a flourish while Corey guided in Onoskelis. The troops, who I'd recognized tomorrow, were setting about cleaning up the courtyard.

I reported to grandmother. "Southeast Battle Leader Norwood defeated the gargoyle with the help of the Scion, who received training in the action. The Dark Fey incursion happened. Command Shevski is reporting to the Atlanta Command Center, and the Dark Fey incursion was handled by the Chesapeake Bay Territory. The Southeast Battle Leader did not take part in the attack of the Dark Fey." This was as I had hoped. My troops came together.

Chapter 29—Rebecca

The opulent formal dinner hall surrounded me with its elegant grandeur, yet I couldn't shake off the restlessness that had taken hold.

In the elegant ballroom, anticipation filled the air. The room brimmed with vibrant energy as we gathered for a night of enchanting revelry. Excitement fluttered in my chest, eager to embark on this extraordinary evening.

"Excellent. Fantasy girl," the fallen angel said. "I know you and your date possess dance training. When Freiherr Reiser and I transition to a fast Waltz, please join us. That should serve as an invitation for others to join in."

"Freiherr Reiser, would you accompany me to the dance floor?" Her voice, soft and alluring, caressed the room as she extended her hand to Corey.

He accepted her hand. "Gräfin Schorgl, you honor me." In that moment, Corey transformed before my eyes, shedding his warrior guise and assuming an air of elegance and grace. He moved with practiced finesse.

"What on earth?" Nicole's hushed voice barely made it to me.

I couldn't believe what I witnessed. Corey, known for his strength and valor, now navigated the dance floor with unparalleled grace and elegance. It was a mesmerizing sight that defied all logic. It took him months to learn the 'two step' and he wasn't that good at it. This morning's fleckeris was not an aberration.

Christopher leaned in, his voice above a whisper. "She referred to him as a Baron, with a common Warrior surname. And he addressed her as a Countess, with a surname associated with a love for the land."

Grandmother engaged in a quiet conversation with the conductor.

Baron addressed Nicole. "Nicole, Candice has injured her ankle, and a waltz would be too much for her. Would you do me the honor of dancing with me until your fiancé claims you?" Baron's persuasive tone elicited a radiant smile from Nicole.

"That would be lovely, Baron," she said with delight. "Perhaps we should assign ourselves grand titles as well?"

"I believe those two held those titles," Christopher said. "The way they speak and move... it seems genuine."

As the leader of the Chesapeake Bay Territory took the stage, a hush fell over the room. Her commanding presence demanded our attention. "Good evening, everyone," she addressed the gathering. "Tonight, we are in for a special treat. Our esteemed new ally desires a traditional Vienna Waltz and believes that the Battle Leader of the Southeast Territory possesses hidden dance skills."

Corey's focus shifted to his dance position; his right arm extended toward Onoskelis. With an elegant bow exchanged between them, they embarked on a captivating journey across the dance floor.

The conductor stood and bowed. "Without further ado, allow me to present Dorfschwalben aus Österreich."

The resounding melodies of the small orchestra filled the room, weaving an enchanting tapestry of sound. As the fallen angel and Corey glided over the dance floor in a closed position, their movements exuded a vibrant energy. Natural turns propelled them forward, their pace quickening as they navigated the floor.

I struggled to keep up, her eyes widening in astonishment. How had Corey gained such extraordinary dancing skills? The intricacy of the fleckeris left me spellbound, each step executed with a precision that defied expectation.

"Your ex is a master of the Viennese waltz?" Christopher's hushed words lingered in the air. "I thought I would be the best dancer here, but those two are beyond incredible."

I reached for my phone to capture the performance. This might be my only chance to witness his grace and skill. Rachel will want a copy of this.

"Alright, they've transitioned into a fast waltz," Christopher said. He extended his hand towards me. Eagerly, I kicked off my shoes. The girls at school had always danced barefoot.

With measured steps, we made our way to the dance floor, positioning ourselves just behind Corey and the fallen angel. The intricate turns and three-step patterns commenced, demanding our full attention. Dancing with Christopher was effortless, a harmonious interplay of movements. There was no need for pretense or cover-ups; we danced as one, his graceful presence elevating my own abilities. "You dance beautifully," he said, his words blending with the music.

"The feeling is mutual," I said. "You bring out the best in me." With a gentle spin, I moved into his embrace, reveling in the moment's magic.

Nicole and the Baron trailed behind us, her kitten heels emphasizing her confidence. A pang of self-consciousness washed over me as I was the only one barefoot. Yet, the flowing gown concealed my feet, allowing me to immerse myself in the evening's enchantment.

After what felt like an eternity of captivating dances, Corey and Onoskelis concluded their performance. They shared a last kiss before she departed through the courtyard, leaving Corey to make his way back towards our table. But Nicole seized his arm, her gaze directed at him as she pointed to the floor in front of him. Corey would dance with Nicole.

Eager dancers joined the fray as Nicole danced with Corey. As Christopher and I broke, we were caught up in the dance and kissed before returning to our seat.

THE NIGHT HAD BEEN magical, but I had an early meeting and had awakened in time to eat breakfast before meeting in grandmother's office. Baron, Commander Goseling, and Lieutenant Shevski were on either side of me inside. The air was heavy with anticipation as Lieutenant Shevski handed me a prepared report, his voice breaking the silence.

"I've confirmed with the Atlanta Command Center that we have neutralized the threats," he said. "The Chesapeake Bay Territory can now rest easy, free from tier one and tier two incursions for at least a month. The remaining tier one threat lies in Buford, Georgia, on New Year's Eve."

A nod of approval from my grandmother, the matriarch of our family, acknowledged Lieutenant Shevski's report. "Well, Tactical Leader Adams," she said, her voice carrying a mixture of pride and acknowledgment, "you have stepped into your role with remarkable grace. Enemies defeated, corruption uprooted, a burgeoning alliance established, and four attacks handled within your first week. Congratulations."

I nodded in gratitude, my eyes reflecting determination. "Thank you, grandmother. But now, we must focus on the tasks at hand."

"Indeed," she agreed, her voice brimming with conviction. "I understand you haven't had time to prepare a comprehensive report, but I must ask, what can I expect in terms of our end goals?"

"The ultimate objectives," I said, my mind racing with strategies and possibilities, "are: achieving battle readiness, bolstering morale, and transforming our forces from mere recipients of aid to reliable providers of help." It was in that moment that I embraced my new-found role and committed myself to giving it my all.

"And what about professionalism?" asked grandmother.

"Defining professionalism in Realized powers will be a complex task," I said. "Our judgment of the Southeastern team, based on traditional military standards, exposed the need for a distinct approach when dealing with individuals who possess magical abilities. It will take time to forge a new understanding of professionalism."

"Fair enough," my grandmother acknowledged. "What are your next steps?"

My mind brimmed with a multitude of plans and contingencies. "We must complete our readiness report and find out the extent of Realized powers within our ranks. Simultaneously, we must address the restoration of our sensors and enhance our early detection capabilities. Second, I task us with designing uniforms that will differentiate us from the traditional military while allowing for seamless collaboration. Last, we must continue nurturing our relationship with the Southeast, solidifying the foundations of our alliance."

"Excellent," my grandmother praised, her voice imbued with approval. "Now, if you could provide orders to these gentlemen, I would appreciate a private discussion with you."

I turned my attention to each of my companions, delivering instructions tailored to their unique responsibilities. "Baron, it is imperative that you find a suitable companion or date for the New Year's Eve party. Remember, appearances in that setting hold considerable significance. Honesty outweighs the need to fit in." I would tell him in private to bring a proper date and not a woman stand in.

Continuing with Baron. "I want you to interview each member of the Southeast team regarding their specific uniform requirements and begin brainstorming ideas for both territories."

Baron's eyes widened in astonishment. "I can design the uniforms?" he asked, his voice filled with a mix of surprise and excitement.

"Will design the uniforms," I corrected.

Turning to Commander Shevski, I addressed him with earnestness. "Lieutenant Shevski, your foremost task is to establish robust communication protocols with the South. Collaborate with them to develop joint titles, cohesive report names, and coherent orders. As we expand our team, we must also prioritize cross-training to foster familiarity with our members. The practices and capabilities of Scions and Druids differ significantly, and we must align both territories."

"Yes, ma'am," Lieutenant Shevski said.

Finally, I directed my attention to Commander Goseling, acknowledging the significance of his role. "Commander Goseling, our highest priorities are twofold: the comprehensive collection of data on Realized powers and troop readiness reports, followed by the repair and enhancement of our sensor network. Building a command structure, while important, takes a backseat to expanding our team for rigorous training."

"Yes, ma'am," Commander Goseling affirmed, his gaze reflecting unwavering dedication. "If I may ask one question, Battle Leader Adams, we have received many requests for hand-to-hand weapons training since your public training sessions. How should we respond?"

A surge of satisfaction washed over me as Commander Goseling posed this question. "We are addressing this demand. We will find local instructors, but we shall coordinate with the Southeast to ensure training opportunities exist in both territories."

"Very well. I dismiss everyone except Battle Leader Adams." My grandmother's authoritative tone resonating through the room.

With swift efficiency, the three men exited, including Baron, who surprised us all with his crisp and disciplined departure. As the door closed, my grandmother leaned against my desk, her expression a mix of awe and weariness. "Goodness gracious, what a week it has been." She spoke with voice tinged with both admiration and incredulity. "I expected some intensity, but I had hoped we could spread it out. Instead, I negotiated with the Council, engaged with a fallen angel, attended an emergency continent meeting in Atlanta. This was while contending with four attacks within our borders. Not to mention firing the head of our territory defenses and uncovering traitors."

"My life has been this eventful for the past few months," I said.

"That it has," my grandmother conceded, shaking her head in awe. "The Rebecca of October would never have fired a person during a call or possessed plans at the ready to issue orders. She wouldn't have led the fight, had the confidence to train in front of the entire estate, or experienced the growth that emerged from the crucible of our recent challenges. You and Corey are surpassing all expectations."

I understood her sentiment. "It was a collective effort. We had a strong team supporting us."

"And that's what makes your accomplishments so extraordinary," my grandmother emphasized, her gaze brimming with pride. "Two remarkable individuals displaying strength is impressive, but when they lead a team and empower it to become stronger, well, that is exceptional."

"You have stood up and taken your destiny into your own hands and excelled," said grandmother. "With that, our Territory is now stable waiting on a succession plan."

A knock on the door interrupted our exchange. My grandmother stood upright, her voice a mere whisper. "Time for me to resume my role as the regal figurehead. I invited your date from last night." With composure, she called out, "Enter."

Christopher Murphy entered the room. "Grace, Rebecca," he greeted us with a nod. I sensed the weighty topic that hung in the air—a topic I had set aside. The implications of our date.

Then I remembered we kissed.

News of that kiss, as it was between the two of the most powerful single Realized in North America, must have circulated to every territory.

"I shared news of your date with Clarissa," grandmother said. "Unsurprisingly, the council approves of a marriage between the two of you. However, it is imperative that you both decide soon if this is a passing fling or the beginning of a substantial relationship. Both of you are running out of time."

"Out of time?" Christopher's confusion echoed through his words.

"I suspect news of our kiss has already spread like wildfire across North America," I confessed.

"It has circulated worldwide. The political implications surrounding both of you extend beyond the realm of norms. The New York team is already struggling to manage the fallout. And for you, Rebecca, it would be even more intense, given your connection to Corey and Nicole."

I recognized the urgency in the air. A decision was necessary. I addressed Christopher, my eyes meeting his. "If you would be so kind as to escort me to the informal New Year's Eve party held by the Southeast Territory, you will have a day to contemplate our situation before our subsequent date."

Christopher's eyes danced with a mischievous spark, and a smile tugged at the corners of his lips. "How about this? You consider our relationship tomorrow, and I shall accompany you to the New Year's Eve party," he proposed, his voice filled with a playful charm.

I didn't need to witness my grandmother's reaction to know that her eyes were rolling at our exchange. A sense of relief washed over me as Christopher and I found a compromise.

I had taken my position of leadership in Chesapeake Bay, found a way I could continue to support Corey, secured the area, and I would lead the charge to tackle Marrianna. I also would make time to consider the curious Christopher and see if maybe he possessed the ability to be the person I would want to be with.

Chapter 30—Rebecca and Christopher

I caught Nicole and Corey in time. "No Corey," I said and grabbed Nicole by the arm and pointed both of them to the stairs.

"He said he had a lot to deal with," said Nicole.

She was almost in tears and I knew this was a time for her to step up. These two had stepped up for me and I was going to step up for them. Corey spoke in German. Something about tomorrow.

"Corey Norwood, put your headset on!" I ordered him, and he looked at me with shock. I met his gaze and stared at him.

The druid rolled his eyes and put on the magical headset. "I wanted to meditate in the Fey Spring Court," he said.

"That's good and this will not take too long, but this is something you have to trust me with." I grabbed his hand and led the two of them up the stairs and into Nicole's room. Once sitting them both on the bed, I shut the door, and pulled up the desk chair to sit across from them.

"You should elevate yourself above people you will chastise—as a leader," said Corey.

"I'm not chastising you. I'm helping three broken hearts," I answered. Nicole, who was barely holding it together, had a look of hope spark in her eyes.

"Three?" Corey held up three fingers in the German manner using the thumb.

"You don't remember this, but before the time bubble you adored Nicole, but hadn't fallen in love yet. You and I were getting over each other. I swore I'd do anything to keep the two of you together, including losing any romantic feelings for you." There, that should kick off the meeting.

"The painter climbed the mountain by himself because he wanted to see you. He cannot get you out of his mind. Did I approve of him as your suitor beforehand?" asked Corey.

"This is the same Corey that changes topics when things get uncomfortable. We're here because you don't want to face me," said Nicole.

"No, no," protested Corey. "You two are the simple parts." He sighed. "In two centuries, I learned a lot and made myself seem smarter. I still have the same brain as before."

"What does that have to do with anything?" asked Nicole.

"I think he's onto something, Nicole. Let's let him finish." This sounded like we had a breakthrough.

He sighed. "You know how the Realm of Shadows sits on our world and shares all the same material items?" He continued after we nodded. "The alternate timeline was a time bubble that wrapped our timeline and shared everything. That means everything I had back then I have now." He said it and hung his head.

"That's a good thing, right?" asked Nicole.

"I didn't understand wealth then and still don't. My estate in Vienna is vast, and contains investment things I don't remember, boxes of gold bars from the new world stamped by Spanish authorities, and who knows what else. If I remember anything, I only ever wanted to be a simple druid." He shook his head. "I don't know what I am anymore," and now he tried to hold back tears.

This is what he alluded to earlier with his finances and legal issues. Okay, that was a wow statement. "Your fiancé." I pointed to Nicole. "Has a degree in Finance."

He continued after raising an eyebrow at Nicole. "I graduated from the Theresianum four times. Once for each of my identities over the years while in the army. Not only am I more experienced in military matters than anyone alive, my education is," he paused. "How about an example? I worked translating Latin, and they considered me an expert. I looked up some of my old work. They're used to teach people now."

Puzzle pieces fell into place. This would be a big deal for Corey. He had never been the educated person or the smart one. He liked his niche as the hard-working druid. This was telling him he was someone new with the caveat that he no longer fit in society. He was struggling to figure who he was and where he fit into the world.

"You're worried about fitting in?" Nicole was incredulous. "And you're looking for help from people other than me? Corey, when Rachel and I lost our second set of parents, you showed up every day to make sure we were taken care of. Eight years you took care of us." She pulled out her phone and showed him pictures. "Here is me when you took me to get my braces off. Here we are, with you intimidating my prom date."

I pointed to his bag. "Hand me your phone."

"What is a phone?" he asked.

I opened his messenger bag and pulled out his phone, then pointed it at his face to unlock it.

"Picture device. The prize-winning garden in my estate is beautiful. I'll take pictures if you show me how." He grinned, and that was better.

"Can I see your estate?" asked Nicole.

"Not unless you can hide your Realized signature. The Freiherr Reiser identity and Corey Norwood identity need to be kept separate. One of my new powers is I can sink my magical signature into the Earth."

Corey had that excuse ready to go. It was a good reason and bulletproof, but I'm glad he did because Nicole would be a wreck seeing pictures of Corey happily married to someone else. I found the picture and showed it to him. He cradled Rachel and Nicole. "This is the day you saved Rachel's life," I added.

"If there is anything I learned from you was if we talk it through and stay together, we can deal with anything." Nicole was emphatic and was holding back tears.

"I remember this day," said Corey and teared up. "Let me gather my paperwork in Vienna, and I'll be back. I promise."

"That's a good plan," I said, standing up.

"Corey. I've crushed on you and loved you for years. Thank you for talking." Nicole stood up with him.

I hugged Nicole after he left.

"Thank you," she said. "You gave me hope."

"It's what friends are for," I answered.

CHRISTOPHER'S HEART pounded in his chest as he surveyed the deserted courtyard. Moonlight cast ethereal shadows across the ancient stones, lending an air of mystery to the scene. Nestling himself against the weathered wall, he positioned himself strategically, allowing a vantage point from which he could detect anyone approaching from either direction.

The anticipation was palpable, his senses heightened, as he counted down the minutes. One-thirty-seven am. The precise moment when his sister would wait by the telephone, ready to answer his call.

Taking a deep breath to steady his nerves, Christopher dialed his sister's number, his fingers trembling. The familiar ringtone resonated through the line until a hushed voice finally answered.

"Hey! Chris," she said with excitement.

"Hey, Sissy." His hushed voice filled with an undertone of exhilaration. "I have something incredible to share with you. I've met someone, and I believe she likes me for who I truly am."

Silence greeted his words, but he could sense his sister's anticipation through the phone. "I heard mother screaming about it earlier. Tell me everything! What is she like?" Her voice carried a breathless whisper.

He couldn't help but smile, his voice barely a murmur. "She is headstrong, competent, and radiates a captivating sweetness. Her movements are as graceful as a dancer, and she possesses an impeccable sense of style. You wouldn't believe it, but she even kissed me—a real, genuine kiss."

"Wonderful! I'm so excited for you!" His sister's excitement was contagious, filling the airwaves with joy. But suddenly, another voice pierced through the background, its tone harsh and intoxicated.

Christopher's heart sank; it was his mother. She was normally passed out at this time

"Who is that? You're smiling! Is it that worthless brother of yours, gallivanting around instead of fulfilling his family's duties? Give me that phone!" The voice bellowed, fueled by alcohol and anger.

Christopher's mother's presence was a dark cloud overshadowing their lives.

Defeated, he acknowledged her accusation. "Yes, Mother, it's me."

The line crackled with tension as his mother unleashed her bitter words. "Listen to you, with your insulting, snobbish attitude!"

Christopher's sister couldn't remain silent any longer. A faint sob escaped her, carried by the wind. "Mother, he is kind. Please, let him be."

But his mother's venomous words continued to spill forth. "Shut up and go to bed, you little whore!" His sister's tears fell, a testament to the pain she endured under their mother's control.

Gathering his strength, Christopher argued, determined to defend his sister's honor. "Mother, you don't allow her to experience life outside your walls. She is a remarkable young lady."

But reason fell on deaf ears as his mother's insults persisted. "Shut up! You're worthless, only thinking of yourself!" The line went silent for a moment, interrupted by a dull thud that signaled his mother's intoxicated collapse.

With his sister's voice back on the line, filled with urgency, she spoke. "Let me call you on another phone."

A voice speaking German told he was sorry he heard all that. The collection of heroic muscles known as Corey sat next to him. Only tonight, the hero looked as bad as Christopher felt.

Christopher could feel the weight of despair pressing upon him. "I feel terrible. I tried to hide these issues, but my mother is difficult."

Understanding and empathy radiated from Corey's eyes as he spoke, offering support.

"You look like you need support." Christopher spoke German fluently and though Corey's accent was Viennese and out of date, the conversation was enjoyable.

"I don't know who I am anymore," admitted a defeated Corey.

"I still see your soul since I will start two paintings with you in it after the holidays. Your soul is that of a hero. Just like it was before." Christopher gave him the truth and watch Corey's confusion turn.

The druid cocked his head as if thinking of this and smiled. "Thank you. I should repay you. Can I help with your sister?"

Christopher's mind raced, knowing the magnitude of the challenge before them. "Unless you can travel undetected to the New York Territory, make your way to western Connecticut within six hours, evade the attack dogs, retrieve my sister and some belongings, all without crossing territory lines—there is little that can be done." He hung his head in despair, feeling trapped by the circumstances that surrounded them.

Corey rose to his feet, determination etched upon his face. "Lift your head and provide me with the latitude and longitude coordinates," Corey commanded.

Looking at the muscular physique before him, Christopher couldn't help but raise an eyebrow in disbelief. "Are you serious?"

"Hypothetically speaking," Corey said with a spark of mischief. "Let's imagine I can prepare a mystical tree in this courtyard, allowing for a single journey. Then I'll transport to my house, entering the Spring Fey Realm. From there, I'll find my way to an Onoganda Indian Reservation. And hypothetically, of course, I'll traverse the realm known as Bright Earth with my magical Fey wings, reaching your sister's residence. I'll navigate past a few friendly dogs, gather your sister and her essential belongings, and then return, connecting a one-use tree there to the one by my house. You come to Atlanta and reunite with your sister, hidden from political fallout." Corey's words spilled forth with an unwavering confidence.

Just as Corey finished explaining his fantastical plan, Christopher's phone jingled, its ringtone slicing through the night. "Sissy, pack a single bag you can carry, and be ready. A remarkable individual, a heroic collection of muscles, is coming to rescue you. Don't be alarmed by his soldier-like appearance; he's genuinely kind."

Hope, like a delicate blossom, blossomed in his sister's voice. "Really? Is this true?"

"Prepare quietly," Christopher urged, his voice laced with urgency and determination.

"I'll pack Snorffil and some clothes, and my pillow," she said as she hung up to pack.

With the coordinates displayed on his phone, Christopher converted them into the precise altitude and longitude.

Guiding Corey through the backyard, he described the back yard and window where Sissy would wait by a tree branch.

Now he needed an excuse to be outside and then he would have another to drive to Atlanta after his meeting with Grade tomorrow morning.

Clutching a blanket and his trusted portfolio filled with supplies. With purposeful steps, his heart beating in harmony with his unwavering resolve, he prepared himself for the inevitable confrontation with Clarissa and his mother. He had prepared himself for this very moment, and all he needed was a single opportunity.

If fate granted him that chance, a glimmer of hope in the darkness, he dared not dream of the possibilities that lay before him.

Being regarded as an outsider, a "freak," had its advantages, and tonight, he would wield his unique gifts to provide subterfuge. With unwavering determination, he took his place beside the tree, preparing to sketch even the most grotesque of trees if it meant reuniting with his beloved sister. He would use this as an excuse to travel to Corey's house for the other half of the tree portal. Really, it was excessive for an excuse, but things were so close.

If only Sissy could escape their mother's clutches. As he waited, pencil poised over paper, he dared not hope. But hope, in its infinite resilience, refused to be extinguished. And so, he drew each stroke of his pencil, a testament to the unwavering love and courage that bound them together.

Epilogue

Madison stood in the small registration office, feeling the chill of the tiled floor through the soles of her shoes. Beyond the frosted windows, she could see the bitter winter cold that had settled in, casting a stark contrast to the warmth she hoped they would find within the Second Chance School.

Outside, workers were busy taking down the school's Christmas tree, captivating the young girls she had brought with her. The tree had also covered up the burn marks from a battle less than a week ago her friends had engaged in, the battle that traumatized Mare and Melinda. They had stripped the once festive office bare of its decorations, signaling the end of the holiday season and the beginning of a new chapter for the students and these girls in particular.

She watched Teesha, the woman who would become their guiding light, as she introduced herself with warmth and compassion. Teesha's presence seemed to cast a subtle glow of hope that contrasted with the chill in the air.

"Hi Teesha," Madison said with a soft smile, taking a step back to let the introductions unfold. "I'd like to introduce you to Mare, Melinda, and Sissy."

Teesha met each of the girls' anxious gazes with her kind eyes. Her handshake with Mare was gentle yet firm, and as she spoke to her, Madison couldn't help but wonder if Teesha could sense the unspoken secrets and pain buried within Mare's heart.

"Hello, Mare," Teesha greeted warmly. "I've heard a lot about you. I know this has been a tough time for you."

Outside, a crash as a large ornament fell to the ground and broke.

Mare smiled weakly with slightly hunched shoulders. The burden Mare carried, beside her role in the attack, was one she hadn't been able to share with anyone yet. Teesha's presence, though, offered a glimmer of hope.

Teesha's next handshake was with Melinda, a girl whose guarded demeanor spoke volumes about the scars she bore. Madison had faith that Teesha's guidance would help Melinda find the strength to open up and heal.

"Hi, Melinda," Teesha said kindly. "It's great to meet you. Madison mentioned that you and Mare have been through a lot together."

Melinda nodded, her eyes briefly flicking towards Mare. Madison could sense the unspoken bond between the two girls, and she knew Teesha would play a crucial role in helping them heal.

Finally, there was Sissy, the youngest of the group. Madison watched as Teesha knelt down to meet her at eye level, her disguise concealing a presence beneath that Madison recognized, but then stopped thinking about it. Sissy's trust in her older brother, Christopher, was heartwarming, but Madison couldn't help but wonder if Teesha knew more about Sissy's unique situation than she let on.

"And you must be Sissy," Teesha said with a gentle smile, her eyes filled with compassion. "I heard you'll be living with your brother and attending a different school?"

Sissy nodded shyly, her small hand trembling slightly as she took Teesha's. "Yes, ma'am. I'm gonna stay with my big brother, Christopher."

Madison knew there was another layer to Sissy's story that politics prevented from being revealed. Corey had sneaked across the country with magic to rescue her from an abusive situation, igniting political turmoil. Teesha's presence gave her hope that these secrets would eventually come to light.

As Teesha addressed all three girls once more, her words of support and guidance resonated. Madison knew Teesha was not just an ordinary counselor but could not put her finger on why. These girls had all been through a tumultuous journey and introduced to magic harshly.

Madison's heart ached as Teesha briefly mentioned three other names: Hannah, Ryan, and Samuel. These were the names of more young souls whose lives Teesha's care would touch. Hannah, like Madison herself had been once, had been in foster care, and the anguish of feeling unwanted still haunted her memories. Madison couldn't bear to look at Hannah's name, knowing that her own presence could put the girl's life at risk—a burden Madison carried.

She didn't know Samuel, but Teesha listed his name alongside Ryan. Ryan was Khalil's younger brother, and Corey knew Khalil from high school.

As she watched Teesha, the path ahead would require confronting obstacles, but it also presented an opportunity for the children to belong in a world that had not always been kind. She just hoped that they could all navigate the complexities of their world and protect those who needed it most, even if it meant making painful choices.

Madison was leaving none of them. Mare and Melinda stayed at a family close by, and the family allowed Madison to help them. Sissy had a strong support network here, but would need help acclimating to a school environment. Last, even if she had to ignore Hannah to save the girl's life, no one else was going to harm that girl—help would need to be discreet, is all.

Don't miss out!

Visit the website below and you can sign up to receive emails whenever Shawn McGee publishes a new book. There's no charge and no obligation.

https://books2read.com/r/B-A-MTXT-ZQZHC

Also by Shawn McGee

The World of Geoe
The Herald
The Regnant
The Vanquisher

Wartime Druid Saga
Wild Eyed Southern Boys
Caught up in You
Fantasy Girl

Watch for more at https://WorldofGeoe.com.

About the Author

Shawn McGee writes fantasy and is an IT professional with hobbies in mathematics and gaming. Along with his current series he is writing a new gaming system.

Please this book as reviews are the life blood of independent writers.

You can join Shawn's discord channel, join his email list, and find out all the book information at https://worldofgeoe.com

Read more at https://WorldofGeoe.com.

www.ingramcontent.com/pod-product-compliance
Lightning Source LLC
Chambersburg PA
CBHW070502160726

48003CB00004B/1381